"IN A CLASS WITH LADY SLEUTHS V. I. WARSHAWSKI AND STEPHANIE PLUM."*

"AN ENTERTAINING DETECTIVE WRITER."
—*The Dallas Morning News*

"[A] UNIQUE SERIES."
—*Seattle Post-Intelligencer*

"FASCINATING INFORMATION about herbs and tempting recipes round out this leisurely cozy with a Southwestern flair."
—**Publishers Weekly*

Susan Wittig Albert's exciting mysteries have been praised as "unique" (*Seattle Post-Intelligencer*) and "fascinating" (*Booklist*). Now, a dead man's bones are uncovered—and Texas ex-lawyer and herbalist China Bayles must dig into a pair of murders separated by time but connected by motive . . .

When China's teenage son finds some skeletal remains during a local cave dig—remains that show a not-so-accidental death—it's a disturbing development. But China doesn't let it distract her from the opening of the new community theater donated by the elderly Obermann sisters. Unfortunately, the haughty, bullying Jane Obermann—and her frail, frightened younger sister—made the donation with a condition: that the first production be a play written by Jane about their aristocratic family history.

The premiere party ends with a bang when a ne'er-do-well local handyman is shot dead by Jane while breaking into the Obermann estate. It seems like a clear-cut case of self-defense. But China senses something else going on behind the scenes. Now, the key to catching a killer might be the mysterious bones in the cave—a clue from the past that could help China solve a mystery in the present . . .

"ONE OF THE MOST ENDEARING AND PERSONABLE AMATEUR SLEUTHS."
—Midwest Book Review

"SUCH A JOY . . . AN INSTANT FRIEND."
—Carolyn G. Hart

continued . . .

Acclaim for Susan Wittig Albert's *Dead Man's Bones . . .*

"China's warmth and sensitivity . . . will endear her to readers, while her investigative skills make her a leader among female sleuths. Fascinating information about herbs and tempting recipes round out this leisurely cozy with a Southwestern flair." —*Publishers Weekly*

"China Bayles is always trying to teach us stuff: it's not annoying at all but somehow soothing and fascinating . . . An enjoyable journey." —*Booklist*

A Dilly of a Death . . .

"More than just a whodunit . . . readers will relish this more-sweet-than-sour adventure." —*Booklist*

"Add another fragrant bloom to the dozen already in the bouquet of Albert's herbal cozies." —*Publishers Weekly*

Indigo Dying . . .

"Albert's skill in weaving everything together into a multilayered whole makes the reading smooth, interesting, and enjoyable." —*San Antonio Express-News*

"Accomplished . . . The heart of the book is the detailed depiction of small-town life in Indigo, which separates the novel from genre fodder by providing a rich context for the mystery. The satisfying ending is icing on the cake." —*Publishers Weekly*

Bloodroot . . .

"Albert has created captivating new characters and a setting dripping with atmosphere." —*Publishers Weekly*

Mistletoe Man . . .

"Ms. Albert artfully uses Texas language patterns to bring the down-home town of Pecan Springs alive with eccentrics in abundance." —*The Dallas Morning News*

"Breezy . . . The characters are an appealing bunch . . . Albert also provides lots of interesting lore about mistletoe . . . A nice book to curl up with on a blustery day, perhaps with a cup of Christmas tea." —*Chicago Tribune*

"The pace is as peppy as a Texas two-step, Albert's dialogue and characterizations put her in a class with lady sleuths V. I. Warshawski and Stephanie Plum, and her writing sparkles." —*Publishers Weekly* (starred review)

Praise for the China Bayles mystery series . . .

"[China Bayles is] such a joy . . . an instant friend." —Carolyn G. Hart

"A treat for gardeners who like to relax with an absorbing mystery." —*North American Gardener*

"One of the best-written and well-plotted mysteries I've read in a long time." —*Los Angeles Times*

"Albert's characters are as real and as quirky as your next-door neighbor." —*The Raleigh News & Observer*

"Mystery lovers who also garden will be captivated by this unique series." —*Seattle Post-Intelligencer*

"Realistic, likable characters." —*Chicago Tribune*

"Lively and engaging." —*Fort Worth Star-Telegram*

"Gripping." —*Library Journal*

"Cause for celebration." —*Rocky Mount (NC) Telegram*

China Bayles Mysteries by Susan Wittig Albert

THYME OF DEATH
WITCHES' BANE
HANGMAN'S ROOT
ROSEMARY REMEMBERED
RUEFUL DEATH
LOVE LIES BLEEDING
CHILE DEATH
LAVENDER LIES
MISTLETOE MAN
BLOODROOT
INDIGO DYING
AN UNTHYMELY DEATH
A DILLY OF A DEATH
DEAD MAN'S BONES

With her husband, Bill Albert, writing as Robin Paige

DEATH AT BISHOP'S KEEP
DEATH AT GALLOWS GREEN
DEATH AT DAISY'S FOLLY
DEATH AT DEVIL'S BRIDGE
DEATH AT ROTTINGDEAN
DEATH AT WHITECHAPEL
DEATH AT EPSOM DOWNS
DEATH AT DARTMOOR
DEATH AT GLAMIS CASTLE
DEATH IN HYDE PARK
DEATH AT BLENHEIM PALACE
DEATH ON THE LIZARD

Beatrix Potter Mysteries by Susan Wittig Albert

THE TALE OF HILL TOP FARM
THE TALE OF HOLLY HOW

Nonfiction books by Susan Wittig Albert

WRITING FROM LIFE
WORK OF HER OWN

SUSAN WITTIG ALBERT

DEAD MAN'S BONES

BERKLEY PRIME CRIME, NEW YORK

THE BERKLEY PUBLISHING GROUP
Published by the Penguin Group
Penguin Group (USA) Inc.
375 Hudson Street, New York, New York 10014, USA
Penguin Group (Canada), 90 Eglinton Avenue East, Suite 700, Toronto, Ontario M4P 2Y3, Canada
(a division of Pearson Penguin Canada Inc.)
Penguin Books Ltd., 80 Strand, London WC2R 0RL, England
Penguin Group Ireland, 25 St. Stephen's Green, Dublin 2, Ireland (a division of Penguin Books Ltd.)
Penguin Group (Australia), 250 Camberwell Road, Camberwell, Victoria 3124, Australia
(a division of Pearson Australia Group Pty. Ltd.)
Penguin Books India Pvt. Ltd., 11 Community Centre, Panchsheel Park, New Delhi—110 017, India
Penguin Group (NZ), Cnr. Airborne and Rosedale Roads, Albany, Auckland 1310, New Zealand
(a division of Pearson New Zealand Ltd.)
Penguin Books (South Africa) (Pty.) Ltd., 24 Sturdee Avenue, Rosebank, Johannesburg 2196,
South Africa

Penguin Books Ltd., Registered Offices: 80 Strand, London WC2R 0RL, England

DEAD MAN'S BONES

A Berkley Prime Crime Book / published by arrangement with the author

PRINTING HISTORY
Berkley Prime Crime hardcover edition / April 2005
Berkley Prime Crime mass-market edition / April 2006

Cover art by Joe Burneson.
Cover design by Judith Murello.

For information, address: The Berkley Publishing Group,
a division of Penguin Group (USA) Inc.,
375 Hudson Street, New York, New York 10014.

ISBN: 0-425-20425-1

BERKLEY® PRIME CRIME
Berkley Prime Crime Books are published by The Berkley Publishing Group,
a division of Penguin Group (USA) Inc.,
375 Hudson Street, New York, New York 10014.

PRINTED IN THE UNITED STATES OF AMERICA

10 9 8 7 6 5 4 3 2 1

A NOTE TO THE READER

Some of the herbs in this book have traditionally been used in the treatment of human illness, and I often refer to these practices, usually as a matter of historical interest. Before you start using any plant medicines, however, you should read as much as you can and consult with professional herbalists. Please do not use this novel as a guide to herbal therapy. China Bayles and I have a great deal of confidence in the healing qualities of plants, but neither of us would presume to prescribe them to treat whatever ails you.

It's my job to make Pecan Springs, China Bayles, and her friends seem very real to you, and I hope I've succeeded. Please note, however, that this book is a work of fiction, and all names, characters, places, and incidents are either products of the author's imagination or are used in a fictitious manner.

Nobody can write a mystery series without a lot of help from friends. For this book, I relied on special dental advice from John L. Wilbur, D.D.S., of Austin, Texas; and (as always) the editorial assistance of my husband and coauthor (in our Robin Paige series), Bill Albert. Thanks, guys. I would also like to thank the women of the Story Circle Network, who are my constant friends and supporters, always ready to offer a cup of tea and a cookie (real or virtual) when I need it. China, Ruby, and I would especially like to thank Peggy Moody and Paula Yost, best girlfriends.

—Susan Wittig Albert

Chapter One

"Dead Man's Bones" is the folk name given to the herb Greater stitchwort (*Stellaria holostea*), a perennial plant found in damp, shady places throughout Europe. It grows to about three feet, with long, dagger-shaped leaves. The starry white blossoms appear in late spring, when thickets of the blooming plant brighten the shady woods.

I've been thinking a lot lately about hidden things, things that are enclosed, interior, inner, concealed. Things that are absolutely necessary to survival, but invisible. Things we can't do without, but things that nobody sees, nobody remembers. Things like bones.

Now, it may seem to you that bones are a strange thing to think about, unless you're an orthopedic surgeon, or you've broken an ankle on an icy sidewalk, or someone you love has osteoperosis—brittle bone disease. Bones have a way of calling attention to themselves only when they disappoint us, when they let us down.

On the whole, though, maybe we ought to give more thought to our bones. While we're alive, they hold us up, allow us to walk and climb stairs, enable us to work on the job or in the garden, give us the strength to make war and make love. When we're dead, our bones will be around for a great deal longer than our soft parts—the parts to which we pay more attention: our faces, our brains, our hearts. And when we've been dead for centuries, we may still have a voice, for our bones can speak, can tell who we were when we were alive: our gender, size, race, the state of our health, even, perhaps, the cause of our death.

Like the bones that were recently discovered in Mistletoe Springs Cave, in the Texas Hill Country about fifteen miles south of Pecan Springs. The man and child had slept together in their quiet resting place for a hundred centuries, while the glaciers melted, the mammoths wandered past, and the splendid Meso-American civilizations flared into a transient glory. The Spaniards came and went, and the French, and then the Mexicans and the Anglos and the Germans came and stayed, and still they slept, silent and secure, undiscovered by any of these. Their bones were joined by other bones, small animals, larger animals, and finally, by more human bones. Still the man and the child slept on, until at last a chance discovery opened the grave to the light, and their bones, and the bones that were found later, began to speak.

A dead man's bones may have secrets to share.

We are compelled to listen.

I wasn't thinking about bones on the day it all began—an ordinary Friday, in an otherwise unremarkable October, a couple of weeks before Halloween.

To be embarrassingly frank, I was thinking about money, or more precisely, the lack of it. It was late afternoon, and Ruby and I had just been to the bank with the daily deposit of checks and cash from our three enterprises: Ruby's shop, the Crystal Cave; my herb shop, Thyme and Seasons; and our tearoom, Thyme for Tea.

"Depressing, isn't it," Ruby said. With a lingering sigh, she fingered the deposit slips.

"Yeah," I said, as I pulled out of the bank's drive-up and onto the street. "Definitely depressing."

I'm no mind reader, but I didn't have to ask what Ruby was talking about. It had been a slow week, and there was just enough in that deposit bag to pay our bills: hers, mine, and ours, with a little left over for groceries. The problem is the decline in tourist traffic, which is probably related to the general downturn in the economy. Pecan Springs, which lies at the eastern edge of the scenic Hill Country, halfway between Austin and San Antonio, is a tourist town, and the local businesses depend on those extra dollars to smooth out the bumps and potholes on the road to economic prosperity.

But tourist traffic dipped this year, and our bottom lines began to look a little red. Not a pretty red, either. Not cherry red or lipstick red or Victoria's Secret red. More like the mottled red of your loan officer's face, or . . . well, you get the idea.

This challenging situation has been much on my mind lately, and on Ruby's, too. However, not being the sort of women who sit and sigh when things start going to hell in a handbasket, we've expanded our enterprises and gone looking for more business. Ruby has created the Party Thyme Catering Service, a traveling show (a traveling circus, she jokes) that takes the tearoom on the road, with the help of our cook, Janet Chapman. Last month, Ruby and Janet catered the annual Pecan Springs Women's Club brunch and a couple of wedding luncheons, and they're doing the cast party for the opening of *A Man for All Reasons*.

For my part, I've taken on garden planning and some extra gardening work. This effort has been moderately successful, I'm glad to say. In the past few weeks, I've helped an Austin church plant a garden of Biblical herbs, installed an herb garden beside a pioneer museum in Kerrville, and designed the herbal landscaping at the new Merrill Obermann Community Theater in Pecan Springs.

The theater landscaping was the current job. Marian Atkins, a longtime friend and the chairman of the Community Theater Association board, had asked me to do the layout and obtain the plants, and a group of volunteers would get together to do the planting. Which is why Ruby and I were driving Big Red Mama, the buxom, beautiful van we bought a few months ago, used, to help us cart our stuff around. Mama, whose previous owner painted a colorful blue, green, and yellow design on her red sides, is sassier than a Sweet Potato Queen. She was toting a big load of plants bound for the new theater. We were delivering them on Friday night so we could get an early start Saturday morning. Opening night—a Denim and Diamonds gala—was only a week away.

While Mama is taking us to the theater, I'll take a few minutes to fill you in, just in case (as the folks in Pecan Springs say) you ain't from these parts and you need some help knowin' who's who and what they've been up to lately.

Ruby is Ruby Wilcox, my best friend and business partner. She's six-feet-plus (her exact height depends on whether she's wearing flat sandals or three-inch wedgies) and slim as a willow wand, with a curly mop of carroty hair, freckles to match, a dramatic disposition, and a show-off sense of style, manifested this afternoon in chic red hibiscus-print overalls and a green tee, green-and-red plastic bangle earrings and matching bracelets, and red tennies. Woo-hoo. Ruby is divorced, with two grown daughters: Shannon, who coaches girls' sports at a San Antonio high school; and Amy, who works at a vet clinic in Pecan Springs and is expecting Ruby's first granddaughter in December. I should also add that when you meet Ruby, you may sense something . . . well, different about her. She is highly intuitive, and she often knows things about people that they scarcely know about themselves. To tune in to these messages, she says, she's using her right brain, the side of the brain that is hard-wired into the universe.

My name is China Bayles. I am definitely not tall and willowy—in fact, I am middling-short and slightly hefty—there's a wide gray streak in my brown hair, and my fashion taste runs to jeans and T-shirts. I'm not very intuitive, either. My brain works more or less linearly, jogging along from fact to fact in a boring, methodical way, while Ruby tends to leapfrog over facts as if they weren't there at all. I am definitely a left-brained person.

Of course, it was this methodical fact-based brainwork that made me a good attorney, and when I was young and foolish, I worked as a criminal defense lawyer in Houston, for a large firm that mostly represented the bigger bad guys, the ones with bucks. Then I grew older and smarter and thoroughly sick of the fast track and the Houston rat pack. I cashed in my retirement, scraped together my savings, and invested everything in the Thyme and Seasons herb shop, at 304 Crockett Street in Pecan Springs. The century-old limestone building houses my shop, Ruby's Crystal Cave (the only New Age shop in town), and, in the back, our tearoom.

Two years ago last month, I married Mike McQuaid, a former Houston homicide detective. It was a two-for-one package deal, since McQuaid's son Brian, now fourteen, was included. The three of us are living happily ever after (well, mostly) in a big white Victorian house on Lime Kiln Road—the one with the rosemary bushes along the fence and the grumpy old basset hound asleep on the porch step.

There's a great deal more to tell about both Ruby and me, of course, but that's enough to get you started. Anyway, Big Mama's gotten us where we needed to go, and it's time to unload her.

The Merrill Obermann Community Theater is located on the outskirts of Pecan Springs, in what used to be a large stone stable at the rear of the old Obermann mansion, a sprawling Victorian, badly maintained and with a sadly overgrown yard and garden. The two-story stable, big enough to house the dozen horses that belonged to the family in the 1920s and '30s, is a wonderful example of the architectural use of locally quarried limestone, the sort of building you frequently see in Pecan Springs or Fredericksburg or New Braunfels. Last year, the Obermann sisters, the last survivors of a wealthy family of philanthropists, donated the stable, several acres of adjacent property, and the funds for renovation to the Pecan Springs Community Theater Association—a generous gift that created more than a ripple of interest around town.

The first production in the new theater—*A Man for All Reasons*, written by the elder Miss Obermann—was scheduled to open a three-weekend run next Friday night, so the landscaping needed to look presentable by that time. Mama was toting five or six dozen pots of perennial herbs: rosemary, cassia, lavender, santolina, various salvias, bee balm, artemisia, and tansy, with thyme, southernwood, and creeping germander for borders and blooming marigolds and chrysanthemums for color. It would have been nice to have gotten the plants established earlier, but in Texas, October planting has a higher success rate. Anyway, nobody thought of it. The Theater Association was too busy managing the renovations and getting the play into production, both of which proved to be almost undoable jobs. Landscaping was a low priority, until somebody noticed how bare the place looked and pushed the panic button.

"There, that's done," Ruby said, as we pulled out the last five-gallon rosemary plant and stashed it with the others, ready for the next day's garden-planting party. She dusted off her overalls and pushed a floppy red curl out of her eyes. "What's next?"

"You have a choice," I replied, opening Mama's door. "I can take you home, where you can spend the evening practicing your lines." Ruby has the female lead in *A Man for All Reasons*. "Or you can drive out to the Flower Farm with me to pick up Brian and then come home and have dinner with us. McQuaid's cooking tonight, so I can't promise anything more exotic than Tex Mex. But it'll be hot, whatever it is. As in spicy." McQuaid has asbestos tonsils, and habanero chile powder—produced from the habanero chiles he grows himself—which is his favorite seasoning.

"I'll take a rain check," Ruby said, as she climbed into the van. She grinned. "Nothing against McQuaid's cooking, though." The grin got wider, happier. "Colin called just before we left. I'm having dinner with him tonight."

I turned on the ignition and started the van. Ruby started seeing a new guy a few weeks ago, and I was glad. She's an attractive woman with a dynamite personality, a generous helping of brains, and a warmly compassionate nature. Unfortunately, she has been blighted in love. Her erstwhile husband ran off with a young woman half his age, and several men with whom she's been temporarily enraptured have proved, on closer acquaintance, to be jerks. Somehow, her intuitive self seems to wear a blindfold when it comes to men—well, certain men. The ones she falls in love with.

Recognizing her perilous propensity for choosing the Wrong Guy, Ruby went into a self-imposed retirement awhile back, to get her act together, as she put it. Colin Fowler is the first guy she's dated for quite some time. Tall and athletic, with reddish-brown hair and regular features, he's nice-looking, in a comfortable, Kevin Costner, guy-next-door way. He moved to Pecan Springs a few months ago and opened a new store on the square, Good Earth Goods, which sells environmentally friendly household stuff, pet products, energy-efficient lighting, pest control, that sort of thing. I've been in the shop a couple of times and I've glimpsed him around town. He's not a standout—he doesn't have a memorable face—but he's definitely attractive. I can see why Ruby is interested.

"So I have to get home and do my hair and nails." Ruby regarded her hands disapprovingly. "I chipped one when we were unloading those plants."

Since Ruby's manicured nails, even chipped and broken, are far more sightly than my stubby, grubby ones, I didn't comment. I shifted into third gear and remarked, "I hope you and Colin have a good time tonight."

"So do I," Ruby said, with a fierce energy I hadn't heard in a while.

I turned to look at her. "Already?" I asked, trying not to show my alarm. Ruby has been known to fall in love with passionate abandon at a moment's notice and with never a backward glance. From the intensity of her voice, I guessed that it was happening again, heaven help us.

"Already," she said with a sigh. "Although I don't hold out much hope."

"Why not? Colin's not married, is he?"

"Oh, gosh, no," Ruby said in a shocked tone. "I mean, he's been married before, of course—everybody has. But they've been divorced for eons, and they don't have any children." She paused. "I don't really know much about his past, to tell the truth. And I don't want to. It's just that—"

She didn't finish her sentence, but she didn't have to. Both of us knew that her love affairs have mostly been painful ones. Maybe she was measuring the paradise she hoped for against the purgatory she feared, and coming up with a negative number. We pondered this matter in silence for the rest of the drive to her house. As we pulled up in front, I leaned over and patted her hand.

"You don't have to go completely overboard, you know, Ruby. You can date this guy without handing him the keys to your heart."

Ruby's mouth looked vulnerable. Her chin was trembling. "Not Colin, I can't," she said, and got out of the van. "This is serious, China. Big time, I mean. Major passion." She raised her hand. "But thanks for the suggestion. I appreciate it."

Feeling apprehensive, I watched her as she went up the walk to the porch. Ruby hasn't fallen in love lately, and she was probably overdue. I don't know whether it's chromosomal, or situational, or just Ruby's thing. But when love comes into her life, it comes on like gangbusters. Caution to the wind, full speed ahead, damn the torpedoes, and every woman for herself.

I sighed and pushed in Big Mama's clutch. This was none of my friggin' bidness, as we say in Texas. If Ruby wants to fall in love, that's her lookout, and I wouldn't do anything about it, even if I could. Privacy is and has always been one of my big hot-button issues. I have to admit to a certain queasy ambivalence when it comes to criminal matters, but in general, unless there is an overwhelming reason to suspect that a law has been broken, I believe that governments have no right to pry into the private lives of citizens, and that citizens have no right to intrude on other citizens' affairs. I resist attempted invasions of my own personal privacy. I wouldn't invade Ruby's unless she got herself into some sort of serious trouble and asked for my help.

Anyway, what was I worried about? What, specifically, was my problem? Was it Ruby's speckled history, where love was concerned? Or was it Colin Fowler, about whom I knew almost nothing at all?

I shook my head. I couldn't answer these questions, and I had no business asking them. It was time to go on to other things.

I was headed out to the Flower Farm, about fifteen miles south of town, where I was to pick up Brian. His latest passion is archaeology, and he's been taking part in a cave dig that's being carried out by the Central Texas State University Anthropology Department at Mistletoe Springs Cave, which is on Flower Farm property.

Most of the people in my life seem not to change very much, except for my son—McQuaid's son with his first wife, Sally (from whom Brian hears only in intermittent and incoherently passionate bursts), but now my son, as well. Brian is taller and heavier than he was just six months ago, and his body has a new authority. I can see a more confident set to his shoulders and the shadow of a mustache on his upper lip, and hear a deeper, more manly voice. Sometimes. Some of his sentences start off in that startling new man's voice, but end in his child's voice, and

I'm reminded that the boy is moving through the between years, when he is still a bit of both.

Cavers get dirtier than anybody else in the world, but since Brian is well on his way to becoming a scientist of one sort or another, I try not to mind. His passions are worth supporting, even when it comes to washing those unspeakable jeans or ferrying him back and forth to the dig.

Anyway, I was enjoying the drive. October brings autumn and cooler weather to most parts of the United States, but in the Texas Hill Country, it's the tail end of summer, no matter what the calendar says. The temperature this afternoon had spiked to a warm eighty-five. The limbs of the pecan trees were sagging under a heavy load of nuts, the prickly pear cactus sported their fruit like plump red fingers on green mittens, and the fields and roadsides blazed with sunflowers, purple asters, and snakeweed. Off to my right rose a high, steep limestone bluff; a little farther on, the same rock had been carved by eons of flashflooding into a broad ravine, shaded by sycamore and cypress. We'd had a couple of substantial tropical rains in late September, and water stood in emerald-green pools in the shade of the trees. Still farther, when I drove over the low-water crossing on Mistletoe Creek just before I reached the farm, water was spilling across the road, bright and clear and sparkling like liquid crystal. Texas Hill Country creeks are here today and gone tomorrow, but when they're running bank-full, there's nothing quite as beautiful.

Mistletoe Creek Flower Farm belongs to a pair of sisters—Donna and Terry Fletcher—and their aunt Velda. Terry is in California right now (actually, she's serving out a prison term, but that's another story). Donna and a crew of day-workers produce a glorious three-season harvest of cut flowers—painted daisies, sunflowers, snapdragons, phlox, sweet William, and a great many more—which they sell to the florists in Austin and San Antonio, and at markets and festivals around the Hill Country.

There's money to be made in the flower business, even in hard times, and Donna can prove it. However, she and Aunt Velda got a big bonus awhile back, when Aunt Velda got lost and found a treasure trove in a cave on the ridge above Mistletoe Springs—booty from a bank robbery cached by the Newton boys, who made a tidy fortune raiding Texas banks in the 1920s. The gold certificates and other bills in Jess Newton's leather saddlebags had crumbled to dust, but the gold coins were still as good as the day they were minted. Better, even, when those twenty-dollar double eagles got into the collectors' market, with a confirmed provenance as genuine pre-Depression bank robbery loot. When all the hoorah was over, Donna and Aunt Velda had ended up with a sizeable profit from this fortunate find—about two hundred thousand dollars, enough, in fact, to fix up the barns, buy equipment, and put in a new irrigation system. Thanks to Aunt Velda, the Flower Farm is turning into a showplace.

But it was Brian and his passion for archaeology that brought me to the farm this evening. As it happened, gold wasn't the only thing Aunt Velda discovered in that cave. She had also found a handful of arrowheads and, when she went back later, two old skulls. Very old skulls. When the archaeologists from CTSU began to study these, and the two skeletons that turned up as they searched, they realized that they were dealing with a pair of Paleo-Indians, an adult male and a child who had lived and died on Mistletoe Creek about ten thousand years ago—a very long time, in terms of human history, just after the last major North American ice age. This was obviously a burial site, for with the pair (I can only think of them as father and son) was an array of grave offerings: seashell beads, turtle carapaces, red ocher, and a bone awl. The skeletons and artifacts had gone to CTSU for study, but the archaeological team was still conducting exploratory excavations in the cave, which is far more extensive than anybody had expected. It's beginning to look like Mistletoe Springs Cave is the largest in the area, and it's entirely possible that the archaeologists will find other evidence of human occupation.

As I pulled to a stop and got out of the van, Donna, dressed in cut-offs and a plaid sleeveless blouse, came out of the barn. "Hey, China," she said. She yanked off her red bandana sweatband and wiped her face with it. "I'm ready for a break. Join me in some iced tea while you're waiting for Brian to come down from the cave? Aunt Velda will be glad to see you. She's been to Mars and back since the last time you saw her."

I grinned. Aunt Velda is my kind of woman. She was abducted by Klingons a few years ago, and she hasn't been the same since she got back from her grand tour of the galaxy. She was treated like royalty, she says, with a window seat for the whole trip, champagne and movies and little felt booties to keep her tootsies warm. And no dishes to wash, which is a very big point with her. The money she found in the cave was left there by the Klingons for her to discover, her reward for being such an entertaining passenger. Hey, what do I know? Maybe it's all true. Aunt Velda is brash. She's got plenty of chutzpah, and I imagine that the Klingons enjoyed her just as much as I do. I was anxious to hear about her round trip to Mars.

But I didn't get the chance. I heard a truck engine and the crunch of tires on loose gravel, and turned to see a dusty pickup lumbering around the curve of the old road. Brian jumped out of the back, gave a wave, and the truck drove off.

"Hey, Mom," he yelled, and ran up to us, his caver's helmet in one hand. His face and arms were generously plastered with gray, gooey mud, and his orange UT Longhorns T-shirt and jeans were grimy. But through the mud, I could see the likeness to his father. He has the same dark hair, the same blue eyes, the same quirky grin. Except that he wasn't grinning now. He wore a half-scared look, and his boy's voice was scratchy and high-pitched when he said, "Hey, Mom, guess what?"

"From the look of you, I'd guess you discovered the biggest underground mud hole in the entire state of Texas," I replied, in an admiring tone. "Must have been a whopper."

"Yeah," he said soberly. He took a breath. "Hey, listen, Mom, I found something. Something really bad!"

Living with a teenager teaches you a great deal about the contradictory and often bewildering nuances of the English language. *In your dreams,* for instance, means *never. Bad,* I have been instructed, means *good,* as in *cool* or *awesome*.

"More stone points?" I guessed, thinking about the very good ones he had already found. "A new bat roost?" In Brian's ordering of the universe, bats rank right up there with tarantulas, lizards, snakes, and girls, and the caves of the Edwards Plateau contain some of the largest maternity roosts for bats—mostly Mexican free-tailed bats—in the entire world. It's pure heaven for bat lovers.

"No, really bad," he said, shaking his head and frowning. "Really, really bad."

"I give up," I said, raising and dropping my hands. "I can't think of anything badder than bats."

"I found more bones," he said seriously. "Real bones, I mean."

"More buffalo bones?" Donna asked. That had been the big archaeological find the week before. Buffalo have been extinct around here since the U.S. Army wiped them out in order to deprive the Indians of their main source of food. But the buffalo bones found in the cave were a good deal older than the U.S. Army. Older than Moses, maybe.

Brian shook his head again. "Human bones," he said, even more seriously.

"Another Indian skeleton?" Donna asked excitedly. "Hey, Brian, that's fantastic! Aunt Velda will be so excited."

Aunt Velda says that the Indian bones are really the bones of Klingons, transported back through time. Watching the expression on Brian's face, though, I didn't think he was talking about Klingons, or another historic find. I was right.

"He's not an Indian," Brian said. His mouth tightened. "At least, not an old one, like the others we found. He's nothing but a skeleton, but he's wearing clothes. Jeans and a shirt, it looks like." His eyes darkened and he swallowed, a young boy confronted with the very real, intensely personal mystery of death. "Must've been a caver. His skull was . . ." Another swallow, his adolescent Adam's apple bobbing. "It was smashed."

At that moment, another truck came down the road, pulled to a stop, and Alana Montoya, one of the anthropologists on the dig, climbed out. I met her for the first time last week, although she's been on the CTSU faculty for a year or so. Her primary interest is forensic anthropology, although the program hasn't gotten under way yet. Alana is an attractive woman, with alert, searching brown eyes and the dark hair and olive-brown skin of her Mexican heritage. She wasn't quite as muddy as Brian, but almost. It looked like they'd been prospecting the same mud hole.

Alana nodded at me, flashed Brian a rueful grin, and turned to Donna. "Okay if I use your phone, Donna? I need to call the sheriff."

"Sure," Donna said. "I'll show you where it is."

"Hey, Alana," I said. "What's this about a skeleton?"

"Ask Brian," Alana tossed over her shoulder. She was already on her way to the house. "He knows as much about it as I do."

I turned to Brian. "So the skull was smashed?"

"Yeah. Looks like a big rock fell on him." Brian hunched his shoulders, suddenly small and vulnerable. "Dying in a cave like that . . ." He shuddered.

I put my hand on his shoulder. The dry bones of ten-thousand-year-old humans are one thing, the skeleton of a caver is quite another, especially when you're just fourteen and a caver yourself. "You need to be careful when you're poking around in caves," I said. Mom-speak, with love. "Your dad and I don't have any Brians to spare."

We were back on accustomed territory now, a landscape that both of us knew, a vocabulary that we shared. He flashed me a quick grin. "Yeah, sure," he said. "I'm always careful. Can we go home now, Mom?"

Chapter Two

Stichwort (*Stellaria holostea*) got its name because it was traditionally used to treat a pain (a "stitch") in the side. The name "Dead Man's Bones" was perhaps derived from a confusion with another plant that was traditionally used to treat fractures, or because the stems were brittle and easily snapped, like the dried bones of the dead. In lore and legend, Dead Man's Bones was a plant that belonged to the elves and goblins, and children were warned that if they picked the flowers, the Little People would drag them off to their houses under the hill.

Although he was more relaxed now, Brian was obviously spooked by his find, and talking about it as we drove home seemed to help him. I was curious, too, about what he had found. His enchantment with Mistletoe Springs Cave and its various subterranean life forms—cave-adapted salamanders, snails, spiders, beetles, bats, and rats—not to mention its rocks and crystals and deposits of mineral salts, has made the cave a frequent topic of family conversations, and his room is crowded with cave stuff he's carted home to add to his collection. I had the feeling that we'd be talking about the bones he had found for a very long time.

The Hill Country looks solid enough when you walk on it, but looks are deceptive. Underneath, it's like a chunk of Swiss cheese, riddled with big and little caverns—what scientists call *karst* topography. Some of these caverns are isolated, others are interconnected; some are filled with water, others are bone dry. Some are explored, a few are mapped, and many others lie secret and undiscovered. Of the explored caves in the Hill Country, five or six are open to tourists, and you can pay an admission fee and take the naturally air-conditioned underworld tour, a cool thing to do on a blistering August afternoon.

Mistletoe Springs Cave, however, was unexplored and almost unknown when Aunt Velda stumbled into one of its two or three subsidiary openings—the same one that Jess Newton had stuck his saddlebag into the night after he and his brothers robbed the Pecan Springs bank. Because the cave is on private property, only a few of the neighbors knew it was there, and these folks—ranchers, mostly—had no idea that it might have any special significance, scientific, archaeological, or otherwise. To them, it's always been just a curious and not very attractive hole in the ground, hardly worth the effort it takes to reach it, which is considerable. The main opening lies at the far end of a craggy, rock-rimmed ravine, created by Mistletoe Creek. You can get there by following the badly rutted road that loops through what used to be the Swenson Ranch, or you can take the shorter but equally rutted road that parallels the creek. Both roads are private, though, which makes the site inaccessible to the merely curious.

I've been in the cave only a time or two, and I've gleaned most of what I know of it from Brian's dinner-table reports. The cavern is long and snaky, its labyrinthian network of mazelike passageways eaten into the soluble limestone by eons of seeping, dripping, trickling, flowing water. The archaeologists recovered the Paleo-Indian skeletons at the rear of the arched main opening, which is something like a large shelter carved into the limestone bluff. A rockfall had almost closed off a narrow passageway that, once opened and entered, proved to branch off in several different directions. Brian and a college-student helper from the dig had been exploring one of those passageways. Since the route had not yet been documented, the boys were not sure where they were going and were moving forward cautiously, mapping as they went.

They encountered the mud hole—the product of an underground seep—about thirty yards from the main cavern, Brian told us at dinner that night. Not far beyond that, the passageway pitched steeply upward and curved to the right. The boys were moving single file through the close, dusty darkness, with Brian in the lead. As they turned a corner, the light on his caver's helmet illuminated a splintered human skull beside a large rock.

The skeleton was hardly more than a heap of disarranged bones, webbed with shreds of what had once been clothing. The light glinted on a metal zipper, Brian said, startling him, and he realized that the skeleton was wearing jeans. It was this bit of modern technology that made the bones seem less like an archaeological discovery and more like the remains of a person—a cave explorer, he thought immediately, struck and killed by a falling rock.

The two boys had beat a nervous, hurried retreat to the main cavern. Brian didn't believe in ghosts, he said, but secrets seemed to hang like dust in the air over the silent, grinning skull. He was glad to get out into the light. He told his story to Alana Montoya, who went to have a look for herself before she drove down to Donna's to call the sheriff.

The longer Brian talked, the more comfortable he became, and I stopped worrying that he was going to be permanently scarred by his discovery. He went back to the cave on Saturday, but the people who were running the dig told him that it had been temporarily closed down. They weren't able to answer any of his questions about the skeleton.

Blackie could, though—Blackie Blackwell, the Adams County sheriff and a longtime fishing and poker buddy of McQuaid's. On Monday afternoon, he dropped by the house to talk to McQuaid about their annual fall hunting trip—they're partners in a deer lease near Brownwood—and ended up joining us for an early supper.

The friendship between Blackie and McQuaid goes back to the time when both were lawmen, McQuaid a Houston homicide detective and Blackie the newly elected sheriff of Adams County. I met McQuaid somewhat later, when he was testifying for the prosecution against the woman I was defending, a much-battered wife who had finally taken a fatal revenge on her husband. The jury found that the woman had acted in self-defense and acquitted her, but McQuaid didn't let that come between us. I was hardly suprised when, after I had moved to Pecan Springs, he walked into Thyme and Seasons and told me that he had left the force and taken a teaching position in the Criminal Justice department at CTSU.

But McQuaid has learned from experience that academic politics can be just as deadly as street fights (even deadlier, sometimes), and that classroom teaching, without the stimulus of real-world investigation, can get tiresome. A few months ago, he reduced his teaching load to part-time—he has just one class this semester, seven to ten on Monday nights—and hung out his shingle as a PI. *M. McQuaid and Associates, Private Investigations.* (By "associates," he doesn't mean me, of course. He plans to use people like Bubba Harris, a retired Pecan Springs police chief.)

This change in career direction has also changed our lives. There's less money, which is rather worrisome, especially since the shop isn't bringing in very much just now. And there are other worries. McQuaid's first case, in which I became inadvertently involved, began with a routine investigation of an embezzlement at Morgan's Pickles and included two murders and an exchange of gunfire. The second—a missing teenager found living with her new boyfriend in Houston—was far less thrilling, and the third (on which he is currently working) is a blood-chilling, spine-tingling case of résumé fraud. He hasn't confided any details, but this ho-hum stuff is definitely okay with me. I nearly lost McQuaid to a bullet several years ago. He still walks with a limp and, when he's tired, with a cane. As far as I'm concerned, the more commonplace and less life-threatening his investigations, the happier I'll be. I can get all the drama I want in my life, and then some, from watching reality cop shows on television.

The shop is closed on Mondays, which means I'm not as rushed as I am on other nights. Since we were having a guest, I was making curried chicken. McQuaid and Blackie like theirs extra hot, so along with curry, rice, veggies, and a large green salad, I opened a jar of McQuaid's six-alarm chutney and spooned it into a red bowl. Martha Stewart I'm not, but since we had company, I set the pine-topped kitchen table with my favorite antique Appleware. I added red placemats and napkins and a vase of autumn wildflowers and felt pleased with the way it looked.

Blackie and McQuaid are both big guys, and when they're in the same room, even as large a room as my kitchen, it feels a little crowded. Blackie is still a bachelor (although he and Sheila Dawson have been engaged for almost two years), and the closest he's likely to come to a home-cooked meal is Lila Jennings' meatloaf, at the Nueces Street Diner. So he sat down at the table with an enthusiastic grin and a thank-you for me.

Blackie Blackwell is quintessentially a cop, as though all the copness in the world has become concentrated in this one man. He's as square as they come—square shoulders, square jaw, square chin, military posture, sandy haircut in regulation style. You almost expect him to salute.

But in spite of his by-the-book look, Blackie knows when to set the rules aside and act on his gut instinct. He comes from a family of lawmen—his father, Corky Blackwell, was Adams County sheriff before him, while his mother Reba ran the jail and the sheriff's office. He's smart and tough. He's compassionate, too, when compassion is required. Even people who aren't overly fond of cops (and there are plenty of those in the Hill Country) have to admit that Blackie Blackwell is one of the good guys.

The men were already seated when Brian came barreling into the kitchen, Howard Cosell right behind him, and dove for his chair.

"Hands," I said, without turning around from the counter, where I was pouring iced tea. There was a silence. "And wiping them on your jeans isn't good enough," I added.

The chair scraped against the floor. "How'd you know?" Brian asked.

"Eyes in the back of my head," I replied, and Blackie chuckled. I put the filled glasses on the table. "Vamoose, kid."

While Brian was washing and McQuaid and Blackie were helping themselves to curry, I fed Howard Cosell, who gave me one of his doleful "surely-there's-more-to-life-than-this" looks when he saw the dry dog food in his dish.

I hardened my heart. "That's all you're going to get, Howard, old boy," I said firmly. "You heard the vet. You need to lose four pounds, before the next visit."

Bassets are almost too smart for their own good, and Howard is certainly no dummy. He inhaled his dry dog food with one scornful breath, then padded over to take up his station under the kitchen table, where McQuaid promptly dropped a chunk of curried chicken in front of him. Howard licked it up and thumped the floor gratefully with his tail, a performance that earned him another hunk of chicken as soon as McQuaid thought I wasn't looking. At the rate we're going, that four-pound loss isn't likely to happen in Howard's lifetime.

I sat down, Brian joined us, and a few moments of silence followed as we all heaped our plates. We were digging in to our food when McQuaid said, "Have you ID'd your John Doe yet, Blackie?"

Brian looked up quickly. "You're talking about the dead body in the cave? My body?"

"It can't be your body that's dead," McQuaid deadpanned. "Your body looks very much alive to me."

"Do we need to talk about dead bodies while we're eating this wonderful dinner I've cooked?" I inquired.

"It's not really a body, Mom," Brian explained, with a touching concern for my sensibilities. "It's just a bunch of dusty old bones."

"A distinction without a difference," I said, but I could see I was backing a losing horse. Judging from their expressions, all three of the guys wanted to pursue the subject.

"There was no wallet, so IDing Brian's caveman won't be a piece of cake," Blackie said, with a half-apologetic glance in my direction. He ladled a generous spoonful of McQuaid's chutney onto his curry. "I think we might've narrowed down the date of death, though."

"Oh, yeah?" McQuaid asked. He raised his eyebrow as Blackie took a second spoonful of chutney. "Watch that stuff—it's a little hot."

"Yeah," Blackie said. "There were a few coins lying under the skeleton, like maybe they'd been in a pocket when the cloth rotted. They were mostly from the 1950s and '60s. The latest was a 1975 penny with a crisp rim, no scratches. Looks like it hadn't been in circulation for more than a few months." He forked curry into his mouth.

"So you're putting the date of death somewhere after 1975?" McQuaid asked.

Blackie sucked in a breath, his eyes watering. "Wow," he said reverently. "Oh, man, this is good stuff. Did you make this, China? Will you marry me?"

"She's already married," Brian explained, with a teenage literalness.

"You'll have to marry McQuaid," I said. "The chutney in the red bowl is his. Mine's in the green bowl. It has more flavor and less firepower."

"He can't marry him, either," Brian explained. "Guys

don't marry guys." He frowned. "Except that I saw something on TV about these guys in Massachusetts who—"

"Thanks, Brian," McQuaid interrupted in a meaningful tone. Dad-speak.

"Didn't know you could make stuff like this, McQuaid," Blackie said. "Hotter'n an El Paso sidewalk in August." He spooned more chutney onto his curry, adding, "We're putting the date of death after 1975. We checked the regional missing-person reports for that time period, and came up with a list of possibles. Nobody local, though, which strikes mc as a little odd."

"Yeah?" McQuaid asked.

"Yeah. That cave's never been on the tourist trail, and only a few of the locals knew about it—until that crazy old lady stumbled onto the robbery cache." Blackie shook his head. He and Aunt Velda do not get along very well. He had a little trouble swallowing her tale about the Klingons, when she found that gold in the cave. I wondered what he would say if I told him she had recently been to Mars.

"Brian said the guy's skull was crushed," McQuaid remarked.

"Like maybe that big rock fell on him," Brian put in, looking up from his plate. "It weighed ten pounds, at least." He dropped a piece of chicken for Howard Cosell, who shot out his tongue and snapped it up. Howard may look slow and lazy, but where food is concerned, he's as fast on the draw as Billy the Kid.

"That's what it looks like." Blackie sounded cautious. "We don't know for sure that this is a man, though."

"He was wearing jeans," Brian said definitively. "And sandals. At least," he amended, "I thought I saw a sandal—like a Birkenstock, I mean. It had somc foot bones in it." He shivered. "I didn't stick around to have a look."

"Oh, *please,*" I said. "Lots of women wear jeans." At that very moment, I was wearing jeans and one of my Thyme and Seasons T-shirts. I stuck out my right foot. "And sandals. My sandal has foot bones in it, too," I added, wiggling it.

"Yeah, Brian," McQuaid said, mock-stern. With a wink at me, he added, "The devil is in the details. If you're going to be a scientist, you have to learn not to jump to conclusions." He turned to Blackie. "So you think it was a caving accident?"

"I'm not so sure," Blackie said, in a tone that sounded unusually cautious, even for him. "It's those sandals that've got me wondering." He frowned. "Brian, if you were going caving, would you wear sandals?"

"Heck, no," Brian replied, with the disdain of the expert. "I always wear leather boots. Anyway, it's not just the cave. First, you've got to get there, which usually means a hike. Most caves are in the backcountry, and hiking in sandals is no fun. You can't tell when you might stir up a rattlesnake."

"That's what I was thinking," Blackie said. "And that cave is way back, just off the ridge, on what used to be the old Swenson Ranch. A caver would have to drive ten miles across the ranch—which raises a question about his vehicle. He'd have to have left it, but how come nobody's spotted it, during all these years?"

"Maybe he came in at the Flower Farm and hiked up the road along the creek," Brian suggested. "That would be a lot shorter."

Blackie shook his head. "The road that's there now wasn't built until the early eighties. Which means that this person had to hike up the creek bed and climb the bluff in sandals. That'd be some rugged hike." He frowned. "And either way, there's still the question about the vehicle."

"Well, then," Brian said, "maybe he rode a horse across the ranch."

"In sandals?" I asked. Even in boots and chaps, riding across that ranch wouldn't be any picnic. I've been there, and it's nothing but miles and miles of prickly pear, mesquite thickets, and scrub cedar.

"There's the missing wallet, too," McQuaid said thoughtfully. "No matter how he got there, a caver wouldn't have any reason to leave his ID at home."

"You didn't mention finding a flashlight," I said.

"That's because there wasn't one," Blackie replied.

I took an involuntary breath. No light? I visited Mammoth Cave once, and the guide—with appropriate warning—turned off the lights. The darkness that abruptly engulfed me was not just the absence of light; it had weight and texture and movement and intention, and I suddenly knew why, in every culture, darkness is a symbol for consummate evil. I'm not especially claustrophobic, but I was glad, very glad, when the guide turned the lights back on.

I let out my breath. "You know what this means," I said quietly. "Somebody else was on the scene. Somebody who brought the person there in a vehicle, then left with the light."

"And that rock," McQuaid said. He turned to Brian. "Isn't it a little unusual to find a large rock lying loose in the interior of one of the limestone caves around here?"

Brian stared at his father. "Yeah, I guess it is, Dad. I'd have to go back and look, but it may have been the only loose rock in that corridor. And the ceiling was rounded from water action. Now that I think about it, I don't see how that rock could have fallen from that ceiling."

"So somebody carried the rock in from outside," I hazarded. The same somebody who had driven the vehicle and carried the light.

Blackie nodded. "It's a fossiliferous limestone. There are similar chunks lying just outside the cave. In other words, we're not dealing with a natural rockfall."

"Why didn't I spot that?" Brian muttered, chagrined.

McQuaid grinned. "Devil's in the details, kid."

"Well," Blackie said, "given all these questions, you can see why I'm not ready to file this case under 'Accidental death.' I want a forensics expert to take a look at those bones and give us an opinion on the cause of death."

"A forensics expert," Brian said in an awed tone. "You mean, I discovered a crime scene? Wait'll Jake hears about this!" Jake is Brian's current girlfriend. Her full name is

Jacqueline Keene. She's a cheerful, athletic girl, high-point scorer on the girls basketball team and a champion soccer player. Somehow, "Jake" seems to fit.

"Brian," McQuaid said darkly, "this is not a video game."

"That's exactly the point, Dad." Brian looked gleeful. "This is for real. We're talking murder here. Which makes it a lot better than a video game. Or a movie, even."

I thought of the solitary bones in the cave, and the human body—energetic, adventuresome, full of dreams and longings—that had once encased them, and bit back my reprimand. In a few years, Brian would be mature enough to hear the insensitivity in his response. Until then, admonitions from me would probably have the opposite effect.

McQuaid must have come to the same conclusion, for he only shook his head. "Who's doing the forensic work on this one?" he asked, turning back to Blackie. "The Bexar M.E.'s office? Or Travis?" Adams County is a small county, and can't afford its own medical examiner's office. Blackie sends his work to either Bexar or Travis County, whichever has the shortest waiting list.

"Neither," Blackie replied. "Both are stacked up from here to Christmas, and since this is obviously a cold case, it'll go to the bottom of the list." He reached for the curry dish and took a second helping. "On this one, I'm getting some help from CTSU."

"Oh, yeah?" McQuaid said, with interest. "Who?"

"Alana Montoya," Blackie said.

"Oh, sure," Brian said eagerly. "You know, Dad. Alana. The woman who's working at the cave dig. She's good." He grinned. "She's got a Ph.D. in bones. People call her the bone doc."

Blackie nodded. "She's agreed to do a forensic analysis of the skeleton." He looked quizzically at McQuaid. "You probably know her, McQuaid. The Anthropology department hired her last year to set up the new forensic anthropology program. Some of the courses must be cross-listed with Criminal Justice."

"I've met her," McQuaid said, in a curiously guarded tone. He added, slowly, "In fact, I was on the search committee that hired her."

"Then you know that she's got first-rate credentials." To me, Blackie said, "Edited a big textbook or something like that. She was on the research staff at Louisiana State University before she came here, in the FACES laboratory—that's Forensic Anthropology and Computer Enhancement Services," he added, for Brian's benefit. "One of the top forensic labs in the country. I figure Alana will get the work done a lot faster than the folks at Bexar or Travis, and cheaper, too." He grinned. "She's one smart gal, if you ask me."

"Oh, she's smart enough," McQuaid said, and pushed his plate away. "And experienced."

I looked at McQuaid, hearing something caustic in his tone. Blackie's head came up. "What's that supposed to mean?" he asked.

"Nothing," McQuaid said, with a quick shrug. "Nothing at all." He looked at his watch and got up. "Sorry guys, but I've got to go, or I'll be late to class."

"There's dessert," I said.

McQuaid dropped a kiss on the top of my head. "Save it for me, babe," he said. "See you later, Blackie. Brian, don't forget your homework." More Dad-speak.

Chapter Three

An herbal bath was used in centuries past as an excellent preparation for an aphrodisiacal feast of love. Erotic oils used in herbal soaps include clary sage, jasmine, rose, ylang-ylang, orange blossom, cardamom, juniper, sandalwood, vanilla, and patchouli.

Christian Ratsch
Plants of Love

Blackie insisted on helping Brian with the kitchen chores—the rule at our house is that anybody who doesn't cook is obliged to wash the dishes. I left the two of them to their work and went out to the herb garden behind the house to cut some lavender.

When we moved here three or so years ago, I didn't plan to have a large garden. But the herb gardens around the shop are more for display than actual production, and every year, I seem to want more of something—more lavender, more sage, more parsley, more thyme. So the backyard garden has become the place where I grow the herbs I dry to sell in the shop, or package fresh and sell in the produce section at Cavette's Grocery, the old-fashioned market at the corner of Guadalupe and Green, just a few blocks from the shop. I always smile when I see those neat little raffia-tied cellophane packages of Thyme and Seasons basil and rosemary and marjoram, and think of somebody cooking with them, making soup, maybe, or a salad, or a main dish. Somehow, it's like spreading the wealth. I'll never get rich, but I'm doing good work.

As the evening deepened into dusk and the nighthawks began to dart through the sky, I spent a pleasant half hour gathering lavender, which I would dry for use in potpourri and sachets. The evening was warm, the soft hum of satisfied honeybees vibrated in the air, and the lavender fragrance wrapped itself around me like a perfumed shawl. The scent of lavender is known to relieve stress, calm anxieties, and promote sleep, and in the evenings, when I'm working among the lavenders, I always feel languid and lazy and loose, as if the sweetened air has softened my bones. Tonight, I moved through the garden slowly, forgetting my worries about the business, about McQuaid's new enterprise and Brian's caveman, just breathing in the therapeutic scent of lavender.

I had finished filling my basket and was on my way back to the house, still feeling mellow and calm, when Blackie came down the path toward me.

"I'm heading home," he said. "Thanks for the dinner, China."

"Oh, you're welcome," I replied. He fell into step with me and we went up the path together. "Thanks for giving Brian a hand with the dishes."

"He's a super kid," Blackie said. "Got a good head on his shoulders."

I agreed, and added, "We don't see enough of you these days, Blackie. Why don't you and Sheila go out to dinner with us next weekend?" I grinned. "We could do some country dancing. McQuaid and I haven't been to Pistol Pete's yet." Pistol Pete's is a new dance hall north of town, on the Old San Marcos Road.

Blackie slowed, stopped, his hands in his pockets. His face was serious and his gray eyes were steady, sober. "You haven't talked to Sheila in the last couple of weeks?"

I shook my head. "Nope." I'd phoned her office to see if she'd be available for lunch, but she'd said she was busy. "Is something wrong?"

"Well, you might say so," Blackie replied. His voice grew taut and bitter. "We've called it off. The engagement, I mean."

"Again?" I chuckled. "Is this the third time, or the fourth?" I stopped laughing when I saw the way his mouth had tightened at the corners, and my mellow, lavender-flavored mood began to evaporate. "Serious, huh?"

"Yeah, serious. It's just not going to happen, China. And the problem isn't our jobs, either. That's just an excuse that Sheila finds convenient."

Sheila Dawson, Blackie's fiancée—Smart Cookie, to her friends—has served for the past two years as Pecan Springs's chief of police, and a darn good one, too, although she has her share of enemies. Their law enforcement work gives Blackie and Sheila a great deal in common, but it's also been a continual source of friction. For one thing, the sheriff is elected, and Sheila has been concerned that some of her unpopular moves—such as insisting on early retirement for certain older officers who had gotten lazy and complacent—might cause him to lose votes. For another, Blackie worries about Sheila's safety and is apt to go out looking for her if she doesn't show up when she's expected. And both have a tendency to poke their noses into the other's cases, giving advice where it isn't necessarily welcome. Altogether, a difficult set of issues to handle.

But Blackie had said that work wasn't the problem. "If it isn't your jobs, what is it?" I stopped. "Sorry. I don't mean to pry. It's none of my business."

Blackie turned, looking out over the garden, so I couldn't see his face. His shoulders were slumped. "I'm just tired of her shilly-shallying, that's all." He sighed heavily. "We've been engaged—if that's what you want to call it—for nearly two years. Two years of nothing but on-again, off-again, will-she, won't-she." His voice became rough. "Damn it, if she hasn't made up her mind by now, she's not going to. I'm the marrying kind. I'm tired of hanging around, waiting."

For Blackie, this was an unusually long speech. The sheriff is not a talkative man, especially when it comes to matters of the heart, and he had taken me by surprise. I said the only thing I could think of.

"I'm sorry." It didn't sound good enough. "I'm *really* sorry, Blackie," I amended. "It must hurt like hell."

"It does. Sheila's a great gal. Whoever gets her will be a damn lucky man." Blackie's mouth went crooked. "I've just got to face up to the fact that it ain't gonna be me, that's all."

I put my hand on his sleeve, feeling the muscular strength through the sleeve of his shirt. "You okay?"

He turned. His gray eyes met mine, and I could see the hurt and anger shadowing his glance. "Not yet," he said, his voice husky. "But I will be. Thanks for asking." Unexpectedly, he put his arms around me and gave me a quick hug. "It's nice to see McQuaid so happy, China. You're good for him. I guess I've been hoping that Sheila and I would have something like what you guys have. But it's over now, and I've got to get on with my life."

He held me for a moment longer, not speaking, as if he had run out of words, or the words still left in him were too painful to speak.

Then he dropped his arms, stepped back, and was gone.

"WELL, it's a damn shame, if you ask me," McQuaid said, tossing his shorts into the laundry hamper. It took nearly two years for him to learn that little trick, and I see it as a sign that we're getting used to living together. He'd probably say the same thing about my remembering to check Big Red Mama's tire pressure when I fill her up at the gas pump. I'm learning that if you give a little, you get a little.

"Yeah." I cinched my white terry robe tighter and began to brush my teeth. "Definitely a shame."

McQuaid stepped into the shower and closed the glass door. We were talking about Sheila and Blackie. The sheriff hadn't told McQuaid, of course—as I said, he doesn't talk easily about emotional matters. I had been the one to break the news.

"I don't want to take sides," I said, raising my voice, "but I can understand Sheila's situation."

"Sure you can," McQuaid said, turning up the volume on the shower. The steam began to rise toward the ceiling, and I could see his shadow through the opaque glass. "You can understand Sheila because you had the same problem. On again, off again." His voice grew muffled and burbly as he stuck his head under the running water. "I don't blame Blackie for calling it quits." He shut off the shower, conserving water, and began to shampoo his hair. "What *is* it with you women? Why can't you make up your minds?"

We had arrived at the edge of a difficult terrain, full of booby traps and land mines, and I wasn't eager to go there. McQuaid had asked me to marry him a couple of years before I actually agreed—and when I did, I couldn't quite bring myself to believe that I was doing the right thing. It took a lot of anguished soul-searching before I felt even halfway ready.

Ruby, of course, had made the whole thing into a joke. "Most of my friends have been married and divorced twice in the time it's taken you to make up your mind, China," she'd say with a laugh.

But it wasn't very funny, after all. When McQuaid was shot, I realized that I cared more for him than for my independence, my self-determination, or even my privacy and personal space. I still sometimes long for the old days, when I was my own boss, when I could close up the shop and go home and have only myself and my own needs to cope with—like those female private eyes in detective novels. Kinsey Millhone, for instance. Kinsey doesn't have a husband and son to cook for, and when her place gets cluttered, she can pick up her stuff and it stays picked up. *Her* stuff, not his. She doesn't rub up against anyone else in her personal space, and all her time is *her* time.

But those old longings are usually displaced by the rich, real pleasures of my life with McQuaid and Brian. I suspected that Smart Cookie would discover the same satisfactions, if she gave herself half a chance. Work, however exciting, is not the only wonderful thing in the world.

All that did not make me want to criticize her, though, and especially not to McQuaid. I rinsed my mouth. "Maybe she just doesn't think it's the right thing to do."

The shower came back on, and McQuaid ran his hands through his hair, vigorously. I could see the shape of his lean body through the translucent glass of the shower door, and the sight of it made me shiver. We've been lovers for a long time, but that hasn't diminished the pleasure I take from his touch or staled the excitement of his body against mine. I can never get enough of him.

"If that's it," he went on, beginning to soap himself, "Sheila oughta tell him so, and stop all this mealymouthed monkey business. How the hell is Blackie supposed to make plans for the future if she keeps stringing him along?"

McQuaid was speaking out of his own needs. He's the kind of person who likes to look for answers, likes to make plans, likes to organize the future, likes to leave nothing to chance. He's good-looking, in a craggy sort of way: dark hair, dark brows, steely blue eyes, a broken nose earned when he threw for extra yardage against Texas A & M on Turkey Day, a zigzag scar across his forehead, relic of a fight with a doper in a parking lot at the Astrodome. But it isn't just McQuaid's looks that you notice when you meet him. It's his commanding presence, his self-confidence, his boldness, his personal authority. He always knows what he wants, what it will cost, and how to go for it. And he has a nice tight butt.

I could smell the erotic fragrance of ylang-ylang and

sandalwood, rising in the steam. I had already taken my shower, but I let my robe slide off my shoulders and slid back the glass door.

"I can see Blackie's side of it, too," I said, stepping into the shower. "You're right. It isn't fair. Maybe calling it off is the best thing to do. For both of them."

McQuaid looked down at me, smiling. "Hey," he said. His eyes lightened with pleasure in a way that gives me goose bumps. "You're naked. Naked wife."

"Naked husband." I put my arms around him. He was slippery with soap, and I moved my hands over his back, his shoulders. The warm water ran over both of us.

"Mmmm," I murmured, licking a trail of scented suds from his shoulder. "You taste good. Smell good, too."

His voice was husky. "You know where this leads, don't you?"

I feigned innocence, about as successfully as Jack the Ripper. "No, where?"

He chuckled. "Wild, unruly, uncontrollable *sex*." He brought his head down and kissed me, hard, his fingers kneading my neck, my shoulders. I arched against him, loving the feel of his hands, his chest, his narrow hips, his thighs, feeling our hearts beginning to pound together.

"Show me," I said.

"You don't have to ask twice," he said, reaching over to shut off the water.

LATER, when we were lying together among the damp, tumbled sheets, he went back to the previous subject.

"About Blackie and Sheila," he said. He kissed the tip of my nose. "I guess I just wish they had some of what we've got. Remember that Kenny Rogers' song? 'I feel sorry for anyone who isn't me tonight.' "

"I remember," I said, and ran the tip of my finger across his dark eyebrow. "Me, too."

Chapter Four

Pumpkins aren't just for Halloween jack-o'-lanterns or pumpkin pie. In central America, the seeds (*pepitas*) of this native American herb were used to cool fevers, treat kidney and bladder ailments, and purge intestinal parasites. And recently, scientists have begun to investigate the use of pumpkin seed oil as a treatment for osteoarthritis, or degenerative joint disease. In osteoarthritis, the cartilege breaks down, causing the bones to rub together. Animal studies suggest that adding pumpkin seed to the diet may be as effective in reducing joint inflammation as the use of nonsteroidal anti-inflammatory drugs.

At the shops, Tuesday got off to a slow start, which gave me time to put out some Halloween decorations. I piled a half-dozen pumpkins beside the front door, making a mental note to ask Brian to carve them into jack-o'-lanterns, hung a few spiderwebs, and put up some autumn wreaths. Before long, it would be time to start thinking about Thanksgiving, and then Christmas. I don't know what it is about the autumn months, but they seem to fly past faster than I can chase them.

Business picked up later in the morning, since we were hosting a lunch for the Friends of the Library. Thirty people showed up to feast on green pea soup with mint (served cold, always delightful), wild rice chicken salad with avocado, focaccia with herb butter, and lavender tea cakes. After their gourmet lunch—without a doubt, the very best that can be had in Pecan Springs—the guests wandered through the shops and the gardens, so we had a better-than-usual afternoon at the cash registers. Not only that, but Ruby handed out Party Thyme cards and snared two more catering jobs. Things were looking up.

Tuesday evening was free for me, since McQuaid and Brian were going to a Dad's Night event at school. Thinking about what Blackie had told me and feeling regretful, I called Sheila to see if we could get together for dinner, but she didn't return my call. Ruby had to leave early to meet Cassandra Wilde, the volunteer costume director for *A Man for All Reasons*, so I closed up both shops at the usual hour, then drove over to the theater to add a few last-minute plants to the landscaping: more rosemary, some lemongrass, and several santolina, and another dozen chrysanthemums. In my opinion, it is theoretically possible to have too many chrysanthemums, but I have personally never reached that point. When they're in bloom, they're bronze and red and gold and pretty; when they're not, they're green and pretty. Such a deal.

The evening was warm and clear, the sun dropping into the western sky, the wind a dry whisper in the trees. It was nearly six-thirty, and I was watering the new plantings when Ruby, a bundle of costumes over her arm, came out of the theater with Cassandra. *A Man for All Reasons* was set in Pecan Springs during four distinct eras: the First World War, the Roaring Twenties, the Depressed Thirties, and the Post-War Forties. The period costumes were a challenge, obviously, but from what I had already seen, Cassandra and her crew of costumers—the Wilde Elves, they call themselves—had been equal to it.

I turned off the hose. "Hey, how's it going, guys?"

Cassandra grinned. "It'd be a whole lot easier if Ruby would just put a lid on her bright ideas."

"But I'm playing Mrs. Obermann," Ruby said, with a

playful pout. "I'm the leading lady. My ideas ought to count for something."

"Oh, they do, they do," Cassandra replied, rolling her eyes. Cass is in her mid-thirties, maybe five-feet-three-inches tall, round and bountifully shaped, with curly blonde hair, creamy skin, and a cheerful, oversized smile. Ruby's friend and sometime astrology student, she's a regular at the shops and the tearoom. "I just absolutely adore the way you redesigned the costume for the second part of Act One," she added dryly. "And only a week before opening night. Good planning, Ruby."

"But I did all the sewing, Cass," Ruby protested.

"And I was happy to let you," Cassandra replied. "I like your new look, really, I do—it's very Twenties, and that slinky fabric and fringe looks wonderful on you." She threw up her hands. "I just don't know how Miss Jane's going to feel about it, that's all. She had already approved the first designs, and you know how hard it is to please her."

"I doubt that she'll notice," Ruby said. She grinned, adding cryptically, "And if Miss Jane wants to find fault with the production, she'll have plenty to hold her attention."

"I'll agree with that," Cassandra said. She glanced around at the landscaping. "Looks good, China. Wish my thumbs were as green as yours. I can cook and sew and cast an astrological chart, but when it comes to gardening, I'm at a loss."

"Thanks, Cass." I picked up a rake and made a few adjustments. "A little mulch covers a multitude of sins." My mantra.

"Can I quote you on that?" Cassandra smiled brightly, showing off very white teeth. "Gotta go, guys. I'm volunteering at the women's clinic tonight." She waved good night and headed toward the new parking lot behind the theater. Cass's queen-size energy matches her queenly amplitude.

"Don't you just loathe women who don't have to get

their teeth whitened?" Ruby muttered enviously, watching her go. "And when she says she can cook, believe her. She brought some lemon bars for the crew this evening. They were gone in a twinkle. But I hate her teeth."

I chuckled. Ruby has been debating the merits of whitening her teeth for the past six months. Not that whiter teeth would attract any more attention than her outfits. This evening, she was wearing skintight black leggings, black leather flats, and a bronzy silk tunic with a flowing scarf, exactly the right complement to her flaming hair. The tunic looked like it cost more than a new set of tires for Big Red Mama, but I knew that the material had come from the sale bin at Menzy's Fine Fabrics and had taken Ruby all of an hour to whip up. It was easy to see why Cassandra had been pleased to let Ruby design and make her own costume.

"How does Cass like her new job?" I asked. Cassandra works at the CTSU campus food service, where she's recently been promoted to a management position.

"I don't think she likes doing paperwork," Ruby said. "She says she misses hands-on cooking. She's been talking about quitting and setting up her own business as a personal chef. You know, somebody who comes into your kitchen and cooks up a batch of tasty meals for your freezer."

"A personal chef," I said with a laugh. "Now, that's what I need. Tell Cass to get cookin'."

She nodded. "Actually, I was hoping she might be willing to give Party Thyme a hand on weekends and evenings. Janet is complaining about her knees again. And yesterday, her elbow was bothering her."

This is becoming a difficult situation. Janet, who has been with us for nearly two years, suffers from osteoarthritis, degenerative disease of the joints. The cartilege breaks down and the ends of the bones begin to rub painfully against each other. She's been taking some of the herbs that have traditionally been used to treat arthritis—devil's claw and boswellia—and using capsaicin cream (made from red peppers), and her condition seems to have improved. But she wants time off, and she's been dropping broad hints that she would like to start working part-time in the kitchen. And as far as the catering is concerned, sometimes she will and sometimes she won't. Lately, she won't. We're obviously going to have to find somebody else to help out with Party Thyme, and probably in the kitchen, as well. But locating a replacement for Janet won't be easy. She's a good cook.

Ruby glanced around at the landscaping. "I'd offer to help, but it looks like you're all finished."

"Yeah," I said wryly. "Perfect timing." Frowning, I added, "Listen, Ruby, have you talked to Sheila in the last few days?"

It's an unfortunate truth that marriage and family activities are subtracted from the time I have to spend with friends. Ruby, Sheila, and I used to go out for dinner at least once a week, take an occasional weekend trip, and hang out together whenever we got the chance. Ruby and I work under the same roof, so I still manage to see her every day, even if we don't have time for the long, leisurely talks we used to enjoy.

But Sheila and I have to make a date to get together, and for the past month—tonight, for instance—we hadn't seemed able to connect. Now that I had some time to think about what Blackie had told me, it occurred to me that Smart Cookie might be avoiding me because McQuaid happens to be Blackie's best friend and she doesn't want to put me in a tough spot. But I had to see her in order to correct this misunderstanding, and if she wouldn't return my calls—

"Sheila?" Ruby said uncomfortably. "Well, yes. We went for a bike ride the other evening."

Time to go bike-riding with Ruby, but no time to phone me. "Did she mention anything about Blackie?"

Ruby gave me a cautious look. "Sort of . . ."

I leaned on my rake. "It's true, then? They've broken off their engagement?"

"How did you know?" Ruby countered.

"Blackie told me last night. He's pretty upset."

Ruby scowled. "Well, I should hope so. If you ask me, he's being a horse's patootie. A real grade-A jerk."

That surprised me. I have seen the sheriff when he was preoccupied, consumed by his work, and uncommunicative, but I would never characterize him as a jerk, and especially not grade-A. And Sheila herself is often preoccupied and work-focused. You can't be a female chief of police without a certain amount of toxic fallout in your personal life.

"I wouldn't call Blackie a jerk," I said defensively. "He loves Sheila very much. The problem is that she can't seem to make up her mind."

Ruby gave a scornful chuckle. "The pot calling the kettle black."

"So?" I retorted. "Maybe that makes me an expert. Been there, done that, not just once but over and over again. Maybe all Smart Cookie has to do is stop worrying, trust her gut instinct, and just let herself love him." It sounds simplistic, maybe, but that's the way I managed to ease into marriage. If I could do it, Sheila could, too.

"But it's not like you and McQuaid, China." Ruby put her head to one side, regarding me with an uncharacteristic soberness. "You knew all along that he was the right guy, and you knew that you loved him—you just weren't ready for marriage, that's all. It's different for Sheila. She's realized that Blackie isn't the right guy. She knows she doesn't love him."

I stared at her, suddenly seeing things in a whole new light. "Oh," I said, feeling like all kinds of a fool. "Oh, gosh, Ruby. That's too bad."

"Yeah," Ruby said. "She's been trying to tell him for the last couple of months, but he just wouldn't listen. You know Blackie. When he gets a thing in his mind—" She shrugged.

Ruby didn't have to finish her sentence. I understood.

Blackie is a great guy, rock-steady, sincere, completely dependable. If he says something, you can stake your life on it. But he has a tendency to a certain inflexibility. When Blackie settles on a view of something, it's not easy for him to change. Sheila had loved him once. It would be difficult for him to believe that she wouldn't love him forever, that she might have actually stopped loving him.

"So the engagement is definitely off?" I said sadly.

"According to Sheila, it's been off for a couple of months," Ruby replied in a pragmatic tone. "Blackie just wouldn't take no for an answer." She looked up. "Uh-oh," she said, under her breath. "Here comes trouble."

I followed her glance. Coming toward us from the direction of the Obermann mansion were two old ladies, one tall and autocratic, the other short, stooped, and fragile, with the look of someone whose bones can barely support the weight of flesh. The Obermann sisters, Jane and Florence. I had never been introduced to them, since they have been reclusive in the years I've been in Pecan Springs. They obviously knew Ruby, however, since she was playing the role of their mother, Cynthia Obermann, in Miss Jane's play.

"Good evening, ladies," Ruby called, raising her voice.

"Good evenin', Ruby." Miss Florence's voice was high-pitched, shrill, and Southern. She's the younger of the two by several years, but she is tiny and frail, and her halo of thin white hair is almost ethereal.

Miss Jane, on the other hand, makes a more substantial impression. I saw first her impressive height, her sturdy frame clothed in a supple garnet-red pantsuit. And then I was struck by her features—the aristocratic nose, the large and astonishingly brilliant black eyes—and her steel-gray hair, coiled on top of her head. She gave me the impression of a poised, self-contained, and autocratic woman, so different from the dithery Miss Florence that it was hard to imagine them as sisters.

Miss Jane nodded shortly to Ruby, then fixed me with those piercing dark eyes.

"Who're you?" Her voice was brusque, deep, startlingly masculine, without a hint of a Texas drawl. "I don't know you, do I?" I immediately regretted my dirty hands and grubby-looking jeans, hardly appropriate garb for paying homage to the queen.

"You've never met China?" Ruby asked smoothly, prodding me forward. "Miss Jane, Miss Florence, this is China Bayles, from Thyme and Seasons Herbs, here in town. Marian Atkins asked her to take care of the landscaping." She gestured toward the plants that filled the gracefully bermed L-shaped bed in front of the theater. "We all think she's done a wonderful job." She added a bright, slightly artificial smile to this commercial endorsement.

"Thank you, Ruby," I said. I glanced at Miss Jane, suddenly apprehensive, like a nine-year-old called to confess her misdeeds to the all-powerful headmistress. What would I do if she didn't approve of the landscaping? Tear it out by the roots? Cover myself with sackcloth and ashes and mulch?

"I hope you like it," I said, appealing to Miss Florence but not expecting much. It is widely reckoned in Pecan Springs that Florence Obermann has not once in all of her seventy-plus years been allowed to have an opinion, since all opinions rightfully and naturally belong to Miss Jane.

I was not disappointed. "Well," Miss Florence said tentatively. She shot a glance at her sister. "What do you think, Jane?" she asked in a quavering voice.

Miss Jane glanced around, her gaze resting, sphinxlike on first one plant, then another, measuring each one and finding it lacking. "Roses would have been far better," she said at last. "Father always liked roses." Her deep, dry voice took on a sarcastic edge. "Of course, no one thought to ask me what he would have wanted, in spite of the fact that Florence and I donated the theater in his honor."

There was no reason for me to be surprised by this response, given Miss Jane's reputation for making life difficult for others. She ruled the social roost in Pecan Springs in the 1950s and '60s, although in the past several decades, she and her sister have turned into virtual recluses. Neither of them drive, and they haven't been seen at a social function in years.

There was a great deal of surprise, verging on incredulity, when it was first learned that Miss Jane and Miss Florence had offered to donate the Obermann stable, the funding for renovations, and a sizeable chunk of adjoining property to the Community Theater Association. No one would have been surprised if this generous gift had come from their father, of course, for Dr. Merrill Obermann, a general practitioner and doc-of-all-trades, had supported a variety of Pecan Springs arts projects. In addition to the hospital wing that bore his name, he had funded the library, a community orchestra, and a summer arts program for disadvantaged children, back in the days when little towns didn't dream of such luxuries. Doctor Obermann may have been a stern authoritarian and not very likable, but by the time he died, in the mid-1950s, he was much admired for his altruism.

The same could not be said for his four offspring. Dr. Obermann's sons, Carl and Harley, and his daughters, Jane and Florence (who inherited the entire family fortune after both brothers' deaths), inherited at least some of their father's philanthropic inclinations. The two sisters have been known for their willingness to say yes when asked to contribute to a worthy cause, especially when that cause involves the hospital, United Way, or the Adams County Republican Club, where they are big-time supporters of every political campaign. They haven't continued their father's support of the arts, however—a major disappointment to several local organizations. The summer arts program and the symphony orchestra both came to an end when the doctor died, for his daughters failed to continue to support them.

So when Jane announced last year that she and Florence were prepared to donate a theater to the Community Theater Association, the news was greeted with pleasure. And with some astonishment, since the sisters had rejected an earlier appeal from the association for funding to renovate the old movie house where they staged their productions. The Pecan Springs *Enterprise*, presenting an editorially grateful face to the public, described the gift as "remarkable and magnanimous," although Hark Hibler, the editor, slyly added that it was gratifying to see one of Pecan Springs oldest families stepping forward at last to take a major role in arts philanthropy.

It didn't take long for the real motive behind the Obermanns' gift to emerge, however, since the promised theater came with some pretty serious strings attached—in Hark's memorable phrase (not for publication), this was a gift horse whose teeth needed counting. In order to get their new facility, the Community Theater Association would have to agree to stage as their first production a play written by Jane Obermann herself, about the life of her father. The play, entitled *A Man for All Reasons*, was to be performed for at least three weekends, so that everyone in town would have an opportunity to attend. What's more, Jane Obermann reserved the right to approve the casting, the costumes, and the scenery. *Quid pro quo*, y'all. If the association accepted these conditions, it would get a spiffy new theater. If it didn't, it wouldn't.

You probably won't be surprised to hear that for the Community Theater Association, this set of conditions felt like a deal breaker. Ruby, who serves on the board of directors, told me what happened when Lance Meyers, the chairman of the board, heard about Jane Obermann's demands.

"Stage her play? Over my dead body!" Lance had thundered angrily. "I'm not going to let some damned amateur playwright—who's never published a thing in her entire life—impose a silly, sentimental script about her father on us. Why, this is nothing but blackmail, and I'm not going to stand for it. No self-respecting theater company would accept such conditions. Theater or no theater, we are *not* doing her play!"

Since Lance is a man who means what he says, this might have been the last word. But the Grande Cinema, the old movie house on the square where the theater association has been staging its productions for the last ten years, was falling down around their ears. It had finally been condemned. Unless the association could arrange to borrow the high school auditorium or fit their productions into the Methodist church annex, there would be no more community theater in Pecan Springs. The situation was nothing short of desperate, and everybody—including Miss Jane—knew it.

So a few other members of the board, reluctant to let this stunning opportunity slip through their fingers, quietly went to work. Within a week, Lance Meyers had announced his resignation from the board, and several others had resigned in sympathy with his position. Marian Atkins—who told me that she hated like hell to do it, but didn't have any choice—reluctantly stepped into Lance's shoes, and it was announced that the board was "seriously considering" the Obermann sisters' offer. Marian took Miss Jane's script home to read over the weekend, and came back with her recommendation, which was hardly a surprise, under the circumstances.

"The play is a little . . . well, amateurish," she told the board, "and it certainly needs some cutting and tightening up. But I think we can manage to stage it. In fact, it might work very well as a house opener, since it's basically the story of Doctor Obermann's life. There are a lot of people in town who still remember him."

"Not always favorably," somebody reminded her. "He gave away a lot of money, sure. But he screwed a lot of people along the way. A lot of important people, with long memories."

Marian had waved the remark away. "Of course, the production isn't going to be easy. Unless I miss my guess, that old woman is going to be the very devil to work with. We'll all be screaming bloody murder."

The board didn't disagree, but as Marian reminded them, they were running out of options, fast. So after a long discussion of the pros and cons (the playwright herself headed the list of cons), they gritted their collective teeth and said yes, thank you kindly, Miss Obermann, we'll stage your play, and we'll take your playhouse, and we'll even pretend that this whole thing is a wonderful idea and we're having a whale of a wonderful time.

True to their word, the two Misses Obermann signed over the property and, with appropriate ceremony and picture-taking, deposited a very cool three hundred thousand dollars into the Merrill Obermann Theater Renovation Fund. A local architect drew up the plans, and the contractors went to work. The attractive old stone building was gutted and refloored, then reroofed and rewired. New plumbing was installed, along with the necessary heating and air-conditioning. One end was turned into the stage and dressing room space; rows of plush seats were set up in the middle; and the front became an entrance lobby. The theater was on its way to becoming a community showplace.

There was an irony here, some observers would have said, for the grand new theater stood in sad contrast to the run-down mansion in which the Obermann sisters lived. They had stopped entertaining decades before, and apparently had no pride of place. The house needed paint and repair, and the gardens were a weedy jungle. Once the most beautiful house in town, the old place was now a derelict relic.

But most people were too busy to notice the sad state of the Obermann mansion. While the renovations were going on, the play's script was rewritten and Jean Davenport, the director, began the casting. Sets and costumes were discussed and designed, and rehearsals got underway.

All this was not without its problems, of course. Most of them were created by Miss Jane herself, who proved, as Marian had foreseen, the very devil to work with. Of course, nobody expected that the old lady would take the revision of her precious script lying down, and she didn't disappoint. Carleton Becker, who was in charge of the rewrite, told me, in a tone of quiet desperation, that he couldn't wait for the play to be over and done with.

"And if that doesn't happen soon," he'd said dramatically, "I promise you I am going to kill her." He raised his fists. "With my bare hands."

But Miss Jane's meddling went far beyond the script. In the end, she managed to alienate everybody, from Marian and Carleton and Jean to the roofer and the plumbers and the people who installed the theater seats. Because she was constantly getting in everybody's face, the construction took far longer and cost much more than planned, and dozens of tempers were frayed to the breaking point. As Marian put it, they were finding it harder and harder to pretend that they were having fun.

"If this drags on much longer," she said through clenched teeth, "I am personally going to bash that old bird right square in her beaky nose."

But at last the theater was ready and the play was as good as it was going to get. The dress rehearsal of *A Man for All Reasons* was scheduled for Thursday night, and the Denim and Diamonds Opening Night Gala for Friday, followed by the cast party, which Party Thyme had been hired to cater. The costumes and sets were finished, and the actors had been rehearsing for almost two months. The landscaping was done, too—except that Miss Jane didn't like it, maybe because it made the overgrown garden around her house look like a tangle of weeds.

So what else was new?

I summoned a smile, knowing that I had to humor the old lady. "I certainly understand how you feel about the roses, Miss Jane. Actually, there's plenty of room to add other plants." I pointed to the top of the low berm. "We could put two rosebushes right there, and a couple more at the corners of the building. We might even add a rose arbor off to one side for a larger planting, if you like. The plants won't be in bloom for Friday night, of course, but come spring, they'll be gorgeous. Did your father have any particular favorites?"

"He liked Cecile Brunner and Duchess de Brabant." Miss Jane spoke reluctantly, but her deep voice had lost some of its sarcastic edge.

"Those are both shrub roses, so we could use them at the top of the berm," I said. "We might plant a Cecile Brunner climber at one corner of the theater. How about a Zepherine Drouhine at the other corner?"

"I'll give it some thought," the old lady said grudgingly. "How can I reach you?"

I fished a card out of my pocket and handed it to her. Maybe roses were the way to the lady's heart. "That's my shop number," I said. "I can also have some little signs made up, identifying the roses as Doctor Obermann's favorites."

Her wide mouth curved into something that might have resembled a smile, although it might just as easily have been a grimace. "Very well, Ms. . . ." She glanced down at my card, as if it had been too much effort to remember my name, and she needed a prompt. She probably wouldn't remember my face, either. "Ms. Bayless. You may expect to hear from me."

"Actually, it's Bayles," I said quietly. "Rhymes with nails."

Miss Florence tugged at her sister's sleeve. "The sign, Jane," she whispered. "You were going to ask Ruby about it."

"I was just getting to that, Florence," Miss Jane said irritably. She turned to look at the building. "The sign will be installed before opening night, I assume." It wasn't a question.

I shot an inquiring glance at Ruby, who said, quickly,

"Oh, I'm sure it will. Would you like me to ask Marian Atkins to give you a call? She can fill you in on the details."

"It's a little late now, wouldn't you say? I should have thought that Mrs. Atkins would have consulted with me about the sign before this." Miss Jane's face was stern and forbidding. "However, yes, she should call me. And when you speak to her, remind her to tell those who are attending the cast party on Friday night that there is to be no loud music or other revelry after eleven o'clock. Florence and I retire early, and do not wish to be disturbed."

She gave me one more censorious glance and said, in a tone that showed that she classed me as a little lower than the gardener, "Put that hose away before someone trips over it."

And that was it. Without another word, Miss Jane turned back toward the house, trailed by her acquiescent sister. When they had gone, Ruby let out her breath with an outraged snort.

"That old dragon! How the dickens did she manage to reach seventy-five without somebody bumping her off?"

"Beats me," I said. "I'm glad I'm not playing her mama. I couldn't do justice to the role. Has she given you any pointers?"

"Jane doesn't give two hoots about the way I play her mother," Ruby replied in a practical tone. "As far as she's concerned, Mrs. Obermann's sole function in life was only to make Doctor Obermann's existence easier and happier. Jane idolized her father, you know. In fact, Duane Redmond was first cast in that role, but Jane nixed him. She didn't think he had enough dignity and personal authority to play her father, she said. He didn't look the part."

"Oh, yeah?" I chuckled as I began coiling up the hose. "Bet that really frosted him." Duane, who also owns Duane's Dry Cleaners, is one of the mainstays of the community theater group and has garnered more male leads than any of the competition. Being bumped from a role for a lack of dignity and personal authority would send him into convulsions. If I knew Duane, he was probably gunning for Miss Jane.

"Oh, you bet," Ruby said emphatically. "Duane thinks he's God's gift to the American stage. He ranted and raved and made a huge fuss, but Jane was unmoved. She decided that Max Baumeister should have the part." She made a little face. "Seems that he was the family dentist until he retired last year."

"I'm surprised that Jean allowed that to happen." I dumped the hose in the wheelbarrow. "Nothing against Max Baumeister, of course, although he's always struck me as . . . well, a little stiff." His fellow actors called him "Field Marshal Max"—not to his face, of course—and he was mostly given roles where his one-dimensionality wasn't a problem. Offstage, he was a nice enough guy, and a pretty good dentist, too. He'd done some work for me, just before his retirement. I collected my digging tools and put them in the wheelbarrow, too. "Isn't casting the director's job?"

Ruby laughed shortly. "Not in this case. We're talking total control here, you know. Duane was doing all he could to make Herr Doctor a little more human. But Her High and Mightiness showed up at rehearsal one day and announced that Duane was out and Max was in. Duane was mad enough to chew nails, but it didn't do him any good. Miss Jane got her way, as usual."

I picked up the empty plastic pots and added them to the wheelbarrow, looking around to make sure I hadn't left something behind to upset Miss Jane—although how she could criticize my landscaping when her garden looked like the Great Texas Wilderness was beyond me.

"I imagine Jean was unhappy, too," I said.

Ruby rolled her eyes, intimating that *apoplectic* might have been a better word. "And Max is so stiff, he's positively wooden. The poor guy has about as much depth and complexity as a piece of blank typing paper. But he reminds Miss Jane of her father—he's stout, and his mustache and glasses give him that Teddy Roosevelt look. I guess that's all she cares about."

"Must make it kind of hard on you," I said. "It's no fun to be onstage with somebody like Max, in a play that wasn't any great shakes to begin with."

"You're not kidding." Ruby's eyes glinted. "But in an odd way, all this has made my part rather more interesting—although not exactly what Miss Jane intended."

"Oh, yeah?"

"Yeah." She laughed impishly. "Jean and I have come up with a new approach to the problem." She smoothed the costume over her arm. "Come opening night, I think Miss Jane may be surprised."

"Surprised?" I frowned. "But I thought she attended rehearsals. Whatever you're doing, hasn't she noticed?"

"Now that she's satisfied with Max, she only comes once in a while. And when she comes . . ." She shrugged. "I just tone it down, play it straight." To my quizzical look, she added, "It's a little hard to explain. You'll see what I mean on opening night."

"I'm looking forward to it," I replied with a laugh. "Hey, listen, I'm finished up here, and I haven't eaten yet. How about going over to Bean's for some dinner with me?"

Ruby flashed me a quick, bright smile. "Oh, thanks, China, but I'm on my way over to Colin's place. He's going to help me rehearse some of my scenes, and he's cooking. We're having grilled salmon."

"Now, that's a real man for you," I said, pretending to be envious. "He's good-looking, he has his own business, and he's a gourmet." I gave her a teasing grin, and then said something I shouldn't have. "I'll bet he's good in bed, too." The minute the words were out of my mouth, I regretted them. Ruby would think I was prying, and tell me to go to hell.

But she didn't. "Oh, absolutely," she said without hesitation. "He's the kind of lover every woman dreams about."

Her voice softened and her eyes grew blurry. "He makes me feel like a young girl again, China, all soft and romantic. For me, it was one of those wonderfully instantaneous things—love at first sight."

"Don't get carried away, Ruby," I said cautiously, wishing she hadn't been so quick to climb into the sack with him. I've done my share of that in my time, and have learned that sex never fails to complicate an already complicated situation. It's a lot harder to get out of bed than it is to get in. "Nobody's perfect. And love isn't instant, you know. You don't just add hot milk, stir, and serve."

"Colin might not be perfect, but he's close enough. If only he . . ." Her voice dropped, her shoulders slumped, and she looked away. "If only I could make him love me."

I began to be alarmed. This was dangerous stuff. "Listen, Ruby, I know how you feel, believe me. But please don't rush into anything."

"How can I rush?" Ruby wailed plaintively. "It takes two to rush."

"Not necessarily," I said. From one love affair to the next (and there had been several), Ruby never quite remembered that for her, falling in love was like falling over a precipice, and with just about the same result. Smashed dreams, splintered hopes, and a broken heart. I took a deep breath. I didn't want to violate her privacy or get involved in her intimate life, but I could at least try to plant a question in her mind. "Maybe it's not very smart to commit yourself before he—"

"I wish you wouldn't try to tell me what's smart and what isn't, China Bayles!" Ruby flared angrily. "You've got McQuaid. I don't have anybody. Not a soul!"

"That's not true," I objected. "You've got Amy and Shannon and me and Sheila and—"

"Amy and Shannon are kids, for Pete's sake!" Ruby cried, flinging her hair back. "They're my daughters! And you and Sheila are just friends, and both of you are always busy. I want a lover, China! I've been living alone for years, and I'm sick of it. I'm lonely down to the very bone. I need somebody to love." Her voice quavered and tears filled her eyes. "And I need somebody to love me. Somebody like Colin, who doesn't care whether I have one boob or two." She gulped back a sob. "You're not going to tell me there's something wrong with that, I hope."

Ah. So that was it. A while back, Ruby had breast cancer. She had elected to have a mastectomy and had said no to reconstructive surgery because she didn't want an alien substance inserted into her body. Colin's willingness to accept and admire her as she was, complete with one breast rather than the standard-issue pair, would be enormously important to her. He would be important to her, and nothing I could say would make one iota of difference.

I felt myself overwhelmed by compassion, mixed with both fear and hope. I had found McQuaid; I hoped that maybe this time, Ruby had found someone who would fill her needs, fulfill her desires. But something inside me was frantically waving a red flag, and I couldn't help feeling afraid for her, too. I didn't know Colin Fowler well enough to make judgments about him, but—

I stopped. Ruby was sweet and vulnerable and very dear to me. For better or worse, she had launched herself wholeheartedly into another passionate love affair. All I could do was cross my fingers, hope for the best, and hang on for the ride, which was guaranteed to be bumpy.

Without another word, I put my arms around her and held her very tight.

Chapter Five

Comfrey (*Symphytum officinale*) is also known as "knitbone." The leaves and root of this perennial herb contain allantoin, a protein with hormone-like qualities that stimulates cell growth. As a poultice or a salve, the plant has a reputation for helping to heal broken bones and reduce the swelling associated with fractures. External use of comfrey is safe; internal use in large amounts is not recommended because the plant also contains potentially carcinogenic alkaloids that may damage the liver.

Bean's Bar & Grill takes up most of an old stone building with a tin roof, between Purley's Tire Company and the railroad tracks. Every time a Missouri and Pacific train goes by, everything in the place shakes, rattles, or sways, from the dishes on the wooden tables to the cigar store Indian in the corner, the rusty iron wagon-wheel chandelier, the neon-lit jukebox, and the racks of pool cues in the back room.

There are some things you should know about Bean's. It's not a good idea to go there if you want to be alone, for you're bound to see three or four of your best friends, all of whom will want you to sit down at their table. Don't go there with somebody you don't want your partner to know about, for somebody else is bound to notice and carry tales; if not, your clothes, saturated with the unmistakable *eau d'Bean's* blend of beer, tobacco smoke, and mesquite-stoked barbecue fires, will tattle on you. And don't go for lunch or supper unless you're willing to load up on carbs and fat grams, since Bob Godwin's famous chicken-fried steak—smothered in cream gravy, with french fries, fried onion rings, and Texas toast on the side—is totally irresistable. Down-home comfort food, no doubt about it, soaked and swaddled in the sweet, down-home comfort of friends, fun, and familiar music.

Down-home comfort, that's what I was after tonight, having been rebuffed by Sheila and rejected by Ruby, both on account of love gone wrong. I went into Bean's, stood for a moment while my eyes adjusted to the agreeable gloom, and looked around. Hark and several of his buddies, gathered around their usual table, motioned me to join them. Bubba Harris, Sheila's predecessor, now retired to the more docile business of beekeeping, grinned at me from the bar. And at the back of the room, I saw Barry Hibbler, a local real estate broker and a member of the Community Theater board of directors, throwing darts at a poster of a man who had once been our governor and has since somewhat widened his sphere of influence. Barry was with his longtime gay partner, George, who is writing a mystery about an ex-lawyer who opens a florist shop. Both gave me a wave and a mouthed invitation to join their game. Tossing darts at ex-guvs is a favorite sport at Bean's, and every now and then, somebody comes up with a new poster.

But my eye had been caught by a woman seated in the back corner, with what was left of a margarita on the table in front of her. Alana Montoya looked tired, she looked lonely, and I was glad to see her. I didn't have the patience for Hark's horseplay tonight, a little bit of Bubba goes a long way, and George keeps pumping me for background information for his mystery. Anyway, I've wanted a chance to get better acquainted with Alana, and I was curious about the bones Brian had found in the cave. She might be able to bring me up to date.

"Hi, Alana," I said, approaching the table. "I'm China

Bayles. We met at Mistletoe Springs Cave—remember? My son Brian found a skeleton out there last week."

"Oh, sure, I remember," Alana said with a half-smile, perhaps not altogether welcoming. She was wearing khaki pants and a plain white shirt with the neck open and the sleeves rolled to the elbows, the color attractive against her olive-brown skin. Her long brown hair was pulled back loosely at the nape of her neck and hung in a braid down the middle of her back.

"May I join you?" I asked.

There was a slight hesitation, long enough to be noticeable. I was just about to add, "Or maybe another time would be better," when she shrugged and said, "Yeah, sure, why not? I haven't ordered yet." Her English was strongly accented, and I remembered that Brian had mentioned that she'd grown up in Mexico.

"Thanks," I said, and sat down. I barely had time to put my elbows on the table when Bob Godwin hustled up with a basket of warm tortilla chips and a crockery cup of salsa. Bob has tattoos on both muscular arms, thick auburn hair, and eyebrows like a pair of fuzzy ginger-colored caterpillars, trading insults with one another across the middle of his face. He was wearing a black T-shirt with a skull and crossbones over the words "Recon Marines." Bob is a Vietnam vet and proud of it. He rides his Harley-Davidson to Washington to visit the Wall every Memorial Day.

"Greetin's, ladies," he said affably. "What kin I do you fer tonight?" He put down his load and looked at me. "Where's yer old man, China?"

"At school, with Brian," I said. "It's Dads' Night."

"Oh, yeah," Bob said, turning gloomy. "Me, I ain't never had no kids, y'know. Jes' Bud and the goats, is all. Maria's got six—never figgered I wanted to take on that bunch, though." Maria Zapata is Bob's girlfriend and a heck of a good cook. He pulled his order pad out of his apron pocket, brightening. "Y'all jes got lucky. Maria's fryin' up a batch of pickled jalapeños. Got cheese in 'em."

"Sounds good to me," I said. I nodded at Alana's margarita. "And I'll have one of those. Except make mine a single."

"I'll have another," Alana said. She looked around. "Speaking of Bud, where is he? I haven't seen him tonight." Budweiser—Bud, for short—is Bob's golden retriever, and a familiar sight at Bean's. He wears a leather saddlebag over his back and totes beer bottles and wrapped snacks from the bar to the tables, and cash and tips from the tables to the bar. Sometimes he runs errands for customers to the Circle-K on the other side of the railroad tracks.

"That Bud's a lazy bastard." Bob made a disgusted noise. "Can't get him out of the kitchen when Maria's here. Allus hangin' around, beggin'. Loves them jalapeños. Eats 'em like they was Snickers." He paused, getting down to business. "I got some great barbecue comin' out of the pit tonight." He smacked his lips to demonstrate his enthusiasm for this culinary triumph and waited expectantly, pencil poised over the pad.

I weighed the relative merits of chicken-fried and barbecue. It was a tough choice. "Make mine barbecue," I said finally. "Sausage and brisket, with slaw and beans." Bob rubs garlic, rosemary, salt, and pepper on his brisket and smokes it for ten or twelve hours over mesquite coals in an old propane-tank pit out back by the railroad tracks. He says it's the mesquite that gives it the unique flavor. I credit the garlic and rosemary.

"Taco salad for me," Alana said. Bob finished scribbling, stuck the pencil behind his ear, and sauntered off.

"So," I said, dipping a chip into the salsa, which is only comfortably hot, not searing, like McQuaid's. "How are you liking it here in Pecan Springs?"

Alana was just starting her second year on the Anthropology faculty at CTSU. As Blackie had mentioned, she'd been hired to set up a program in Forensic Anthropology. The program seemed a good idea to me, since the field is growing fast and there are only a couple of similar programs in Texas. Eventually, McQuaid says, there'll be a thirty-hour, master's-level track of courses—some taught by Criminal Justice faculty—in forensic osteology, forensic entomology, forensic anthropology, and criminal investigation, with internships in the Travis and Bexar County Medical Examiners offices that would allow students to gain hands-on experience. When they graduate, they'll go on to positions in coroners' offices and police departments in Texas and around the country.

Alana seemed to be giving my question some serious thought, turning it over in her mind as if it were not just an invitation for small talk. "I like living here," she said finally. "Pecan Springs is pretty and the people are friendlier than they were in Baton Rouge. Some of them, anyway."

Her smile was lopsided, and I noticed for the first time the hard lines around her mouth and the wrinkles at the corners of her eyes. I had thought she was in her middle thirties, but now I revised my estimate upward. A young forty, perhaps. Nearer my age than otherwise.

"When I first came here from Houston," I said, "it was easy to make friends. People kept inviting me to take part in all kinds of community events. Pretty soon, I had more invitations than I had free evenings."

"You're Anglo," she said flatly, and the bitterness in her tone caught me by surprise. I was embarrassed, too. She was a Latina, but that hadn't registered as "different" with me. Ethnicity isn't something I think consciously about, although maybe I should. I'd certainly put my foot into it this time. I could feel myself flush.

Alana saw my discomfort. As if to soften the blunt edge of her remark, she added, with a carelessness that seemed affected, "I was hoping that Texans would be more accustomed to working with Latina professionals."

"I think they are," I said. From Alana's nuanced remark, I gathered that she had encountered some racial bias in Baton Rouge—and here, too. If so, it had probably happened at CTSU, not in Pecan Springs, where Hispanics have always played an important role in the community.

The silence lengthened while she drained her drink and put it down. "What about CTSU?" I asked finally. "How's it going with the new program?"

Her answer was almost weary, as if she'd thought about this a lot and didn't especially feel like going over it again. "It's slow. The master's degree was supposed to be approved by now, but the process wasn't as far along as they told me when I was hired—that, or it's stuck somewhere in the bureaucratic process. Most of the new courses aren't in the catalogue yet, and I've had a hard time getting the money for lab equipment. It has to come out of the department's budget."

"It takes a long time to get a new program through the system," I said, as Bob appeared with our margaritas, frosty cold and rimmed with salt, a single for me and a double for Alana. "When McQuaid was trying to get approval for the Criminal Justice master's degree, it took forever."

That happens, sometimes. Faculty are committed elsewhere, or the program isn't widely supported. Mostly, though, it comes down to dollars. Every new program—especially when it involves expensive lab equipment and a hiring budget—takes a bite out of somebody else's funding. I wasn't suprised to hear that Alana was already fighting budget battles within the Anthropology Department.

Alana reached for her glass and took a solid swig, while I sipped at mine. Somebody put coins into the jukebox and began to play Garth Brooks' "Friends in Low Places." "You call your husband by his last name?" she asked.

"We met when he was a homicide detective and I was a criminal defense attorney," I said. "It was an adversarial relationship—to start with, anyway."

"You *were* a defense attorney? You're not doing that now?"

"Right," I replied. "Now, I own a business. An herb shop called Thyme and Seasons, and a tearoom and catering service, with my friend Ruby Wilcox. It's a lot of work, but a gentler lifestyle. Less competition, less stress. Less money, of course, but money isn't everything." I grinned. "The nice thing about plants is that they don't give you any smart talk. And they don't start yelling malpractice if you neglect them."

"People think there isn't much competition and stress in the university," Alana said, her face serious. "But it's not true."

"I know," I replied. "McQuaid tells me about what goes on in his department. Sounds brutal, sometimes. It must be even tougher for women, especially in fields dominated by men."

"Yes," she said emphatically. "Like anthropology." Her mouth tightened. I thought she might be going to say more, but she took another swallow of her margarita and changed the subject. "I was hoping that your husband would be available to teach one of the courses in my new program, but his department chair told me he's teaching only part-time now. He's a private investigator?"

I nodded. "Investigation is the thing he's missed most since he left police work and started teaching. He's not happy unless he's ferreting something out." I chuckled. "So far, his cases have run the gamut—from embezzlers to runaway teens to people who doctor their résumés." I dipped another chip into the salsa. "You grew up in Mexico, I think he told me."

She was reaching for her glass again, but her hand had frozen in midair. Her eyes narrowed, and I could feel the involuntary tenseness in her muscles, a sudden remoteness. It was as if my words—the mention of Mexico, perhaps—had dropped a curtain between us, and she had disappeared behind it. My question—which she probably connected to the ethnic thing—was obviously unwelcome, and I felt clumsy and tactless. On the other hand, we are who we are, and we'd better get used to it. Alana Montoya was a professional woman, and she'd been around for a while. I would've expected her to have grown callouses over the tender places.

She picked up her glass and spoke over the rim, her voice as frosty as her drink. "I came from Cueranavaca. That's where my parents live."

"Oh, I've been to Cuernavaca," I said, with a forced brightness. "Such an interesting place. The Palace of Cortes, the Borda Gardens." I'm sure I had seen other sights, but I couldn't remember what they were. I fumbled for something else to say. "You got your undergraduate degree in Mexico?"

She looked away, then back at me, her glance veiled and unreadable. "I studied at the National Autonomous University in Mexico City." She didn't seem inclined to say more, and the silence, laden with implication, grew increasingly uncomfortable. It must be time to change the subject again.

"Blackie—Sheriff Blackwell—mentioned that you edited an important textbook in forensic techniques."

A corner of her mouth quirked. "One of my chief claims to fame. The contributors gave me some outstanding chapters, and I added one of my own." With undisguised pride, she added, "The book just went into another edition."

Not only a claim to fame, I thought, but a rung or two on the promotion ladder. A strong textbook, along with other publications, can lead to tenure. The Anthropology Department might have hired her on the textbook alone, although there was of course her work at the LSU forensics lab. She didn't sound eager to talk about her accomplishments, though—odd, for an academic. They're usually spilling over with news about the articles they've published, the conferences they've attended, the kudos they've received from their peers.

I reached for another topic. "The sheriff also mentioned that you're doing some forensic work on the bones Brian found."

The curtain pulled aside, and she was totally there

again. "Oh, yes," she said, probably as eager as I to have something we could talk about easily. "Yes, indeed, the bones from the cave. They present some very interesting problems." She leaned forward, her words coming faster, a little slurred, maybe, but that was no surprise, given the amount of tequila she'd been putting down. "Of course, the cave dig itself has been fascinating. Did Brian tell you that the first two skeletons we found are from the Paleo-Indian period? They're close to ten thousand years old."

"Yes," I said. "It's hard to imagine ten thousand years, somehow." Those bones predated the Pyramids, the Great Wall of China. They were very old bones. I imagined that they had some stories to tell.

She nodded. "We've also found several Folsom points, and one very fine Clovis point, and quite a bit of detritus from later periods. I'm sure there's much more to be discovered in other parts of the cave. Everyone in the department is quite excited about the finds, of course. But these recent bones—"

Our dinners arrived then, her taco salad and my barbecued brisket and sausage, spicy and fragrant, and we ate while she told me about the skeleton Brian had stumbled on to the previous Friday. It had been moved to her laboratory at the university, but she hadn't yet had an opportunity to study it in detail, she said. She'd need time, and she'd have to use equipment in other labs around the campus, since she didn't have much of her own. She had already formed some preliminary conclusions, though. Gender, for one.

"The narrow sciatic notch, the short pubic bone, the small pelvic inlet—I wouldn't say it definitively yet, but I'm fairly confident that we're dealing with a man here, rather than a woman."

Her voice had taken on confidence, assurance, authority; her shoulders had straightened; her expression had become lively, animated. I could easily picture her as an expert witness, talking to the jury, commanding their attention. If I were in the courtroom with this woman, I'd much rather have her on my side.

"As to age," she went on, "I'm guessing that the individual wasn't much older than thirty. I'll have to do more osteological analysis, of course, but the auricular region of the hip bone doesn't reveal the kind of pitting and wear that we would expect to see in an older person, and the medial end of the collarbone—the end closest to the spine—exhibits the raised ridges that are usually associated with a young adult. There's a rather distinctive and visible gold tooth—the right central upper incisor—that may help with identification."

"A gold tooth?"

Alana nodded. "Now, restorations are made of tooth-colored porcelain or resin. But this didn't become common practice until the 1970s." She paused. "There are also a number of severe injuries to the femur and tibia of the right leg and to the right humerus, probably within three or four years of death. Difficult repairs, too. As to the skull—"

I stared at her. She had taken a fragmented collection of speechless bones and given them a voice—a fascinating, if somewhat macabre skill, this speaking for the dead. And equally fascinating, perhaps even more, was the way she had come to life as she talked about what she'd learned, as if the dead man's bones had given *her* a voice.

Catching my expression, she stopped in midsentence. "Oh, sorry. It isn't exactly dinner table conversation."

"It's not that," I said. "I'm impressed, Alana. No wonder they call you the bone doc. Brian told me that," I added, in explanation.

That brought a smile. "I like that title."

I paused. "So how did you get into forensic anthropology in the first place? It seems like a strange field for a—" At the bar, somebody broke a glass. The noise obliterated the rest of my sentence.

"For a woman?" Her expression darkened. "Or for a Latina?"

Damn. There was that sensitivity again, and it was getting to me. Life is one long challenge under the best of circumstances. If you're balancing a heavy chip on your shoulder, and you go around daring people to knock it off, the challenges multiply.

"Of all the forensic anthropologists I worked with in court or out," I said, deliberately ignoring her second question, "I don't think any were women. You must have to love bones."

She seemed to relax a little. "And you have to learn not to throw up at the smell of rotting flesh. It helps if you don't mind working forty-eight straight hours on a case, and sleeping in the lab, either. And it also helps if you can tolerate snakes, skunks, and poison ivy." She smiled wryly. "I tell my female students all this. And then I show them photos of me, soaked to the skin and up to my knees in mud. And if they continue to be interested, I give them a list of all the biology and chemistry they'll need—almost as much as if they were planning to go into medicine. Then I tell them that fewer than half of the women who start the program are likely to finish it. If they're going to drop out, I'd rather have them do it at the beginning, before they've invested a couple of years of their lives. A lot of them quit." She raised a hand and let it drop, half-amused. "Maybe they don't love bones enough."

At the dart board, Barry scored big and let out a triumphant yell. Somebody at the bar called, "Way to go, Barry," and there was a round of applause. George wins a dozen games to Barry's one, so this was cause for community celebration.

"But you made it," I pointed out, over the ruckus. "Were you always interested in anthropology? Was that your undergraduate major?"

She nodded. She was talking more easily now. I couldn't decide whether it was the subject or the alcohol—the second double had disappeared while I was still on my first single. "I did a couple of summer field schools while I was an undergraduate. Then I married an American and came to the U.S., to Baton Rouge, where my husband was a professor. I applied to the master's program in anthropology. When I finished, I went to work in the forensic lab. I was there for over ten years. I got the chance to work with police departments and to serve as an expert witness." She paused, then added bleakly, "My husband and I divorced. It turned out that he didn't like the idea of another anthropologist in the family, after all."

The spare understatement, rich with significance, told a familiar story of professional competitiveness, complicated by ethnicity. Perhaps Alana had been his student, and he had liked her better when she was clearly his subordinate, his inferior. Perhaps, when she grew to be his professional equal, she became competitive, a personal threat. Perhaps—

But I was speculating, trespassing where I had no invitation to enter. I pushed my plate away and went back to the subject of Brian's caveman. "The sheriff said he thought the bones were fairly recent—the late 1970s, maybe. He said he discovered some coins."

If she wondered how I had come to discuss the matter with Blackie, she didn't let on. "The latest, I think, was from 1975. Those coins were a lucky find," she added. "It's next to impossible to date a skeleton like this by the bones themselves."

"The guy died of a crushed skull?"

"Well, the skull was certainly crushed," she said cautiously. "Whether that was the cause of death—it's too soon to tell. I won't know until I have time to look more carefully at the interior of the skull."

She had only half-finished her taco salad, but she pushed her plate away. There was another silence, a longer one. Willie Nelson and Julio Iglesias were crooning to all the girls they'd loved before. I like Willie, but this particular song is so charged with macho bravado and sexual exploitation that it makes me want to go kick the jukebox. In the back room, there was the sharp crack of a pool cue and somebody yelled "Gotcha, you sumbitch!"

Alana picked up her margarita and took another swallow. "You asked how I got into forensic anthropology. Are you still interested in hearing the story?"

I nodded.

"It happened because of a young mother in New Orleans, who was murdered several years before I came to the States. I never knew her, of course, but by the time it was all over, she was like a friend. Her bones told me things about her that even her mother didn't know."

She looked at me, checking to see whether I was listening. I was, so she went on, her words definitely slurry now. There was no doubt about it, Alana was looped.

"The first year of graduate study, I took a summer job as an intern in the LSU forensics lab. I'd been there a couple of weeks when a woman's remains were brought in for analysis. Somebody was putting in a new sewer line, and the skeleton had been dug up by a backhoe. As we pieced the bones together, you could see that her skull had been badly fractured, as well as most of her ribs, the bones in both arms, one ankle, even her foot." Her mouth tightened. "A great many fractures, with various degrees of healing. Obviously, they occurred over quite a few years, some of them shortly before her death. It was the skull fracture that killed her."

"Abuse," I said. It wasn't a question.

She nodded. "Yes, years of it. The police didn't have to look very far for the abuser, either. The woman, a black woman, was identified as a former resident of the house on the property where her remains were found. She had simply disappeared one day, about fifteen years earlier. Her mother reported her missing, and the police questioned her husband, who had a history of domestic violence. But he told them she'd been having an affair with another man and had simply taken off. And without a body . . ." She shrugged, her face impassive now, stony. "Well, you know."

"Yes," I said. "I know." Without a body, it's sometimes hard to get the police to make a serious investigation—unless of course, the family begins calling press conferences. And even when an investigation leads to an arrest, it may be difficult to get a conviction. Not impossible, but definitely not easy. Not a gamble that most prosecutors want to take.

"Anyway, the police didn't push it," Alana went on, "until the body turned up, that is. Then they arrested the husband—by that time, he was married again—and charged him with his first wife's murder, citing the extensive evidence of abuse. The evidence of the bones."

She took another drink, then fell silent, as if she were engrossed in the story, playing it over in her head. As if she had gone back there, to that time and place.

After a minute, I nudged. "Go on. What happened, Alana?"

She focused on me, on the present. "What happened? The guy had a good defense lawyer, that's what happened. A very aggressive woman, very smart and good with words. She argued that the backhoe broke up the woman's bones in the process of digging them up."

A logical strategy for the defense. "Is that what happened?"

"Of course—that is, some were damaged during the excavation. But the perimortem fractures could be easily identified by the staining on the older trauma and the way the bones had been broken and displaced. The damage caused by the backhoe was recent and entirely different." She turned the stem of her glass in her fingers. Her voice was sharp, dry. "Any fool could see it."

"Any fool. Except for the jury, that is."

"Right. But they had help. The forensics expert—my boss—botched his testimony, and the defense attorney caught him on a couple of inconsistencies." Her eyes had become dark, her voice fierce. "He'd just gotten back from a long trial in St. Louis, where he was the expert witness.

This case seemed like an easy one, so he didn't bother to do his homework. He made some mistakes, stupid mistakes, and the defense attorney pounced on him. She completely destroyed his credibility. The jury acquitted a guilty man."

"It happens," I murmured. I wanted to say that the defense attorney was only doing the job she was paid to do, the job that the system demanded, but I thought better of it. "So this was the case that made you decide to go into forensics?"

"Not quite." Pain etched her face. "The man who had been acquitted—six weeks after he walked out of that courtroom, he beat his wife to death with a baseball bat. He didn't break every single bone in her body, but he broke quite a few of them. Most of her ribs, all four bones in her forearms, her skull, her jaw."

Alana was leaning forward now, but her voice had dropped to a grating whisper, and I had to lean forward, too, to hear her over the music, the sound of Willie crooning those abominable lyrics, "To all the girls I've loved before." Love. Love and exploitation. Love and violence. Love and death.

I shivered, suddenly chilled to the bone, the image of Ruby rising like a ghost in my mind. Ruby, who was no longer listening to her common sense—or her uncommon sense, either. Ruby, who was joyfully falling in love again, abandoning herself to another wild leap off the precipice. But love didn't mean living happily ever after. Love could mean betrayal. Love could mean—

I gave myself a hard shake. This was silly, totally and completely stupid. The story that Alana was telling me, grim as it was, had nothing to do with Ruby. The only danger she faced was another broken heart, and that wouldn't take more than a month or two to mend.

Alana was going on, and I tuned back in. "Only this time," she said grimly, "the bastard didn't get away with it. This time, there was a witness, the woman's ten-year-old daughter, his stepdaughter, who watched through the keyhole of a closet door. The prosecution didn't need a forensics expert. The girl told the jury how her mother had cried and pleaded and screamed, until her stepfather finally crushed her skull, and she stopped screaming."

She blew out her breath in a shuddery puff. More words came out on that breath, too, propelled by a bitter anger. "I'll always remember the way that little girl cried, up there on the witness stand. That was what made me decide to stay in the business. If that damn fool of a forensics man had done his job right, the second victim would still be alive, and that little girl would never have had to witness her mother's murder." She gave me a penetrating look. "There's only one consolation."

"What's that?"

"I felt bad that the forensics man lost the first case." Her mouth went hard, her look was accusing. "But I'm willing to bet that the murderer's defense attorney—the woman who convinced the jury to acquit—felt a whole helluva lot worse."

I doubted it. When you're a defense attorney, you disconnect your brain from your heart. You've got to, or you won't survive. You know sometimes that your client is innocent, and if he's convicted you feel like a failure for not saving him. And sometimes you know that your client is guilty as sin, and when you get him off, you feel like a criminal. To keep from feeling rotten all the time, you have to stop feeling, period. I'd bet that defense attorney just chalked another one up to experience.

I looked at Alana. "It's time I called it a night," I said. I hesitated, balancing the obligation I felt against the risk of offending her yet again. "I wonder—maybe you'd like a ride home."

She regarded me blurrily. "Think I can't drive, do you?" She hiccupped, then giggled.

"I think," I said, suppressing my anger, "that you don't want to risk losing your license. The cops around here keep a close watch." Sheila takes a very hard line when it comes to drunk drivers.

"You're just trying to scare me," she said. She pushed back her chair and stood, wobbling. "But maybe I'll take you up on the offer."

As we went together out the door, Bob gave me a rueful grin and a high sign, and somebody else laughed. I had the feeling that this wasn't the first time some good Samaritan had driven Alana home.

She fell asleep the minute after she gave me directions. I had to wake her up to get her into her apartment—not an easy job, since it was on the second floor, and by this time she was leaning on me, dragging her feet and muttering something incoherent. I steered her to the bedroom, dumped her on the bed, pulled off her shoes, and found a blanket.

I stood for a moment, watching her face as she slept, letting myself feel the anger I'd kept out of my voice a little earlier. This woman had career recognition, challenging and rewarding work, people who believed in her, a bright future. What was driving her to drink? I thought of my mother, Leatha, who had been an alcoholic until just a few years ago. I'd been angry with her, too, until I began to understand that she suffered from a genetic tendency to addiction, and that her need for drink had been kindled and stoked by an overwhelming sense of inadequacy and imperfection, especially where my father was concerned. Leatha could never meet his expectations, could never measure up to his standards.

Was it something like this that kindled Alana Montoya's need for drink? Or was it a failed marriage, or the competitions that came with being a Latina in an Anglo world, a woman in a man's field?

But there were no answers to these questions. I watched her a minute more, feeling the anger soften and dissolve into a kind of perplexed pity. Maybe she was drinking out of frustration at the delay in getting her program started. Now that I thought about it, that delay didn't make any sense, either. CTSU had hired her with fanfare; a Latina added to the faculty is one more politically correct plus in a column that used to be called Affirmative Action. (God only knows what it's called now.) And the program was needed, too. So why wasn't the department putting more muscle, more money, behind it? Why were they dragging their feet?

I made a mental note to ask McQuaid about this. I turned off the lights, locked the door, and left Alana to sleep it off.

Chapter Six

Horsetail (*Equisetum arvense*). This herb has been used in many cultures as an externally applied poultice to stop bleeding and speed the healing of broken bones and wounds. Its effectiveness derives from the plant's high level of silica and silicic acid, which is absorbed directly into the blood and cells. The herb has also been used internally (usually drunk as a tea) as a source of minerals, especially silica and calcium, in a form that the body can use in the repair of skin, connective tissue, and bone.

I went home, crawled into bed beside McQuaid, and dreamed of bones.

In my dream I am lost in a dark labyrinth deep under the earth, have been lost for hours, days, weeks, maybe a century. In the dark, time is meaningless, my breath and the hard pounding of my heart the only measures of moments passing. I have a flashlight in my hand, but it keeps flickering out, the fragile light fading, brightening, dimming, finally dying altogether. I am totally wrapped in the smothering dark, my mouth dry as dust. I am so frightened, I can hardly catch my breath.

Then, through the utter blackness, I glimpse a phosphorescent glow, faintly, eerily green, far away down the pitch-black, rock-strewn corridor in front of me. As I grope my way forward, the glow becomes brighter, and I realize that it emanates from a heap of broken, splintered bones piled on the dusty floor. On the top of the heap sits a grotesquely grinning skull, vacant-eyed and ghastly, its one gold tooth glinting. Somewhere far beyond, in the deathly silence of the cave, I hear a child's anguished weeping, the crystal echoes breaking around me like the rising and falling of distant music.

But there is something more. Beneath the sound of weeping, I realize that the skull is speaking to me, whispering my name, telling me something important, something I need to know. Something about the bones themselves, who they belong to, how they got there. But more, I realize that these bones know the way out of the labyrinth, the way to the entrance, the way to safety, to the light. Desperate to hear, I lean forward, lean close, lean closer, my eyes on the empty-eyed skull, listening, so intent on hearing the words that I don't realize that someone is creeping up stealthily behind me, until suddenly I feel a hand on my shoulders, shoving me forward, and I am falling into the bones; falling, falling—

"Hey, China," McQuaid said urgently, shaking me. I was lying half off the bed. "Wake up. You're having a bad dream."

I sucked in my breath, marooned halfway between the fearful cave of my dreams and the familiar comfort of our bedroom. "Oh," I breathed, and scooted back on the bed, grabbing for McQuaid's hand. "Oh, wow."

"Yeah. Some dream." McQuaid squeezed my hand, gave me one last pat, and rolled over, already half-asleep. "Must've been Bob's barbecue," he said drowsily. "It's potent stuff."

But I didn't go back to sleep, not right away. I lay on my back, watching the twiggy tree shadows on the ceiling. I was still thinking about bones. Broken bones, buried bones, bones that lay in limbo, waiting to be discovered. Bones that talked. And people who listened.

* * *

"THAT was some dream you had last night," McQuaid said again, the next morning. "It took a long time to wake you up."

Brian had already gulped his cereal and orange juice, grabbed his book bag, and galloped out the door to catch the bus to school. Howard Cosell, his morning duties done, had flopped onto the porch step, where he would wait for the school bus to bring Brian back again. And McQuaid and I were enjoying a quiet cup of coffee together before we separated and went off in different directions.

"Yeah," I said. "I was dreaming of bones. A glow-in-the-dark skull. It had something to tell me, but you woke me up before I could find out what it was." I shuddered, not wanting to remember that vast dark emptiness under the earth, the eerily phosphorescent bones, the whispers I couldn't quite make out. "It wasn't the barbecue that brought on that dream, though," I added. "It was Alana." Alana, the bone doc.

"Montoya?" Something in McQuaid's tone caught my attention, and I looked up.

"Right. I ran into her when I went to Bean's for supper. We had quite a talk."

He was studiedly casual. "Personal stuff?"

"Oh, maybe a little. She said she's divorced—but I suppose you already know that, since you were on the committee that hired her." I frowned. "How come the Anthropology Department has been so slow in implementing her program?"

"Dunno." He stirred coffee. "Maybe they've got other priorities."

"But that doesn't make sense, McQuaid. They hired her to develop the new Forensic Anthropology degree, but they haven't given her money for lab equipment or pushed her courses through the approval process. What's going on?" Now that I thought about it, it seemed to me that there was something fishy here. "Is somebody deliberately holding up the process?"

"I said I don't know, China." His voice was sharp, and he made an effort to soften it. He leaned back. "Was that all you talked about? Just the program?"

I shook my head. "Mostly, we talked about bones. Brian's caveman." I summarized what she had said, adding, "She also told me how she decided to go into forensic anthropology." I shuddered. "Two women, beaten to death by the same man. The first woman was dug up by a backhoe. The second one—her daughter saw it all." I pulled in my breath. "A ten-year-old girl, McQuaid."

"The world's an ugly place," he said, but not without sympathy. "That shouldn't be news to you, after your courtroom career. You specialized in dirt, didn't you? It didn't seem to bother you then."

McQuaid was right, although that wasn't exactly the point. I had spent a great many years in a dirty world, full of crime and corruption, and I'd had to grow callouses over my conscience just to do the ordinary stuff that had to be done to defend people who might or might not be guilty of the crimes with which they were charged. Which is maybe why I love what I do now. The shop is sometimes hectic and stressful, especially when it's not making money, but while I may get my hands dirty, my conscience is clean. I—

"What?" I asked, realizing that my thoughts were taking me on a detour and I'd just missed something. "I'm sorry. I was thinking about the opposite of ugliness."

"I asked," McQuaid said, "whether she mentioned anything about her undergraduate work."

"Undergraduate work?" I asked blankly.

He was patient. "The university where Montoya got her degree."

"Oh, that. Mexico City. National something university. But you know all that." I frowned, thinking that I had not told him about Alana's getting drunk, or my taking her home and putting her to bed. Was I afraid it would affect his opinion of her, professional or otherwise? Was I protecting her? Why?

"Oh, sure," McQuaid said carelessly. "I was just wondering." Then he got serious. "Listen, China, I'm seeing a couple of new clients this morning, somebody you know. Maybe you can give me some background on them."

New clients. Hey, that was good news. At least one of us was bringing in money. "Somebody I know? Who?"

He paused for effect. "Jane and Florence Obermann."

I stared at him in astonishment. "Jane Obermann is hiring a private detective? What in the world for?"

"She says she's afraid that someone plans to kill her and her sister. She wants me to keep it from happening."

"Kill them?" I laughed grimly. Why was I not surprised to hear this? "Kill her, you mean. Florence is a sweet old lady who looks like she might fall apart any minute, but Jane is a genuine fire-breathing dragon. Don't get too close, or she'll scorch you."

With a chuckle, McQuaid picked up both our cups, went to the coffeemaker, and poured. "I don't know yet whether there's been an actual threat—I'll find that out when I see the women today. And I don't know whether the threat, if there is one, has anything to do with the theater association. But there's a chance that it might." He brought our cups to the table and sat down. "I know you've been doing some landscaping at the theater. I was wondering whether you might have picked up something—a bit of gossip, some information, maybe—that could help me."

"What I have picked up is that Jane Obermann is the very devil to work with," I replied. "She won't give you the information you need. Whatever information you give her, she'll find something wrong with it and probably refuse to pay you for it. And if somebody does succeed in bumping her off, she'll come back from the dead and sue you for malfeasance."

McQuaid chuckled. "The client from hell, huh?"

"Laugh now," I retorted. "You won't be laughing later."

His eyebrows were amused. "You're not serious."

"I'm serious."

"Well, if she's that kind of person, maybe she's got something to worry about, after all." He pulled a scrap of paper toward him and turned it over to the blank side. "Who might have it in for the old lady?" He took a pencil out of the ceramic cup where the writing implements live when they're off-duty. "Why?"

"Who? Why?" I began counting off on my fingers as McQuaid made notes. "Well, you could start with Lance Meyers, who was forced to resign as president of the theater board because he refused to stage Miss Jane's play. Or Marian Atkins, the current president, who told me a couple of days ago that if she'd known what the board was getting into, she never would've accepted the offer of the theater. And then there's Jean Davenport, the director, who has to put up with Jane's constant meddling. And Duane Redmond, who got fired from his role as leading man because he didn't meet Jane's expectations. And her sister, who seems innocuous enough but has probably been carrying a grudge for decades. And—"

McQuaid looked up. "Well, go on. And who else?"

But my cautious lawyer-self had taken over and warned me against charges I had no way of backing up. "I'm exaggerating, McQuaid. Nobody in Pecan Springs would actually kill that old witch. People are too civilized, or too afraid of getting caught, or both." I grinned maliciously. "Of course, I wouldn't rule out a little bodily injury, or maybe aggravated assault with a deadly weapon."

"Well, I have to start somewhere," McQuaid said, pocketing the list.

"Good," I said, and gave him a dazzling smile. "You can start with hamburger, anchovies, and mozzarella."

"Excuse me?"

"And don't forget milk and bread. But it's all on the list."

He frowned. "The list? What list?"

"The list you just put in your pocket, on the other side of which you have jotted the names of five potential killers, none of whom, I hasten to say, has what it takes to do something really nasty." That was certainly true of Marian and Jean, and probably true of Lance. Duane, however, is impulsive and unpredictable, and he doesn't handle frustration well. He might—

"Oh, yeah." McQuaid had pulled out the list and was turning it over. "Sorry, China."

"No need to be sorry, babe," I said sweetly. I got up, circled around behind him, and put my arms around his neck, my cheek against his. "At least, not about the groceries. Working for Jane Obermann, you'll have plenty else to be sorry for."

AFTER breakfast, I drove to the shop. No matter how I'm feeling, the sight and scent of Thyme and Seasons always gives me a lift. The place isn't large, but every inch of it is filled with something that looks pretty, smells good, or does something nice for my soul. Herbal wreaths and swags and bundles of dried herbs are draped against the stone walls, and braids of garlic and peppers hang from the ceilings. The wooden shelves hold gleaming jars of bulk herbs, handmade soaps, herbal cosmetics, bags of potpourri, vials of essential oils, sparkling bottles of herbal vinegars, boxes of fragrant herbal teas, and books about herbs and gardening. On the flagstone floor, the corners and aisles are crowded with baskets of dried celosia and goldenrod, salvia and sweet Annie, tansy and yarrow. Thyme and Seasons is a treasure trove of wonderful, natural things, and I love it. I would even pay for the privilege of working here, although that hasn't been necessary. Not yet, at least.

I propped the door open, took the cash register drawer out from under the cache of dust rags where I always hide it, and filled Khat's bowl with some of his low-cal kitty food. Khat K'o Kung, as Ruby has christened him (in honor of her favorite sleuth cat, star of the Cat-Who mystery series) is an eighteen-pound Siamese who enjoys the run of the shops, the tearoom, and the gardens. His Largeness takes a fiendish delight in playing mountain lion, peering down at startled customers from the top of a shelf and frightening them with an imperious "I-do-not-suffer-fools-gladly" growl. The rest of the time he spends dozing on a sunny windowsill, his charcoal paws tucked symmetrically under his tawny bib, his charcoal tail wrapped around his plump and satisfied self.

One of my tasks this morning was seeing to the completion of the deck just outside the tearoom. When I first stepped on the wooden step and broke it, Ruby and I had thought that replacement would be a minor do-it-yourself job. But after we'd pried up a couple of boards and had seen what was underneath, we changed our minds and called Hank Dixon, the handyman who helps us with the repairs we can't handle for ourselves. Hank had shaken his head when he came to look at the deck and give us an estimate on the cost of the work.

"Looks t' me like y'all got yerselfs a big problem here," he said, in his raspy Texas drawl. "Some stupid sumbitch went 'n' built this here deck outta untreated lumber."

I sighed. The deck had been designed and constructed by the architect who owned the building before I did, and who should have known what kind of lumber to use. But we had run across some of his cost-cutting efforts before, so this one didn't surprise me.

"That sounds bad," Ruby said apprehensively.

"You betcher sweet boobies it's bad." Hank shifted his cud of chewing tobacco from one side of his mouth to the other, and winked at Juan Gomez, his helper. Hank is probably pushing sixty, although he began looking older and grayer while he was nursing his father, Gabe Dixon, through an extended battle with lung cancer. Gabe had died, at last, a couple of months before.

Sixty or not, Hank is still strong as an ox and twice as stubborn. If you hire him to do a job for you, don't bother to sketch out any plans, and forget about giving directions.

Hank will do it his way or not at all—although in fairness, it ought to be said that his way is usually better than anything you could've come up with, even if you are an architect. He has a reputation as the finest handyman in all of Pecan Springs.

Hank also has a reputation for a quick temper, and he's been known to go on titanic drunks of several days' duration, which often land him in the hoosegow. Ruby and I have had a firsthand acquaintance with both these unfortunate traits because Hank has done several jobs for us, both at the shops and at home, occasionally missing work to sober up or sit out a spell in jail. I'm also acquainted with him through his helper, Juan, who came from Guadalajara to CTSU to get his education. Juan was one of McQuaid's students last spring and came out to our house for the party McQuaid always throws when classes are over. He wasn't in school just now, I understood. But he was still in town, working with Hank and staying with him, too.

The day Hank bid our project, he was sober and in an uncharacteristically good mood, probably because the work was easy, and was mostly in the shade of a large pecan tree. He grinned as he regarded the deck.

"Yup," he said, with a pitying shake of the head. "Best thing fer y'all to do is to tear up this whole dad-blamed piece o' shit and rebuild it with treated lumber." He handed one end of a tape measure to Juan and measured the deck, which I had already told him was sixteen feet by twenty. "'Course, it's gonna cost you out the wazoo," he added, reeling in the tape. "But the wood'll last longer'n you will, and it's a damn sight cheaper 'n gittin' yer butts sued."

This statement was inelegant but true. Ruby and I had already agreed that it was a very good thing that I had been the one to put a foot through that rotten board and fall flat on my face. Luckily, I didn't break any bones. But if this had happened to a customer, and she had broken an ankle and fractured her nose—well, the thought of it makes me shudder. A repair bill wasn't welcome just now, but it was better than the alternative.

So we accepted Hank's recommendation that the entire deck be ripped up and replaced, haggled over the bottom line, and finally agreed to a price. The work wouldn't take long, happily. When Hank agrees to do a job, he doesn't usually mess around, unless he's drunk or in jail. He and Juan had started on Monday and were finishing up this morning.

I opened the door, went out onto the new deck, and looked down at the clean, straight, strong boards. I could stop worrying about somebody falling through them.

"It's beautiful," I said admiringly. "Nice work, you guys."

"Thanks, Ms. Bayles," Juan said, with a smiling flash of white teeth. He's short and slender, with dark skin and dark hair. He's a personal favorite of Ruby, who seems to have a motherly attitude toward him. She always makes sure that he leaves with his pockets full of cookies.

Hank slung his hammer into his tool box and straightened up. "Yup," he said, putting his hand on his hip as if his back might be bothering him. It was probably time for him to go on another drunk. "I'll bring you the bill in the mornin', and you kin write me a check. I don't take no credit cards." He tipped his battered straw hat onto the back of his head, a hat that he had worn as long as I'd known him. "I don't like to wait fer my money, neither, but I reckon you remember that from before."

"Sure," I said absently. Actually, I was remembering my conversation with McQuaid at breakfast, and what he'd told me about the Obermann sisters. I was also remembering something I had known and forgotten, one of those odd bits of random fact that pop into your mind when it's busy processing other information. "Hank, didn't your father work for the Obermann sisters awhile back? He lived in the stable, too, didn't he?"

Somewhere I had heard—maybe it had been Marian Atkins who told me—that both Mr. and Mrs. Dixon had worked for the Obermann family, he as a yardman and handyman, she as cook and housekeeper. Mrs. Dixon had died fairly young, in the 1960s, and Gabe Dixon had stayed on, doing the sisters' shopping, running their errands, taking care of the yard and the house, and driving them around in their gleaming-white 1964 Cadillac, complete with fins, vinyl top, whitewalls. Now, they didn't go out often; when they did, the Cadillac—still gleaming white—was driven by their housekeeper, a grim-faced, dark-haired woman who never smiled.

A dark look crossed Hank's face. "Yup," he said gruffly. "Pop worked fer them fer goin' on forty years. Lived in that old stable, too. And then that damn ol' bitch tossed him out like a piece of stinkin' garbage." Juan put a cautioning hand on Hank's arm, but he shook it off. "Damn bitch," he repeated sourly. "Meaner 'n a stuck rattlesnake."

"Tossed him out?" I asked, surprised. By "ol' bitch," he had to mean Jane Obermann.

"Yup. Pop, he'd got too sick to work, so they stopped payin' him. Didn't stop chargin' him rent, though. The place needed fixin' bad—floorboards was rotted clear through, roof leaked like a sieve, plumbin' was stopped up. Gas heater didn't work, neither. Place was allus cold as a witch's tit in January and hot as a whore in July." He gave an exasperated snort. "All he'd done fer them women, you'd think they'da built him a palace. But Miz Obermann, she said she didn't have the money to fix things up. And Pop, he didn't have money fer rent cuz she'd allus paid him under the table, so he didn't have no Social Security. She told him she was fixin' to tear the stable down, and he had to get out."

Somehow I wasn't surprised by this bit of information. It fit with the image I had already formed of Jane Obermann.

Juan gave me a sideways glance. "She did pay some of his medical expenses, though," he put in—tentatively, as if he wanted to correct the record but didn't want to rouse Hank's wrath. "You gotta give her that, Hank."

"Oh, yeah? 'Some' is right. Like maybe a coupla thousand measly bucks, which wadn't a drop in the damn bucket." Hank was scornful. "She shoulda done a helluva lot more 'n that, seein' wot he did fer her. Her 'n that sister, they wouldn't be where they are today, wasn't fer old Pop. But I aim to see that they set things right, and quick, too." He stopped as if he had said too much, and spat a mouthful of tobacco juice into the flower bed.

"It was good of you to take your father in, Hank," I said. It was not an idle compliment. Hank could have done what most men would do and checked Gabe into the Manor, the local nursing home. The old man would have qualified for Medicaid, and Hank wouldn't have had to nurse him.

Hank isn't one to accept a compliment. He just grunted. "Yup," he said, picking up his tool box. "Next thing I know, the ol' bitch up an' give Pop's place to them damn actors. She had money enough to fix it up then." He shook his head disgustedly. "Pop, he missed that old place somethin' fierce. Him and Ma, they was happy livin' there. It was home fer him. Reckon that was why he died. Jes' couldn't see any reason to go on livin'. And all on account of that ol' bitch."

"I'm sorry," I said, wondering just how many enemies Jane Obermann had accumulated during her seventy-five-year tour of duty on this earth. More than most people, I'd guess.

Hank put on his cap and pulled the brim down. "No call fer you to be sorry, Miz Bayles. Man's gotta die sometime." He grinned briefly, showing tobacco-stained teeth. "Woman, too, for that matter, I reckon. Ever'body's gotta die."

"You're right there," I replied to this philosophical remark—cheerfully, since the prospect of death seemed far away on this bright, beautiful morning. I was to think about this exchange in a much different light later, though.

And I was to wonder just how philosophical Hank's remark really was.

I opened up the Crystal Cave for Ruby, then spent the morning peacefully and productively dusting the shelves, balancing the checkbook, and doing the dozen or so little odds and ends that tend to get ignored during busy weeks. I also ordered another dozen of Theresa Loe's herbal calendars, which are always a big hit with my customers. They love the illustrations, as well as the unique crafts and recipes.

Around ten-thirty, Ruby stuck her arm through the connecting door between my shop and hers, called out a hello, then disappeared again. I did not take this to be a good omen. If she'd had something wonderful to tell me about her date with Colin, she would have been bubbling over with the news.

At noon, I locked the door and hung up the OUT TO LUNCH sign. Unless there's a special event, the tearoom is closed on Wednesdays. But there was plenty of good food in the kitchen fridge. I split two croissants and spread them with chicken salad and lettuce, ladled two cups full of cold tomato-basil soup, and poured two glasses of rosemary lemonade. Then I put everything on a tray with napkins and tableware and added a half-dozen lavender cookies. When the tea shop is open, you'll pay $9.95 for this elegant little lunch; Ruby and I were getting it free, one of the perks of owning the tearoom.

I carried the tray into the Crystal Cave and set it on the counter. Like Thyme and Seasons, Ruby's shop is a delightfully restful place. The prisms displayed in the front window reflect shimmering rainbows against the walls, the air is gently scented with jasmine incense and resonant with whale songs, and the shelves and tables are filled with New Age toys and books, all aimed (as Ruby says in her newspaper ad), "to give you strength, wisdom, and insight for your inner journey." Of course, you can't embark on your inner journey without a natural crystal wand, a selection of mystic oils, a scrying mirror, a lunar candle, your astrological chart, and six lessons on developing your intuition. This week only, half-price.

"Thought you might like to join me for lunch," I said.

Ruby was perched on a stool behind the counter, studying her playscript. She was wearing a long black skirt and a black T-shirt featuring the galaxy, with a silver arrow pointing to one of its spiral arms and a legend that read, "You are here." Her hair was arranged dramatically across the left side of her face, like Cher, and she wore large silver earrings of concentric circles that looked like the solar system, with the sun in the center and the planets represented by tiny colored beads. Ruby Wilcox, Girl Guide to the Back of Beyond.

"Thanks, China," she said casually, not looking up, "but please don't bother about lunch for me. I'm really not hungry."

"Too late—I've already bothered." I reached under the counter and turned down the volume on the whales. "Tomato soup with sour cream, and chicken salad, mayo, no mustard, just the way you like it. Eat. It will give you strength for your inner journey."

"Oh, all right," Ruby sighed. "If you insist." As she reached for the cup, her hair swung back and I caught a glimpse of her face.

I gasped. "Ruby! What's wrong with your eye!"

"It's black," she said calmly, and dipped her spoon into her cup.

"I can see that it's black, you goony-bird!" *Black* wasn't an accurate description. Ruby's left eye was a dark purple-black, trimmed with a greenish-yellowish border, and swelled. "How the hell did it get that way?"

She dipped again. "I ran into the pantry door at Colin's house." Her voice was serene, but her freckles were like copper flecks against her pale cheeks, and her mouth was nervous. "I put on some makeup," she added. "Can you still see it?"

"I don't mean to be cruel," I said cruelly, "but the only way to hide that eye is to put a bag over your head." I sat down on the other stool, thinking of Alana's story of the night before. The story about domestic violence that had ended, twice, in murder. I pushed the thought out of my mind. "The pantry door?"

"I knew you wouldn't believe it." She put down her soup and picked up half a croissant and added, in a joking tone that sounded so false it made me wince, "I told Colin you'd probably think he slugged me."

I frowned at her. I didn't really think Colin would do something like this, did I? But since she had brought it up—

"Well?" I asked.

"Of course not!" she flashed indignantly. "That's absurd! Even the thought of it is totally ridiculous."

I regarded her closely. "I don't suppose you'd tell me if he did."

She sniffed. "Well, he didn't, so I don't have anything to tell."

We ate in silence for a moment, until I said, "Honest Injun, the pantry door?"

Ruby held up three fingers, solemn. "Brownies' honor. It was halfway open and the hallway was dark. I just banged right into it." She sighed. "I'm hoping it won't be so noticeable by tomorrow night. And anyway, Chris is pretty good with makeup. She can fix it, I'm sure." Tomorrow night was dress rehearsal, and Chris Delaney is the makeup person.

We didn't say any more about Ruby's eye. I didn't ask about her dinner with Colin, either, and she didn't volunteer, an omission that spoke louder than words, I thought. Mostly we talked about the play—about Max Baumeister's inability to loosen up onstage—and about the shops, and Hank's repair of the deck, and paying the bills. Ah, yes, the bills. About as pleasant a topic of conversation as whether Ruby's boyfriend had socked her in the eye.

At last, I stacked the plates and cups on the tray and stood up.

"I have to get back to work," I said. "But first, a hug." I put my arms around her. "I'm really sorry about your eye," I said softly.

"Yeah." She was rueful. "I just wish you'd believe me, that's all."

"I believe you," I protested. I did, too. I couldn't picture Ruby taking a fist in the face without slugging the guy back. And if she'd done that, she would definitely have told me.

She sighed again, an exaggerated, pretend sigh. "No, you don't."

"I am not going to argue with you," I said loftily, and picked up the tray. "If you don't want to believe that I believe you, that's up to you." And with a chuckle to show that both of us were joking, I took our plates back to the kitchen and rinsed them off.

In the afternoon, Ruby watched both shops and I went out to the garden, where I weeded the bed of culinary herbs and cut the basil. We'd had a huge crop this fall, and it looked like we'd have plenty right up until frost. I took enough to make pesto for supper, filled a plastic bag for Ruby, and another one, and took all three bags inside. It was just four-thirty.

"You opened up the shop for me this morning," Ruby said, "so if you want to go home early, I'll close up for you."

"You've got a deal," I said. "Thanks." I handed her a bag of basil, seeing that the purple of her eye had become noticeably more garish, and the yellow-green ring seemed to be expanding, like a flower coming into full bloom. I suppressed a *tsk-tsk*. Chris's makeup artistry would be challenged.

I was leaving the shop when I met Alana Montoya coming up the walk. She seemed subdued and pale, and her face was puffy. She looked like somebody who'd been to a heck of a party the night before and had lived to regret every minute of it.

"You got your car okay, then?" I asked. That had been one of the points of discussion as we left Bean's—what to do about her car.

She nodded. "I guess I had a little too much to drink. I seem to be doing that a lot lately." Her smile was crooked. "Anyway, thanks."

"You're welcome," I said. "I'm just on my way out, but Ruby Wilcox can help you find whatever you need." Maybe some powdered ginger. A teaspoonful stirred into hot water, with honey and a shot of lemon. A tried-and-true hangover remedy. Or there's the old Southern plantation favorite, Jezebel Tea. Fresh mint, parsley, celery leaves, a few cloves, a piece of cinnamon stick, and some freshly grated ginger steeped in boiling water for ten minutes or so. It's supposed to cure what ails you, and it doesn't taste bad.

Alana's glance evaded mine and slid down and away. "I'm not really shopping for—" She stopped. "That is, I came to see you. I thought maybe you could help me with . . ."

There was a longish pause. Across the alley, I could hear Mr. Cowan's little Pekingese yapping ferociously. Lula is about the size of a possum, but when it comes to her territory, she's a grizzly bear. She was probably defending her pecan tree against an invading squirrel.

The barking went on. "Help you with what?" I prompted finally.

Alana swallowed. "It's . . . it's personal, and . . . well, kind of a long story. If you're in a hurry . . ." Her voice trailed off weakly.

I was in a hurry. I wanted to get somewhere before five. And I had the feeling that she wanted to talk about her drinking problem. Well, if that's what it was, she could count me out. I had to deal with Leatha's alcoholism because she was my mother. I didn't have the patience to deal with Alana's.

"Another time would be better for me, if you don't

mind," I said briskly. "We could try for lunch next week. I've got a catering job tomorrow night, and I'm hoping to get some time to relax this weekend."

A look—of desperation, perhaps?—crossed her face, and her shoulders slumped imperceptibly. "Thanks," she said. "Next week. I'll give you a call."

She turned, and I fell into step beside her, feeling half-guilty for disappointing her and wanting to make it up.

"How's the analysis going?" I asked conversationally, as we walked. "The bones from the cave, I mean. Have you had the chance to get a closer look at that skull?"

Her expression brightened. "Yes, I spent a couple of hours working with it this afternoon." She turned to face me. "The victim—his skull was fractured, probably by the rock that was found beside him. But that's not what killed him." She was animated now, excited, and I knew that the bones had spoken to her, had told her their story. "He was shot."

"Shot!" I said, startled. And then, somehow, I wasn't. I already knew from the conversation with Blackie on Monday night that the victim—a young man, Alana had said—hadn't come to that cave alone. Someone had come with him, someone who drove a vehicle and carried a light—and a gun. Someone who had brought in a rock from the cave's entrance and who had then taken the light, and the gun, and gone away, leaving a corpse behind. The bones had told their story. What we had here was a murder mystery.

Alana was nodding, almost eagerly. "The rock—it weighs just under ten pounds—was slammed against the base of the skull, with force. That's what caused the post-mortem trauma."

"So he was already dead when his skull was crushed," I said thoughtfully. "Shot in the head?"

She nodded. "I found a smooth-edged circular hole with internal beveling, consistent with a bullet's entrance, in the lower left section of the occipital. There was an exit fracture, externally beveled, in the right frontal bone above the eye orbit."

Shot in the back of the head, then smashed with a ten-pound rock, probably in an effort to obliterate the gunshot wound and make the death look like a caving accident. I didn't have to ask Alana how she could tell the sequence of these terrible events. I'd listened to enough courtroom testimony—and questioned enough forensics experts on the stand—to know what she'd say. The radiating and concentric fracture lines from the blunt impact of the rock had terminated into the radiating fracture patterns caused by the bullet. Alana had read the story of the victim's murder in his bones.

"You've reported this to Sheriff Blackwell, I suppose," I said.

She nodded. "I've talked with him by phone. I'll send him a report tomorrow."

"That's good," I said. Blackie would be pleased at the fast turnaround on this cold case. If he'd sent the bones to Bexar or Travis, he'd still be waiting for a receipt, and the report itself wouldn't be along until after the first of the year, or the year after that.

We had reached my car, and I stopped. "Give me a call, and we'll do lunch," I said.

"I . . . I'll try," she said, not looking at me. The energy that had charged her story of the bones had fizzled, and her voice was flat, without passion or even interest.

I like to think that, if I had known what Alana Montoya was going to do in a matter of days—might have been thinking of, even now, as we discussed getting together for lunch—I would have put my other errand on hold and sat down and listened to her, would have tried to hear her story, to get to the bottom of what was troubling her. Or maybe I would have sent her to see Pam Neely, the therapist Ruby talks to when she's feeling low. Surely I would have done something, wouldn't I?

I hope so.

Chapter Seven

For over three thousand years, *Cannabis sativa* was regarded as a Godsend to the human race. It was one of the world's most important all-purpose plants, producing essential fiber for fabric, rope, and paper; indispensable oil for lighting and for food; vital plant protein for humans and animals; and a valuable pain-relieving medicine. Since the 1940s, in the United States, it has not been possible to grow this herb without penalty.

My mind had two puzzles to play with as I drove the couple of blocks to the square and parked in front of Hoffmeister's Clothing Store. One was the skeleton in the cave, known now, some thirty-plus years after the fact, to be a murder victim. Unknown, still, who he was and why he was killed. Perhaps forever unknown, who had killed him.

But that was an old, very cold case, and the killer, for all I knew, might be long dead. Far more immediate and puzzling was the matter of Alana Montoya, and this urgent business that she wanted to discuss with me. But there wasn't anything I could do about it at the moment, was probably nothing I could do, ever. I laid it aside. I had other things to think about.

Pecan Springs' town square used to be the town's center of gravity, although more recently, this seems to have shifted east to the malls along I-35. That's where Wal-Mart is, and Home Depot and Office Depot and The Gap and the chain supermarkets and the branch banks. That's where the new people, residents of the bedroom communities that are springing up like toadstools everywhere, do their shopping. Still, the tourists like the square for its turn-of-the-century look, and lots of townfolk still do all their business here. The shopkeepers are friendlier, the service is more personal, and you don't have to trudge a mile of aisle to find what you want.

The centerpiece of the square is a pink granite wedding cake of a courthouse, built of rock that was quarried near Marble Falls, at the southern tip of Burnet County, and transported to Pecan Springs via the Missouri and Pacific Railroad. It sits on a square of straggly grass, worn by the summer's foot traffic, with a pot of petunias and a bench for the old guys anchoring each of the four corners. Around this center are arranged a motley collection of stone buildings, several of them built in a style called the German Vernacular: the Ben Franklin Variety Store, Beezle's Hardware, the *Enterprise* office, the public library, the Library Thrift Shoppe, the Sophie Briggs Historical Museum, Mueller's Antiques and Fine Crafts, Krautzenheimer's Restaurant, and Hoffmeister's Clothing.

If you're guessing that Pecan Springs was settled by Germans, you've guessed right. These sturdy, God-fearing people came to Texas in the 1840s and '50s, taking passage on wooden ships to Corpus Christi, then trekking overland by wagon and horseback. They brought with them their axes and knives and plows, their Bibles and bags of seed, their skills in carpentry and smithing and wagon building, their disciplined habits of work and their stern morality. They came in search of self-determination and a better life, but most of all, land. The ones who survived—those who were adaptable, resourceful, and lucky—got all three.

They settled first at New Braunfels, on the Balcones Escarpment. The rich blackland prairie lay flat and fertile to the east and the hills and canyons of the Edwards Plateau rose to the west, the uplands blanketed with cedar, with pecan and hackberry and cypress growing green along the creeks. Life wasn't easy, for the settlers hadn't watched any reality TV shows or read any do-it-yourself books and weren't quite prepared to be pioneers. This can be a brutal land, especially when you don't have air-conditioning in the summer and central heat in the winter. But there were plentiful artesian springs and a long growing season, and some of the settlers were adventurous enough to move west and north, building towns like Boerne and Fredericksburg and San Marcos. They also built Pecan Springs, and eventually the courthouse square and the shops around it.

It was one of those shops I had come to visit, Good Earth Goods, which is owned and operated by Colin Fowler. I had dropped in before, when the shop first opened, and came away with a fairly favorable impression. In general, I think it's smart to buy environmentally sensitive products, although the Good Earth items struck me as pricey. I prefer to find less expensive ways to be kind to the environment. However, I was on a reconnaissance mission this afternoon—to get a clearer fix on Colin—and price was no object. How much can a couple of environmentally friendly lightbulbs cost, anyway?

Thirty-seven bucks, that's what.

"These are CFLs," Colin Fowler told me, noticing the telltale pain of sticker shock on my face. "Compact fluorescents. They use about a quarter of the electricity to provide the same amount of light, so they significantly lower the pollution and carbon dioxide emissions that result when fossil fuels are burned to make electricity. Not only that, but they lower your electrical bill. And since they last several times longer than ordinary bulbs, less raw material is required to make them."

"Well, I'm for that," I managed. I took out my environmentally insensitive plastic credit card and handed it to him, along with the bag of basil. "From my garden," I said. "Live long and pesto."

"You brought this for me?" he asked, looking pleased. He put his face in the bag and inhaled deeply. "Hey, this is terrific! Thanks, China."

"A natural high," I said, "and legal."

"There aren't enough of those," he said, smiling. Studying his face, I could see what had attracted Ruby. Colin Fowler is definitely a good-looking man, with a strong-featured face, high cheekbones, chestnut-brown hair worn a little long, and dark eyes. He's six-feet and then some, which makes him taller than Ruby (a real plus for her, I'm sure). He has the build of a man who works out regularly and often. He smiles easily and seems outgoing and friendly, although it seemed to me that the smile on his mouth wasn't quite reaching his eyes. He was wearing jeans and rope sandals and his T-shirt, naturally green, said "Legalize Hemp."

Legalize Hemp. It's not a slogan you see much of around here, where the T-shirts promote Lonestar Longnecks and the Pecan Springs Panthers. Most guys wear cowboy boots, too, not sandals, and they'd rather chew tobacco than sniff basil—in fact, most of them wouldn't be caught dead sniffing basil. But all this was probably part of Colin's attraction for Ruby, who doesn't have much use for your average Pecan Springs macho male.

However, as I glanced from his T-shirt to his dark eyes, I caught a glimpse of something unsettling. It wasn't just the absence of smile, but a distrustful, watchful wariness, the look of a man whose life has taken him into the shadows, who has seen a great many ugly sights and would not be surprised when he saw them again. It was just a glimpse, so brief that I could not be sure what I had seen. And then he lowered his glance.

"Did you see Ruby's shiner?" he asked casually, running my credit card through the machine.

"Hey, how could I miss it?" I made my voice light, matching his. He was still looking down, punching numbers, and I couldn't read his expression. "She's hoping that some stage makeup will take care of the problem tomorrow night, but I have my doubts."

He handed back my card. "I feel just awful about it. The whole thing was my fault, you know."

"It was?" I felt distinctly uneasy.

"Yeah. It wouldn't have happened if I'd turned on the light in the hall. Or if I hadn't left the bathroom door open. Poor kid walked right into it."

I managed a laugh. "The oldest story in the world."

He gave an odd, quirky shrug, then echoed my laugh, tore off the credit card slip, and pushed it toward me. "An old story but true, so help me God." He was making this into a joke. "I'll admit to my share of skirmishes, but I've never yet cuffed a woman."

"Of course not." I gave him back the slip, signed. "Trouble is, Ruby said it was the pantry door. You guys had better synchronize your stories." Without giving him time to respond, I glanced at his T-shirt. "You're a hemp activist, huh?"

"You bet," he said, straight-faced and serious now. "There's our display." He pointed. "If you're into subtle ironies, we've even got a U.S. flag made of hemp."

I turned around. One whole wall of the small shop was devoted to a display of hemp products. Shirts, shorts, pants, sandals (exactly like the pair Colin was wearing), fabric, paper, rope, soaps, food products. And the flag.

"Quite a collection," I said, meaning it. "How are people taking it?"

Pecan Springs is, by and large, a conservative town, and some people would be suspicious of hemp products, "all-natural" or not, legal or not. It's illegal to grow hemp in the U.S., but it's not illegal to sell or purchase hemp products imported from other countries. Go figure.

However, CTSU is just up the hill, and no doubt the hemp items were popular among students. And among the liberals in town and in such nearby art colonies as Wimberley and Gruene, who would be delighted to show off their new pair of hemp shorts, or their "Legalize Hemp" T-shirt. Some of them would even be happy to wear a cap that said "Legalize Marijuana," although we have our share of drug problems here, close as we are to the border and to the drug pipeline that runs from Mexico through Texas to points north. Tons of high-grade Colombian dope—hidden in boxes of clothing, cheap coffeemakers, made-in-Mexico furniture—are smuggled through the border checkpoints by *pasadores,* border crossers, with the connivance of a few inspectors and crooked cops. McQuaid had been investigating just such a criminal arrangement when he was shot, and although his work put an end to one bunch of bad guys, there were plenty more where they came from, living and dealing in the dark places.

Colin was pointing to a poster behind the counter. "As you can see," he said, "I'm an active member of the Hemp Industries Association. Hemp has been legalized in Canada, and we're working for legalization here." He leaned against the counter, regarding me. "You're into herbs, China. So I suppose you know the story." He grinned a little. "Or maybe you don't. Cannabis doesn't exactly qualify as a poster plant for the Herb Society of America."

"I know the story," I said, "or at least, the outline."

For thousands of years, *Cannabis sativa* was one of the world's most important all-purpose plants, yielding fiber, oil, food, medicine—and, yes, a psychoactive narcotic—to cultures around the globe. It was primarily the fiber, called hemp, that made this plant so vitally important to humans. Throughout our existence, far more clothing has been produced from hemp than from cotton, flax, or wool—comfortable clothing, too, clothing that absorbs moisture, softens with washing, and doesn't need much ironing. And until the late nineteenth century, all the sails, ropes, riggings, and nets carried on all the ships of the world were made from hemp. In fact, our English word *canvas* is derived from the Latin word *cannabis.* Without hemp,

Columbus could not have discovered America; Magellan wouldn't have had a prayer of sailing around the world; and the English fleet would not have defeated the Spanish Armada. Without hemp, it is safe to say, there would have been no British Empire.

The American colonies relied on hemp, just as did the Old World. Thomas Paine listed hemp as one of the new nation's four essential natural resources, which also included iron, timber, and tar. Thomas Jefferson thought it was far more sensible to grow cannabis than to grow tobacco ("which is never useful," he remarked judiciously, "and sometimes pernicious"). And when Benjamin Franklin started his first paper mill, the fiber he used was hemp, thereby allowing America to have a colonial press without having to obtain paper (and permission) from England.

It's a different story in America now, of course. The legitimate and valuable uses of cannabis were ended in the United States by the Marijuana Tax Act of 1937—special interest legislation that, many historians say, was aimed to boost the synthetic fibers and pulp-timber industries by criminalizing their major competitor, hemp.

Meanwhile, hemp is legally grown in over thirty countries, including Canada, England, Germany, Australia, and France. Its proponents call it a "miracle" plant—not far off the mark, for hemp fiber is now used to produce a strong, lightweight fiberglass-like material, as well as textiles, paper, building materials, carpeting, even circuit boards.

But Colin was right. Cannabis will never be celebrated by those of us who think of herbs as the teddy bears of the plant world: sweet little warm-and-fuzzies that brighten our gardens, perk up our food, heal our ailments, and offer nothing but good. We can't think of cannabis that way, or the other two powerful herbal narcotics, opium and cacao.

I picked up my sack of thirty-seven-dollar lightbulbs. "Thanks, Colin."

"Sure." He grinned. "And thanks for the basil. I've got

some salmon left over from last night's dinner—it'll be perfect, cold, with pesto mayo."

Not just a gourmet, but a creative gourmet. And, despite the slight inconsistency in their stories, I seriously doubted that Colin was responsible for Ruby's shiner. I could be wrong, but I met plenty of abusers in my career as a lawyer, and this man didn't strike me as quite the type. There was that odd, watchful wariness, though, as if he were mentally watching his back—hardly the look of a man who was completely comfortable with his life. I had the feeling that, one way or another, Ruby's love affair wasn't destined to run smoothly.

COLIN'S mention of pesto mayo—a simple thing, really, just mayonnaise, homemade or store-bought, blended with pesto—gave me an idea. I had planned to have spaghetti for supper, but on the way home, I stopped at Cavette's Grocery—a family store that has somehow survived the supermarket blitzkrieg—and bought chicken breasts, sourdough rolls, and fresh spinach. While I was picking up a bottle of zinfandel, I ran into Marian Atkins and Jean Davenport. Marian was trying to decide between a red and a white wine. With a puzzled look, she held out both.

"Jean and I are having chicken cacciatore tonight. Jean says white for chicken, I say red for tomato sauce. What do you think?"

"Well, if it were me," I said, pointing to the cabernet sauvignon in her right hand, "I'd go for that nice dry red." It bore the Falls Creek Vineyards label, one of our fine Texas wineries. "I'd use it in the cacciatore, too. But I'm not much of a wine connoisseur," I added, as she put the white wine back on the shelf. "You might prefer something else."

"I'll take your word for it," Marian said. She's in her early forties, shorter than I, with broad shoulders and practically no waist. Her blonde hair, darker at the roots and permed to a crinkle, was disheveled, and her flushed face was the color of her cranberry shirt. A pale sheen of perspiration shimmered on her forehead, whether from heat or stress, I couldn't tell.

"Let's get both." Jean reached for the bottle of white and put it into their basket, pointing to a package of frozen chicken cacciatore. "We're not actually cooking the chicken. All we have to do is stick this stuff in the microwave—which is just about all either of us can handle these days." Jean, too, looked hot and disheveled, which is unusual for her. She's a cool lady. When the whole play cast is losing their collective and individual heads, she keeps hers.

"Play's got you guys down, huh?" I asked sympathetically. "Hang in there. It'll all be over in three more weeks."

Marian waggled her hand. "The play is . . . well, we've done everything we can do. It's in the hands of the gods."

"And it may not run for three weeks," Jean said wearily. "It may close after opening night."

Marian pressed her lips together and narrowed her eyes with a look of combined irritation, impatience, and annoyance. "The problem is Jane Obermann. I suppose you know she sacked Duane Redmond and replaced him with Max Baumeister?" Her tone grew bitter. "Max reminds her of her father. It's that mustache, I suppose, and his little gold glasses. And the fact that he's an old acquaintance. The family dentist, as I understand it."

From the tautness of her voice, I'd say that Marian was definitely stressed out. She needed to go home, open that wine, and put her feet up. "Ruby said Max was having some trouble getting into the role," I remarked.

"Trouble!" Marian gave a disgusted snort. "I'll tell you, China, if it weren't for Ruby, we'd be in a helluva mess. She's taken her role and made it into something special—with Jean's help, of course."

"Oh?" I turned to Jean. "Ruby hasn't said much about it, except that you've made some changes in the script. What have you done?"

Jean gave me a mysterious look. "You'll see," was all she said.

Marian bent over and took a package of Parmesan cheese out of the cooler next to the wines. "Of course, we don't know what Jane is going to say. She'll probably close us down." She dropped the cheese into her basket. "And today, she ripped me apart over the damn sign. The big one, that was supposed to go on the front of the theater."

"Uh-oh," I said softly.

"Uh-oh in spades." Marian's voice rose, her tone hot enough to fry fish. "Turns out that she wanted *'Merrill G. Obermann'* on the sign, rather than just plain old Merrill Obermann."

"G," Jean put in, "stands for *Gustav.* It distinguishes Merrill G. from his ne'er-do-well cousin, Merrill T."

"T," Marian said, "stands for *Tobias.* Never mind that both of these old farts have been dead for half a century, or that the sign cost nearly a thousand dollars. It has to be done over again. With a *G.* Which stands for God help us."

"What a pain," I said.

"You said it. I—" She glanced at her watch. "Holy smokes, we've gotta go, Jean. You're coming to opening night, aren't you, China? You'll see what Jean and Ruby have cooked up then."

"Of course I'm coming," I said. "Have you forgotten that Party Thyme is catering the cast party? And since Ruby will have her hands full with the play, I'm helping Janet with the food."

"Good Lord, yes." Marian ran her hands through her crimped curls. "Jane's got me so rattled that I'd forget my head if it wasn't nailed on."

Jean's laugh was short and bitter. "If we can just get through opening night without somebody shooting that wretched old bitch, we'll be lucky."

It was the kind of thing people say without meaning, of course, meant to express impatience, exasperation, even anger. One of those trivial remarks that we forget as soon as the words themselves have dropped into silence.

But given my conversation with McQuaid that morning, I didn't forget them. They were the first words that would come into my mind on Friday night, when I heard the shot.

Chapter Eight

CHINA'S PESTO MAYO

1/3 cup basil leaves, lightly packed
1/3 cup spinach leaves, lightly packed
2 Tbsp. grated Parmesan cheese
1 Tbsp. pecans (you can substitute pine nuts or walnuts)
2 Tbsp. lemon juice
2 Tbsp. olive oil
2 garlic cloves, mashed
salt and freshly ground pepper to taste
1 1/2 cups prepared mayonnaise (low-fat, if you prefer)
1–2 Tsp. prepared horseradish (if desired)
2 Tbsp. diced sun-dried tomatoes

In a blender, combine the basil, spinach, cheese, garlic, and nuts. With the blender running, add the lemon juice and olive oil. Process until smooth. Place in a bowl and stir in mayonnaise. Add horseradish to taste (more if you like a zesty bite, less or none if you don't), and salt and pepper. Add diced sun-dried tomatoes and stir just to mix. Cover and refrigerate until serving time. Excellent on hot or cold chicken, or on cold salmon or cold sliced beef. Makes about 2 1/2 cups.

Brian had gone to Jake's house to eat and do homework and whatever else teenagers do when they're out of sight of adults, and I had planned a pleasant supper *à deux* on the screened-in back porch. The porch was one of the jobs Hank Dixon had done for us, two summers before. A shady, breezy spot, it's become our favorite for lazy weekend meals, when the hottest days of summer are over.

I tossed a green salad and mixed up a batch of basil pesto mayonnaise and sliced some Swiss cheese for the chicken, while McQuaid built a pecan-wood fire in the barbeque, grilled the chicken breasts, and toasted the sourdough rolls. I watched him through the window, loving him, worrying a little because he looked tired and he was whistling between his teeth in the way he does when he's feeling pain and doesn't want to take the medication that makes him drowsy. We had been enormously, miraculously lucky. A fraction of an inch, and the bullet that only nicked his spinal cord would have killed him; as it was, the doctors hadn't given him much of a chance to walk again. But they hadn't counted on McQuaid's determination. He no longer jogs but he walks easily, except when he's tired or in pain, and he manages his other physical activities with enthusiasm.

When he brought the chicken in from the grill, I spread a cloth on the low, green-painted table, put out the food, and filled our wineglasses. "I ran into Alana Montoya today," I said, as we helped ourselves to salad. "She's finished her preliminary work on Brian's caveman." I told McQuaid what she'd said about the bullet hole in the skull and the postmortem fracture.

"I guess I'm not surprised," he said, layering grilled chicken and Swiss slices on a toasted roll. "Wonder if we'll ever find out who he was." He slathered pesto mayo over the top. "Kind of a coincidence, huh? You seeing her last night and today, too." He paused. "You going to see her again?"

"We're having lunch next week," I said, withholding my suspicion that Alana wanted to talk about her drinking. I frowned. Lots of faculty members drink too much. So why was I protecting her? Was I afraid that McQuaid would think less of her if he knew? But why should that matter to me? Enough already, China.

We settled into the porch swing, eating and drinking in companionable silence, enjoying the cool evening breeze that blows in from the cedar-covered hills. Howard Cosell sprawled at our feet, one vigilant eye open for any little treat that might come his way, and in the sycamore tree, a wren celebrated the advent of cooler weather with a spill of song.

McQuaid leaned forward, picked up the zinfandel bottle, and refilled his empty glass. "Oh, by the way," he said, "I'm flying to New Orleans on Friday morning. I'll be back around lunchtime on Saturday."

"Well, drat," I said. I held out my glass and he refilled it, too. "That means you'll miss opening night, and the Denim and Diamonds gala. Ruby will be brokenhearted." And I had been counting on him to help me tote the boxes of food for the party. Janet balks at carrying anything heavier than a tray of sandwiches.

"Yeah," he said ruefully. "Tell Ruby I'm sorry to miss her big night. But I'll catch the play later. It's on for three or four weekends, isn't it?"

"Three, if it doesn't fold. Marian and Jean didn't seem too confident when I saw them today." I paused. "What's taking you to New Orleans?"

"The . . . other case I'm working on."

I eyed him. "The résumé fraud thing? What's that all about, anyway?" McQuaid usually shares at least the outline of his cases, but he hadn't told me anything at all about this one, not even the name of the client. The case itself was an oddity, since lying on a résumé doesn't usually warrant the hiring of an investigator. Unless, of course, the liar happens to be a chief honcho of a major corporation. I had read recently of a software company whose CFO had lied about having an MBA from a prestigious Western university. When a reporter uncovered the truth and the wire services got hold of the story, the company's stock fell thirty-five percent. If there were a potential downside of that magnitude in this case, it would make sense to hire McQuaid to look into the suspected problem.

McQuaid eased back into the swing with a grimace that told me that his back was bothering him. He answered my question with one of his own. "Aren't you going to ask me how it went with the Obermann sisters this afternoon?"

"Oh, right," I said, with interest. "So you saw them today?"

He nodded. "If Jane is the client from hell, she hasn't shown her true nature—not yet, anyway. The interview went very well."

"Jane must have been on her best behavior," I said dryly, thinking of my conversation with Marian and Jean.

"I suppose. We didn't finish—I didn't get all the information I needed, and I don't yet have a signature on the retainer agreement. But Jane certainly seems cooperative enough. And this is a job she wants done. She's definitely afraid."

I pushed the cloth aside and put my feet up, turning the table into an ottoman. "So what happened? Let's have the blow-by-blow. And don't leave anything out."

McQuaid obliged. He had gone to the Obermann mansion at two o'clock that afternoon, parking in the circular drive in front of the house and going up the walk to the front door.

"It's an imposing house," he said, "or at least it must have been, once upon a time. It needs a lot of fixing up, though—painting, repair, garden work. There's enough to keep somebody busy full-time for a year or more. It's an odd place, with those turrets and towers and chimneys and weird dormers." He frowned. "It has a strange feeling about it, too, if you ask me. I don't think I'd want to live there."

"Maybe it's the widow's walk," I offered. "The Obermann mansion is the only house in town that has one. And Cynthia Obermann is the only woman in Pecan Springs history who killed herself by jumping off her own roof."

"No kidding." He made a face. "Well, I'm not surprised. Maybe taking care of that enormous place drove her crazy." His grin was lopsided. "It has a certain authentic spookiness, I'd say. It would make a great set for a vampire movie. You can picture them flying out of those turret windows."

"Or a haunted house for Halloween," I said, "featuring Miss Jane as the chief haunter—although I'll bet you couldn't persuade the neighborhood kids to go inside. They'd be scared to death of the old lady."

But McQuaid, not being a scared kid, had gone inside. He had banged the heavy, old-fashioned door knocker, and eventually the door was opened by a grim-faced woman in her fifties, her hair done up in a ragged knot—the housekeeper and sometime-chauffeur, he surmised. He gave his name, she nodded, beckoned him in, and closed and locked the door behind him.

Without a word—"Eerie," McQuaid described it—she showed him to the book-lined library, which had French doors that opened onto a brick patio, littered with leaves and surrounded by a tangle of unkempt bushes. The room's windows were tall and elegant, but the green velvet drapes were faded and dusty. The Edwardian furniture—a velvet settee, carved tables, beaded lampshades—would have been at home on the set of *Upstairs, Downstairs*, but most of it was shabby, and the Oriental rug on the floor was worn to the bare threads. The focal point of the room was a fireplace, over which hung a gilt-framed oil portrait of Doctor Obermann.

"Imposing man," McQuaid said. "Teutonic to the mustache and gold-rimmed glasses." He grinned. "I wondered what that testy old German would think of his daughters' inviting a private detective into his library. He'd probably view me as a little lower than dirt."

There was one more thing in the room that caught McQuaid's attention, quite naturally: a glass curio case with curved legs that might have held crystal and china, but instead held three pistols, each on its own glass shelf. Because McQuaid collects guns, he sauntered over to take a look. They were vintage guns: a broom-handle Mauser, a Luger, and an M1911 Colt .45 automatic, all antiques, but still quite lethal-looking. He was examining them through the glass when the door opened and the Obermann sisters made their entrance.

"Amazing," McQuaid said with a chuckle. "Jane was wearing something queenly. She is remarkably aristocratic."

"An understatement," I said.

"All statements are understatements, when it comes to that lady," McQuaid said. "The other one, Florence, looked pretty frail. She didn't seem well—or perhaps she just didn't want to talk to me. Jane did all the talking."

"Apparently, she always does," I said.

The first order of business was the family history. Of course, it wasn't relevant to the present situation, Jane told him, but she thought it might be helpful for him to know something about the Obermann background. McQuaid, who had the feeling that family history was a source of pride for her, had let her talk.

I knew the story, or part of it, anyway, from *A Man for All Reasons*, and from the tales I'd heard about the family since I had come to Pecan Springs. Merrill Obermann—Merrill Gustav Obermann—had been born in 1896 and was twenty-three when, a decorated war hero, he returned from combat in France to marry his sweetheart, Cynthia. From his mother's side of the family, he inherited a couple of thousand acres of East Texas oil land, where his first gusher spouted in 1925. From his father's side, he had inherited the intelligence and determination to finish his medical degree and the financial shrewdness required to steer the family fortune, battered but mostly intact, through the angry seas of the Depression.

Jane then pointed out the photographs of Merrill and Cynthia's four children, arranged on one of the tables. Carl had been the oldest, followed by Jane, then Florence, and finally, Harley. The young family had fit comfortably into the Victorian mansion on Pecan Street that Merrill Obermann (Doctor Obermann by now) had built. The doctor, obviously a man of talent and energy, divided his time between his oil-related East Texas business activities, his medical practice, and his growing philanthropic interests. Cynthia Obermann, if a trifle flighty and eccentric, was a devoted mother and widely admired Pecan Springs socialite who entertained lavishly and with enthusiasm.

But while the senior Obermanns managed to have four children, the junior Obermanns failed to match their parents' conjugal fecundity. The four of them, taken altogether, produced only one offspring, and that one was destined for a tragic end.

The girls didn't have an opportunity to bear children. Jane and Florence had never married, although Florence was once engaged—her suitor, I had heard it said, was cruelly and unconscionably banished by her sister. After their mother's death, the two women continued to live with their father, managing the servants—a diminishing number, as time went on—and assuming their mother's role as hostesses for Doctor Obermann's social engagements. Their father had died of a heart attack, quite suddenly and unexpectedly, in 1955.

The boys fared only somewhat better than the girls when it came to producing progeny. Carl came back from the Second World War, married, and moved to San Antonio, but he and his wife were killed in an auto accident the year after Doctor Obermann died. They had no children. Harley was more fortunate. He married, took up residence in Houston, and produced a son. The boy, however, enlisted in the Marines and went to Vietnam. He was badly wounded and spent a year or more in military hospitals. After his release, he roamed around for a while, visited briefly in Pecan Springs, and then took off for California. Nothing had been heard from him since, and no one ever knew what had become of him. He was ruled legally dead in 1983.

"So Jane, Florence, and Harley are all that's left," I said.

"Nope," McQuaid replied. "It's just the two women. Harley died in 1969, and when his son was declared dead, the sisters were next in line. Jane and Florence must be worth millions. They could afford to fix up that house out of petty cash."

Jane had not told him all of this, of course, but McQuaid, who likes to have as much information as he can about his clients, had made his own independent inquiry. Apparently, Doctor Obermann had been of the old school in more ways than one. He did not believe in giving women control over the family money—either that, or he feared that his daughters might have inherited their mother's eccentricities. The old man had given some of his wealth to the Pecan Springs hospital and the public library, but divided the bulk between his sons, with a sizable annual allowance for each of his daughters. Carl got what was left of the property in East Texas, while Harley got the house in Pecan Springs, with instructions to allow his sisters to live there as long as the house remained in the family. But with both sons dead, the old man's intentions had been thwarted. The girls got the money, after all.

"And with no direct descendents," I said, "Jane and Florence are going to have to decide who gets those millions. Let's hope they continue their philanthropic interests. The theater is certainly a step in the right direction." I paused, regarding him curiously. "So what's this threat that's got these ladies' tails in a tizzy? Is somebody from the theater association making nasty noises at them? Lance, maybe, or Marian, or Duane?" I chuckled, not really taking this seriously.

McQuaid shook his head. "This has to do with a former employee, somebody who worked for the family for twenty or thirty years. The old man lived in an apartment in the stable."

Somewhere, a woodpecker began tapping at a tree. I was staring at McQuaid, a startled interruption on the tip of my tongue. I swallowed it and let him go on.

"Then he got to the point where he was sick and couldn't work any longer. The sisters had already come up with the idea of giving the property to the Community Theater Association, so they asked him to move. They offered him a room in their house, but he turned them down. They even offered to find him an apartment of his own, but he decided to move in with his son. He was pretty sick—lung cancer, Miss Jane said. They paid all his doctor bills, but—"

He stopped. I was open-mouthed. "Why are you looking at me like that, China?"

"Because," I said. "Didn't Jane tell you that this man is *dead*? He died a couple of months ago."

"I got that idea, yes. You know who I'm talking about?"

"Uh-huh. Didn't they tell you?"

He shook his head. "We didn't actually get that far. The frail one, Florence, became distraught and had to leave the room. She has heart trouble, Jane said after her sister went upstairs, and apparently this whole affair has been traumatic for her. So we cut the interview short. Jane asked me to come back Saturday. She said she'd finish the story and give me a check for the retainer then." He paused. "She did tell me, though, that it's the old man's son who has threatened them. She's afraid he'll try to kill them."

"Yeah, right," I said dryly. "She's talking about Hank Dixon, you know."

"Hank?" It was McQuaid's turn to stare. "The guy who screened in this porch?"

I waved my hand. "And repaired the roof over your workshop, and fixed the drain in the kitchen." All good jobs, done competently and with a minimum of fuss, with only a couple of days out for boozing and sobering up.

McQuaid frowned. "How do you know this, China?"

"Somebody—Marian, I think—told me that old man Dixon had worked for the Obermanns. Hank was finishing the deck at the shop this morning, and I asked him about it. He told me the same story you've just related, although some of the facts don't quite match." I grinned wryly. "He put a very different spin on it, of course."

"What kind of spin?"

I told McQuaid what I'd heard from Hank. That his father Gabe had worked for the Obermann family for a long time, and that he'd been paid under the table, so he'd had no Social Security. That Gabe's apartment was in bad shape and the Obermanns refused to make repairs. That they had essentially evicted the old man, although they had given him a couple of thousand dollars toward his medical expenses.

"Jane said they paid all his medical bills," McQuaid said thoughtfully.

"She also said they offered him a room in their house or an apartment of his own, which Hank didn't mention."

"Hard to say who's telling the truth. Hard to check, too. It's one of those she-said he-said things."

I agreed. "I guess I'm not surprised to hear that Hank has threatened the Obermanns. He certainly resents the way they treated his father. And if his story is anywhere close to the truth, I'd have to say I don't blame him."

"Oh, yeah?" McQuaid inquired dryly. "You mean, these aren't the compassionate, public-spirited women people think they are?"

I laughed shortly. "Nobody ever gave Jane Obermann

points for being compassionate." I paused. "Hank's got a bad temper. He might fling a rock through a window, especially if he got drunk. But I don't think he'd actually attempt anything . . . well, really serious." I looked at McQuaid. "Do you?"

And then I thought of something Hank had said, something to the effect that the Obermann sisters wouldn't be where they were today if it hadn't been for his father. And, he had added, "I aim to see that they take care of that, and right quick, too." Or words to that effect. It didn't sound like a death threat, exactly. More like blackmail.

McQuaid was shaking his head. "If it's Hank the women are worried about, I don't see that they've got a serious problem. I agree—the guy is hot-tempered, but he's not stupid."

"These threats the women received," I said. "Were they oral or written?"

"A phone call, I think. As I said, though, we didn't get into the details." He frowned a little. "Somehow, I had the feeling that the situation wasn't terribly urgent. Florence certainly seemed distraught enough, although that might have been her illness. But Jane was pretty cool about the whole thing. Detached, actually. I don't think I've ever seen a woman who is quite so . . ." He threw up his hands, unable to find a way to describe her.

I nodded. "It doesn't sound to me as if they're actually afraid. If they thought they were in real danger, they'd have called the police, instead of hiring a PI." They hadn't actually hired McQuaid, either, when you got right down to it. That had been put off until the weekend. So whatever Jane thought Hank might be planning, she didn't believe it was imminent.

"They might not want the cops involved because they don't want to get Hank in trouble," McQuaid said in a reasonable tone. "Maybe they feel sorry for him, for his father's sake. After all, the old guy worked for the family for a lot of years."

I frowned. "I can imagine Florence feeling that way. But Jane?"

McQuaid drained the last of his wine. "Or maybe they're nervous about dealing with the police. Who knows? They're just two little old ladies who find themselves in a situation they don't know how to handle. Maybe all they want is for somebody to weigh in on their side, but without the brass knuckles."

I chuckled. I hadn't thought of Miss Jane as a little old lady, exactly. But if she wanted a two-ton gorilla with a soft touch, McQuaid was her man.

We sat for some time as dusk gathered gently around us, bringing the sights and songs of an October evening. A whip-poor-will shrilled his monotonous two-note tune from the open field, *poor-will, poor-will, poor-will.* A great horned owl hooted breathily in the woods, like somebody blowing across the neck of a bottle. A nighthawk executed precision loops and turns on its evening patrol, snatching bugs and dragonflies out of the still, honeysuckle-scented air. Snout to the earth, an armadillo wandered along the stone fence and disappeared through a veil of goldenrod.

"So what's the plan?" I asked finally. "What are you going to do?"

McQuaid put his arm across my shoulders and pulled me comfortably against him. "Nothing, until I see Jane and Florence on Saturday, and they officially hire me. Now that I know it's Hank, I'm not concerned that they're in any real danger. When I have all the details, I'll have a straight talk with him. Let him know that whatever he's been up to, he has to stop before he digs himself a hole he can't climb out of. I'm sure he'll listen."

"I'm sure, too," I said. McQuaid wouldn't use the brass knuckles, of course, but as a gorilla, he can be pretty convincing.

What neither of us knew, though, was that it was already too late for talking and listening. The events that created this tragedy had been set in motion long ago. By Saturday, we wouldn't be dealing with threats.

By Saturday, somebody would be dead.

Chapter Nine

Chrysanthemums (*Chrysanthemum sp.*) were first cultivated in China, where the roots were used to relieve headaches, young sprouts and flower petals were sprinkled over salads, and the leaves were brewed as a drink for festive occasions. Other members of the chrysanthemum family have proved themselves useful, even into modern times. Feverfew (*C. parthenium*) has been scientifically demonstrated to be a remedy for migraine headaches and rheumatoid arthritis. Pyrethrum (*C. cinerariifolium*) contains a chemical that paralyses and poisons insects; it is used as the basis for many botanical insecticides.

On Thursday morning, I called Sheila Dawson's office and left a message. When she hadn't called me back by lunchtime, I decided to stop by. I like Sheila very much, and I wanted to clear the air. As a peace offering, I chose a pot of bronze chrysanthemums from the display in front of my shop, wrapped the pot in green foil, and took it along.

If you ever need to visit the Pecan Springs Police Department, you'll find it on the northeast corner of the square, in the basement of an old brick building that also houses the Tourist and Information Center (on the first floor), the Parks and Utilities Department (on the second), and (in the attic) a summer colony of Mexican free-tailed bats that swarm out at sunset like voracious baby vampires, making some tourists nervous. For years, the first-floor Tourist people encouraged the second-floor Parks people to exterminate the bats in the attic, until somebody pointed out that they eat their weight in mosquitoes and then some every night. In fact, the largest bat colony in the world—a million and a half bats, so many that you can actually see their flight on Doppler radar—hangs out for the summer underneath the Congress Avenue Bridge in Austin and nightly slurps up some thirty thousand pounds of mosquitoes and other insects. Hearing this, Tourist and Parks surrendered, although the staff sometimes wear clothespins on their noses in protest. Guano stinks, especially at the end of a long, hot summer. (If you're a gardener, of course, you don't mind the smell—bat guano makes great fertilizer.)

Dorrie Hull, the police department's receptionist and day-shift dispatcher, was drenched in so much perfume that she couldn't have smelled the guano if somebody had shoved her face in it. When Sheila was hired as chief of police a couple of years ago, she made Dorrie start wearing a uniform and stop smoking at her desk. She gave in to Dorrie's plaintive pleas, though, and allowed her to keep on wearing perfume and a nonregulation hairstyle.

"Mornin', Miz Bayles," Dorrie said cheerfully. She patted her pagoda of platinum-blonde, Dolly Parton–big hair, courtesy of Bobby Rae's House of Beauty. Piled so high I'd have to stand on a chair to see the top of it, the hair was an interesting contrast to her regulation gray uniform shirt and blue tie. "Ya here t' see the boss lady?"

"Is she available?" Dorrie's perfume was as overpowering as her hair. I was filtering the air through my teeth.

"Lemme check." Dorrie picked up the phone and punched an extension with an inch-long blue fingernail, the same shade as her blue tie, with a silver stripe down the middle. Dorrie had been allowed to keep her nails, along with her hair and perfume. "Hey, ya there, Chief?" she asked perkily. "It's Miz Bayles, wantin' to see ya."

There was a silence. I couldn't hear what Sheila said.

Dorrie frowned. "But she already knows—" Another silence, then a heavily aggrieved sigh. "Yes'm. I'll tell her. Sorry fer botherin' ya." She put down the phone and looked up at me. "Two minutes is all ya get. She's got city council this afternoon, and that Ben Graves is after her scalp again."

Ben Graves would love to get Sheila fired. He almost managed it when it took the department a while to nail old Mrs. Holeyfield's killer. Now, he was probably looking for something else, and Sheila was unhappy about it.

I grinned at Dorrie. "Chewed you out, did she?"

Dorrie grinned back. "Some days she is ornerier than others." She leaned forward and lowered her voice. "Dunno what's eatin' her, but it's bad."

In Sheila's office, I took a deep breath, shut the door, and leaned against it. "I prefer guano to Torrid Shoulders or Sexy Secrets or whatever the hell Dorrie's wearing."

Sheila closed a folder and looked up. Whatever you were expecting a female police chief to look like, Smart Cookie is not it. She was dressed for her appearance at the city council meeting: shell-pink silk blouse, crisp cream-colored linen blazer and slim skirt, pink-and-gold jewelry. Her ash-blonde hair was sleek and classy, her makeup perfectly subdued, her nails pink and pearly. If you haven't encountered her on the firing range, or if you don't know she's packing a .357 Magnum in her Gucci shoulder bag, you'd swear she was a CEO at Mary Kay Cosmetics and start checking the curb for her pink Cadillac.

Sheila frowned. "I give Dorrie the sniff test when she comes in every morning. Trouble is, she keeps the stuff in her drawer, like a flask of moonshine, and soaks herself in it the minute my back's turned." She put the folder on a stack, not meeting my eyes. "Did she tell you I'm running behind? A couple of minutes is the best I can do."

I put the pot of chrysanthemums on her desk. "Smart Cookie," I said quietly, "you are not running behind. You are running from me. And it's high time you stopped. I may sleep with McQuaid, but that doesn't mean that what you say to me will get back to him, or to Blackie. You ought to know me better than that."

Sheila let out her breath as if she'd been holding it for about three months. "You've heard, then."

"I heard. I'm sorry." I sighed, too. "I'm really sorry, Sheila."

"So am I." She picked up a pen and fiddled with it. "I'd rather not go into the details just now, if you don't mind." Her voice was tight. "Maybe later, when I'm not feeling so much like a female black widow spider. He must absolutely hate me." She looked at the pot of chrysanthemums. "Those are pretty. Thank you."

"You're welcome," I said. "And you don't have to go into the details at all, ever, if you don't want to." I reached into the back pocket of my jeans. "I've brought you something else." I put it on the desk in front of her.

She picked it up. "A ticket?"

"To tomorrow night's opening of *A Man for All Reasons*. I want you to dress up in your finest denims and diamonds and help me cheer for Ruby. It's her big night, you know, and she's planning something special—what, I don't know. She's being very mysterious about it. Also," I added, "you're invited to the cast party afterward."

I didn't want to say so, but I knew it would be a safe evening for Sheila. If there was one thing I could count on, it was that Sheriff Blackwell would not be at the performance. He isn't keen on the arts, although Sheila is, and he would much rather be fishing on Canyon Lake than going to the theater or the Austin symphony or the ballet in San Antonio. This attitude was probably one of the hidden reefs their relationship had foundered on. The two of them may have a common interest in law enforcement, but otherwise, they couldn't be more different. Now that I'd had time to think about it, I was surprised that they'd lasted as long as they had.

Sheila looked at the ticket and her face lit up. "Oh, China, I'd love to," she exclaimed. "Thanks for thinking of me."

"There's just one catch," I said. "Party Thyme is catering the party. Ruby will be celebrating, so I'll have my hands full. But that needn't stop you from enjoying yourself."

Sheila was smiling. "I'll be glad to help." She pushed her chair back and stood.

"You don't have to do that," I said. "You can just hang around and look decorative. I only wanted you to know so you wouldn't expect me to—"

"But I want to help," she insisted. She came around the desk and hugged me. "Evenings are sort of miserable just now. I sit around hating myself for causing Blackie so much pain—or I waste time fantasizing about the best way to clean Ben Grave's clock. The play and the party will give me something productive to do."

I certainly wasn't going to argue with somebody who was volunteering a pair of willing hands, even if those hands were so pretty and well-manicured that they made me jealous. I hugged her back.

"White Linen," I said, sniffing appreciatively. "A great alternative to guano. And to Sordid Secrets." I held up my wrist and looked at my watch. "Two minutes and thirty seconds, Chief. I'm outta here."

To mend fences, the telephone just doesn't work. You have to *go* there. Flowers and a ticket to a play don't hurt, either.

SOME years back, when the community theater group was just getting started, it wasn't easy to get people to come out to see a play. It wasn't that Pecan Springs lacked culture; after all, CTSU always scheduled a full calendar of cultural events on campus every year, and lots of people from the community made it a point to attend. Maybe it was the idea that community theater is amateur drama, and people didn't want to pay to see their neighbors making fools of themselves onstage. Or maybe Pecan Springers, at heart, were like Blackie: they'd rather go fishing or hunting, or drive to San Marcos and listen to country music at the Cheatham Street Warehouse.

But things changed when the Community Theater Association announced its first Denim and Diamonds Opening Night, and a Pecan Springs tradition—now a decade old—was born. The tickets are priced as if this were Broadway, the Theater Auxiliary ladies serve champagne punch and chocolates before curtain and at intermission, and the patrons gussie themselves up in their most dazzling (and mostly fake) jewelry, their fanciest cowboy boots, and their dressiest denims. There's even an armed security guard, usually an off-duty cop, who makes a big show out of protecting the showgoers from thieves out to steal their jewelry; one year, they even staged a fake robbery. It's all very over-the-top, but it works. Most people come to strut their stuff and show off their rhinestone-cowboy outfits, rather than out of a love for the theatrical arts. But who cares, as long as they pay the tariff and act like they're enjoying the performance?

Since this was the first time a play had been staged in the new Merrill G. Obermann Theater, tonight's gala was even more of an event than usual. All the Pecan Springs bigwigs were there, togged out in their best denim bibs and diamond tuckers. The mayor, the entire city council, the Chamber of Commerce, and all their spouses. Brian Ducote, our state representative, and his toothy wife Beulah. The Hill Country Ladies Club and their husbands, and the Myra Merryweather Herb Guild, *en masse*. The architect who had designed the building, and the contractor, and Colin Fowler, who was standing off to one side, watching with a bemused look.

The event was being documented by a photographer from the the *Enterprise*, who crept in close to chatting patrons, snapping candid photos. He took several of Sheila, and no wonder. Smart Cookie looked like an ice cream sundae in white jeans, a fringed silk shirt, rhinestone-trimmed white boots, and outrageous faux pearls the size of marbles—hardly the sort of look you expect from your local chief of police. I was wearing a red shirt, jeans, an embroidered denim vest, and my favorite red cowboy boots. I had on makeup, too, and—between finishing the sandwiches and starting on the appetizers, I'd sneaked off to Bobby Rae's House of Beauty for a shampoo, cut, and blow-dry. It was too bad McQuaid wasn't there to see it. It was the most dolled up I'd been since the two of us got married.

Jane and Florence Obermann were there, too, of course, and although they weren't wearing denim, they had taken the Obermann family jewels out of the bank vault for the occasion. Jane was wearing a regal blue silk dress with a diamond-and-sapphire choker and matching earrings and bracelet. Florence, in pearls, wore a flowing gray dress and kept to her sister's shadow. Both seemed pleased with the way the playhouse looked—and it did look splendid. Just goes to show what money can do, if it's put in the right places. You never would have guessed that we were gathered in a stable, which was gussied up just like the rest of us.

Before the curtain went up for the first act, Marian Atkins gave a speech on behalf of the theater association, praising the Obermann sisters for carrying on their father's legacy of community philanthropy and thanking Jane for the playscript—"a masterpiece of dramatic creativity," she said. Marian laid it on a little too thick for my taste and didn't say a word about the grief the old lady had caused. But of course, the truth would have spoiled the illusion that the occasion was designed to produce: that Pecan Springs is devoted to the arts (which isn't true, unless you number country-dancing and barbecuing among the arts) and that the Obermann sisters are selfless, tireless supporters of the theater (in your dreams).

Jane rose to the occasion with a few gracious remarks about how much Dr. Obermann would have enjoyed this night, and how delighted she and Florence were with the renovations and with the play itself.

Applause. House lights down, curtain up. Act One. I could finally sit back and take a breath.

As things had turned out, I was very glad for Sheila's offer to help with the cast party. That afternoon, back at the tearoom, Janet and Ruby and I had assembled the food—appetizers, sandwiches, dips, crackers, raw veggies, cookies, cakes, and desserts. The centerpiece was a hollowed-out pumpkin filled with chive dip, an idea that we borrowed from Theresa Loe's Herbal Calendar. And then Ruby went off to get ready for the play and Janet . . . well, Janet announced that her knees were acting up, and she was going home.

Sheila, bless her, came through. After the shops had closed, she helped me load all the food into Big Red Mama and get it to the theater. Everything was backstage, now, and ready for the party. And I was ready to relax in my seat and applaud for Ruby—for the other players, too, of course, but mostly for Ruby.

And she didn't disappoint us. Chris had worked a makeup miracle, and if you didn't know that Ruby was still sporting a shiner, you wouldn't have noticed it. The three-act play followed the fortunes of the Obermann family from 1918 to 1948, and the characters—the Obermann parents and children, several servants, and a few others—aged accordingly, their changing costumes reflecting the changing eras.

But throughout, the spotlight was on Dr. Obermann and his wife Cynthia. And as Ruby and Jean had reshaped the drama, Cynthia had become the most important character. Ruby was simply terrific in that role, her spontaneity and slightly flighty, discombobulated charm a marvelous comic foil for her cautious, stiffly dignified husband.

And Max? Well, yes, he was predictably stilted, stodgy,

and wooden. But something interesting happened on stage, for these attributes seemed somehow natural to the character he was playing, rather than to any deficiencies of the actor. As Max played him, Herr Doctor Obermann might be a dedicated physician, a devoted father, and a generous philanthropist, but he was first and foremost a genuine Germanic stuffed shirt. Quite unconsciously, Jane had cast the perfect man for the role of her father.

And while Max pontificated, Ruby danced, flinging herself into her role with a sparkling and inventive energy, an almost manic abandon. Oh, yes, she delivered the lines Jane had written, or very nearly, but she delivered them with a life that Jane had never intended or even imagined. She was sweet, gay, wacky, wild, and poignantly human, and by the end of the third act, she had stolen the show right out from under the nose of the man who was meant to be the star. Flushed and happy, eyes sparkling, Ruby was summoned back for applause several times, the last time, with a standing ovation. Everyone loved her.

Everyone, that is, but Jane Obermann. It was clear that the playwright had not meant her play to have this effect, and that this unexpected outcome—this upstaging of her idolized father by her frivolous and upstart mother—was an unpleasant surprise. I'm no expert on drama, and I don't know how often the playwright's intention is altered by the way an actor creatively interprets a role. But I could see that Jane, who must not have witnessed a full rehearsal of the play in its present form, was both surprised and angered. Her face wore a thunderous scowl, and she kept to her seat while everyone else was standing, cheering. She swept out of the theater even before the curtain calls began, a study in sheer rage, with Florence like a frightened puppy at her heels.

I smiled as I saw that. The director and most of the cast (I doubted that Max was aware of what was happening) had obviously taken revenge on the old lady for imposing her script, her conditions, and her casting on them. Marian and Jean were going to hear about this—but, of course, it was too late. Jane Obermann was stuck with her bargain. Anyway, she was the one who had insisted on casting Max in the role of her father. Poetic justice, it seemed to me.

But there wasn't time to think about that now. While the audience was leaving the theater, Sheila and I were already on the stage, behind the curtain, setting up the tables for the buffet supper. As Party Thyme's catered events go, this wasn't a major production—especially since somebody else had volunteered to handle the drinks and another person had brought a CD player and a stack of CDs. It didn't take long to unload our boxes and trays and put out the food, and by the time the actors were out of costume and the curtain was raised on an empty house, we were ready to party. People began to migrate to the drinks table, then filled their plates, all the while talking about the play.

"—muffed his lines, but she came right on back. What a trooper, that Ruby!"

"—so then he picked up the wrong prop and put it down in the wrong place, halfway across the stage from where I was standing, and I had to—"

"We'd better get the electrician to look at that second light bar. Couldn't bring it up, no matter what I—"

"Gotta hand it to Jean. She took a bad play and made it pretty damn good."

"—the look on old lady Oberwhozit's face? Worth a mint, just to see that scowl."

"—magnificent, Ruby, absolutely, utterly—"

"Duane? Dunno, didn't see him. Was he here?"

I stepped forward, took a cigarette lighter out of my pocket, and relit the Sterno under the dish of meatballs. The success of a cast party always depends on the success of the play, and tonight's party was obviously already a smashing success.

Even Max was having a good time. Face flushed, eyes twinkling behind his gold glasses, he came up to me. "Well, Ms. Bayles?" he asked. "How did you like it?" He was formally polite, as always—a formality that strikes me as odd, when you consider that this man, before he retired from his dental career, had had both hands in my mouth.

"I thought it was great," I enthused. "Your performance was perfect, Max. Couldn't have been better." I spoke truthfully, albeit with an ironic twist.

Max looked pleased. "I thought I captured old Merrill G. quite well," he said, in his gruff voice. "I didn't know him personally, you understand. He died while I was away at college, before I came back to Pecan Springs to start my practice. But my father was acquainted with both him and his wife, and I know his daughters, in a professional way, of course. I'm glad to have had this opportunity to—"

"I'm terribly sorry," I said, "but I'm afraid I have to see Ruby about something."

Impolite or not, I made my escape. Once Max gets started, he's a little difficult to stop.

Cassandra caught me as I went around the table. "My compliments to the caterers," she said, her round face crinkling into a wide smile. Cass has a strong sense of style, and she doesn't believe in trying to camouflage her size, which I like. "Got it, flaunt it," I've heard her say. Tonight, she was flaunting it, in a red-and-purple draped dress that flowed with her movements. She's heavy and rounded, but she carries herself with a grace that seems to be an expression of spirit, as much as a mannered way of moving. "You've done a terrific job on this party," she added, tilting her head. Her eyes sparkled. "Any chance a girl could get a job with you?"

"Are you serious?" I asked, startled.

"Oh, heck, yes," she replied, without hesitation. "I'm tired of pushing paper and dealing with the food service bureaucracy. I want to cook again. Would you like me to bring my résumé by the shop?"

"As a matter of fact," I said, thinking of Janet's arthritis, "I would. Of course, I have to talk to Ruby, but—"

"I already did," Cassandra put in. "She said she had to

talk to you." She hesitated, her face becoming sober. "But to tell the truth, I'm looking for more than just a job. I have a proposal I want to make to you. I've been thinking of opening my own business as a personal chef and—" She raised her hand to wave at Marian, who was giving her a high sign. "But let's talk about this later, when we have more time. How about Monday afternoon? I can be at the shop by four-thirty."

"That'll work," I agreed, wondering what "more than just a job" might mean.

Ruby was standing with Colin, and Marian had just joined them when I came up. "You were terrific, Ruby," Marian said excitedly. "Great, incredible—"

"Let's not overdo it," Colin said, straight-faced. "She's already about nine feet off the ground. Another compliment or two, and she'll be in the stratosphere."

Ruby gave him a playful push, then turned to survey the table. "Gosh, China, you and Sheila did a great job with the food. Thanks for taking over tonight." She turned to me. "How'd my eye look?" she whispered. "Could you see it from where you were sitting?"

"It wasn't noticeable at all," I said truthfully. "Anyway, you were larger and brighter than life. Nobody could possibly spot a little shiner."

Colin laughed and put his arm around her shoulders. "She was wonderful, wasn't she?" he said, and looked down at her fondly. "She was the star, no doubt about it."

"Oh, please," Ruby said. She lowered her voice under the party chatter. "Max will hear you, Colin. I don't want to hurt his feelings."

"Hurt his feelings?" Colin asked, opening his dark eyes wide. "Why? Max was super. It's no fun to play a little tin god, especially when your leading lady has all the great lines."

I raised my eyebrows at Ruby. She gave me back a smirky little smile, and I knew that Colin was playing straight man. "Hey," I said, sotto voce, "Cassandra wants to talk to us. About some sort of proposal she has in mind. Monday at four-thirty. Okay?"

"Fantastic," Ruby said. "I'm hoping that—" Whatever she was about to say was drowned out by a burst of raucous laughter from the group behind us.

Sheila came up to us. "Where's Duane Redmond?" she asked over the hubbub. "Didn't he come tonight?" She paused. "Or maybe he didn't want to watch Max trying to fill his shoes."

"So you know about that?" I asked.

"You're surprised?" Sheila countered. "The chief of police is supposed to know what's going on in her own town, isn't she? Sure, I heard that Miss Obermann fired him."

"Chief of police?" Colin asked. He had turned to her when she came up. Was I mistaken to think that he was taken aback by the sight of her? Now, I noticed, he was eyeing her, quite appreciatively, I thought.

Ruby grinned. "Chief Sheila Dawson, meet Colin Fowler, owner of Good Earth Goods, on the square."

"You're kidding," Colin said with an almost exaggerated disbelief. Deliberately, he dropped his glance to Sheila's silk shirt and faux pearls, then back up to her eyes. "You're a cop? Pardon me all to hell, ma'am, but that's kinda hard to believe."

Ruby, busy with a cracker on her plate, had missed the glance. "Don't you read the newspapers?" she asked Colin. "Sheila makes the headlines at least twice a month." She put down her plate, held up an invisible newspaper, and pretended to read. " 'Courageous Chief Collars Parking Meter Thief.' 'Awesome Dawson Does it Again.' "

"Ruby, you're a scream." There was a perceptible tension in Sheila's voice, and her eyes were on Colin. This time, it was her glance that I intercepted. It held surprised recognition and something like a covert signal, not quite a head shake, but clearly a warning. There was something taut and still about both of them, and just for an instant, all the sound and motion in the room seemed to stop, as if somebody had hit a freeze-action switch, to allow the two of them to exchange silent, secret messages that the rest of us couldn't hear.

But then it started up again, both motion and sound. Glasses clinked. Somebody laughed. Colin bent to whisper in Ruby's ear, then took her glass and his own and went in the direction of the bar, stopping to exchange a complimentary word with Max Baumeister.

As Colin moved away through the crowd, my eyes went back to Sheila. I was suddenly, apprehensively, convinced that she and Colin knew one another. And that neither one of them was anxious to let Ruby in on the secret.

But I knew it. Where did that leave me? And eventually, Ruby would have to know it, too. Where would that leave her?

Jean and Cassandra came up with plates of food. "I think Duane must be sitting this one out," Jean said to Marian, and I suddenly realized that I wasn't the only one who might have seen the exchange between Sheila and Colin. "Poor guy. I don't think he'd ever been fired before. It must really have hurt his feelings—otherwise he'd be here."

Cassandra turned to Ruby, her round face animated, her eyes sparkling. "Ruby, you were brilliant! You did it. You saved the play."

"It was all of us," Ruby said earnestly. "Not just me." She looked troubled. "Jane was not thrilled, though. I saw her marching out while we were still taking our bows."

"Miss Obermann must not have seen the whole production ahead of time," I remarked to Jean. "Otherwise, you'd never have gotten away with it."

"She saw it all," Jean said, chewing appreciatively on a meatball, "but not all at once, just in bits and pieces. And she said she didn't want to come to dress rehearsal, since it would mean being up late two nights in a row."

"Thank God for old ladies' bedtimes," Marian said in an aside, popping a stuffed mushroom into her mouth. "Hey, guys, this food is terrific. You can cater my parties any day."

"Thanks," I said, and grinned. "We'll phone you about a date. We're definitely looking for work." I couldn't help glancing at Sheila. Her head was half-tilted, and she was watching Colin, who was returning from the bar with a glass of wine in each hand. Fierce, undisguised feeling was written on her face. Whatever their relationship had been, it had obviously not been merely a flavor of the month. It had meant something to her.

Ruby had gone back to the subject. "And when Jane was here, we tried to distract her with trivial mechanical problems, so she'd concern herself more with the renovations to the theater and less with the play."

"And we kept asking her opinion about Max's scenes," Jean added, "to make sure that he was playing her father exactly the way she wanted him played. I even took notes about what she said, so we'd be sure to get it right."

"And to cover your asses," Colin suggested helpfully, handing Ruby her drink.

Jean's grin was mischievous. "I didn't want her to come back later and accuse us of making her father look like a dodo bird on its way to extinction."

"But that's exactly the quality that Jane caught—quite unconsciously—in her play," Marian said. "And the only way it could actually be staged, without the risk of boring the audience to death, was to remake the Cynthia character."

"Where Cynthia was concerned," Jean said, "we only had to tweak the actual script a little—it was mostly in the way Ruby played her. Of course it's hard to say for sure, but she was apparently quite eccentric. Manic-depressive, we'd probably say today. She killed herself, you know. Dove headfirst off the roof of her house. Broke her neck."

"Her husband probably drove her to it," Colin said. Sheila carefully did not look at him. "Or maybe her daughters."

"It's not known for sure that she jumped," Jean objected. "She didn't leave a note. And the family insisted that she fell."

Ruby took the wineglass from Colin. "Oh, right," she said, heavily sarcastic. "Cynthia just happened to fall off the roof of her house at three-thirty in the morning. And how do we know she didn't leave a note? If she did, neither Jane nor her father would voluntarily hand it over to the police."

"Well, if you ask me," I said, "it's a very good thing that the Obermann sisters can't take back their theater. If they could—"

"What was that?" Sheila held up her hand.

"What was what?" Marian asked.

"It sounded like a shot," Colin said. His mouth had gone tight, his eyes alert, his muscles tensed. I remembered the look I had seen the other day, the look of a man watching his back.

"A car?" Jean hazarded. "A door slam?"

"Maybe. But—" Sheila shook her head. "Sorry. What were you saying, China?"

I was watching Colin. His head was turned, as if he were still listening. Listening and assessing his next move.

"Only that it's a good thing the Obermann sisters can't take back their play and their theater," I repeated. "If they could—"

There was a commotion in the theater lobby. "Chief!" The uniformed security guard—the one who had been hired to make sure that none of the faux gems were filched—came running down the central aisle. "Chief Dawson," he yelled. "You'd better get out here. There's been a shooting."

Conversations stopped. People turned and blinked and sucked in their breaths. Sheila put her plate on the table and turned, peering down the dark aisle. "Lonnie? Is that you? What's going on?"

Lonnie vaulted onto the stage. "I was in the parking lot, getting ready to leave." He was breathless. "I heard a gunshot, then another one, right close together. And then a woman screaming. It came from the Obermann mansion."

Marian pulled in her breath with an audible gasp. Jean let hers out with a dismayed puff. Marian put down her glass, her face suddenly white.

"Oh, my God," she breathed. "It's finally happened! Somebody has murdered that wicked old woman!"

My thought, exactly.

Chapter Ten

Oleander. This tree, being inwardly taken it is deadly and poinsonsome, not only to men, but also to most kinds of beasts.

John Gerard
***The Herbal, or General History of Plants,* 1633**

Sheila was suddenly all business. Taking charge, she ordered Lonnie to call for EMS and a squad car and to keep everybody in the theater. She told Ruby and Jean to make a list of the people who were at the party—as well as the people who should have been there and weren't. She picked up her bag, pulled out a small flashlight and her gun, and beckoned to me and Colin to follow her to the house.

Colin? If I needed a confirmation of their acquaintance —or whatever it was—that was it. What did this suggest about Colin's past? That he had done police work? And where did this leave Ruby? But I couldn't do anything with this stuff just now. I let it go and followed Sheila.

It had rained during the performance, and the air was chill and fresh. The fitful wind chased fallen leaves across the damp grass and tossed the thick oleander bushes that lined the flagstone path to the back of the house, where a single bulb, haloed by mist, shone languid yellow, like a blob of liquid amber.

The enormous house itself seemed to loom over us with an angry and poisonous presence, and I remembered McQuaid's remark about vampires. The place was mostly dark, except for a dim glow on the second floor and a spill of red-tinted light shining through the shrubbery. It looked as if it came from a pair of French doors standing open at the side of the house, near the front. The only sound was that of a woman's desperate, keening cry, not loud, but wordless and shrill, like a knife cutting wind. I shivered.

Sheila and I circled the house in the darkness, hunched over and moving fast, keeping to the shrubbery where we could, hugging the wall where we couldn't. Colin, without a word, had gone freelance around the house in the other direction, moving as if he knew exactly what he was doing. I certainly didn't. I kept close behind Sheila; not because I was afraid, exactly, but because she had the flashlight and the gun, and she was the boss. I was just there for . . .

My arms were breaking out in goose bumps and a distinct uneasiness had settled in my stomach. I had no idea why I was there, except that maybe Sheila wanted company, or she thought I knew the layout of the house and was acquainted with the Obermann sisters, neither of which was exactly true. And I didn't *like* being there, either, for that matter. Cops-and-creeps drama is okay in the movies, but I can think of any number of things I'm better and braver at than skulking through rainy darkness in the direction of gunshots and the eerie sound of a woman sobbing, in the menacing shadow of a haunted house.

So while Sheila was moving forward, intent on capturing whoever had fired those shots, I was nervously watching our flank and our rear, and listening with all my ears. But there wasn't much to hear, just wind, and faraway thunder, and the sound of our stealthy movements, and that awful, shuddery wailing. Anyway, the guy who had shot that gun was probably long gone, chased off by the sound of Lonnie's shouts, if not by the woman's dreadful crying.

I was wrong. The shooter was still there when Sheila and I finally pushed through the overgrown jungle around the house, reached the open French doors, and peered around them into the room lined with books and lit by a lamp with a red silk beaded shade.

And it wasn't Jane Obermann who had been shot. She was the one who had done the shooting, and somebody else was dead.

THE gun still in her hand, still wearing the blue silk dress she'd worn to the play, Jane Obermann was standing in the center of the room, her dark eyes glittering, her mouth set and hard.

Miss Florence, also still dressed, was half-sitting, half-lying against the wall beside the open door to the hallway. She was the one who was crying, the powder on her face streaked with tears.

The victim was sprawled faceup on the Oriental carpet, a battered straw hat on the floor beside him. Under his hand was a wicked-looking wooden-handled butcher knife with a five-inch blade.

"Hank," I breathed, and knelt beside him, feeling for a pulse. I didn't expect one; there were two bullet holes in his chest, a handsbreadth apart. His shirt was blood-soaked and blood had puddled on the red carpet under him.

Sheila had already identified herself to Jane Obermann and had taken the gun from her unresisting hand. Now she turned to me. "You know this guy?" she asked tautly.

"His name is Hank Dixon," I said, thinking of McQuaid and the sisters' plan to hire him to protect them against Hank. And thinking of what Hank had said to me a few days before, when I'd remarked that I was sorry about his father.

"No call for you to be sorry, Miz Bayles. Man's gotta die sometime. Woman, too, for that matter, I reckon. Ever'-body's gotta die."

I'd taken his words as a philosophical musing, a comment on the transient nature of life. Now, as I looked down at Hank's body on the floor, the remark seemed prescient, prophetic, heavy with another kind of meaning. Hank must have already known what he intended to do tonight.

"There's a story behind this, Smart Cookie," I said in a low voice, wishing that McQuaid were here, instead of in New Orleans. He might have prevented this from happening—although at the moment, I couldn't quite think how. "I'll fill you in later."

Colin stepped into the room through the open hallway door, taking in the scene with a glance. "Everything under control?" The tone of voice was casual, but the confident authority behind it was not. Colin had been here, done this before. At some point in his past, he had been a cop.

Jane Obermann had folded her arms across her chest and was eyeing Sheila with unmasked suspicion. "You hardly look like a policeman. Let alone a chief of police."

"I will be glad to show you my identification when I get my bag," Sheila said, putting the gun on the fireplace mantel, out of easy reach. "In the meantime—"

"If you intend to ask me whether I shot this man," Jane interrupted, with some asperity, "the answer is yes. He was breaking in. He had threatened us. My sister saw the whole thing. She'll tell you what happened."

Florence Obermann moaned weakly, and Colin bent over and put a hand on her shoulder. "Let me help you get to the sofa," he said, and began to lift her.

"Don't!" Florence gave a scream of pain. "My . . . my hip," she gasped. Her face was the color of paper. "I . . . I fell just as I came through the door. I think my hip is broken."

"I expect she's right," Jane said, in a tone of mixed pity and scorn. "She has brittle bones. She's always breaking something. Last time, it was her wrist and several ribs." She lowered her voice as if she didn't want Florence to hear. "She has a bad heart, too."

Colin took a pillow and a knitted afghan from the velvet settee. He placed the pillow under Florence's head and covered her. "We've called an ambulance," he said gently, smoothing her straggly white hair back from her forehead. "It'll be here in a few moments."

Sheila went over and knelt beside her. "I know you're in pain, Miss Obermann," she said, "and I'm sorry. But maybe you can tell me what happened here."

Florence lay back against the pillow. "She . . . my sister shot him," she managed. "He was . . . coming through the door. He had a . . ." She closed her eyes, and her voice began to fade.

"A knife," Jane Obermann said firmly. "Tell them, Florence, so there's no mistake."

"He . . . he had a big knife," Florence whispered. "In his . . . hand."

In the distance, I could hear the wail of sirens. Sheila stood up. "Thank you," she said. "You just rest now. Everything will be all right." She turned to Jane. "The gun you used, Miss Obermann. Where did you get it?"

Jane gestured to a glass curio cabinet, the one McQuaid had described to me. The door was ajar, and one of the glass shelves was empty. The other two shelves displayed guns.

"It was my father's gun," Jane said, raising her voice over the sirens that now sounded very close. "I'm so glad that the case wasn't locked. When I saw that wretched man coming through the French doors, I opened the cabinet, seized the gun, and shouted at him—to frighten him, of course." She shuddered. "I had no idea the gun was loaded."

Both sirens cut off abruptly, one right after the other, and her next words sounded too loud.

"I don't even remember pulling the trigger. I suppose I was under a great deal of stress."

Sheila glanced at Colin, who nodded shortly and left the room. "Very well, then," she said, turning back to Jane. "We'll be busy here for the next hour or two. The ambulance can take your sister to the hospital. You may go with her if you like. But of course, I must ask you not to leave Pecan Springs until our investigation is concluded."

Jane gave a small, hard laugh. "So I'm not under arrest?"

"No," Sheila said quietly. "You're not under arrest. I'd like to take your statement tomorrow morning at the station. I can send a car for you, if you prefer. And of course you're free to ask your attorney to join us, if that would make you more comfortable." She paused. "I'll also want to take a statement from your sister, when the doctor gives us permission."

Jane crossed the room and bent over Florence. "I'll go to the hospital with you, dear," she said in a solicitous tone. "I'll stay with you. You won't have to go through this alone."

As Florence opened her eyes, I caught her look. It reminded me of a frightened rabbit. "Oh, no," she managed, putting up a trembling hand. "It's so very late, and you must be under a terrible strain. Don't make it worse by coming out to the hospital, Jane. I'm . . . I'm sure they'll take good care of me."

"Such a dear," Jane said, and patted her shoulder. "Always thinking of me, before yourself. But I must go with you," she added briskly. "And, of course, we need to put the jewels away for safekeeping before we go. Here—let me unfasten yours." With a little effort, she unclasped the pearls around Florence's neck and took the bracelet from her wrist. "I'll take these upstairs to the safe," she said to Sheila, "and get my purse and a wrap."

I heard footsteps and voices, and Colin came into the room leading the EMS personnel. In a few more moments, Florence was on a gurney and loaded into the ambulance. Jane came back downstairs. There was a brief discussion at the back of the ambulance, and then Jane was allowed to climb in with her sister. I moved to an out-of-the-way corner and watched while Sheila's crime scene team—a photographer and a couple of investigating officers—arrived and conferred with their chief, then set about their work.

While her team settled down to the task, Sheila came over to me. "Okay, China. You said there's a story. What is it?"

I told her what McQuaid had told me: that the sisters intended to hire him to deal with somebody who was threatening them, that they hadn't gotten to the point of naming the man, but that I had recognized him from McQuaid's description as Hank Dixon, the son of their long-time family servant, Gabriel Dixon.

"I was aware that Hank was angry about the way the women treated his father," I said. "He even made a remark that, looking back on it, seems like a threat." I repeated what Hank had said. "At the time, I thought he was just . . . well, speaking philosophically. After McQuaid and I talked, I thought he might have blackmail in mind—but nothing involving bloodshed." I glanced regretfully at the body.

Sheila frowned. "Blackmail?"

I considered. "Maybe leverage is a better word. Hank said something to the effect that the Obermann sisters wouldn't be where they were today if it hadn't been for his father. He said he aimed to see that they took care of that."

"Took care of it how?"

"Money, I guess." I shrugged. "That was my impression when McQuaid and I discussed it."

"What was McQuaid planning to do?"

"Talk to Hank, after he'd been formally retained." I pushed away the thought that McQuaid had just lost a client—with Hank dead, Jane Obermann would hardly need a private investigator. Somehow, it didn't seem a worthy thought, now that a man had lost his life.

Sheila bent over, raised the body slightly, and worked Hank's wallet out of his back pocket. "Do you know Dixon's family?"

"I don't think he has one. A young man named Juan lives with him—a former student of McQuaid's, actually.

Hank and Juan just finished replacing the deck outside the tearoom. I talked to both of them day before yesterday."

Sheila flipped the wallet open and took out Hank's driver's license. "Looks like he lives on East Brazos. Can you go over there with me? Now?"

I sighed. This wasn't the way I'd planned to end the evening, but Juan would probably rather hear the bad news from me than from a police officer. And he might know something about Hank's motive for coming, armed, to the Obermann mansion tonight.

"Yeah, sure," I said. "But I have to let Ruby know what's happening, and make sure that she has help with the party cleanup." I looked around for Colin, but he was gone—back to the party, I guessed.

"You do that," Sheila said, "and come back here. We'll take one of the squad cars." She looked down at her faux pearls and grimaced, then pulled them off. I hid a smile. Even without the pearls, she didn't look much like a cop. "And I'll change," she added. "I keep a uniform in my car."

Fifteen minutes later, I was riding shotgun in the squad car, as Sheila, now properly uniformed, drove through the silent streets. It was nearing midnight, which is the witching hour for most of Pecan Springs. But the east side of town has more than its share of neon-lit bars and late-night cafés and pool parlors, featuring the occasional small-time prostitute and the big-time drug deal—the sort of dirty work that goes on after sundown in every town, no matter how squeaky clean and cozy it looks in the daytime. The rain had moved on, and we could see people hanging out under the streetlights and cars cruising slowly down the dark streets.

Sheila, I noticed, was keeping a wary eye out, assessing every car, every pedestrian, as a possible problem. The cop curse, I've come to call this tendency to generic mistrust and suspicion. McQuaid has been out of law enforcement for quite a few years, but he still watches the world out of the corner of his eye, as if he's waiting for somebody to pounce. Colin had done it, too.

We stopped for a red light at Fifth and Brazos, and I broke the silence with a question, abrupt and unplanned, and right off the top of my mind, where it had been buzzing like an angry fly for the past several minutes. "How'd you happen to know Colin Fowler?"

"Who?" Sheila swiveled to face me, her face half-shadowed, half-lit by the glow of the dash. "Oh, Fowler."

"Right. Ruby's new boyfriend." When she didn't speak, I prompted her. "Where'd you meet him?"

She was looking straight ahead, both hands on the wheel. "I don't know where you got the idea that we know one another," she said, with an attempt at casualness. "Tonight was the first time we've met."

I didn't believe her. But there wasn't any point in my saying so, or in attempting to persuade her to reveal whatever she was concealing. Some truths, I have learned from bitter personal experience, are better left uncovered, when the knowledge can only lead to pain and distress. But it certainly didn't make me happy to think that Sheila's past connection with Colin, whatever it was, might get in the way of Ruby's current relationship with him.

A couple of minutes later, we were pulling up in front of Hank's place, a two-story duplex with a small, scrappy piece of grass in the front. It was Hank's, all right. A sign in the yard said HANK THE HANDYMAN, CHEAP, QUICK, GOOD, and the motorcycle parked in the driveway had "Juan" painted on it in flaming red letters. And if I needed further confirmation, there were several ladders leaning against the garage and a couple of five-gallon paint cans on the small front porch.

When we parked the squad car and went up the shrub-screened walk, I saw a dim light glowing in the front window upstairs, as if it came from a room farther back. With the light on and his motorcycle in the drive, I expected Juan to appear. But after several moments of knocking, it was obvious that nobody was going to open the door.

"Must be out for the evening," Sheila said. She took a departmental notepad out of her pocket, scrawled a brief message on it asking Juan to call the police station, and signed her name.

"If we don't hear from him by morning," she said, as she tucked the note under the door knocker, "I'll send somebody out to find him. I'm hoping he can shed some light on this situation."

To tell the truth, I was relieved. Juan had been one of McQuaid's favorite students, and I had liked the boy, who struck me as honest and hardworking. I suspected that he was sending most of his money back to his mother and sisters, who still lived in Mexico. I hated to be the one to tell him that Hank had been shot to death while trying to break into the Obermann mansion.

But as I got into the squad car, I happened to look back up at that window. The light I had seen was gone, and the window was completely dark.

Somebody—Juan?—was in that house.

Chapter Eleven

Some herbs contain chemical compounds that act like estrogens. These phytoestrogens can help to minimize the effects of estrogen loss after menopause, which results in lower bone density and the condition known as "brittle bones." They include dong quai, blue cohosh, black cohosh, burdock root, sage, alfalfa, and motherwort. Of these, the native American herb black cohosh (known as both *Actaea racemosa* and *Cimicifuga racemosa*) has received the most scientific attention.

Both Ruby and I were a little bleary-eyed when we opened up the next morning. It was Saturday, which is usually our busiest day of the week—especially this Saturday, with people dropping in or phoning to let Ruby know how much they'd enjoyed her performance.

I had gotten home very late the night before, to an empty house. McQuaid wouldn't be back from New Orleans until Saturday afternoon, and Brian was away for the weekend on a Boy Scout camping trip near Utopia, in the western part of the Hill Country. Howard Cosell and I were batching it, and in honor of the occasion, Howard had decided it was his prerogative to take over McQuaid's side of the bed. He was already there, lying on his back with all four paws in the air, snoring sonorously—something of a surprise, since I had expected the bed to be empty.

But that wasn't the only surprise. When I went to the

basin to brush my teeth, I discovered one of Brian's chameleons, sitting on a green cake of soap, staring gloomily at me.

"Drat," I muttered. I don't know how many times I've told Brian to keep his creatures penned up properly, instead of letting them wander around the house, where they have a way of attempting to drown themselves in the washing machine, dropping unexpectedly from the top of a door, or lurking in various odd corners. But when I picked the lizard up to take it back to Brian's room, I saw that it had taken its last safari. It was stiff and cold, and dead as a doornail. At least it had died in its green phase, rather than its usual muddy brown color. For a dead lizard, it was rather pretty.

I took the deceased downstairs and stuck it in the refrigerator freezer, thinking that Brian would want to give it a proper interment when he got back from his camping trip. Back upstairs, I climbed into bed next to Howard Cosell, and rolled him over on his side in an effort to stop his snoring.

It didn't work. He twitched, grunted, snorted, and the snores began again. Howard the Loud. Tonight, though, I'd probably sleep through it. The evening had been long and full of disquieting events. I was exhausted.

Ruby had already heard the story of Hank's shooting from Colin, so I didn't have to go into the details when we talked the next morning. She kept shaking her head in puzzlement, though, as she unlocked her front door and set up her cash register for its first sale.

"What in the world could Hank have been after?" she asked. "The Obermann jewels?"

"I don't think it's as simple as that," I said. I sketched out what Hank had told me—that he was angry over the way his father had been treated—but I omitted McQuaid's involvement in the matter. Ruby wants to be Nancy Drew when she grows up, and since McQuaid has hung out his shingle as a private investigator, she's volunteered several times to work for him as a "freelance operative," as she puts it. Talking about his conversation with the Obermann sisters would only heap fuel on her fire, so I kept my mouth shut.

"Well," she said in a practical tone, "it sounds like Jane did what she had to do. She must have been terrified, seeing Hank burst through those French doors with a knife in his hand. I can't say that I blame her for shooting him—although I keep thinking that there has to be more to it than a simple break-in."

Nobody else would blame Jane, either. Texas is one of the few states where you can shoot someone to keep him from committing arson, burglary, robbery, aggravated robbery, theft, or criminal mischief. And according to Chapter 9, Section 42, of the Texas Penal Code, you can shoot the thief when he has broken into your house in the dead of night, taken your stuff, and is climbing over the back fence—as long as you "reasonably believe" that's the only way you're going to get it back. This case wouldn't even get to the grand jury. Jane Obermann had killed a man, but it was justifiable homicide.

"Terrified?" I asked, picking up on Ruby's comment. "Not when I saw her. Jane Obermann is one cool character." I paused. "Florence is another matter, of course. She was terrified. She could hardly describe what happened."

Ruby made a little face. "Well, the whole thing is a tragedy, that's all. A tragedy. Hank was crusty, but he was a good worker. I can't believe he meant any harm." She paused thoughtfully. "Maybe I should call the hospital and ask how Florence is doing this morning."

"One of us could run over there with some flowers from the garden," I said. "If she's broken her hip, it might be a long time before she's back home. According to Jane, there have been other fractures."

"Osteoporosis," Ruby said with a troubled look. "It's such a scary disease. I just found out last week that my mother has it. She's allergic to dairy products, and her low calcium intake is catching up with her. I've been meaning to ask you about herbs that might help."

"That's a tough one," I said. "It depends on how much bone she's already lost—and only a bone scan is going to tell her that. To prevent any more bone loss, she might try horsetail and alfalfa. Licorice and mallow have also been used. Some people suggest a salve made from wild yam, which is supposed to contain a chemical that has progesterone-like properties. The Chinese recommend dong quai and ginseng. I can give your mother the names of a couple of experienced herbalists who could take a look at her situation and make some detailed recommendations."

"I'll tell her," she said. "And I'll go pick some flowers to take to Florence, poor thing."

Ruby brought in the flowers—some Michaelmas daisies, chrysanthemums, calendula, and some rosemary, tansy, and fern for greenery—and I was arranging them when Sheila came into the shop. She was uniformed, with a gun on her hip and a business-like look on her face. Her don't-mess-with-me look.

"Juan hasn't shown up at the house," she said without preamble. "Any idea what his last name is, and where he might be?"

"His last name is Gomez," I said, "but I have no idea how to locate him. Have you asked the neighbors?"

"Yes, but no luck there. Everybody knows Hank, but Juan must have kept pretty much to himself, because nobody knows him."

"You took Jane Obermann's statement?"

She nodded. "This morning, first thing. She and Florence were in the library, about to go to bed. The door was unlocked. Hank shoved it open and stumbled in, brandishing the knife and muttering something incoherent. Florence tried to run and fell. Jane grabbed the gun out of the cabinet and shot him. I don't think Howie wants to touch this one." She looked at the flowers I was arranging. "That's pretty."

Howie Masterson is the recently elected Adams County

D.A. He is further to the right than Archie Bunker, and not nearly so harmlessly amusing. He campaigned on an anti-crime agenda, but the kind of crime he had in mind involved drug deals, convenience store heists, and parking lot muggings by lowlife interlopers from the big city. Jane Obermann's shooting of Hank Dixon was exactly the kind of citizen's self-defense that would thrill him down to the pointed toes of his ostrich-skin cowboy boots.

"They're for Florence Obermann," I said, adding a sprig of rosemary. In flower arrangements, rosemary is better than fern, if you ask me. It's fragrant and it holds up much longer. "Have you been to the hospital this morning?"

"I haven't, but one of the officers tried to take her statement. She was barely coherent, and her sister insisted that he leave. I'll send him back later."

"Maybe she's sedated," I said, tucking a daisy into the arrangement.

"Maybe I should phone McQuaid," Sheila said restlessly. "Do you think he might know where we could locate Juan?"

"Won't do you any good," I said, as the door opened and three older women came in. Ah, customers. I raised my voice. "Good morning, ladies. Please take your time looking around. I'll be right here if you have any questions."

"What time will the tearoom be open?" one of the women asked.

"Eleven-thirty," I replied, and added, with a smile, "the menu's on the wall. Will you be joining us for lunch?"

Janet was in the kitchen making crepes, and one of the girls would be here in a few minutes to set things up and handle the service. Ruby and I take turns playing hostess at lunch, and it was Ruby's turn.

"Look, Jessica," one of the women said, "they're having chicken crepes. Oh, let's do stay. I had them last time I was here, and they're wonderful."

Sheila leaned forward. "What do you mean, it won't do me any good to call McQuaid?"

"Because he's out of town," I said. "Won't be back until this afternoon. You could try his cell phone, but he almost never leaves it on."

And then, just to make a liar out of me, the door opened and McQuaid came in, followed by another little gaggle of customers. Several of them had potted plants in their hands from the rack outside the door.

I was busy for the next few minutes, answering questions, making suggestions, pointing out plants, and ringing the cash register, which is something I always like to do. Several other people came in, and when I finally got time to take a breath, Sheila had left and McQuaid had disappeared. I found him on the patio with a glass of herbal iced tea and a magazine.

He looked up at me with a smile that said he was glad to see me. "How about some lunch?"

"I'm glad you're back," I said. "I'd rather have you in my bed than Howard Cosell. He snores." I brushed the dark hair out of his eyes and bent to kiss the tip of his ear. "If you don't mind waiting a few minutes, we can eat here. We're having chicken crepes today."

His smile became less enthusiastic. "I skipped breakfast so I could get an early plane. I was thinking of something more substantial. Sauerbraten, maybe. How does Krautzenheimer's sound?"

"Sounds fine. I need to check the kitchen and let Ruby know when I'll be back." I paused. "Did Sheila tell you?"

"About Hank?" His blue eyes were serious, and I saw pain there. "Yes. Not good. I wouldn't have thought he'd try a damn-fool stunt like that. What the hell was he thinking?" He put his hand on my arm. "You okay? Sheila said you were with her when she went to investigate."

I nodded. "Since we're going out for lunch, I'd like to drive over to the hospital and leave some flowers for Florence. Maybe I'll even get to see her for a minute or two—if you don't mind, that is."

He swigged the last of his tea. "The truck is out front.

You can tell me about the shooting as we drive."

There wasn't much to tell, actually, since Sheila had given him the official story. I added the bit about Colin, since I doubted if Sheila had mentioned it, but since McQuaid hadn't met him, it didn't mean much to him. The name didn't ring a bell, either.

At the Adams County Hospital, the charge nurse—Helen Berger, a friend and fellow member of the Myra Merryweather Herb Guild—took the flowers and the card Ruby and I had signed, but told me that Miss Obermann wasn't permitted to have visitors until the next day. So McQuaid and I drove back into town and parked in front of Krautzenheimer's Restaurant, which is located on the square between the Sophie Briggs Historical Museum and the Ben Franklin Store. It's a favorite lunchtime hangout for people who work nearby.

"Ah," McQuaid said with a gusty sigh, as we sat down in a high-backed wooden booth and opened our menus. "Real food for real men."

I pointed out that chicken crepes qualified as real food, but he said he didn't think so. One of the Krautzenheimer granddaughters, costumed in a perky red skirt, suspenders, and embroidered Bavarian apron, danced over and took our orders: sauerbraten for McQuaid and a bowl of goulash for me, with spaetzle, tiny German dumplings that are put through a sieve into a pot of simmering stock. If you haven't had Mrs. K's spaetzle yet, you have to try it the next time you're in Pecan Springs. You'll also get a tasty earful of German polka music with your meal. While we were waiting for our food, the music system cleared its throat and Oma and the Oompahs began to play a bubbly rendition of the "Beer Barrel Polka."

The Oompahs are a popular polka band from New Braunfels, where they always entertain at Polka Fest. Their framed photos decorate the Krautzenheimer walls, along with dozens of photos of other local bands wearing German vests and walking shorts and red kneesocks and jaunty green felt hats, brandishing their accordions and clarinets and saxophones and big brass tubas. The Bohemian Dutchmen, the Jubilee Polka Band, the Happy Travelers, the Cloverleaf Orchestra. Eat your heart out, Lawrence Welk.

McQuaid stirred his tea. "Sheila said they haven't been able to locate Juan Gomez."

I thought of the window that had gone dark. "Maybe he's away for the weekend. Or maybe he's got a girlfriend, and he's staying with her."

"Maybe," McQuaid said. "He's a good kid, with a lot of promise. I was sorry when he dropped out of school. Now that Hank's out of the picture, maybe I can talk him into coming back." He picked up his glass and looked at me over the rim. "Sheila said that the old lady used one of her father's guns."

I nodded. "It's too bad the cabinet wasn't locked. It might have slowed her down, given her a minute to think about what she was doing. She knows Hank. She should have realized that he wasn't a serious threat." The minute I said that, though, I realized how silly it was. When a man armed with a butcher knife breaks into your house at eleven o'clock at night, you're probably glad to have a gun handy.

McQuaid was looking at me strangely. "But the cabinet was locked when I was there. I know, because I tried the door. I wanted to have a closer look at that Luger."

I didn't have time to respond. A uniformed figure stopped beside our booth, and I looked up.

"Hey, you guys," Blackie said, and clapped a hand on McQuaid's shoulder. "Is this a private conversation, or may I join you?"

"We're just talking about last night's shooting," McQuaid said. He got up and moved over to my side of the booth, giving Blackie a seat by himself. "Nothing private."

"I heard about that," Blackie said, hanging his white Stetson on the hat rack at the outside corner of the booth. He sat down, his square bulk filling the space. "Bad news. I knew Hank Dixon—he did some work for the sheriff's office when we were still at the old location." The Adams County sheriff's office has recently moved to a spiffy new building just outside of town. "Would've thought he was smarter than that."

"Folks do stupid things," McQuaid said. "Maybe he was on drugs." He gestured to the other Krautzenheimer granddaughter. The conversation stopped while Blackie, without bothering with the menu, ordered a plate of bratwurst with red cabbage and home fries. The "Beer Barrel Polka" ran out of oomph and a cheerful accordion took up "The Happy Wanderer."

"I just got Alana Montoya's preliminary report," he said, propping his elbows on the table. "On the bones in the cave," he added, catching McQuaid's querying look. "Looks like we've got a male, about six foot three or four inches tall, age around thirty, with one gold tooth, right front upper."

"Anything show up yet through missing persons?" McQuaid asked.

"Nothing locally. Nothing statewide, either, at least nothing that matches the general time period, gender, size, et cetera. An Adams County girl disappeared in 1968, probably put flowers in her hair and headed for San Francisco. A Mexican national, a field worker, in 1971, five-foot-four. A couple of years later, another woman, in her sixties. None of these are possibles for our caveman."

"A transient," McQuaid said, as a Krautzenheimer grandson appeared with a tray full of dishes and began parceling out the food.

"Maybe. But somebody was hosting him, and that somebody had to have been a local." His host and murderer. "Have you talked to the dentists in town? If he was from around here, somebody ought to remember installing a gold tooth in a mouth that belonged to a six-foot-four-inch man."

"That looks like our best lead," Blackie agreed. "I was

pleased at Montoya's quick turnaround." He grinned. "She's a helluva lot easier to work with than either Bexar or Travis counties."

"Easier on the eyes, too," I said lightly. I was only joking, but Blackie blushed and ducked his head.

Uh-oh, I thought. I knew that look, and I knew Blackie, who may not say much but is transparent about certain things. The poor guy hadn't even completely untangled himself from his relationship with Sheila, and he was already on the verge of romantic involvement with another woman. And a woman with serious psychological problems of her own, if Alana's drinking was any indication. Blackie didn't need this.

McQuaid obviously agreed, because I could feel him stiffen. But guys rarely tell other guys that they should stay the hell away from a woman. He only said, "Montoya doesn't have much of a lab. Her program hasn't been funded yet."

"All the more reason to be pleased at the way she handled the analysis," Blackie said, and began paying attention to his bratwurst and cabbage. It was obvious that he didn't want to talk about it.

It was Saturday, and Krautzenheimer's attracts tourists who enjoy the German ambience of Pecan Springs, so the restaurant was busier than usual. We ate quickly, didn't talk much, and adjourned to the street, to the tune of the "Pennsylvania Polka." Blackie put on his Stetson, nodded courteously to me, and headed for the sheriff's car parked next to the courthouse.

"I hope he doesn't get involved with Alana Montoya just now," I said, watching him go.

"Not ever," McQuaid replied, with an odd emphasis. I turned, catching a hard look as it crossed his face.

"Why?" I asked.

McQuaid gave me his I-don't-want-to-talk-about-this shrug. "I'm going home. When is Brian getting back from his camping trip?"

"Not until Sunday night. I—"

"Hang on," McQuaid said, looking over my shoulder. "There's Sheila. It's probably not important, but I want to mention that business about the unlocked gun cabinet."

I turned. Sheila was disappearing through the door of Good Earth Goods, which was just down the street from the restaurant.

"I'll wait in the truck," I said. I didn't feel like confronting Sheila and Colin Fowler, after she had lied to me the night before. There was no doubt in my mind that she knew the man, and knew him with some intimacy.

McQuaid was out again in a couple of minutes. He was frowning.

"What's the matter?" I asked, as he yanked opened the door and climbed in, shutting it with a hard bang. McQuaid's blue truck is about twenty years old. The driver's side door doesn't always want to open, and when it's open it likes to stay that way. You have to use brute force.

"That guy in the shop," McQuaid said, putting the key into the ignition. "I know him."

I remembered my speculation that Colin was a cop. "Colin Fowler, you mean?"

"Yeah. That's the name Sheila gave when she introduced us, anyway." The engine turned over, then quit. McQuaid pumped the gas and tried again. This time it caught. "But it's not his real name."

I turned to face him. "It's not?" Somehow, I wasn't surprised.

"Nope. Trouble is, I can't remember it, or where I met him." He narrowed his eyes. "I'll think of it, though. He had something to do with a case I was on once. I just have to remember which one." He put the truck into reverse and backed out onto the street.

I settled back uneasily for the short drive to the shop. This definitely did not bode well for Ruby.

Chapter Twelve

Another herb that is often recommended for the prevention of osteoporosis is red clover (*Trifolium pratense*). In a recent study published in the journal *Menopause*, it was reported that isoflavone extracts of this phytoestrogenic herb significantly increased bone mineral density, as well as raising the HDL cholesterol level ("good" cholesterol).

Herbalgram
Number 56, Fall, 2002

In the north of England, leaves of red clover were also employed as a charm against witches and evil.

Geoffrey Grigson
The Englishman's Flora

Sunday morning dawned bright and shiny, the cedar elms glowing gold against a cornflower-blue sky, the clean, crisp scent of cedar in the air: the sort of day that is Texas at its best. McQuaid and I were lazy and slept late on Sunday morning, then had a leisurely breakfast of bacon, eggs, and pancakes, which I make with a tablespoon of chopped chives stirred into the batter. The meal was only slightly marred by McQuaid's discovery, when he opened the refrigerator freezer, of the frozen lizard corpse.

"What the devil—" he yelped, jumping back.

I grinned. "How cool is that?" I asked, borrowing one of Brian's phrases, and adding, guiltily, "Sorry. I should have warned you."

He picked up the frozen beast by the tail. "If I've said it once, I've said it a thousand times. Brian has to keep his animals in his room. How in hell did this lizard get into the freezer?"

"I put it there," I said, and related the story of finding the creature, dead on the bar of soap in the bathroom.

"Doesn't change anything," he muttered, putting the glaciated lizard back in the freezer and taking out the ice cube tray. "That boy's got to remember to keep track of his animals."

"Speaking of remembering," I said tactfully, "have you come up with any more thoughts about Colin Fowler—or whatever his real name is?"

"Nope." He dropped a couple of ice cubes into our orange juice glasses, shaking his head. "But I'm working on it. It'll come to me when I'm doing something else. Eating breakfast, yelling at Brian." He bent over and dropped a kiss on my head. "Making love to my wife." He put my glass in front of me and sat down. Howard Cosell licked his bare foot, and he reached down. "Petting my dog."

"Well, I hope it comes to you soon," I said. I told him that Ruby thought she was in love with Colin, and that I suspected that Sheila and Colin had shared some sort of personal history. I wasn't specific.

"Oh, yeah?" McQuaid asked, interested. "I guess I did have the feeling that I was walking in on something yesterday, when I went into that shop of his."

I looked up sharply. "They weren't—"

"No, they weren't, but it looked like they might have been." He shook his head, frowning. "I keep thinking he was involved with a case. Drugs, maybe. But damned if I can remember what it was. Trouble is, he's got such an ordinary face. You sort of remember it, but nothing stands out enough to give you a good fix."

I reached for the blueberry syrup. "I didn't ask how your New Orleans investigation turned out," I said, pouring it over my pancake. "Seems kind of strange that somebody would send you all the way there just to check up on a résumé."

McQuaid growled something I couldn't catch.

"I'm sorry," I said, looking up. "What was that?"

His eyes were chilly. "Don't ask," he said distinctly.

"Well, okay," I said, "if you feel that way about it. Have some more bacon."

After breakfast, McQuaid put on his cowboy hat and went out to drive the riding mower around the back lawn, work he seems to enjoy. I did some serious housecleaning: vacuuming and dusting and picking things up, while I kept a wary eye out for Brian's roving *reptilia*. I don't know why, but—now that I'm living in a place I like, with people I care about—chores don't feel like chores. I'm not wild about housework, but it doesn't bother me the way it used to. And I had plenty of stuff to process while I was working.

Hank and the Obermann sisters. What had he been after? What was he trying to prove? And why was Florence Obermann afraid of her sister? Of course, I could have been wrong, but that's how it had seemed to me when I saw that look on her face.

And there was Ruby and Colin to think about, and Sheila and Colin. Not a pretty triangle, or one that promised good things for the future.

And Alana Montoya, too, and Blackie. Was he seriously interested in her, or was it just a rebound relationship, the sort of thing you fall into when you're feeling vulnerable? And what did McQuaid have against her? An illogical dislike, it seemed to me. And her department—why were they so slow in getting her program set up? Was she running into some sort of ethnic discrimation?

No answers, of course, just questions, the kind of questions that loop endlessly through your mind as you push the vacuum cleaner around the house. I finished, put my cleaning equipment away, and was heading out to the garden when the phone rang. It was Blackie.

"Hi," I said. "If you're looking for McQuaid, you'll have to hang on while I fetch him. He's mowing the grass."

"Don't," Blackie said. "I need to talk to you, China."

The urgency in his voice stopped me, and I immediately thought of Brian, on his Scout camping trip. "Is everything okay?" I asked, as my stomach muscles contracted.

"It's Alana. Alana Montoya. She's . . . in the hospital."

"Oh, gosh," I said, feeling relieved that Brian was safe, and then feeling guilty for my relief. "That's too bad. What happened? An auto accident?"

"No." He was gruff and harsh. "They pumped her stomach. Alcohol and antidepressants, they said. Could have been an accident. Could have been . . ." He didn't finish the sentence, but I understood. It could have been a suicide attempt. Had he been the one to discover her and get her to the hospital?

I felt a sudden sympathy for him. "Is there anything I can do?" I asked, meaning: Is there anything I can do for you? There was nothing I could do for Alana.

"She was asking for you," Blackie said. "She's sleeping it off just now, but I thought, well, maybe in a couple of hours, you could come over and see her. They're just keeping her overnight, I think. She'll be going home in the morning."

"She was asking for me?" I said warily. "But I barely know her."

I wasn't being honest. I remembered Alana's visit to the shop the previous week, remembered it more clearly than I wanted to admit. She had wanted to talk to me—about her drinking, I had suspected. And I had put her off. I'd been too busy with my own stuff to pay attention to her. The guilt wrapped itself around me like a gray blanket. But I had offered Alana an alternative, a chance to sit down together and talk over lunch. That was enough, wasn't it? Wasn't it?

Blackie cleared his throat. "I know you don't want to get involved, China," he said heavily. "But I'm asking you to do this as a personal favor—to me. Something's bothering Alana, and I can't help her. She seems to think you can."

"I . . . guess so," I said, thinking once again that I was reluctant to get involved with an alcoholic. The only thing I could tell her was that she needed to get help—and I wasn't the person to get it from. I'd been there and done that, with my mother, and I wasn't eager to go there and do that again.

On the other hand, I had to admit to some curiosity. People attempt suicide for all sorts of reasons, some deeply profound, others as superficial as a bid for attention. What was Alana's reason? Was it somehow connected to McQuaid's dislike of her? And what made her think that I could help?

I heard myself say, with evident reluctance, "I was planning to go to the hospital today, anyway, to see Florence Obermann." This was something of a surprise, since I hadn't consciously made this plan. But it sounded like a good idea, and having said the words, I couldn't very well take them back.

"I'm glad," Blackie said, and I could hear the relief in his voice. "About five or six? I'll be here when you come, and then I'll leave the two of you alone. But I'll stick around. Maybe, after you've seen Alana, we can talk."

I held my breath for the count of three, and then said it anyway. "Blackie, why you?"

There was a silence. "Because," he said. More silence. "Because she's in trouble." After a moment he spoke once more, so low I could barely hear him. "And because I care what happens to her." He broke the connection.

I distrust two-bit psychologizing, which often reduces

multilayered emotional situations to an oversimplified and formulaic explanation. But this situation seemed pretty clear, on the face of it, anyway. Alana, rejected by her colleagues, lonely and friendless, needed somebody to stand by her. Blackie, rejected by the woman he had loved, sad and vulnerable and lonely, needed to be needed. All the ragged, hurting pieces fit together. It was a perfect match.

Perfectly toxic, that is.

I took my apprehension out to the garden and put it to work cutting red clover blossoms and leaves, for tea. According to the weather forecast, we were due for some rain, and I wanted to cut the herbs before they got wet.

THE sky was growing dark in the northwest when I left to go to the hospital late that afternoon, but the rain still hadn't arrived. I had told McQuaid only that I was going to see Florence Obermann. He didn't like Alana, and he had made it clear that he wasn't in favor of Blackie's getting involved with her. He wouldn't be delighted to know that I was about to get involved as well—and for that matter, neither was I.

Then why are you doing it? my hardheaded, lawyerish self wanted to know, as I started the car and drove off.

Because Blackie asked me to, my softer, more compassionate side replied, with (it must be admitted) a touch of smug superiority.

Bullshit, my lawyer side hooted sharply. *You're doing it because you're curious about the woman. Confess!*

My softer side, recognizing that there's no arguing with a lawyer, shut up.

THE Adams County Hospital has two contrasting architectural components, the two-story main building and a one-story wing that was built in the late 1950s with a bequest from Herr Doctor Obermann. It is called, naturally enough, the Obermann Wing. The main building is built of red brick and set back from the street behind a row of sweeping live oaks. It has a mannerly, gracious look about it, unlike the tacked-on wing, a long, narrow stucco affair that angles off from the main building like a broken arm in a plaster cast, bent at the elbow. The hospital board has planned to build a second matching wing when they've raised the money. Rumor has it that the Obermann sisters have promised to donate a million dollars after the first million has been raised—a promise that may never be fulfilled, since nobody's stepped forward yet with that first million. In the meantime, the space is occupied by a lawn and an herb garden, maintained as a public service by the Myra Merryweather Herb Society.

There are fifty-plus patients' rooms in the Obermann Wing, which sports gray walls and a gray floor waxed to a glossy sheen. To liven things up, the corridor was decorated for Halloween, with crayoned pictures of witches and pumpkins lovingly drawn by Pecan Springs elementary school artists, and sheafs of decorated cornstalks in the waiting area, along with a grinning skeleton—a veteran of a medical school classroom, most likely—with a stethoscope dangling playfully around his neck. More dead man's bones.

I stopped at the desk, where Helen Berger was on duty again. "Hi, Helen," I said. "I'd like to drop in on Miss Obermann for a few minutes."

Helen looked up from her chart, peering at me over the tops of her glasses. "Oh, hello, China," she said. "She's in 107. Ruby's there now, I believe."

I hesitated. "Okay for both of us to visit?"

"Sure—for a little while, anyway. If she seems tired, one of you might leave." She put the chart down and poked her pencil into her brown hair. "Oh, by the way, you haven't forgotten that you're giving the talk at the November herb guild meeting, have you? What's your topic?"

Helen is an active guild member and as competent an

herbalist as she is a nurse. Last year, she presented a slide show and talk on toxic plants. Most of her audience were surprised to hear that lantana, yellow jessamine, and Mexican poppy—our native prickly poppy—are poisonous to animals and humans. I suppose her interest comes with being a nurse.

"I haven't forgotten," I said. "I'm going to talk about native dye plants." I sighed. "If I can get the time to dye some sample skeins."

Helen rolled her eyes. "Time," she said, "it's always in short supply, isn't it?"

I went to see Florence first. The witch on her door wore a jaunty hat and bore a child's inscription, "Happy Halloween, from Janna J." The door was ajar, and I saw that the private room was as nicely appointed as a hotel room—the privilege of the wealthy, I thought, or perhaps the prerogative of the hospital benefactor's daughter. You wouldn't want the blue bloods to mingle with the riffraff, especially when they're sick.

And Helen had been right—Ruby was there, sitting beside the bed, looking like Little Miss Sunshine: yellow tunic, yellow leggings, yellow wedgies, and a flowing yellow scarf tied around her carroty hair. A walking Happy Face.

"Oh, now I have two visitors," Miss Florence said, with evident pleasure. "How nice of you to come, Ms. Bayles. And thank you for the flowers." She waved a thin, dry hand toward the vase on the windowsill. Her voice was trembly, and her face was almost as white as the sheets of her hospital bed.

"I've just come from the matinee performance," Ruby said with a bright smile. "We've been chatting about the play." She held up the Saturday *Enterprise*, which had been enthusiastic about the new theater and the performances, if not about the play itself. "I read her Hark's review."

Florence made a little face. "I'm afraid my sister didn't like the way Max Baumeister played Father. But I thought it was him, to the very life. He was always so . . . well, so formal, you know. To tell the truth, Mama used to say he was—" She giggled and lowered her voice as if she were telling a secret. "Stodgy. We loved him, but he was stiff as a board."

"Men were very formal in those days," I said. I smiled and put my hand on Ruby's shoulder. "Did you like the way Ruby played your mother?"

"I've already told her I thought she was perfect," Florence said, smiling. "Somehow, she managed to catch my mother's sense of fun. I remember especially how much Mama loved playing hide-and-seek with Andy when he was a little boy. She was a child herself, always laughing and giggling." She paused, puzzled. "My sister didn't portray Mama that way—I know, because I read the script. What made you decide to do it like that, Ruby?"

Ruby smiled a little. "To tell the truth, it was a strange experience. The more I played her, the more I understood her—understood what wasn't there in the script, I mean." She leaned forward and dropped her voice. "Jean Davenport and the others, they thought I was making it up, but I wasn't. It was almost as if . . . as if your mother were speaking to me."

Ruby ducked her head self-consciously, and I knew what she wasn't saying out loud. She had gone inside Cynthia Obermann. She had made some sort of psychic connection with the woman and gotten some insights about her character—and she didn't want to say so because she was afraid that Florence would think she was weird.

But maybe this isn't as far-out as it seems. Doesn't a good actress have to become the person she plays? Doesn't she have to reach down and find that character within herself, somehow? Ruby had reached down into herself and found Cynthia. And Florence was confirming that she had gotten it right, in spite of the constraints and limitations imposed by the script.

"Mama was an . . . unusual woman," Florence said in a halting voice. A shadow passed over her face, like a remembered pain. "Father was terribly stern with her, of course. He had to be, because sometimes she couldn't control herself. She went too far. And then she . . . she—" Her voice trembled, and she turned her head away.

I patted her hand, knowing that she was thinking about her mother's death and not quite knowing how to respond. What do you say to someone whose mother jumped off the roof of the house?

I seized on something else. "You mentioned Andy," I said. "Who is he?"

"My brother Harley's son," Florence replied. "He was such a lovable child, with so much promise. We all thought that he was the hope of the family. The only grandchild, you know. The only one who could carry on our father's name." Her old face crumpled, and her pale eyes, the color of water, filled with tears. "It was a tragedy," she whispered raggedly. "Poor, sweet Andy. Such a terrible—"

"Florence," Jane said sharply. Her stern shape appeared in the open door. "You shouldn't tire yourself with too much talk."

"Oh, but I was only—" Florence began, flustered. "I mean, I wouldn't—"

"Please don't, Florence," Jane said sharply. "I told you about Doctor Mackey's orders. She even wrote it on your chart. You're not well enough to have a visitor." Her glittering glance raked Ruby and me. "Let alone *two*."

"I'm afraid it's my fault," Ruby put in, pushing her chair back and standing up. "But I asked at the nurses' station, and the charge nurse said I could—"

"The nurse didn't read the chart," Jane snapped.

I thought of Helen Berger, with her precise and careful competency. "I really don't think—" I began, but stopped. An argument would only upset Florence.

Jane stood aside from the door, with a gesture that plainly ushered us out. "I'm sorry," she said, in a softer tone, "but I'm sure you can appreciate the situation. My sister not only has a fractured hip, but a delicate heart.

Even the slightest upset makes her very ill. We're all terribly worried about her."

Florence lifted her head and began to protest. "There's nothing wrong with my—"

"Now, dear," Jane said, in the soothing tone one uses to a child. "Don't excite yourself."

There was a small sound from the bed. Before Florence turned her face away, I saw it again, that look of frightened helplessness, like a mouse cornered by a combative cat. But this time, there was something almost defiant about it, as if the mouse might be on the verge of fighting back. Good for Florence, I thought. It was about time she stood up to her sister.

Ruby bent over the bed and dropped a kiss on Florence's cheek. "I'll keep in touch," she said softly, smoothing the straggly white hair back from the parchment forehead. "When you're well enough, we can go on with our conversation. China and I would like very much to hear more about your family."

"Get well soon," I added.

Florence lifted her glance to us. "I'll try," she said. There were tears in her eyes. "And do come back, please." Her glance darted to her sister, then slid away. Her voice dropped to a whisper. "I'd like to . . . to talk," she said. "I have something to tell you."

"Florence!" Jane said. There was a sharp note of warning in her voice. And as we went out the door, she said to Ruby, in an even sharper tone, "I intend to talk to you soon about your performance in my play, Ms. Wilcox. I found it nothing short of disgraceful."

Chapter Thirteen

Lavender. In the Victorian language of flowers, this herb represented distrust. The allusion is based on the old belief that the asp, the small, venomous, hooded snake which killed Cleopatra . . . habitually lurked under a lavender plant, and it was highly advisable to approach a lavender clump with caution.

Claire Powell
The Meaning of Flowers

Out in the hall, the door safely shut behind us, Ruby stamped her foot.

"What an old witch!" she exclaimed. "That Jane is nothing but a bully. Poor Florence hasn't drawn an independent breath since she was born. And now Jane is trying to bully me!"

I frowned. "Did you get the idea that Jane doesn't want her sister to talk to us? Wonder what that's about?"

"You felt that, too, huh?" We began walking down the hall, Ruby's yellow wedgies clicking against the tile. "I thought at first that Jane just didn't want Florence to open the family closet and let the skeletons out." She frowned. "But somehow I think there's more to it than that, China. I'm going to ask the charge nurse about visitors. That business about the chart just doesn't make sense to me."

"Andy," I said, still turning Florence's words over in my

mind. "The little boy Cynthia Obermann played hide-and-seek with. What was the tragedy?"

"He got shot up in Vietnam and spent a lot of time in hospitals. He was around off and on for a while after he got out, but then he went off to California, and nobody ever heard from him again."

"Oh, right," I said, remembering what McQuaid had told me. "The grandson." Ruby grew up in Pecan Springs and went to high school here, so she knows a great many people. "Were you acquainted with him?"

"Not really. He was older, and he lived with his family in Houston. But he visited in the summers, sometimes. I'd see him playing in the yard when I was riding my bike, on my way to the river to swim." She shook her head. "You know, that house was spooky even then. Kids would run up and peek in the windows after dark. And people thought the Obermann sisters were weird—maybe because of the way their mother died."

"Well, yes," I said. "Jumping off the roof is pretty bizarre. It would tend to make the neighbors wonder."

Ruby's laugh was subdued. "Are you free this evening? Want to do dinner?" She wasn't looking at me.

"I'm sorry, but I can't, Ruby. I'm here to make another visit." I expected her to ask who I was visiting, and began to grope around for an explanation that wouldn't bog us down in details about Alana.

But she seemed to be focused on her own distress. "That's too bad. I wanted to talk to you about . . ." Her voice gave out and her face was gloomy. Not much sunshine here.

"About Colin?"

"How'd you know?"

"A wild guess." I sighed. I didn't want to talk about Ruby and Colin until I knew more about Sheila and Colin. Until I knew more about Colin, period. But that wasn't likely to happen anytime soon, and in the meanwhile,

Ruby was in love. She needed a friendly ear, or maybe a shoulder to cry on. "Want to have lunch tomorrow?" We usually try for Monday lunch anyway—it's a good day to get together, since the shops are closed that day.

"Yes," she said, sounding relieved. "My house? And don't forget that we're seeing Cass at four-thirty."

"I haven't forgotten, believe me," I said. Ruby's house. A good place for the kind of girl talk that might turn into a sobbing spree. "Noonish for lunch?"

She nodded. "Thanks for understanding, China."

"No problemo," I said, waving my hand airily.

I wished.

ALANA'S room was at the far end of the hall, behind a door with a crayon drawing of a black cat riding a witch's broom. I tapped lightly. After a minute, Blackie came out into the hall, closing the door behind him. I almost didn't recognize him, because he was wearing street clothes; khakis and a plaid shirt with the sleeves rolled up.

"How is she?" I asked.

He lifted a shoulder and let it fall, not quite meeting my eyes. "Physically, she's okay—or she will be when she gets over the discomfort. Getting your stomach pumped isn't fun. Otherwise, she's depressed. Or maybe she just doesn't want to talk—not to me, anyway."

"Have you found out how it happened?"

"She told the doctor it was an accident. She lost track of how much she was taking. But maybe she'll tell you a different story. Who knows where the truth is." His square jaw was working, and I suddenly felt sorry for him. Cops have to build a psychic barrier against other people's pain. It must be very hard for them to acknowledge their own. But I could hear it in his voice when he added, "Go easy on her, will you, China?"

I gave him a wry grin. "You mean, don't chew her out for

being careless enough to mix drugs and alcohol?" I didn't think she'd merely been careless. Women who drink the way Alana had been drinking the other night have a death wish, whether they know it or not. They can get behind the wheel and kill themselves. Or they can kill other people. Or they can go home and pop a handful of antidepressants.

"Yeah." His smile didn't reach his eyes. "Don't chew her out, period. She's got enough to deal with."

Alana had a double room, but the other bed was unoccupied, its sheet and blanket stretched tight, the bedside table empty. A television set, tuned to CNN but muted, sat on a shelf on the wall, and a remote control lay on the table beside Alana's bed, along with a pitcher and a half-empty glass of water with a plastic straw in it, a box of tissues, a kidney-shaped stainless steel spit-up pan, and a small lavender plant wrapped in cellophane—a gift from Blackie, perhaps. A clock hung on the wall, its second hand jerking around the dial in audible spasms. The chair Blackie had vacated, a metal straight-backed chair, sat beside the bed. A couple of magazines—*Texas Monthly* and *Cosmopolitan*—were lying on the chair.

Alana's bed was cranked up to a half-sitting position. "I didn't think you'd come." Her voice was gritty, and she spoke with an effort—not surprising, since she'd had a tube down her throat. Her white hospital gown wasn't exactly *haute couture,* and her hair, rumpled, was dull and lifeless. Her skin was gray, her cheeks hollowed. Her eyes had a haunted look.

I picked up the magazines and put them on the table. The words "My Friend Stole My Lover" were emblazoned across the *Cosmo* cover, beneath it, "I'll never trust him again."

"I'm sorry we didn't get to talk the other day," I said uncomfortably. I sat down in the chair. What else should I say? Should I apologize for not being there when she needed me? Or should I—

"It's okay," she said. "Don't worry about it."

I shifted uncomfortably. "Blackie said you wanted to see me."

She looked away from me, at the wall, at nothing. "I need to talk to you. About . . . about your husband."

"My husband?" I couldn't have been more surprised if she had said that she wanted to talk to me about the condition of my appendix, or where I planned to spend my retirement. "What about him?"

My question was answered by a long silence. In the stillness, I discovered that the second hand on the clock was not only audible but noisy, *tick-tick, tock-tock*, that it repeated itself on every beat, but that time itself had seemed to stop. Unbidden, unwanted memories rose up and began to click through my head, measured by the metronome of the irrevocable clock.

Tick-tick. I remembered Margaret, the woman with whom McQuaid had an affair before we were married. Margaret had been dark like Alana, pretty like her, too. And young, oh so young.

Tock-tock. I remembered McQuaid's studied casualness when he'd questioned me about running into Alana at Bean's, about the topics of our conversation. Was he trying to find out whether Alana and I had become friends, whether she had revealed anything about the two of them? Was he trying to guage my suspicions?

Tick-tick. I remembered his irritation—no, it was more than that, it was anger—at the idea that Blackie might be romantically involved with Alana. I'd wondered at that. Now I wondered if I had been mistaken, if what I took for anger might have been a secret jealousy.

Tock-tock, tick-tick. I remembered that old cliché, that one person can never truly know another. McQuaid has been my lover, and then my husband, for . . . what? Seven years? Eight? For a long time. But how well do I know him? Do I know what he's doing when he isn't with me? What he's thinking when he's silent? How he feels when I can't read his feelings on his face? The fierce, sweet intimacy that binds us—does he share that same intimacy with someone else? With this woman, who, in one way or another, has tried to kill herself?

"Your husband is . . ." Alana's words splintered the silence, like glass breaking against a metallic surface. She reached for the glass of water, sipped through the straw, put it back, tried again. This time, she got it out. "He's . . . investigating me."

I stared at her. "Investigating . . . you?" I asked blankly.

And then I understood. McQuaid's other case. His questions to me about Alana's undergraduate work. His trip to Louisiana—he'd flown to New Orleans, and then driven, most likely, to Baton Rouge. His refusals to answer my inquiry about the department's slowness to fund her new program. She wasn't a friend or a lover. She was the subject of an investigation.

"For résumé fraud?" I asked, in a voice that sounded almost normal.

"You knew." Two red spots glowed on her cheeks. "He's told you, then."

I shook my head. "I guessed, just now. I knew the kind of case he's been working on, but I had no idea that it had anything to do with you."

I paused. The question, "Do you want to tell me about it?" was on the tip of my tongue. But did I want to hear? Would my listening to Alana's story in any way compromise McQuaid's case? Not in any legal way, of course. But morally? Ethically?

"I want to tell you about it," she said urgently. "I need to ask your advice. About what I should do next."

I sat forward in the chair. "I can't act as your lawyer. I can refer you to someone else, but I can't take your case."

"No," she said hurriedly. "That's not what I want. But I thought, with your legal background, you might be—"

"And I can't promise not to share what you tell me with my husband."

A shadow of pain crossed her face. "He already knows . . . everything. There are no more secrets."

I was suddenly overwhelmed by a feeling of pity. Whatever she had done to bring her to this place in her life, whatever choices she had made, voluntary or involuntary—that was all in the past. She was facing a difficult, painful future.

"I'm sorry," I said quietly.

She was silent for a few moments, her fingers pleating the sheet in her lap. "I lied about my undergraduate degree at the University of Mexico." She spoke slowly, as if she were testifying in court, as if every word had to be measured, had to be verified against some internal catalogue of facts. I said nothing.

She took a deep breath. "I was in my last semester, twelve—no, thirteen—hours away from graduation, when I met my husband, the man I later . . . married." She came to a stop, as if the word *married* had surprised her, had tripped her up.

The silence lengthened. Was this all she was going to tell me, or was there more? "He was an American?" I prodded.

She nodded. "His name was Thomas. He was an anthropologist from LSU, doing a dig near Mexico City. We fell in love." She stopped. It was as if she was listening to herself say something she'd said many times before, but hearing it, really hearing it, for the first time. She bit her lip.

"No, I want to tell the truth. He didn't love me. For him, it was entirely sexual. For me, it was . . . wanting to go to the United States. To become a U.S. citizen." She looked at me. "Can you understand that?"

"Yes," I said cautiously, although I couldn't understand marrying someone in order to become a citizen. Marriage is dicey enough when you do it because you love someone. For any other reason—

"Then you understand that I couldn't say no. I couldn't even say, wait. Thomas wouldn't have waited, of course."

She scrutinized my face, as if trying to discover how I felt about what she was saying. "I didn't think it would ever matter. About the degree, I mean."

"When did it begin to matter?" I asked. "When you applied to graduate school?"

She shook her head. "Not then. Thomas was the department's graduate adviser, you see. He said he'd fix my transcript so it wouldn't raise any questions. It didn't even matter later, when I began to work in the forensics lab, and they asked me to teach a class. Then they asked me to join the faculty. By that time, Thomas and I . . ."

She paused, her lips twisting in what might have been a smile. "By that time, he'd found someone else, someone younger. Another sexual thing. And I had found the work I wanted to do for the rest of my life. It seemed like a fair trade. I had my work. He had his . . . lover."

"But to get the faculty position, you had to give them a undergraduate transcript, didn't you?"

She shook her head. "They already had it on file. The one Thomas 'fixed.' And of course they had the transcript of my graduate work—all A's, with outstanding recommendations. And I had several major publications. One on forensic three-dimensional facial reconstruction, another on the use of the computer in facial reconstruction. And then I edited the textbook, and I was all set. For life, I thought."

"What happened?"

She tilted her head. Her eyes glinted. "I came to CTSU. Ralph Morgan—a faculty member who lost some of his funding to my program—began to ask questions. He met Thomas at a conference, and the two of them got drunk together. Thomas . . ."

"Spilled the beans," I said.

She held out her hand, flat, and turned it over. "I'm sure he didn't do it on purpose. It reflects badly on him, too, of course. Altering the transcript, I mean."

"This man, Ralph Morgan—he went to the department head here at CTSU?"

"And the dean. That's when they asked your husband to investigate. I learned all this," she added, "from a secretary in the department, somebody who's had problems with Morgan. She overheard them say that McQuaid was going to LSU to interview Thomas. I . . . I felt desperate. I would lose everything. My whole life was wrecked . . ." She ducked her head. "I couldn't think of any way out, except . . ."

So it wasn't an accident. The silence dragged out like a long punishment, aching and heavy. Finally, in an effort to bring us back to some sort of practicality, I asked, "What are you thinking of doing? Will you try to fight it?"

Her smile was bleak. "I don't suppose it would do any good. Do you?"

"No," I said, with an honesty that matched hers. "You falsified the transcript—if not you, then your husband, acting for you and with your consent. LSU can choose to revoke your graduate degree. CTSU can certainly end your employment."

"In either case, it's the end of my academic career," she said bitterly. "And my career in forensic science. I can never testify as an expert witness—I'd be discredited in an instant." Her voice was ragged. "Any report I file can be challenged on the grounds that I falsified my credentials."

I nodded. The university and the courtroom are both brutal places, where small falsehoods can destroy large reputations. "It might be easier to submit your resignation before they convene a formal hearing. Easier on you, I mean."

Her lips trembled. She suddenly looked very young, very vulnerable. "I don't know what to do."

"You can go back to Mexico and finish your degree," I said. "I'm sure you'll find other opportunities in anthropology." I was reaching, and I knew it. Finishing her degree wouldn't be easy, since most of the course work was out of date by now and would have to be repeated. And short of working as a lab assistant—

"I'm not sure that finishing the degree is the answer," she said. Her voice was flat, resigned. "But I've already decided to go back to Cuernavaca, at least for a while. My mother's ill. She's been asking me to come home."

I regarded her for a moment. I could think of only one other question. "Have you told the sheriff?"

It wasn't just their relationship—whatever it was, or might have been—that was at stake here. It was the report she had submitted on the bones in the cave.

Alana shook her head, and I saw the pain in her eyes, a pain that matched the pain I had seen in his. It told me that there was probably more between them than either of them could or would acknowledge, to me, anyway. Blackie is a scrupulously honest man who cannot tolerate deceit. She probably knew that much about him, and knew that it would mean the end of their relationship.

"Do you want me to tell him?" I asked.

"He has to know." I heard the catch in her voice. She let out her breath as if she had been holding it for a long time. "I would rather you told him than your husband."

It wasn't an easy thing to do, but I didn't try to soften the blow. I knew that Blackie would want to hear the story straight up and clear, not muffled with efforts at explanation.

He listened without saying anything, his jaw rock-hard, his eyes on my face. When I finished, he looked away.

"Too bad," he said. I heard the finality in his voice. He is a man who draws lines in the dirt, and once they're crossed, there's no going back. "What's she going to do?"

"I suggested that she submit her resignation, rather than wait for the university to take action. Her mother's ill and wants her to come home."

"Best thing." He straightened his shoulders. "Too bad," he said again, and now there was a startled regret in his voice, as if crossing the line had cost more than he expected.

I studied his face, thinking that—this once—he might say more. But he straightened his shoulders, gave me a tight smile, and said, "Thanks. I'll walk you to your car."

* * *

"ATTEMPTED suicide!" McQuaid stared at me in astonishment. "Sweet Jesus. Is she going to be okay?"

"Depends on what you mean by 'okay,' " I said dryly. "I imagine this sort of thing is like an earthquake, or a flood. Your house is gone, and your livelihood, but you're alive. She's alive."

"It's a bad business," McQuaid said, shaking his head. "It's been making me sick for a couple of weeks, ever since Morgan began raising the issue and the dean asked me to look into it."

"I suppose there's nothing Alana can do that will change the situation at the university," I said. "Negotiation? Some kind of a deal?"

The storm had arrived just as I got home, with hard rain blown at an angle to the road by a fierce wind. Brian had called to say that he was at Jake's, and he'd stay there until it let up and Jake's mom could drive him home—which from the sound of it, might be a while.

"No deal." McQuaid shook his head. "Morgan's got a real burr in his butt and a couple of his buddies are siding with him. The dean made a big mistake on this one. Instead of coming up with new money, he moved fifty thousand out of Morgan's program and put it into a fund for Montoya's lab equipment. So Morgan is out to sink her *and* the program, and he's got the ammunition, too. My investigation only confirmed what Morgan told the dean. Alana Montoya is history."

"Academic politics," I said resentfully.

"It's not just politics," he replied, in a reasonable tone. "Universities take a dim view of forged credentials, which is what this amounts to. If you can't trust a transcript, what the hell can you trust? It's the bottom line."

I turned away. "I hope there'll be some action taken against her ex-husband. After all, he was the one who doctored her transcript in the first place. He told her it would be okay." But even as I said the words, I knew it was hopeless. The man would only deny the charge, and there probably wasn't a shred of evidence to prove it.

"They're not going to touch him." McQuaid smiled thinly. "Even if what she says is truc—maybe it is, maybe it isn't—he's a big guy in his field. He brings in a lot of research funding. And there's nothing wrong with *his* transcripts."

"Hell," I said disgustedly. "Talk about ugly."

Chapter Fourteen

In the Middle Ages, students were encouraged to twine sprigs of rosemary through their hair to stimulate their brains; consequently, the herb has come to be associated with remembrance, most famously by Ophelia in *Hamlet*, "There's rosemary, that's for remembrance—pray you, love, remember."

Gretchen Scoble and Ann Field
The Meaning of Herbs

It's true that the shops are closed on Mondays and that my day gets off to a slower start, but I still have plenty of work. This Monday, I stopped at the shop and picked up Big Red Mama. Ruby and a couple of helpers had dealt with the leftovers on Friday night, but they'd left a few things at the theater, serving dishes and things like that. I used my cell phone to make sure that somebody would be there to let me in, and then drove over.

There were several cars in the parking lot, and when I went into the theater, I found a half-dozen people there, doing various odd jobs. There had apparently been some debate about canceling the Saturday night performance, given the shooting, but the board had decided to carry on, and Marian and Jean were in the office, tallying up the take. Chris had stopped by on her way to work to check on some makeup items. Two guys were pushing brooms, and Max Baumeister, dressed in an orange zip-front jumpsuit—not very flattering, with his paunch—was doing some touch-up painting on one of the sets.

There was a loud clamor for an eyewitness account of what had happened Friday night when I followed Sheila to the scene of the shooting. And since the story, most of it, anyway, had appeared in the Saturday *Enterprise*, I didn't see any problem with telling them what I'd seen.

Everyone had a different take on it. Marian and Jean, who had both worked with Hank, couldn't understand what he was doing in the Obermann house with a knife.

"Hank was a really gentle guy," Marian said, with a shake of his head. "He might mouth off when he got mad, or stamp off the job in a huff, but he always got over it."

"He took care of his dad while old Gabe was dying of cancer," Jean put in.

"And she threw Gabe out," Chris added. She works at a beauty shop in Austin, where she does makeovers, and she's a walking advertisement for her makeup artistry. Her long blonde hair was twisted in an artful loop that looked casually gorgeous. "Jane Obermann, I mean. I wonder if Hank was carrying a grudge."

"You know about that?" I asked. Seemed like everyone knew a little piece of the story.

"Well, sure," Chris said, batting her long eyelashes. "Hank was doing some work at my mother's house about that time. I was living there then, and every day he'd give us the blow-by-blow. He was really upset about the way his dad was being treated." She glanced around the theater. "It's good that we have this place, and I certainly hate to look a gift horse in the mouth. But if you ask my opinion, Jane Obermann could have waited for a few months and let Gabe die in peace."

Max Baumeister put the lid on his paint can. "So you think that's what made Hank Dixon do what he did?" he asked, frowning behind his gold-rimmed glasses. "He was angry about the way his father was treated?"

Chris shrugged. "Your guess is as good as mine, Doctor

Baumeister. But I can't think of another reason why Hank would pick up a butcher knife and threaten the Obermann sisters. He got to thinking about his dad and brooding over the situation, and he just lost it."

Man's gotta die sometime, Hank had said. *Woman, too, for that matter.*

"It's so sad," Jean said. "Hank dead, Florence in the hospital. And Jane must feel just awful about what happened."

"Don't bet on it," Marian said grimly. "I wouldn't put it past that old lady to be feeling just ducky about the whole thing." She turned away. "Now, if you guys will excuse me, I need to finish counting the ticket money."

"The theater had a good weekend?" I asked.

"The best opening weekend ever," Jean replied happily. "We sold out both Friday and Saturday nights."

Chris waggled her beautifully plucked eyebrows at Max. "How does that make you feel, Herr Doctor Obermann?"

"I am complimented, little lady." Max bowed at the waist. "Indeed, I am deeply honored to have been given the opportunity to play a man of such stature in our community."

Chris giggled, and Jean suppressed a smile. I loaded the empty chafing dishes and other items into the plastic bins I'd brought. Max offered to give me a hand with them, and between us, we carried them out to Mama.

"Thank you," I said, closing the rear door on the load. "I appreciate the help."

"You are very welcome, dear lady," Max said, in his chivalric way, which I try not to think of as patronizing. He was turning to go when I thought of something. Max was a dentist; he had replaced a crown for me not long before he retired. Brian's caveman had had one gold tooth. It was a long shot, but what the heck.

"Doctor Baumeister," I said, "when did you start practicing in Pecan Springs?"

He turned, looking pleased at the question. "Let's see," he said, considering. "That would have been in 1959, in April. My father retired, and I took over his practice—a fine start for a young dentist, who could barely afford to buy new equipment. That's really why I retired, you know. The new dental technology costs a small fortune, and one must be willing to keep up with all the changes, even when one finds them . . . bewildering." He paused, peering at me over the tops of his glasses. He really did look like Teddy Roosevelt, I thought. "And why do you ask, my dear?"

"I wonder if you remember putting in a gold front tooth," I said. "Right upper incisor. The patient, a man, was tall—six foot three or four. This would have been before the mid-seventies." The penny in the caveman's pocket had been minted in 1975 and had looked new. There was no telling when the tooth had been installed.

"A gold front tooth?" He pursed his lips, clasped his hands behind his back, and rocked back and forth. "I shouldn't think I would have put in a gold front tooth after 1965."

I was surprised by the specific date. "Oh? Why?"

"Because porcelain came into use at that time, and most people preferred it to gold, for cosmetic reasons." He paused, frowning. "Six feet four? My goodness gracious. I pride myself on my memory. In a performance, of course, I must be able to hold all my lines in my head and recite them without difficulty. Memory is a crucial asset as a performer, and I exercise it religiously."

But not briefly, I thought, and waited.

He cast his eyes upward as if consulting the skies, thought for a moment longer, then gave it up as a bad job.

"I'm terribly sorry, but I'm afraid I'm drawing a blank, which suggests to me that I did not treat the gentleman you describe. You might try Doctor Rosenberg—he began practicing about the same time as I did. Poor fellow had to start from scratch, and it took him quite a few years to build up a following, although I believe he's done quite well in his latter years. I've seen some of his work, and it seems quite good."

That's what happens when you talk with Max. He is not

only stiff and formal, he is long-winded. But since I hadn't expected any information, I wasn't terribly disappointed.

"Thanks anyway," I said. "By the way, Ruby and I dropped in at the hospital yesterday and talked to Florence. She was very pleased with your performance on Friday night. She said that you captured her father, to the life."

"Oh, really?" Max's plump face was wreathed in a smile. "How gracious of sweet little Miss Florence to say so, and how very nice of you to pass the compliment along. I'm afraid that our dear Doctor Obermann was a rather stiff gentleman, and exceedingly formal. I had to make his character a little more lively, just to keep up with Ruby, you know." He smiled, as if we were sharing a joke. "Otherwise, Ruby would have upstaged me, and I don't think that was what Miss Jane had in mind."

I tried not to smile. "The play was great," I said truthfully. "And you did a fine job."

"I am truly complimented, little lady." Max lifted his hand in a formal gesture. "I trust that you will have a fine day." He turned to go back to the theater.

I climbed into the van and was inserting the key into the ignition when Max reappeared at the driver's side window. Suppressing a sigh, I rolled it down.

"Something has just occurred to me that may be of some assistance to you," he said. "It was your mention of Miss Florence that jogged my recollection." He paused, with a thoughtful look. "Isn't it fascinating the way memories are connected? Like threads. Pull on one end, and they all begin to unravel. Why, just the other day, when I was rehearsing, I happened to remember something I hadn't thought of in—"

"The recollection?" I asked quickly, since he showed signs of going off in another direction for another two or three paragraphs.

"Ah, yes, the recollection. Quite right. You might be interested in knowing that I fitted a gold tooth on a young lad in the first year of my practice. He was not very tall then, of course, but I believe that he grew up to be an unusually tall man. In fact, I remember seeing him and remarking on how very tall he had grown, six feet three or four. Young people have a way of doing that, I find. Of growing beyond one's expectations, I mean."

"Interesting," I murmured. I could feel the impatience rising in me. I turned on the ignition, thinking ahead to the long list of things I had to do. I needed to take the plastic bins back to the shop, do some bookkeeping and some garden work, and then go to Ruby's for lunch. After that—

"Yes, it is, actually, quite interesting. My patient was Doctor Obermann's young grandson, Andrew. Of course, Doctor and Mrs. Obermann had been my father's patients, and I was enormously complimented when they decided to stay on with me." He looked reflective. "Although to be truthful, they might not have considered the alternative. That would have been Doctor Rosenberg, and I'm not sure that Doctor Obermann would have been entirely comfortable with him." He dropped his voice. "Jewish, you know. That's why it was so difficult for him to start a practice in Pecan Springs. On the face of it, we are a tolerant little town, but when you scratch the surface, you will find all sorts of—"

It is easy to be mesmerized by the flow of Max's words. I stopped him. "You said that the boy was Andrew Obermann?"

"Indeed, yes." He beamed. "Now that it has come to mind—been retrieved from a dusty back shelf of my brain, as it were, the library of my memory—I remember the occasion quite well. Miss Florence brought the boy in. It was summer, the first summer of my practice, and he was visiting here. He had been playing in the stable, which is now our very fine playhouse." He made a sweeping gesture in the direction of the theater. "Apparently, he broke his tooth when he jumped out of the hayloft. It was an upper incisor, as I recall, although I should have to consult my records to be certain whether it was right or left. And if I'm not mistaken, I did a root canal."

"I see," I said, "but I—"

He was in full swing. "You wouldn't have known young Andrew Obermann, of course, because he was gone long before you arrived. And he was not a resident of Pecan Springs, only a visitor. He and his family—his father was one of the Obermanns' two sons—lived in Houston."

I stared at him. "Andrew Obermann. He was the one who went to Vietnam, and then came back and disappeared?"

The light glinted on Max's glasses. "The boy was badly wounded during the war, I understand, and became addicted to opiates during the course of his treatment. The waste of a fine young life. So sad for all concerned. I know that his aunts were devastated, because Miss Florence spoke of it to me."

"When did he disappear?"

"When?" Max wrinkled his forehead, concentrating. "Well, I couldn't answer that with precision. I can, however, tell you when I saw him last, if that would be of any help."

"It might," I said.

"It would have been in 1976, I believe." He pursed and repursed his lips, as he did a serious search of his memory banks. "Yes, 1976, in the autumn, although I can't tell you whether it was September or October. I was working in the election campaign, you see. I have always been eager to participate in the democratic process. Did you know that Mr. Ford was defeated in that year by only two percentage points? A very narrow margin indeed. And as the next election demonstrated—"

"You saw Andrew Obermann during the campaign?" I asked. I am always impressed by people with good memories. I can barely remember my shopping list, and Max Baumeister was recalling the details of a presidential election a quarter-century before.

"Yes, I saw him. Jane and Florence had volunteered to work for the campaign, as they did then, and quite actively, too. That was when they were still venturing out into public, although as you know they have been reclusive in recent years—a pity, I have always thought, for both of them have a great deal to offer the community and—"

"You saw their nephew at a political event?"

"Andrew drove them to one of our campaign functions—a rally for local candidates, as I recall—and was introduced as a war veteran. Somebody from the newspaper was there taking photos, I believe. I remember that he didn't smile, and I wondered if he was self-conscious about that tooth and might want a porcelain replacement. In fact, I believe that I spoke to him about it. He could certainly afford the expense of a replacement."

"Well, thank you, Doctor Baumeister," I said heartily. "You have quite an astonishing memory." I paused. "You wouldn't happen to recall whether you took X rays of Andrew Obermann's mouth, would you?"

"In those days, X rays were not done as a matter of course," he said. "But since I recall doing a root canal for him—one of my first, actually, if not the very first—I'm sure I must have. I should have to look in my records."

"Would you?" I asked. "It might be important." On the other hand, it might not. You never know.

"May I ask why you have this interest?" he inquired curiously. "It seems a rather odd—"

"Goodness gracious, just *look* how late it's getting!" I exclaimed, with a glance at my watch. I cranked Mama's engine. "If you come across those X rays, you'll let me know, won't you?" I shifted into first gear and began letting out the clutch.

He retreated, not wanting Mama to step on his toes. "Yes, of course, but—"

"Wonderful," I said. "Thanks again, Doctor Baumeister. Bye!" And Mama and I took off.

As I said, I had planned to go to the shop. However, my agenda had changed, now that I had these disconnected fragments of information to deal with, retrieved from the dusty back shelves of Max Baumeister's quite remarkable memory. Andrew Obermann had a gold upper-front incisor. Andrew Obermann was very tall, six foot three or four. Andrew Obermann had been in Pecan Springs in 1976, after which he had—it was said—gone to California. Eventually, he was declared legally dead. One possible conclusion: Andrew Obermann was Brian's caveman.

I drove around the square, nosed Mama into a narrow parking space two doors down from the *Enterprise*, and went into the office. Ethel Fritz was behind the front desk, her largish self looming even larger and more cheerful than usual in a bright red polka-dot dress. Ethel does not believe in hiding her light under a bushel.

"Mornin', China," she said, poking a pencil into her blonde beehive, which is balanced on her head like one of those three-foot gilt crowns worn by Indonesian dancers. I haven't a clue how the woman manages to sleep, or how long it takes to assemble her hair for each new day. "Gotcher page ready early, for a change?" she inquired.

For the past couple of years, I have been editing the weekly Home and Garden page in the Thursday edition of the *Enterprise*. My page is due at six P.M. on Tuesday, but I almost never make the deadline, and Ethel never misses a chance to remind me of my delinquencies. However, I happen to know that, since Hark installed the new computers, I can deliver my page, electronically, as late as four P.M. on Wednesday, and it will still make the production deadline. We're not talking the *New York Times* here. The *Enterprise* has come up in the world from the days when it used to be a weekly, but it's still a small newspaper, and Hark is reasonably flexible. Ethel, however, is a different matter. She sticks to the rules.

"You'll have the page tomorrow, Ethel," I said. For some reason, even when I hand in my work on time, I always feel like a freshman with an overdue paper. "I'm finishing it up tonight."

Ethel opened her drawer and took out her advertising receipt book. There's a computer right in front of her, but she still does business on paper. She says that the problem people have with their memories these days comes because they put too much faith in computers. "Use it or lose it" is her philosophy.

"Then maybe you're here because you wanna buy some more ad space," she said, opening the book and reaching for a pencil in the cup on her desk.

Advertising in the *Enterprise* is actually a good deal, since everybody in town reads it from front to back, if only to verify the gossip they just heard at the Nueces Street Diner or the county courthouse. But I shook my head, pretending not to notice the look of disappointment on her face.

"I stopped in to look for something in the morgue. Okay?"

Ethel put her receipt book back in the drawer and stuck the pencil in her hair, opposite the pencil that was already there. "I reckon," she said, resigned. "But you'll have to watch your step. We bin fixin' the floor up there, and most of the boards're gone." She pulled her brows together. "Hank Dixon was doin' it for us. Now that he's went and got himself shot, we're gonna have to find somebody else to finish it, I reckon." She fixed me with a significant look. "You mind where you put your feet, China. I don't want you comin' through my ceilin' and into my lap."

"I wouldn't think of it," I said.

"Guess you know the way." She tipped her golden beehive in the direction of the stairs.

I did. To get to the *Enterprise* morgue, you have to climb the narrow circular iron staircase at the rear of the building. This takes you to the upstairs loft, which is like a sauna for six or seven months of the year. It might be October outdoors, but up in that loft it was definitely still summer, with some of July's humidity and August's heat lurking under the eaves. And Ethel had been right about the floor. To get to the shelves where the old newspaper files are kept, I had to negotiate an eight-inch-wide wooden plankway, with boards laid end to end across the floor joists, like a tightrope walker on a high wire. The air was heavy with the sultry perfume of bat guano, resonant with the soft cooing of the pigeons, who fly in under the eaves and nest in the corners, and thick with dust. I didn't want to breathe too deeply. There was no telling how many bird or bat viruses were riding through the air, piggybacking on the visible dust motes.

When Hark Hibler took over as editor, he started keeping the *Enterprise* issues on microfiche. If you want to read a back issue, you have to locate the fiche and put it into the fiche reader. The newspaper's pre-Hark issues, however, are stored in large cardboard porfolios stacked on plywood shelves, systematically arranged by quarters and years, so that you can find what you're looking for without a great deal of trouble.

But people never put things back the way they're supposed to. It took me fifteen minutes to find the portfolio containing the back issues for September 1 through December 31, 1976, buried between portfolios for the first and second quarters of 1957. By the time I had pulled it out and carried it to the table under the front window, I was hot and sticky, and sweat was dripping off my nose.

I cleared a litter of papers, empty soda pop cans, and cellophane sandwich wrappers from the table and turned on the light, a single flourescent bar that supplements the dusty light filtering through the window. I began with September, turning the pages slowly. The newspaper has never been big on national or international news, figuring (I suppose) that people could turn on the radio if they wanted to know what was happening outside the city limits. But I learned that the *Viking 2* Lander had successfully reached Mars, that the space shuttle *Enterprise* had been rolled out, and the Montreal Summer Olympics were running way over budget. Most of the coverage, however, was local.

Cookie sales and car washes, school lunch menus, a city council dustup over zoning, an article about the positive power of prayer, and the community calendar.

The community calendar. I ran my finger down the list of miscellaneous items. Tickets to the Eleanor Roosevelt Dinner, presented by the Adams County Democratic Women, were $1. The Widowed Fellowship was meeting on Tuesday at the First Baptist Church. Enrollment was open in the Marriage Enrichment Seminar ("Couples' Therapeutic Spark Plug Change"). Lively doings in Pecan Springs, Texas, circa 1976.

Halfway down the list, I found the announcement that the Republican Club would be meeting in two weeks for a rally, starting with a social hour at six P.M. and including featured entertainment by the Promettes, a girls' quartet from Pecan Springs High School. Voters of Adams County, regardless of political affiliation, were invited to come out and rally with the local candidates, who exhibited a standard of high moral character and strong family values and would seek to limit the intrusion of big government into citizens' lives. Nobody had heard of the Patriot Act yet.

Two weeks. I skipped the next week's paper and leafed unsuccessfully through the following issue. In the issue after that, I found the photo Max Baumeister had mentioned, under a banner headline: "Local Candidates Woo Republican Faithful." It showed a stern-featured middle-aged Jane, wearing a slightly ironic smile, and a hefty Max Baumeister, his glasses glinting in the glare of the flashbulb. Between them was a tall, stooped young man in a blazer with too-short sleeves, his mouth set in a straight line. He was shaking hands with a man wearing a saucer-sized button emblazoned VOTE FOR TRACY. The photo was captioned "War Hero." Underneath, I read, "Senator Tracy congratulates Andrew Obermann, nephew of Jane and Florence Obermann, on impressive war record." A drop of sweat fell off the end of my nose and plopped onto Senator Tracy's face.

The article told me that Andrew Obermann, a former member of Echo Company of the First Recon Battalion of the U.S. Marines, had been responsible for single-handedly wiping out a machine-gun nest in the jungle near Chu Lai, thereby saving his squad from ambush. He had, however, suffered extensive shrapnel wounds and had spent a couple of years in military hospitals. He was in Pecan Springs to visit his aunts.

There is, of course, no copy machine in the morgue—Hark wasn't able to haul it up the circular stairs, and I wasn't about to take the newspaper downstairs, copy it, and bring it back up again. So I made notes of the dates and the military information, then replaced the portfolio—in the right place this time, where it could be found again without difficulty—and headed back to the spiral stairs, treading carefully on the planks.

At her desk, Ethel glanced up at the ceiling, as if to confirm that I had not in fact fallen through. "Find whatcher lookin' for?" she inquired. There were now three pencils stuck in her hair.

"Actually, I did," I said, pausing beside her desk. Ethel has worked for the newspaper ever since she got out of high school, and she knows the people in Pecan Springs the way she knows her own family. A lot of them probably are family, come to that. There are a couple of dozen Fritzes in the phone book, and that's only her father's kin. Her mother was a Jones, and the Lord only knows how many of them live in town.

"What do you remember about Andrew Obermann?" I asked.

"Andrew Obermann," Ethel muttered, frowning. She picked a pencil off her desk and began turning it in her fingers. "Andrew Obermann. Lessee, now. He was old Merrill G.'s one and only grandkid, wasn't he? Harley's son?" She gave me a triumphant look. "That's the one. Andrew Obermann. Lived in Houston, spent summers here when he was a kid."

"I believe that's right," I said. "He joined the Marines and went to Vietnam, and—"

"And came back all shot up," Ethel said. She poked the pencil into her gilt pagoda, which was now studded with pencils. "Florence Obermann, she was a close friend of my sister-in-law's cousin Charley. She told Charley how bad the boy was hurt—injuries to his stomach and intestines, legs all cut up with shrapnel—and how they thought maybe he might not live, which was a real pity, 'cause his dad had died just the year before, and Andy was the last male Obermann. And him with all that money, too. I heard he went through it pretty fast after he got out of the Marines, though."

"Did you see him after the war?"

She thought about that. "Maybe a time or two. He wasn't around long, though. Went off to California, was what I heard."

"He was here in 1976," I offered. "There was a piece in the newspaper. He got his picture taken with Senator Tracy."

"Tracy." Ethel made a scornful noise in her throat, and the pencils in her towering hair quivered with disgust. "That crook. He went straight from the statehouse to prison, you know. He was taking bribes. We got way too many like that in this state, especially now that—"

"Does your sister-in-law's cousin know anything about Andrew Obermann, do you think?"

"Charley?" Ethel replied mournfully. "Charley got kilt in a tornado up in Oklahoma a couple of years ago, her and her two kids and their dog. I wouldn't live in Oklahoma, if somebody gave me a house and a hundred acres of land. Tornadoes rippin' through all the time, right, left, and center. Hardly a month goes by, they don't have a tornado up there."

"Well, since Charley's not available, maybe you can suggest somebody else who might know."

"If you're interested in Andy Obermann, you oughtta talk to his aunts." Ethel raised her eyebrows inquisitively.

"This don't have anything to do with what happened at their house Friday night, does it? Hank gettin' shot, I mean."

"No, nothing to do with that. It's something else altogether." I couldn't tell her about the caveman—if I did, it would be all over town by the time Ethel finished her second helping of meatloaf at the Diner, where Lila (the owner) is the Chief Operator of the Pecan Springs gossip switchboard and Director of Rumor Proliferation.

Ethel made a face. "I can't figure out what Hank thought he was doin', breakin' in like that. With a knife, too. I figure maybe he was drunk, but even so, I don't blame old Miss Obermann for shootin' him. Somebody comes into my livin' room like that, I'll blow his head off."

Judge, jury, and executioner. But I didn't say that. I said, "I don't want to bother Jane and Florence with questions about their nephew until I've done a little more research."

Ethel sighed heavily. "I heard this morning that Florence isn't any too good. Broke her hip, I heard. That's not good, y'know. That's ostopersus, that's what it is. Yer bones go bad, you're done for. Spend the rest of yer life in a nursing home." She paused. "If it's research you're after, you oughtta go over to Bean's and talk to Bob."

"Bob Godwin?" I asked, surprised, and then I wasn't. He was a Vietnam vet. The other night, when Alana and I had eaten at Bean's, Bob had been wearing a black T-shirt with a skull and crossbones on it. And over the skull were the words "Recon Marines." I looked down at my notes.

Andrew Obermann had been a member of the First Recon Battalion of the U.S. Marines.

Chapter Fifteen

MARIA ZAPATA'S JALAPEÑO-APRICOT JELLY

3/4 cup red jalapeño chiles, seeded, stemmed
1 red bell pepper, seeded, stemmed
2 cups cider vinegar
1 1/4 cups dried apricots, slivered
6 cups sugar
3 oz. liquid pectin
3–4 drops red food color, if you like it red
few drops Tabasco sauce, or as much as you think you can get away with

Coarsely grind the chiles, bell pepper, and vinegar in a blender, until you have small chunks. Combine apricots, sugar, and pureed mixture in a large saucepan. Bring to a rolling boil and boil for five minutes. Remove from heat and skim off foam. Cool for two minutes, then stir in pectin and food coloring. Taste for heat, then add hot pepper sauce. Pour into six sterilized half-pint jars, seal with sterile lids, and cool.

Bob was out back by the railroad tracks, stoking the mesquite fire in his propane-tank barbecue pit, his face as red as the glowing coals under the meat. He stepped back from the fire, pulling off his red bandana headband and using it to wipe the sweat from his face and neck. He hadn't shaved yet, and his cheeks were covered with a reddish stubble.

"Andy Obermann? Yeah, sure, I knew Andy." Bob wadded up his headband, picked up a fork, and began turning slabs of brisket. "Who wants to know?"

"I do," I said. "He was declared dead . . . when?" I knew, but I wondered if Bob did.

"Long time ago," Bob said. "Middle eighties, mebbe. Around the time I got my trailer." Bob lives a couple of miles out of town with Budweiser and a bunch of goats, a renewable resource.

"He'd been missing for seven years, I suppose." That's the common-law standard for presumption of death.

"Thereabouts, I reckon. The ol' ladies said he went to California. Leastwise, that's where he last wrote from." Bob dropped the cover on his barbecue with a loud clang. "Hot as hell out here. Let's cool off. Anyway, I got something I want your opinion on." He headed for the back door of Bean's, and I followed.

Inside, the place was dark and cool. Somebody was rustling around in the kitchen, and I smelled the rich, spicy odor of simmering beans, layered over the stale smells of booze, tobacco smoke, and yesterday's barbecue. Bob disappeared into the kitchen and came out with several slices of meat on a plate.

"Wanna get you to try this," he said. "Tell me what you think."

He pulled a beer from the tap and offered it to me. Lunchtime was still an hour away, so I opted for iced tea. Bob took the beer, and we sat down at a table. I cut off a bite of meat—it was fork-tender—and chewed. It was sweet and spicy-hot at the same time, unusually tasty.

"Hey," I said, "this is good stuff. What is it?"

"It's a leg offa Rosabelle's kid," he said. "I roasted him up with some rosemary, a couple of bay leaves, garlic, and mustard." He gave me a snaggletoothed grin. "And a secret ingredient."

"A secret ingredient, huh?" I sniffed at the goat meat, which I usually don't care for. "Jalepeño?"

He made a face. "Mighta known you'd spot it." He leaned forward and whispered loudly. "Jalapeño-apricot jelly. Sweet and plenty hot. Maria made it. She put extra hot sauce in it, too."

"No foolin'," I said, opening my mouth and fanning with my hand. "You've got my vote, for whatever it's worth."

"Muchas gracias," he said with satisfaction. "Then maybe you'll put a piece about it in the paper, on your cookin' page. Only you can't have the recipe. I want folks to come here to eat it, not go cookin' it up at home." He thought about that for a second. "Guess they won't, though. They ain't got any of Maria's jelly, and good baby goat is hard to come by."

"We'll just keep it a secret," I said. "And I won't mention that I was eating Rosabelle's kid. That might be too up close and personal for some tastes. What are you calling it?"

"Bob's Best Grilled Goat." He beetled his red brows. "Now, what was it you wanted to know about Andy Obermann?"

"He was in the Marines, I understand. First Recon Battalion. Is that where you knew him?"

"Nah." Bob glugged another swallow of beer. "We was both in Recon and both at Chu Lai, but I got there after he'd already got shot up and was back in the States. I ran into him later, here in town. But you know how guys are when they been through the same war. He was a Marine, I was a Marine, we was buddies."

"When was it you ran into him?"

He cocked his head one way, then the other. "Well, lessee. Would've been, oh, maybe '76, '77, somewhere in there. He was hangin' round town here, tryin' to get some bread outta his aunts."

I was surprised. "I thought he inherited the Obermann family fortune. From his father. Isn't that right?"

"Yeah, well, he did, sorta. But he'd already spent all the loose change. The rest was tied up some way or another and the lawyers wouldn't let him at it for another three, four years. He figgered on gettin' his aunts to give him enough to keep him goin' for a while." He paused, regarding me. "Guy had a big-ticket habit."

I guess I wasn't surprised. It happened to a lot of soldiers who came home from the war and spent time in the hospitals. So Andrew Obermann, looking for money, had come to Pecan Springs, bringing his expensive drug addiction with him. What had happened after that?

"Did he have any friends here? Other than his aunts, I mean."

Bob barked a short laugh. "What makes you think his aunts was his friends? Oh, Florence, maybe. She allus made over him, like he was special, but she didn't count. That other one, Jane, she was always on his case about something or other. Booze, dope, women."

"Women?" I asked. "Anybody in particular?"

He squinted at me. "Hell's bells, China. That was twenty years ago. More 'n that. And I only knew him to drink with."

With a meaningful look, I tapped the fork on the empty plate. Tit for tat.

Bob got the message. "Well, there was Lila," he said after a minute. "We all used to hang out at the old Rodeo Roadhouse, out west of town. Place was torn down long 'fore you got here." He shook his head reminiscently. "Man, oh man, it was some joint. Lotta good times, lotta good dope. And more shootin's and stabbin's in that parkin' lot than anywhere else in Adams County."

"Lila Jennings, over at the Diner?" My voice showed my surprise.

"Wudn't Jennings back then. King, her name was." His eyes glinted. "Damn sight younger and prettier than she is now, and a helluva lot more fun." His grin became sly and his eyebrows were suggestive. "Kinda . . . well, easy, I guess is the way you'd say it, though she ain't gonna own up to it now she's been born again. Yeah. Nice 'n' easy."

Meaning that Lila had slept around. Meaning that she and Bob had probably slept together, and that maybe she'd slept with Andrew.

Ooh-la-la, Lila, the secrets you have kept!

I glanced at my watch as I got in the car. I still had better than a half hour before I was due at Ruby's. Plenty of time to stop at the Nueces Street Diner for a cup of coffee.

Some years back, Lila and her husband Ralph (now deceased, a victim of his long-standing two-pack-a-day habit) salvaged an old Missouri and Pacific dining car and had it installed on the square, catty-corner from the bank. They cleaned it up, prettied it up, and furnished it with vintage items from the 1940s and '50s that they picked up at going-out-of-business sales around Texas: red formica-topped tables, chrome chairs with red plastic seats, old soda pop signs, and a Wurlitzer jukebox loaded with scratchy 45s, songs like "Bye Bye Love," "The Purple People Eater," and "The Battle of New Orleans." Lila herself favors '50s' fashions, with a green puckered-nylon uniform, a ruffled white apron, a flirty white cap perched on her pageboy do, and cherry-red lips and nails.

It was just after eleven, so the breakfast crowd had left and the lunch crowd hadn't come in yet. Lila was behind the counter filling plastic catsup and mustard bottles. Her daughter Docia was in the kitchen, banging pans. Lila and Docia are almost always at war. Today, the dispute seemed to be over something Docia had been supposed to do and didn't.

"—Told you three damn times to order thirty pounds of hamburger last week," Lila was saying as I came in.

From the kitchen, I heard Docia roar, "Did not!"

"Did!" Lila yelled. She looked up, saw me, and modulated her voice. "Hello, China."

"Did *not*!" Docia thundered. "You said you was gonna order that meat yerself, and for me not to bother."

Lila put her head through the kitchen pass-through and said, very sweetly, "We got us a customer out here, Docia, dear. Button your lip."

Docia was not cowed. "So fire me, whydoncha?" she bellowed. There was a bellicose clanging, as if she had slung a saucepan into the metal sink, followed by the slam of the kitchen door. The soda-fountain glasses clinked on their glass shelves.

Lila picked up the coffeepot, rolling her eyes. "These modern girls. Don't know what they're comin' to." She poured coffee into a white ceramic mug and slid it across the counter to me. Lila's coffee is legendary. It's like drinking pure adrenaline. "My mother would never of taken that kinda lip from me. She'da backhanded me across the mouth. I swear, I spoil that girl."

Docia is all of thirty-five and hardly qualifies as a girl, but I wasn't going to argue. I sat down on a stool, wondering how to broach my somewhat delicate subject. I put sugar and cream into my coffee and stirred.

"Hey, Lila," I said, "do you remember a guy named Andy Obermann? I happened to be talking to his Aunt Florence the other day, and she mentioned his name, and something about a tragedy. I thought I'd ask you, since you know more about the people around here than anybody else." With Lila, a little flattery goes a long way. "If you don't know about it, probably nobody will."

Lila put a hand on her bosom and sighed dramatically. "Yeah, I knew Andy. Sweet guy, nothin' but a big kid at heart. It was a for-real tragedy."

"What was?"

"Him bein' on drugs an' all. Wasn't his fault, neither. It was what they give him in the hospitals, while they was fixin' him up. Some of them boys got hooked in the vet hospitals. Pain killers, y'know." She paused. "Say, Docia was messin' around in the kitchen yestiddy and she come up with a new pie. Wanna try a piece, tell me what you think?"

I thought of Bob's Grilled Goat, the effects of which lingered in my digestive system a little longer than I might have liked. "Thanks, Lila, but I don't—"

"Aw, come on," Lila wheedled. "Where's your sense of adventure?"

I considered. Lila might be more likely to talk if I was eating. "Sure," I said. Docia's pies, like Lila's coffee, are legendary. "What kind is this one?"

"Apple, with a little somethin' special. You know how Docia is, always wantin' to be different." She took a one-crust pie out of the cabinet behind her and deftly sliced it into eighths.

I sipped my coffee, feeling the rush almost before the hot liquid was down my throat. "I don't suppose Jane was too happy about that situation with Andrew. His being on drugs, I mean."

Lila slid one of the pieces onto a plate. "Boy, you just said a mouthful there. Jane, she was fit to be tied. Raised holy Ned with him, said she wasn't gonna have no addict in the family." She shook a can of whipped topping, squirted a three-inch mound on the pie, and added a maraschino cherry. With a flourish, she put the plate in front of me. "Florence was a real softie, o' course. She knew Andy was hurtin', and she'd slip him money on the sly. Until Jane caught on, that is. Then there was a such a hollerin' fit, you could hear it clear to Dallas."

I forked up a bite of pie. "You heard them arguing?"

"Well, sorta." She gave a little shrug. "See, me and Andy was messin' around in the stable, and when Jane come lookin' for him, he told me to climb up to the loft." She eyed me. "Whaddya think?"

I blinked. "Hoy!"

"Ya like it?" She leaned forward.

"It sure is . . . different. It's got jalapeños in it?"

"Guess I shoulda warned ya, huh? Docia got some jalapeño-apricot jelly from Maria Zapata. She couldn't figure out what to do with it. Thought it might go good in a pie."

Maria's jelly again. What goes around, comes around. I took a gulp of coffee and sloshed it around in my mouth. "Maybe a little less of it next time," I said.

"I'll tell her," Lila said. "Some folks do like it hot, though."

I grinned. "Guess I'd better not ask what you and Andy were doing, messing around in the stable, huh?"

She batted her mascaraed eyelashes at me. "Don't ask, don't tell," she said ambiguously.

I finished the pie and chased it with the rest of my coffee, shaking my head to Lila's offer of a refill. "So Jane was mad at Florence for giving Andy money?"

"Mad as a mean bull at rodeo time." Lila put down the coffeepot. "And pissed off at him for taking it. See, he'd inherited a bunch from his dad and his grandpa. But with his habit, he was goin' through money like it was water and he was a broke faucet. There was more in stocks and bonds and stuff like that, but his dad had fixed it so he couldn't get it for a while. The old girls had plenty, so he figgered he could get them to loan him some. Or he could sell the house."

"Sell the house?" I asked sharply.

"Well, that's what he said, anyway. I never got the straight of it, but somehow or other, seems like it was his. He was thinkin' it would bring in enough to keep him goin' for a while, until . . ." Her voice died away, and she shook her head sadly. "Until he was dead, I reckon. He was skin and bones then. Big tall guy and skinny as a fence post. And crazy. You know how people get when drugs is all they think about. Little bit crazy." She sighed. "A lot crazy, maybe. He was always lookin' to score—not so easy in Pecan Springs, leastwise, back in those days."

"So what happened to him, Lila?"

"Dunno." She shrugged. "One day he was there, and the next, he was just . . . gone, that's all. Florence told me they got a letter from California, but I never heard from him." There was a silence, as Lila scrubbed an imaginary stain on the counter. "People do that, you know. They just up and disappear, and you never hear from them."

The words were matter-of-fact, but there was sadness in them. I wondered how many other people had disappeared from Lila's life. I thought of Andy, too, craving the release that drugs gave him, desperate to ease old pains.

"And when was that?" I asked gently. "When did he disappear?"

She pushed her cherry-red lips out, pulled them back in. "Oh, about this time of year, I guess. October. But I couldn't tell you when." She sighed. "It all blurs together, doncha know? That's been a lotta years ago."

"1976, maybe?"

"Coulda been." She considered. "Yeah, I'd say that's about right, maybe. How'd you know?"

I gave a vague wave of my hand. "As I said, I was talking to Florence. She must've mentioned it." I pushed the plate back. "That's good pie, Lila. You ought to give it a name, though—something that tips people off to what's coming."

She wiped the counter. "How about Hot Apple Pie?"

"I don't think that would quite do it," I said. I reached for my purse. "How much do I owe you?"

"You gonna write up Docia's pie in your column?" Lila understands tit for tat, too.

I grinned. "Well, I might." Maybe what I ought to do was write up Maria Zapata's all-purpose jelly, if I could get her to give me the recipe.

"You put it in your column, pie and coffee're on the house. Lunch, too." She paused. "Say, speakin' of Florence, what'dya know about Jane shootin' Hank? I heard you showed up with the chief right after it happened."

I told her what I had seen, adding the caution that it was

for her ears only. That was pure foolishness on my part, of course, since that story, with embellishments, would walk out with the next customer. But most of it had already been in the newspaper. And it made her feel good to think there was something secret about it.

"Well, my goodness gracious," she said when I had finished. "Andy allus usta say that Jane had a mean streak in her. She hadda figger that Hank was liquored up, or he wouldn't a come bustin' in that way. All she had to do was pick up the phone and call nine-one-one." She pursed her lips. "Somebody said it was legal, too. Shootin' him like that, I mean."

"The law says you can use deadly force to protect yourself," I said, feeling called upon to defend Jane. "He had a butcher knife."

"Mebbe." Lila looked doubtful. "But you know Hank. He never woulda used it. Leastwise, not on them. Why, his dad worked for them for years. Gabe was their driver, their yardman, ran their errands, did ever'thing he could for them. He was good to Andy, too. Tried to help him out best he could." She shook her head, perplexed. "I just dunno why Jane thought she hadda go and shoot Hank, when all she had to do was go up to him and grab that butcher knife outta his hand."

I went back to something she had said a moment before. "You mentioned a mean streak. What was that about?"

"Oh, I dunno. Just that Jane wasn't what you might call a nice person. Allus givin' her sister a hard time. Florence didn't dare look cross at her for fear of makin' her mad. Jane got her meanness from that old dad of hers. All he cared about was the family name. He was real ugly to their mother, Andy said. That bidness about Cynthia jumpin' off the roof—truth is, Andy said, she never jumped, she was pushed. He said Jane did it, but he never would say how he knew, and I wasn't sure I believed him. Guess it was family talk. Maybe something Florence made up." She grinned, showing crooked teeth. "Lotsa skeletons rattlin' around in them Obermann closets, is my guess."

I glanced at the clock and stood. This had taken longer than I expected. "Listen, if I'm going to mention the pie in my column, it's got to have a name. How about 'Docia's Devil-Made-Me-Do-It Apple Pie'?"

In the kitchen, there was a raucous laugh and a loud banging of pots. Docia was back, and from the sound of it, she approved of the name.

Lila nodded. "Okay by me." She paused, wiping her hands on a towel. "Hey. You wanna stay for lunch? We got meatloaf and fried okra."

I shook my head. "I promised I'd go over to Ruby's."

"Ruby won't feed you fried okra," Lila said.

"I know," I said.

Chapter Sixteen

A number of plants are good for your bones. Dark green leafy plants, such as broccoli, kale, bok choy, collards, and turnip greens are high in absorbable calcium. Beans—soy, white, navy, great Northern, black—are also good sources of calcium. Tofu, a cheeselike product made from soybeans, is a valuable source of both calcium *and* plant protein.

China Bayles, "Bone Food"
Home & Garden Page, *Enterprise*

When you first come into Ruby's kitchen, it takes a little while to adjust. Ruby loves bright colors—oranges, yellows, and reds—and she especially likes them in the kitchen, she says, to liven up the monotony of kitchen work. The wallpaper is red-and-white stripes, and there's a watermelon border above the yellow-painted beadboard wainscot. A green lamp hangs over a red table and four green-and-red chairs, and there's a green-and-red watermelon rug under the table. Vintage tea towels hang at the window, and the sills are filled with red and green bottles that glow like rubies and emeralds in the sun.

"Sorry I'm late," I said penitently, as Ruby answered my rap at the kitchen screen door. "I took a couple of detours."

"Not a problem," Ruby said. Barefoot and without makeup, in jeans and a white shirt with the sleeves rolled up, she looked as young and vulnerable as a teenager. A teenager having troubles with her love life. "Sit down. Lunch is just about ready."

Oh, gosh. I sat down at the kitchen table as Ruby went to the stove. She had set the table with watermelon place mats and her favorite green pottery luncheonware. "I have to confess, Ruby. I've just had a plate of Bob Godwin's grilled goat, a piece of Docia's hotsy-dandy apple pie, and a cup of Lila's coffee. It took the edge off."

Ruby turned and gave me a puzzled frown. "But you knew you were coming here for lunch. Why did you—"

"Because I got snookered into it," I said. "I'm ashamed of myself, and I apologize. It was base and contemptible of me. I am a despicable person. Have you gone to a lot of trouble?"

"I made a salad. And I've come up with a new soup recipe for my mother, and I wanted to try it out on you. It's called 'Bone Soup.' "

"Bone soup?" I asked, keeping my tone carefully neutral. "Beef bones? Chicken bones?" Surely not goat bones. And it had better not have Maria's jelly in it.

Ruby laughed. "It doesn't have any bones at all, silly. It's supposed to be good for your bones, which is why I'm giving the recipe to Mom. If we have any extra, I'll give you some to take home." She paused thoughtfully. "Maybe I ought to call it 'Better Bones Soup,' just to be clear. It's made with kale, bok choy, and tofu—and it proves that you don't have to eat dairy to get lots of good calcium in your diet." She picked up the ladle. "You can skip the salad if you want, but how about a cupful of soup?"

Ah, veggie soup. "I can manage that," I said. "I knew I shouldn't be eating all that stuff this morning. But I was on the trail of something, and I guess I got carried away." I suppressed a burp that tasted like Bob's goat.

"On the trail of something?" Ruby ladled soup into a cup.

"Remember the bones Brian found in the cave? I'm wondering if they might belong to Andrew Obermann."

Holding the cup, Ruby turned to stare at me. "Andy Obermann? You're kidding, China!"

I shook my head. "It's only a guess, but it's possible." Possible, heck. I was already convinced. I tried to make the story as concise as I could, starting with Alana Montoya's description of the bones and dental work (I deliberately didn't mention Alana's trip to the hospital, feeling that this was Alana's private affair). Then I reported Max Baumeister's revelation that six foot something Andy had a gold front tooth; the photo I had found in an October 1976 issue of the *Enterprise*; Bob Godwin's remark about Lila and Andy; and finally, Lila's tale about Andy's abortive attempts to borrow money from his aunts and his idea for selling the house.

"And that was the last Lila saw of him," I concluded. "She said that he just . . . disappeared."

While I was talking, Ruby had put the salad and soup on the table. She sat down across from me and helped herself to salad. To be polite, I took a little.

"You know what it sounds like to me?" Ruby said. "Like a drug deal gone sour. Maybe Andy went out to that cave to meet somebody and buy drugs. Something happened and he got shot, instead."

"That's as good a guess as any," I said. The salad was ordinary, but Ruby's soup was tasty enough to make me forget that I'd already had both the meat course and dessert.

"Well, can you come up with anything else?" Ruby asked.

"No," I admitted. "I guess I'll go out to Blackie's office this afternoon and tell him what I've found out. Max Baumeister will be more likely to hunt for those X rays if the sheriff asks him to do it."

"Probably," Ruby said. She frowned. "So long ago. There's probably no way to find the killer."

"Likely not," I agreed. "But Alana mentioned an exit fracture in the skull. If Blackie searches the cave where the skeleton was found, he might locate the slug. And the cartridge case."

"But that wouldn't do any good unless the gun turns up," Ruby said in a practical tone. "And after so many years . . ."

She was right. Identifying the skeleton might bring a measure of peace to Miss Florence, although I doubted that it would matter much to Jane, one way or another. From what Lila had said, it sounded as if Jane wouldn't have been too upset if her nephew got himself wasted in a drug deal, as long as he didn't dishonor the Obermann name. And even if Blackie was lucky enough to find the bullet that had killed Brian's caveman, it wasn't likely that this very cold case would ever be solved.

Ruby was frowning. "You know," she said, "I have the oddest feeling about Florence and Jane. I stopped at the nurses' station yesterday on my way out of the hospital, and Helen Berger checked Florence's chart for me. There wasn't a word about visitors. Why do you suppose—"

There was a tap at the door, a light "Yoo-hoo!" and Amy Roth came in.

"China!" she said brightly. "How nice to see you. Hi, Mom. Don't get up." She went to stand behind Ruby, put her arms around her mother's neck, and gave her a kiss on the cheek.

With her cider-colored curls, her freckles, and that delicate diamond-shaped face, Amy looks like Ruby must have looked twenty years ago—although she's pierced in a few places that Ruby isn't. She is Ruby's eldest, now twenty-six, but with a childlike fragility that makes her seem much younger. She came back into her mom's life a couple of years ago, and into my life, too, with a bang, waltzing into the shop one day and announcing that she had found her long-lost mother: me. It took some effort to convince her that I wasn't the one she was looking for, who turned out to be Ruby. Ruby had given birth to her out of wedlock and was forced by her mother to give the baby up for adoption.

Recently, Amy jolted us with another couple of big-bang declarations. She announced that she was pregnant, and then it turned out that the father was dead—one of the victims of a double murder that unsettled Pecan Springs earlier in the year. We were still dealing with that when Amy declared that she was going to live with her friend and lover, Kate Rodriguez.

If you're thinking that Amy sounds wild, I don't blame you. She's impulsive and sometimes her judgment is questionable—both of which are fairly normal for young women her age. But her relationship with Kate seems to have settled her down, and the two of them obviously care deeply for one another. Kate owns her own accounting business, and Amy has a good job at the Hill Country Animal Clinic, with insurance to cover the baby's birth. She and Kate recently bought a house together, and it looks like they're planning for the long term. The baby, by the way, is a girl, and Ruby is thrilled, in spite of herself. (Ruby's mother and grandmother, of course, are another generation, and another story. They are definitely not thrilled by any of this.)

"Help yourself to soup and salad, Amy," Ruby said, with a wave at the pot on the stove. "There's plenty." To me, she said, "I'm taking Amy for her checkup this afternoon." Amy is seven months along; the baby is due around Christmas.

"How're you feeling?" I asked, as Amy put her soup bowl on the table.

"Great," Amy said. She patted her belly. "And so is Charity. She's getting feisty, too."

"I forgot to tell you," Ruby said, beaming. "Kate and Amy have decided to name the baby Charity. Isn't that a beautiful name?"

"It is," I said, with real feeling. "With a name like that, she's bound to have a good life." Well, maybe. I once defended a woman named Faith, who was charged with arson. Nice names don't always make for nice people, but I was willing to give baby Charity the benefit of the doubt.

"Excuse me, ladies," Amy said, "but I'd better go pee

before I sit down to eat." She shook her head, bemused. "Seems like I'm always running to the bathroom."

"Goes with the territory." Ruby sounded like an expert, which she is, having had two babies. I kept silent, having had none, by design. I'm always thrilled to hear that someone who wants to be pregnant has gotten her wish, but as for me—well, let's just say that I'm glad that my biological clock is winding down. Pretty soon, I won't have to worry about accidents.

When Amy had gone, I sat back in my chair, feeling delinquent. "I haven't asked what's going on with you, Ruby. Your eye looks a lot better." Actually, I thought she looked pale and tired, but maybe it was just because she wasn't wearing her usual Cleopatra the Colorful makeup. "Everything else okay?"

She shrugged. "Ups and downs." A smile ghosted across her mouth. "I was pretty low yesterday, but Colin called this morning and suggested we drive to San Antonio on Sunday and take a walk along the river."

It occurred to me that it would be healthier if Ruby's ups and downs were her *own,* rather than being triggered by somebody else. But the thought of Colin reminded me of Sheila, and that made me think of the scene McQuaid had walked in on Saturday, in Colin's shop, and what McQuaid had said afterward. I'd already made up my mind not to mention Sheila, but that didn't keep me from saying, "McQuaid thinks he might know Colin. Has he mentioned where he's from?"

"No, not really," Ruby said. She leaned on her elbows, her chin in her hand. "He doesn't like to talk about the past. He says he's starting over."

I fiddled with my soup spoon. "Do you know what he did for a living before he started Good Earth Goods?"

Ruby gave me a narrow look. "Colin has a new life, China. He says he wants to leave the old one behind. So I haven't questioned him." Her voice became firm. "Whatever he's done, I don't want to know. I don't even want to guess."

In my experience, when somebody wants to start a new life, it's because there's something in the old one that they'd like to forget. And I couldn't believe that Ruby didn't want to know what it was. Everybody's got unfinished business, and by the time you get to be thirty-five or forty, there's a trainload of it. How could she be in love with someone who doesn't have a past? How could she hope to understand someone who only has a present?

But I kept all this to myself, feeling that my misgivings wouldn't do Ruby any good. Instead, I said, "Well, I'm glad it's working out for you."

"I didn't say that," Ruby said. She looked away. "To tell the truth, China, I'm having a lot of trouble dealing with this. I want Colin—not just physically, I mean, although there's certainly that. I love him, and I want him to love me. I'm ready to make a commitment."

"But he's holding back?" The image of Sheila came into my mind.

She nodded miserably. "It was a lot worse this weekend. He seemed remote, withdrawn. Like I wasn't there." She turned back to me, her eyes dark. "Maybe . . . oh, I don't know. Maybe he's got a case of commitment-phobia. Maybe he'll never be ready for a real relationship. But he's sweet and gentle and caring, and he seems to like being with me. We're good together—in bed, I mean." Restlessly, she got up and began moving around the kitchen. "In fact, that part is great. But the rest of it is making me crazy, China! I try not to show that I'm hurt, or that I feel needy." Her mouth twisted. "But I do. And I *am*!"

I felt helpless. How could I comfort her? Short of being a smart-mouth, there's nothing much you can say to your best friend when she is stuck in a relationship that looks to you like an extreme dead end.

I did the best I could. "Maybe you could cut him—and yourself—a little slack," I said lamely. "Sometimes things don't happen right away."

And sometimes things don't happen at all. Sex—even

good sex—doesn't guarantee love, and love is not a cakewalk. It's not the Holy Grail, either, although of course Ruby had to know that, having been there and done that several times before.

She managed a wan smile. "I keep telling myself to be patient. To focus on what's right about this relationship, and not to mind about what seems . . . not enough. And as you say, maybe I just need to be patient. Maybe things will change." She came back to the table and sat down again. "In the meantime, I'm lighting an empowerment candle and creating a love-and-commitment ritual. It won't hurt to have the universe on my side."

"Good strategy," I said. There was so much else I wanted to say. *You're too good for this jerk, Ruby.* And *Colin Fowler has a past, and ten to one it ain't pretty.* And *Lighten up a little, babe.* And *I love you, Ruby.*

I cleared my throat. What came out was, "How about letting Amy go to the doctor by herself? You could go with me to talk to Blackie about Andy Obermann and the bones in the cave." True, identifying those old bones was hardly an urgent matter. But an afternoon of playing Nancy Drew might give Ruby a different perspective on life.

"I guess not," Ruby said, sounding more cheerful. "After we get out of the doctor's office, I'm taking Amy shopping. Maybe that will make me feel better."

"Undoubtedly," I said. I was at the end of the line when they handed out shopping genes, but I've seen the magical effect shopping has on Ruby. In the mall, she satisfies her romantic fantasies ("I'll have a double choco mocha latte or, with a sprinkle of cinnamon and extra whipped cream."); allows herself to be waited on ("I'll try the other two blouses now, and would you mind taking this skirt back and bringing me a size ten?"); and indulges in the dream of having it all, or most of it ("I'll take the red silk panties *and* that lacy cream-colored nightgown.")—all of which were denied to her in this relationship. Here at home, in her kitchen, Ruby was the Rejected Lover who could never get enough of her heart's desires. In the mall, she is the Material Girl herself, She Who Will Not Be Denied. Maybe she would bring a little of that shopping spirit home with her. And that, considering the way she was capitulating to Colin Fowler, would be a very good deal.

Amy came back into the room, and I changed the subject. "What kind of a proposal do you suppose Cassandra has cooked up, Ruby?"

"I don't know, but whatever it is, I'm looking forward to hearing it. Janet says she can't work at the Snyders' party on Saturday afternoon."

"But she promised!" I exclaimed heatedly. "Really, Ruby, I know that her knees are bothering her, but sometimes I think that's just an excuse. Anyway, we've got to look out for ourselves and the business. Like it or not, we're going to have to do something about Janet!"

"I can help with the party, Mom," Amy offered. "To be honest, I need the money. I have to start thinking about buying some baby things."

"Thanks, sweets," Ruby said. "I accept. But I'm going to ask Cassandra if she can help, too. It's a big party—fifty or so."

I looked at Ruby. "All I know about Cass is that she volunteers at the theater, she works in the food service at CTSU, and she does astrology. What else do you know?"

Ruby looked thoughtful. "She's from the West Coast, Washington or Oregon, I think. She worked at Yellowstone National Park, in the lodge. She's held other cooking positions, too, but I'm not sure where. She's been married, but her husband was killed—a hiking accident, I think she said. Something like that, anyway. She doesn't have any children." She paused, eyeing me. "Do you like her? I mean, would you like to work with her?"

"I guess," I said. "I'd be willing to give it a try."

We looked at one another in silence for a moment. At last, Ruby said, "I want to help Janet as much as we can, but it feels like it might be time for a change. Let's see what Cass has in mind."

Amy finished her soup and pointed at the clock. "Speaking of time, we'd better go, Mom. The appointment's at one-fifteen."

Ruby stood up. "I'll get you some of that soup to take home," she said. She filled a plastic container with it and handed it to me. "You can put this in the freezer. It'll be even better the second time around. McQuaid might like it, too."

"Not with bok choy and tofu, he won't. Have a good time shopping."

"Right," she said cheerfully. "See you at four-thirty. Maybe Cass will help us solve the Janet problem."

I sighed. Sometimes I think we're trying to do too much. Whatever happened to the simple life?

THE new county jail complex, which includes the sheriff's office, is on the far west side of town, a mile past the high school. It isn't nearly as nostalgic as the old sheriff's office, which was in a building constructed around the turn of the century, with wood floors, dark oak paneling, and ceiling-high windows with stained-glass panels. Somehow, it had an old-fashioned dignity that made you feel that law enforcement, and all that it stood for, was a valued part of the community's life. It deserved to be at the very center, admired and respected by everyone.

The new sheriff's office, in contrast, stands at the margins of the community, and—like the department—has adopted a rather low-profile stance. The building has a great deal of strength and fortitude, but I wouldn't characterize it as dignified. It's a windowless concrete bunker, which has (as Hank remarked in an ironic editorial in the *Enterprise*) about as much personality as a tornado shelter. On the inside, the tiled hallways and white-painted rooms remind me of a hospital, and the thermostat is always set low enough to make me wish I'd worn a sweater. Or maybe the place would make me feel chilly even if somebody nudged the indoor temperature to eighty.

Blackie's office isn't very hospitable, either. There's a gray metal desk, a computer on a metal trolley next to the desk, a row of bookshelves that mostly contains computer printouts, a couple of thinly padded chairs, a fluorescent ceiling fixture that makes people look like corpses, and a stiff plastic philodendron in the corner. I noticed that the photograph of Sheila that used to sit on Blackie's desk was gone, in its place was an untidy stack of manilla folders on which lay a pair of metal handcuffs. There was a metaphor in there somewhere, if I knew where to look.

Blackie glanced up from the computer screen and a welcoming smile crossed his square face.

"Hey, China," he said, and pushed himself out of his chair. He stuck out his hand. "What brings you here?"

We shook. "Oh, one or two items." I paused. "Heard anything from Alana today?"

His mouth tightened, and he shook his head. "Don't reckon I will," he said. It sounded like whatever might have been growing between them was already dead. Blackie is not the kind of man who can imagine building a relationship with a woman who has lied about herself.

I sat down. "She told me she turned in her forensic report on the bones in the cave," I said. "That's what I came to talk about. It's complicated—you might want to take notes."

I repeated for him the same story I had given Ruby, taking a distinct pleasure in the surprise that chased across his face as he jotted items on a notepad. It's hard to impress Blackie, and when I do, I'm pleased.

He put down his pencil, and his chair squeaked as he leaned back. "Good job, China," he said approvingly. "You got any problem with me talking to these people?" He looked down at his notes. "Baumeister, Godwin, Jennings."

"No problem," I said. "I don't think any of them are leaving town."

"Yeah, well, I'm not in a tearing hurry." He grinned bleakly. "Those bones laid in that cave for thirty years, give or take a few. I guess they can wait a little longer." He nodded at the computer screen. "I've got a couple of situations that are a heck of a lot more urgent."

I nodded. "When you do get around to doing the interviews, you might want to start with Max Baumeister. If he can locate those X rays, that should cinch the identification. And you could add Florence Obermann to your list. According to Lila Jennings, she was very fond of her nephew. She gave him money to—" I stopped, frowning at the look on his face. "What's wrong?"

"I guess you haven't heard," he said. "The old lady died this morning."

I stared wordlessly at him, at first shocked and saddened, then puzzled. "But she seemed well enough yesterday," I managed finally, "under the circumstances, I mean. What was it?"

"Heart failure, I understand. Thelma Watkins, who works in Traffic, was at the hospital this morning, visiting her mother in the room across the hall. I heard Thelma telling Gina Mae about it in the cafeteria." He shook his head. "Used to be, we'd close the office and go to the Diner for lunch, or Krautz's. Now, we're so far out of town that nobody wants to drive back in just for a meal. We're stuck with the cafeteria, or we bring our own."

I pressed my lips together. Heart failure. Maybe I could get the details from Helen Berger. "That's too bad," I said. "Florence was a nice old lady— totally intimidated by her sister, but I liked her. I'm afraid she's the second victim of that shooting on Friday night."

"Hank Dixon, you mean," Blackie said. He frowned, clasping his hands behind his head. "Yeah, that was a weird one. I knew Hank. Breaking and entering with a butcher knife is the last thing I would've expected from that guy. But people do crazy things. Things you can't explain." He sighed, and I wondered if he was thinking of Alana.

"Well, that's it for me," I said, getting out of my chair. Ruby was going to be upset to hear about Florence. I wondered how Jane was taking it.

Blackie stood, too. "You've been very helpful," he said. He glanced down at the notes he had taken. "You spent some time on this, didn't you?"

I thought back to the beginning of the day. "Most of the morning. One thing just sort of led to another, I guess." I paused. "Just out of curiosity, Blackie—how thoroughly did you search that cave?"

"Not thoroughly enough," he said. "We collected the items we found with the corpse, but that's about it. When I get some time, I'll take somebody out there and see if we can turn up either the slug or the cartridge case. I don't like loose ends, even in cold cases." He paused, considering. "Maybe especially in cold cases. You never know where something's going to lead."

"If you can't spare one of your deputies to go with you," I said, "I'm sure Brian would be glad to give you a hand. He probably knows as much about that cave as anybody. He thinks he has exclusive rights to it."

"I'll keep that in mind," Blackie said seriously. "Have a good afternoon." He glanced back down at his notes. "And if you happen to stumble over any more of this stuff, you'll let me know, won't you?"

"Oh, absolutely," I said.

Chapter Seventeen

Every American schoolchild learns that the Pilgrims' ship was the *Mayflower*. But few, if any, know that the name refers to hawthorn, a tree known for centuries as a heart tonic and today widely used in Europe as a treatment for heart disease.

Michael Castleman
The Healing Herbs

Hawthorn berries constitute one of the valuable remedies for the cardiovascular system, strengthening the force of the contraction of the heart muscle while also acting to dilate the vessels of the coronary circulation. They can be used in most circulatory problems as they are amphteric (i.e., they will relax or stimulate the heart according to its need).

David Hoffman
The Holistic Herbal

I went back to the shop, phoned the Adams County Hospital, and asked to speak to Helen Berger. When she came on the line, however, her tone was guarded and coolly professional.

"Yes, Miss Obermann passed away this morning." From

the sound of her voice, I knew that someone was with her. There was a pause, and then she continued: "Oh, yes—about your presentation to the Herb Guild next month. I'll call you at home tonight to discuss it, shall I?"

I put down the phone and picked up the list of chores I'd planned for the morning, thinking that Helen didn't need to discuss my presentation and wondering what she did want to talk about. Florence Obermann, probably. I thought again about the old lady. She had seemed childlike and sweet-natured, like her mother, perhaps—and yesterday, at least, had seemed reasonably well. I hoped that death had come quickly, without pain, and wondered what Jane would do without her sister to give orders to.

I thought, too, about Andy Obermann. If his was the skeleton in the cave, the identification answered one question. But it raised another, surely. Who had killed him, and why? Ruby's speculation that it was a drug deal gone sour seemed like the best explanation. A drug dealer—somebody local, probably, somebody who knew about the cave—had agreed to meet him there. There'd been an argument, or maybe a simple robbery, and Andy had been shot.

But I had already given more hours than I could spare to the mystery of Brian's caveman. I put it out of my mind and spent the afternoon getting caught up on the things I'd meant to do that morning. By the time I finished my list, it was nearly four-thirty, and there was no time to tackle the afternoon chores. Oh, well. The good thing about working for yourself is that you can always put things off. The bad thing about working for yourself is that you *always* put things off.

At four-twenty-five, Ruby came breezing in, carrying several sacks and looking happily empowered.

"Ah," I said. "The Queen of the Mall. What'd you buy?"

She began pulling items out of the sacks. "You won't believe, China. I got this blue batik top, blue-and-green pants, green sandals, blue beads—"

"It's the underwater look. The latest fashion fad."

Ruby took this seriously. "I hadn't thought of that," she said, fingering the silky batik fabric. "I have some mermaid earrings at home. They'll be perfect!"

I grinned, then sobered. There was no easy way to break the news. "Ruby, I'm sorry to have to tell you this, but Florence Obermann is dead. She died this morning."

Ruby dropped the sack, her eyes widening. "She . . . died?"

"Of a heart attack, Blackie said."

"I don't believe it," Ruby said flatly. "She was . . . she was so lively yesterday!"

"But her sister said she had a bad heart. And even lively people die of heart attacks. You can be walking across the street and—"

But Ruby wasn't listening. Her eyes had the faraway, unfocused look she gets when she's listening to her Inner Guide. "There's something wrong about this, China. I know it."

"I'm sure you must be surprised," I said, in a comforting tone. "You really liked Florence, didn't you?"

"But I'm not surprised," she said, looking at me. "That's just it, China. Yesterday, when we were in the hospital, I sensed something. Something wrong, I mean. Between—"

But whatever Ruby was about to tell me was interrupted by a rap on the door. I opened it to Cassandra.

"Hi," she said. She gestured to the CLOSED sign. "I didn't realize today was your day off."

"We don't get days off," I said ruefully. I glanced at Ruby, who was still standing there as if she were frozen, gazing off into space with a trancelike look.

"Ruby," I said. "Cass's here."

"Hi, Ruby," Cassandra said.

When Ruby didn't move, I put my hand on her shoulder. "Cass's here, Ruby," I said, in a louder voice.

Ruby came back to life with a start. She blinked and

shook her head. "Oh. Sorry. I was thinking about Florence. I didn't hear you come in, Cass."

Cassandra looked from one of us to the other, frowning a little. "Have I come at a bad time?"

"Ruby and I were talking about Florence Obermann," I said. "She died this morning, of a heart attack."

"Oh, gosh," Cassandra said, with a distressed look. "That's too bad. She never said much, and she was always in the shadow of that sister of hers. But I liked her."

"We all did," I said. "Let's go in the tearoom and sit down, so we can talk around a table."

Five minutes later, we were seated in the tearoom with glasses of iced tea and a plate of lavender cookies. The light fell across our table, and I noticed that Ruby still looked sad and distracted.

Cassandra, on the other hand, was brimming with her characteristic energy and cheerfulness. She was wearing a beige linen jacket with a shawl collar and matching linen pants, a red shell and multicolored African beads, and managed to look both businesslike and smartly casual at the same time. When she began to talk, her words were charged with concentrated energy. In a few short moments, she summed up what she had come to discuss.

After giving the matter a great deal of thought, she had decided to leave her food service management position at CTSU. She had some money she wanted to invest in a business, and she admired what Ruby and I were doing. Ruby had mentioned that Janet wanted to work part-time, and she thought there might be an opportunity for her. She proposed buying in as a working partner in the tearoom and catering businesses.

What's more, she had an idea for a new companion enterprise that would be called the Thymely Gourmet. "You can see how it fits with Party Thyme Catering," she added. As a personal chef, she would go into people's homes and cook healthy gourmet dinners, personally designed for the client's tastes and dietary needs. She would package the meals and leave them in the freezer for later consumption. She would—

"Hang on a minute," I said, raising my hand. "The personal chef business seems like a great idea, Cass. It's something you could easily do on your own. Why do you want to buy into the tearoom and the catering, as well?"

"Because, starting from scratch, it will take at least a year to build the personal chef business to the point where it's a break-even proposition," she replied. "But you already have a client list for your catering—which would also be a strong target market for personal culinary services." She tilted her head, frowning slightly. "But also because I like to cook for people—cook creatively, I mean." She grinned and spread her hands. "And then there's you."

Ruby glanced at me. "Us?"

Cassandra nodded. "Well, sure. That's a big part of it, maybe the most important thing. I admire you, both of you. You're smart and you're focused. You're working for yourselves, which is something I've always wanted to do. You're living your dream. And you always seem to have so much fun together—for you, work is more like play."

"Well, it might look like that," I pointed out, being realistic. "But it doesn't always feel like play. Mostly, it feels like work—good work, but work just the same. And it doesn't pay as much as . . . well, lawyering, for instance. Or managing an institutional food service."

"Oh, I know," she said. "But it does look like fun, at least from the outside. And money . . . well, let's just say that it isn't a big issue with me right now." Her voice took on a wistful note. "I've been thinking about this for a long time, and I know I would enjoy working with you. If three wouldn't be a crowd, that is."

Ruby smiled at her. "I don't think that's an issue," she said. "In some ways, having a third person—a third committed person, I mean—would be a big help. But she would have to be the right person."

"Forgive me for saying so," Cassandra said, "but I think

I'm the right person." She hesitated. "Maybe I sound like a pushy broad—that's what my husband used to say, anyway. But I believe in being up-front about what I want."

I studied her. I'm cautious by nature, and I wasn't sure about taking Cassandra on as a partner. That's a pretty big step—every bit as big a step as getting married. And in some ways, it's easier to get a divorce than it is to get out of a partnership that isn't working.

"I don't know how Ruby feels about it," I said guardedly, "but I think I'd want us to work together for a while before we jumped into something as major as a partnership. Maybe we could come up with some sort of trial arrangement that would give us a chance to see what kind of a team we'd make. That way, we can keep all our options open."

Ruby leaned forward. "Would you be available for cooking in the tearoom when Janet's not here, Cass? We could work it out so that you'd have some days free to develop the personal chef business."

"Of course," Cassandra said promptly. She reached for her briefcase, opened it, and took out two manila folders. "I've put together some materials for you to review. My résumé is here, and a business proposal detailing my ideas for the Thymely Gourmet and for participating as a partner. You'll also find my investment proposal in the package. But if you're more comfortable taking me on as an employee or a contract person, I'm certainly willing to discuss that option."

"Spoken like a true negotiator," I said with a laugh. I had to admire her style. Be clear about what you want, but be willing to dicker over the details.

Cassandra pushed back her chair. "I'm sure you'll have plenty of questions. I do, too, actually. Maybe you could read what I've given you, and we can get together again."

"Sounds like a plan," Ruby said. She seemed more cheerful, as if Cassandra's enthusiasm had lifted her spirits. I felt better, too, knowing that we had an alternative to

Janet. We agreed to another meeting, and Cassandra said good-bye and went on her way.

"My goodness," I said, feeling a little stunned. "Talk about perfect timing. If Janet's knees give out completely, Cassandra might just be the answer." I frowned. "But I don't know about a partnership. That seems like a big step, especially when we don't know her very well."

"How about if we sit down together and read her stuff and talk it over," Ruby suggested.

"How about tonight, then? McQuaid's teaching, and he won't be home until late. You could have supper with Brian and me." I grinned. "Lacking a personal chef, we're having pizza."

"How about if I come over after supper?" Ruby asked. "I've got some errands to do. I meant to take care of them this afternoon, but I figured that shopping should come first."

"There's no arguing with that," I said.

ON the way home, I stopped at Gino's Italian Pizza Kitchen and got a pizza large enough to feed Brian and me, and then went to Jake's house to pick up Brian. The sky was gloomy, and the line of low, dark clouds in the northwest seemed to promise another storm.

"Hey, pizza!" Brian said happily, as he jumped into the car. He'd eat it every night of the week, of course, if we'd let him. But he had other things on his mind.

"Did I tell you about the Halloween dance Friday night?" he went on. "Jake and I need a ride, and her folks are going to a party. I said you'd be glad to take us." He gave me an earnest look. "You will, won't you?"

"I'm sure we can manage," I said, which to my mind committed McQuaid equally. "Especially if you'll guarantee to mow the grass on Saturday morning." More Mom-speak.

I didn't mention the lizard until after we got home. Then I went to the freezer, took it out, and put the frozen corpse on the table. "I found this little guy in my bathroom Friday night," I said. "He was dead."

Howard Cosell padded into the kitchen to ask about the progress of his dinner. He saw the lizard on the table, and his melancholy expression became even more melancholy than usual.

Brian picked up the lizard and looked at him sadly. "Aw," he said. "Too bad. Leopold was a good lizard."

"He might not have died if he'd stayed where he belonged, in his terrarium," I remarked, as I got out the dog food and put it in a bowl.

Brian considered this. "Well, I don't know. Leopold was a pretty old lizard. I've had him since . . ." He thought. "Since sixth grade. And he could have been a couple of years old when I got him. He probably died of old age."

"How do you know it's Leopold?" I asked. I put Howard's dinner on the floor and got out the cling wrap that we usually use as a shroud on such occasions. Brian and I have buried more frogs and snakes and lizards than I care to count.

"From his foot," he said, holding Leopold up. "See? One of his toes is gone. Leonard and Lewis have all their toes, and Lewis has an extra one. So this has got to be Leopold." He sighed as he wrapped Leopold in his shroud. "Guess we better have a funeral after supper, huh?"

Howard was sitting on his haunches, ignoring his dog food and casting meaningful looks in the direction of the pizza. "Absolutely not, Howard," I said sternly. "Don't forget those four pounds."

Howard heaved a resigned sigh, arranged his long ears on either side of his dish, and inhaled his dog food.

With Leopold's funeral arrangements under control, Brian and I ate our pizza and talked. He'd been away for the weekend, and I wanted to hear about his camping trip. He told me about his various adventures; he'd seen the tracks of a mountain lion, had gone swimming in the Frio River, and had slept out under the stars and listened to the coyotes singing to the full moon. The sorts of things that a Texas boy ought to be doing.

When he was finished, I told him, as matter-of-factly as I could, about Alana Montoya's conclusion that his caveman had been the victim of a shooting. I wanted him to hear it from me, rather than pick it up from someone else. I didn't, however, tell him that the skeleton might have been identified. That was still speculative and couldn't be confirmed until Max Baumeister came up with those X rays.

"He was shot!" Brian's eyes got big, and he puffed out his cheeks. "Wow! Gosh, Mom, I never expected *that*!"

"I know," I said mildly. "It's kind of a surprise."

Brian thought about this for a minute. "Next time we're up at the cave, I'll ask Doctor Montoya if I can go to her office and see the bullet hole in the skull."

"Sure," I said, helping myself to another piece of pizza. It wasn't likely that Alana would be going back to the cave. She would either submit her resignation or be fired, and somebody else would take over the dig. But I'd leave it to McQuaid to tell Brian about Alana's situation at the university. After all, he was the one who had confirmed the résumé fraud. I thought fleetingly of Alana and hoped that she would be all right. Going back to Mexico was probably a good idea. She might even be able to find work there, under circumstances where knowledge and experience counted for more than credentials.

Brian wore a troubled look. "Do you know," he said after a minute, "whether the bullet was still in the . . . the skull?"

"It wasn't," I said. "Doctor Montoya identified the exit fracture. Which means," I added, "that if the man was shot where you found him, the slug and the cartridge case ought to be there somewhere. Sheriff Blackwell said he'd try to get out to the cave to look for it."

I expected Brian to clamor to go with the sheriff, but he said nothing, just ate the last of his pizza reflectively, his eyes on the enshrouded lizard that occupied a place of honor beside the pizza.

We held the funeral after dinner. Howard offered to be the pallbearer and carry Leopold in his mouth, but Brian and I agreed that this was not a good idea. We buried Leopold beneath a rosemary bush. Brian always likes to say a few words of farewell over the departed. Myself, I don't mourn much, since my relationship with these creatures is usually an adversarial one. But I respect Brian's feelings, so I bowed my head while he said softly, "Goodbye, Leopold. You were a good lizard. I'm glad you lived long enough to get old. I hope you enjoyed your life."

We had just finished putting a very large rock over Leopold to keep Howard from paying his last respects, when Brian said, "I've got something to give you, Mom." He reached into his pocket, pulled something out, and put it into my hand. An empty brass cartridge casing.

"What's this?" I asked, turning it over in my fingers.

"It's a bullet."

"Let me rephrase the question," I said. "Where did you get this cartridge casing? And why are you giving it to me?"

In the distance, thunder rumbled. The line of low clouds in the north had risen, mushrooming into a gray-blue mass. The promised storm would be here before long.

"Well . . ." Brian looked sheepish. "I found it in the cave. Not far from where I found the skeleton."

"Oh, my gosh, Brian," I said. "The cave is a crime scene. Why didn't you give the casing to the sheriff?"

"It wasn't a crime scene when I found the bones," Brian said defensively. "And I didn't know that the guy had been shot until you told me just now." He looked down and scuffed the ground with the toe of his sneaker. "At first I thought he died when the rock fell on him. Then I thought that somebody bashed him in the head. I never figured that the bullet was . . ." He glanced at me unhappily. "I hope Dad and the sheriff aren't going to be too mad at me." He bit his lip. Being the son of an ex-cop, he knows what his father is likely to say about something like this.

I composed my face in a stern look and put on my lawyer's voice. "Removing evidence from a crime scene . . ."

"But I didn't mean to," he said desperately. "Really, I didn't!"

I saw the look on his face and relented. "I think it'll be okay," I said, putting my hand on his shoulder. "The shooting happened a long time ago, and this is a cold case. The fact that you've had the casing probably won't make any difference in the way the investigation is handled."

There was a flash of lightning and a loud clap of thunder. Brian gave me a grateful look, cast a good-bye glance at Leopold's grave, and we went into the house.

I sent Brian upstairs to do his homework under the watchful eye of Howard Cosell and went into the kitchen, where I turned the kettle on to make myself a cup of tea. Ruby had promised to stop by after supper, and she'd be here any minute.

While I was waiting, I examined the casing. Turning it up and looking at the base, I could make out the letters *USCC* and a number, *18*. Greek to me, but Blackie would be able to decipher it. I put the casing into a plastic bag with a zipper top and stuck it in my purse. I'd drop it off at the sheriff's office on my way to the shop in the morning.

Ruby arrived about ten minutes later, just as darkness fell and the rain began to come down hard. "Whew," she said, shaking herself like a damp puppy. "It's wet out there!"

"Looks like you're dressed for it," I said, as Ruby peeled out of her raincoat. She was wearing the blue batik top, blue-and-green print pants, green sandals, and the blue beads she'd gotten at the mall that afternoon, plus her mermaid earrings. "The underwater look."

Ruby made a graceful pirouette. "Lovely, isn't it? And such a bargain!"

Bargains are always good for Ruby's morale. "You look like a mermaid," I said, "or a strand of kelp. Want some tea? The kettle's hot."

"Lovely," Ruby replied, and sat down at the kitchen table, arranging the blue drapery around her. She took Cassandra's folder out of her bag and put it on the table. "Have you had a chance to look over Cass's proposal yet?"

I shook my head, filling the large tea ball and dropping it into the teapot. Might as well make several cups while I was at it. "I was guest of honor at a lizard funeral. Leopold died."

Ruby chuckled at that. She's aware of Brian's creature passions. "I haven't read it, either," she said. "We can do it together."

Which we did, for, oh, maybe five minutes, while the rain pelted the windows. And then there was a sudden glare of blue-white lightning and a thunderous crash so close that it rattled the windows. The lights flickered like windblown candles, came back on, and then went out, decisively. The kitchen was plunged into darkness as rain hammered against the windows and wind howled in the trees. Somewhere nearby, there was a splintery crack, the sound of a tree breaking and going down. We don't lose our power very often, but I had the feeling that it might be a while before the Pedernales Electric Coop got the lights back on.

From upstairs, Brian called reassuringly, "Don't worry, Mom. I can still do my homework. I've got a flashlight."

"Resourceful kid," Ruby said.

"Yeah," I said. "He's on his good behavior right now." I went to the cupboard, took out the matches, and lit two fat cinnamon candles. I took them to the table and sat down. "Well, what do you think about Cassandra's idea, Ruby? Seems to me—"

But that was as far as I got. I was interrupted by the shrill ringing of the phone on the wall. Ruby pushed her chair back.

"While you get that," she said, picking up one of the candles, "I'm going to visit the little girl's room."

Ack. "Don't flush unless you have to," I said. "With the electricity off, the pump won't work. There's only one flush left in each toilet, and we should probably save it for an emergency."

"Gotcha," Ruby said cheerfully.

The caller was Helen Berger. "I suppose you know that I couldn't talk when you phoned this afternoon," she said. "There were other people at the nurses' station."

"That's what I thought," I said. "Thanks for calling back."

"You were . . . you were asking about Miss Obermann," Helen said hesitantly.

"That's right. I heard Florence died of a heart attack. I wondered whether you had any details."

"A few." Helen's tone was guarded. "In the night, she began suffering severe abdominal pain, nausea, and vomiting. I came on the floor at eight, just after she began to experience cardiac dysrhythmia and hypotension—low blood pressure. She went into cardiac shock and died at nine-thirty."

"I . . . see," I said, frowning. "Was this . . . was the attack something that might have been expected, given her heart condition?"

"Heart condition?"

"Her sister mentioned several times that Florence had a bad heart."

"That's odd." Helen sounded puzzled. "Doctor Mackey—Miss Obermann's personal physician didn't note that in the chart, or point it out to any of the nursing staff. She and I went back over the medications together this morning, thinking that the attack might have been caused by an allergic reaction to one of the drugs. She didn't say anything about a heart condition then, either."

I had a sudden feeling of urgency. "Has an autopsy been ordered?"

A pause. "Yes."

Yes. There was a world of meaning in that single word. If the attending physician had been certain that Florence Obermann had died of natural causes, she would have signed the death certificate, the local justice of the peace would have countersigned, and Florence Obermann's body would have been released to her sister. The fact that an autopsy had been ordered—

"Helen," I said, "what's your feeling about this situation?"

Another pause. When Helen finally answered, her voice was uneasy. "I wish you wouldn't ask me that, China. I'm sure you appreciate my professional position." She cleared her throat. "The autopsy report will be ready in a few days. I doubt that my feelings will have any material affect on its outcome. I just wanted you to know because . . ."

The silence stretched out.

"You wanted me to know," I said quietly, "because you didn't feel comfortable keeping this knowledge to yourself."

She sighed heavily. "I guess that's it. You and Ruby sent flowers and visited. In fact, you were the only visitors that poor woman had—except for her sister, of course." She hesitated, as if she were searching for the right words. "It's the way . . . the way she died, China. There's something—" She swallowed audibly. "I don't know. I'll have to think about this some more, I guess."

I paused, reading between the lines and guessing at what she didn't feel able to say. "What kind of toxicology tests are routinely done at autopsy, Helen?"

"Oh, gosh, I . . . I wouldn't know," Helen said, sounding uncharacteristically flustered. "That's out of my area, I'm afraid."

"Did Doctor Mackey order any special tests?"

"I don't know that, either. I couldn't really ask, you know," she added hesitantly. "That sort of thing is the doctor's business entirely. And while Doctor Mackey is very nice, I don't think she'd like it if I butted in. It wouldn't be . . . professional, you know."

I thought back over what she had said. Nausea, abdominal pain, cardiac dysrhythmia, hypotension—

"Helen, do you remember the program you gave last year on plant poisons?"

Helen sighed. "I was thinking of that, actually. But I hate to suggest that—" She stopped. I imagined her with the phone in her hand, her pleasant face screwed into a worried frown, her lower lip caught between her teeth. "You know what I mean," she said at last. "I could be fired for something like this."

"I know there's a risk. But you have to share your suspicious, Helen. If the autopsy is treated as routine, it might not include testing by a forensic toxicologist—at least, not the kind of tests that would be necessary to identify plant poisons. You know this stuff better than many toxicologists, I'll bet. If you could suggest specific possibilities—"

"I suppose I could make a list," Helen said doubtfully. "But then what? I really don't think I should be the one to . . ." Her voice trailed away.

I paused. I don't usually step back into my lawyer mode, but this was one occasion where it seemed like a good idea. "If you'll give me a list of the plant materials that might have caused this kind of reaction, I'll talk to Doctor Mackey, first thing in the morning. That will keep you out of it." I was momentarily glad that I had just renewed my bar membership. At least I wouldn't be lying when I told the doctor that I was a lawyer—not that it would explain my nosiness. I'd have to think of another explanation.

"Oh, China, would you?" Helen sounded vastly relieved. "I have all my research materials here. I'll go through the list of possibilities right now. Do you have a fax machine? I could fax it to you."

"Sure," I said, and gave her the number. "I don't think the fax machines will work until the power is back on, though," I added.

"Oh, right." Helen gave a little laugh. "I forgot all about

the power. Thank heaven the phone isn't out, too. I guess the phone company must have backup generators, like the hospital's." I was hanging up the phone when Ruby came back into the kitchen.

"That was Helen Berger," I said. "She's the charge nurse at the hospital. She was calling about Florence Obermann."

"Oh?" Ruby put her candle on the table and sat down. "I've been thinking about that ever since you told me, China, and I'm more and more certain that there's something wrong. What did she say?"

"She said that Doctor Mackey ordered an—" The rest of my sentence response was lost in a loud thunderclap, and when the sound had died away, I became aware of a repeated rapping at the front door.

"Is that somebody knocking?" I asked, startled. I hadn't heard anybody drive in, but that wasn't a surprise, with the rain pouring down.

"Sure sounds like it," Ruby said. "Are you expecting anybody?"

"Not that I know of," I said. I picked up the candle and carried it down the hall to the front door, Ruby tagging along behind. I opened it, on the chain, and held up the candle. The flickering yellow light fell on the face of a young man standing on the porch, his shoulders huddled against the rain.

I unhooked the chain and stepped back. "Juan!" I exclaimed. "Juan Gomez! Come in, please—it's wet out there."

Chapter Eighteen

THE SYMBOLISM OF HERBS AND FLOWERS

Falsehood: *Deadly nightshade*. The fruit of which produces poison and death, and cannot be pointed out too soon to the innocent and unwary, that they may be prevented from gathering it.

Entrapment: *White catchfly*. This white flower may be found in almost every sandy field in June; and many a poor fly that is attracted to it by its odour, finds death amid its entangling leaves.

Treachery: *Sweet Bay*.

Bitter truth: *Savory*.

Greed: *Primrose*.

Thomas Miller
***The Poetical Language of Flowers*, 1847**

"Hello, Ms. Bayles," Juan said. He nodded at Ruby. "Ms. Wilcox. I'm sorry to barge in like this, but I need to . . . to talk to Professor McQuaid."

Professor McQuaid? Of course—Juan had been McQuaid's student in the spring semester. The young man—he was hardly more than a boy, I thought, just a few years older than Brian—was drenched and shivering uncontrollably, his thin cotton shirt and jeans soaked through.

"He won't be back for another couple of hours, Juan," I said, noticing that Ruby's and mine were the only cars in the drive. "But I'm not letting you go back out into this weather. Come in and get dried off."

"Thanks," he said, sounding discouraged. "I don't want to—"

"Nonsense," I said firmly. I took the boy upstairs and found a sweatshirt and a pair of sweatpants for him, far too large, but dry, and gave him a towel for his hair. By the time we were back in the kitchen, Ruby was pouring a mug of hot tea.

"How'd you get out here?" I asked, as Juan sat down at the table and wrapped his hands around the mug, still shivering. "I didn't see a vehicle in the drive."

"I hitched a ride part of the way," he said, "and walked the rest." His dark hair was damply plastered on his head, and his voice was weary.

"If you'd called," I said, sitting down across from him, "I'd have come and picked you up."

"I . . . didn't want to call," Juan said. His voice was tense, and his mouth worked nervously. He darted a glance at Ruby. "I don't want anybody to know where I . . . where I'm staying."

"That's okay, Juan," Ruby said in a comforting voice. "I'm trustworthy. Don't you remember all those cookies I fed you?"

He smiled crookedly at that, and I said, "Whatever the reason you wanted to see my husband and me, it must be important. To bring you all the way out here in this awful weather, I mean." I paused, studying his face. "You know that Hank is dead?" I asked gently.

Juan's nod was barely perceptible, his expression miserable. In the candlelight, his eyes, bright with unshed tears, were the color of caramel. "I saw you when you came to the house Friday night. With the lady policeman. Afterward, I figured out that you came to tell me that he . . . that Hank had got shot."

"So you were in the house." That explained the light I had seen upstairs.

"*Sí*. But I didn't know why you were there. I thought—" He glanced once again at Ruby, and then decided to trust her. "I'm illegal, you know."

"Your immigration status?" I asked in surprise. Then I got it. "You were on a student visa?"

"*Sí*. I . . . I had to drop out and go to work because of the tuition increase, and because my mother is sick and can't work, and she and my sisters need money. By the time I saved enough for another semester, my student visa had expired, and I didn't know . . . I mean, I couldn't . . ." He dropped his head as if he were ashamed.

This wasn't a great surprise, of course. Lots of young men and women enter the U.S. on a student visa and then stay on past its expiration. Sometimes they obtain forged documents, sometimes they don't bother. For many years, this was seen as nothing more than a knotty bureaucratic problem, with both the universities and the Immigration and Naturalization Service scratching their heads and admitting that they didn't have the staff to track violators down and deport them. It didn't seem a particularly good use of resources.

But this laissez-faire attitude has changed with the changing times. Universities are now required to maintain an electronic foreign-student tracking system and share the data with the government. The INS is cracking down, and the FBI has gotten into the act, as well, looking for terrorists who might be hiding on college campuses and in campus towns. Generally speaking, the FBI doesn't care whether it snares big fish or little fish in its net, just so long as it catches enough to justify more fishing. A great many foreigners, whether they are in the U.S. legally or not, are terrified of deportation. And those like Juan, whose visas aren't current, have gone underground. It's a difficult situation, all the way around.

"So that's why you didn't want to answer the door Friday night?" I asked.

He nodded. "After you left, I went to my girlfriend's house. When I went home to pick up some clothes the next day, a neighbor told me about Hank. Then I read it in the newspaper." He lifted his head, and I saw that his cheeks were wet with tears. "I came here to tell you that it's . . . it's not true," he whispered brokenly. "Hank didn't go to that house to hurt those ladies. I want to clear his name."

Ruby was watching him with sympathy. "Why did he go there, then?" she asked. "It was kind of late to go visiting, wasn't it?"

"And why did he take a knife?" I added.

"He didn't take a knife." Juan smudged his cheek with the back of his hand. "Somebody's lying."

"But I saw the knife myself, Juan," I protested. "I got to the scene right after it happened. The knife was there on the floor, under Hank's hand."

Juan shrugged one thin shoulder. "He was mad at them, sure. Over the way they treated his father. And he figured to get something from them. But not with a knife." His grin was lopsided, ironic. "Anyway, he didn't need a knife. They'd already promised him."

I frowned, not liking the sound of this. "Promised him what? Why would those women promise Hank anything?"

"You don't believe me!" Juan cried with a sudden violence. He jumped up, knocking over his mug. "I should have known better than to come here. You don't care about Hank. Nobody cares about Hank but me. You don't care about me, either. You'll probably tell the cops—"

"Oh, for Pete's sake." Ruby took the boy by the wrist and pulled him back into his chair. "Sit down and stop being a gooney bird."

I doubt if Juan knew what a gooney bird was, but he obeyed. I got up and found some paper towels and a sponge to clean up the spilled tea.

"Don't go jumping to conclusions," I said. "We can't decide whether you're telling the truth until we've heard the whole story. Start at the beginning. And don't skip anything."

Juan chewed on his lip, debating with himself. "That's the trouble," he said finally. "I don't know the beginning—not really, I mean. I only know what Hank told me." His voice was flat, and his eyes were intent, as if he were trying to sort through the bits and pieces of truth. "The trouble was that he . . . well, he bragged a lot, you know. Sometimes it was kind of hard to figure out whether he was telling you the truth or making stuff up."

Ruby refilled Juan's cup from the teapot. "Well, then, what did he tell you?" she asked encouragingly. "We can start with that."

Juan looked from me to Ruby, his face grim and unsmiling in the flickering candlelight. "He told me that his father did something really big for those old women, a long time ago. They paid him for it, but they didn't pay him enough. At least, that's what Hank said."

"What did his father do?" Ruby asked.

Juan's glance slid away. "I . . . don't want to get into that."

"Do you know what it was?" I asked.

Juan shook his head. "I only know what Hank told me. And maybe he . . . well, maybe it wasn't the truth. It sounded kinda—" He shrugged. "Anyway, he told the old ladies he knew about . . . about what his father did, and they said they'd give him some money. They hadn't done it yet, but they promised."

Blackmail. Ruby and I exchanged glances.

"How much money?" Ruby asked.

Juan shifted uncomfortably. "Ten thousand dollars was what he told me. At least, ten thousand to start with. He said they told him they'd give him more later."

Definitely blackmail. Gabe Dixon, by all reports, had been a good and faithful servant. And although the Obermann sisters may have treated him shabbily, they claimed to have offered him enough—a room in the house, money for his medical expenses—to compensate him for his services. They wouldn't give Gabe's son ten thousand dollars unless they were paying him off.

But when the Obermanns discussed the situation with McQuaid, they told him they were afraid of Hank. If they had already promised to pay Hank off, why would they want to involve McQuaid? What did Hank know that made him a danger to them? And what kind of danger did he actually pose? I frowned, catching at a thought that ghosted through my mind. Suppose—

"Okay," Ruby said agreeably, leaning back in her chair. "So the Obermann sisters promised to give Hank ten thousand dollars. So then what?"

"Hank was supposed to go to their house on Friday night and get the money," Juan said. "Eleven o'clock. That's when they told him to come." He looked straight at Ruby. "He was there because they asked him."

"That may have been what he told you," I said, "but it sounds a little strange to me. Friday night was the first performance of Miss Jane's play. Why would they have wanted him to come then? If they were going to give him money, why didn't they do it on Friday afternoon, or—"

I stopped. There was that elusive thought again. Only this time, it was clearer, its outlines beginning to emerge.

Ruby was being encouraging. "Well, then, let's assume that Hank told you the truth, and that he was asked to be at the Obermann house on Friday night at eleven o'clock. If he was expecting some sort of a payoff, why would he take the knife?"

Juan glanced at me as if he were assessing the truth of my eyewitness report to the fact of the knife. His shoulders slumped. "I don't know why. He knew he was going to get the money." He looked down at his mug. "He *thought* he was going to get the money," he amended, in a lower voice. "But maybe he suspected it was a trick."

"A trick?" Ruby asked interestedly. "What kind of a

trick?" She frowned. "Maybe there's some proof that he was asked to go there?"

I was staring at the flickering candle, and remembering. The gun cabinet. Locked on Thursday, unlocked on Friday night. And Jane's insistence that there be no noise after eleven. No noise, so a shot and a scream could be easily heard.

"Is there any proof?" Ruby asked again, and I refocused.

Juan's tongue came out and he licked his lips nervously. "Well, there's an envelope."

I leaned forward. "An envelope?"

"It's at the house. At least, I think it's there." He pressed his lips together, shaking his head. "I mean, I didn't actually see the envelope. Hank just told me about it, that's all. Then he hid it."

Ruby's eyes narrowed. "What's in this envelope?" she asked. "A note from the Obermann sisters asking him to come?"

Juan shook his head. "Something Hank's father gave him. Hank said it would prove that he—" He caught himself saying too much. "Prove what he did. His father, I mean. Hank said it was important. It was proof. It was the reason the old women said they'd give him the money."

"You said that Hank was going to hide it," I said. "Where?"

"In the back of the downstairs closet. There's an opening there, so you can get to the bathroom plumbing. He wanted me to know, just in case."

"In case of what?" Ruby asked, giving her eyebrows a lift as if she thought this whole thing was just too dramatic. "Was he afraid?"

Juan pushed his cup away, his voice dropping even lower. "Just in case—that was all he said. But he laughed when he said it, so I guess he wasn't really too worried."

"Are you sure Hank wasn't making all this up?" I asked gently. "He liked you, Juan. Maybe he didn't want you to know that he was planning a robbery, and he told you all this in order to explain some unexpected cash." If Hank had a genuine affection for Juan, he might not want the boy to think of him as a thief. Still, there was that unlocked gun cabinet . . .

Juan stared at me, his eyes going dark. I could see him processing my suggestion, weighing it against what he knew of Hank, wanting to find a reason to disregard it, but finally, unhappily, finding it plausible. When he spoke, his tone was ragged and despairing.

"I guess . . . I don't know what to think. Maybe you're right, Ms. Bayles. Maybe Hank was making the whole thing up. About them promising him that money, I mean. Maybe he thought he'd take a knife and go over there and rob them. And then tell me that they gave it to him so I wouldn't ask too many questions."

"You know, there's a way we can settle this," Ruby said in a helpful tone. "If we could find that envelope, it might give us a clue as to what really happened. How about going over to Hank's with us, Juan? You can show us where to look for it."

Juan looked distressed. "I . . . I'm scared to go back there. The cops might be watching for me." His voice was full of earnest entreaty. "I have to trust you to keep me out of the picture, Ms. Bayles. I want to clear Hank's name, if I can. I owe him that. But I hope you can understand—I don't want to deal with the police."

"Okay," I said. "How about this? Ms. Wilcox and I will take you into town and drop you off wherever you say. You give us your key to Hank's place—your place, I mean—and we'll go over there and look for this envelope. Then we'll make sure that you get your key back. We can get you some clothes, too, while we're there."

Of course, there was another way to handle this. We could convey Juan's information to Sheila, and she could take the key and search for the envelope, or whatever it was. But she might argue that the house was Hank's, not

Juan's, and I wouldn't care to debate the point. She'd probably insist on obtaining a search warrant. And she would undoubtedly insist on talking to Juan before she did that, in order to get her facts straight. And it might turn out that there wasn't any envelope, in which case Juan would be jeopardized for no good reason.

No, it would be quicker and cleaner—and safer for Juan—if Ruby and I used his key to make a quick search of the house. His house, I would argue, if the question ever came up. If we found the envelope and it proved to contain pertinent information, we could hand it over.

"How about it, Juan?" I asked. "Is it okay if Ms. Wilcox and I have a look for that envelope?"

"I . . . guess," Juan faltered. His glance, colored with confusion and uncertainty, told me that he was beginning to doubt whether Hank's envelope really existed. But the only way to prove that it did was to find it. "I'll have to get the key out of my jeans." He looked at me. "I think they're still upstairs."

"Good," Ruby said, and stood up. "There's no point in sitting around here, talking about it. Let's go."

As if this were some sort of signal, the lights came on and the refrigerator began to hum reassuringly. I went upstairs to get Juan's wet clothes and to tell Brian that I was going into Pecan Springs for an hour or so, and that he should go to bed at the usual time.

"Although your dad should be home in another hour," I added.

"Yeah, sure," he said absently. He was sitting at his desk, turning on his computer. Ivanova, his tarantula, fat and smug, was on the desk beside the computer, sunning herself under the lamp. Ivanova's name was originally Ivan, until he was revealed to be a she. "It's a bummer when the lights go out," he muttered. "Nothing to do but homework."

I suppressed a Mom-speak observation and went out to the car.

* * *

THE electric power had been restored along Lime Kiln Road, but that wasn't true everywhere. On the east side of Pecan Springs, the streetlights were off, the juke joints and cafés were dark and seemingly deserted, and the wet streets were empty.

We had taken Ruby's car, because it was behind mine in the driveway. Ruby turned the radio on to a rock station. Juan, in the back seat, directed us to Dolores Street, a main north-south thoroughfare through the east side.

At the corner of Dolores and Brazos, he reached for the door handle and said, suddenly, "Stop here. I want to get out." Ruby pulled over to the curb and stopped.

I turned around in the seat. "Where do you want us to leave your key and your clothes?"

"See that café back there?" Juan said, jerking his head in the direction of a glass-fronted shop called Taco's Grill. His voice had become hard, as if, back on his home territory, he felt less vulnerable—or perhaps he thought he ought to sound tougher. "Put a couple of shirts and some underwear and socks in a bag and leave it and the key with Rosie. She works the cash register most days. I'll pick it up." He opened the door.

"Sure thing," I said. Ten to one, Rosie was his girlfriend. If I found out where she lived, I'd probably find Juan. "If you'll call me at the shop tomorrow, I'll fill you in on what we learn—if anything."

"Yeah," Juan said. "Yeah, sure." He got out of the car, then turned around and looked from one of us to the other. He was still wearing McQuaid's sweats, and they hung loose on his slender frame. I rolled down the window, and he came forward.

"I put you on the spot," he said. "I just want you to know that I . . . I—" He gave it up. "Thanks."

"Oh, you're welcome," Ruby said, and smiled.

I put my hand through the window, and Juan took it

briefly. "Be safe," I said, wondering what was going to happen to this young man. There had to be a way to help him out of his predicament.

"I'll try." Juan stepped back, raised his hand, and was gone in the shadows.

Ruby put the car in gear and turned onto East Brazos. We didn't say much on the two-block ride to Hank's house. *Juan's* house, I reminded myself, as we pulled into the driveway beside the red motorcycle, which was still parked in front of the garage. If it was Hank's house, we were breaking and entering. If it was Juan's, we were entering with the occupant's permission—and his key.

The power was off here, too, and the entire neighborhood was dark, except for the pale sheen of candles or oil lamps in a few houses. I could hear the dull rumble of eighteen-wheelers on I-35. Somewhere, a dog was barking, sharp and staccato.

"The key opens the front door, I suppose," Ruby said, as I took it out of my purse. "We didn't think to ask."

"We can try the front first," I said. "Do you have a flashlight?"

"Of course," Ruby said loftily. "Would Kinsey Millhone go anywhere without a flashlight?" She fished through the glove compartment with no luck, then on the floor under the driver's seat. We finally found it, pushed back under the passenger's seat.

"I imagine Kinsey keeps her flashlight where she can find it," I remarked, as we went up the front walk.

"Don't be tacky," Ruby replied in a whisper. She glanced nervously over her shoulder. "I guess there's not much risk of somebody seeing us behind all these bushes. Hank must have liked his privacy."

She was right. The front of the house was shielded by a row of overgrown shrubs, and once we were on the porch, we were virtually invisible. I put the key in the lock and turned. It clicked, and the door opened onto a shadowy hallway.

"Phew!" Ruby exclaimed, wrinkling her nose. "Smells like the garbage hasn't been taken out in a while."

The odor was ripe and rich. "At least a week," I said. The bright beam of the flashlight fell on a pair of work boots—Hank's, probably—on the floor beneath a row of pegs that held jackets and sweaters and a yellow poncho. Next to the boots was a metal toolbox with HANK painted on it in red letters.

Ruby closed the door behind us. "Downstairs closet," she said. She had lowered her voice, as if she might be overheard by somebody upstairs. Or maybe the sight of Hank's boots and toolbox had reminded her—had reminded us both—that he was dead. I thought again of the man, and of what Juan had claimed. Was it possible that—

But now wasn't the time for questions. Now was the time for answers. "There," I said, as Ruby's light fell on a door underneath the stairs, to the left. I went to it, turned the knob, and stepped back, anticipating the cascade of stuff that occasionally falls on my feet when I open the front closet at our house.

But the closet was nearly empty, except for a couple of cardboard boxes off to one side—none of the usual toys and clutter of a man's life, fishing gear, tennis rackets, golf clubs, skis, life jackets, things like that. It looked as if Hank had had neither the time nor the inclination for recreation.

"Do you see the opening?" Ruby asked, peering over my shoulder.

I took the light and flashed it around. "That's what we're looking for," I said. The opening was cut into the wall to my right, which probably backed up to the downstairs bathroom. It was covered with a panel of painted plywood, screwed to the narrow framing. "We're going to need a screwdriver."

"I'll check the toolbox," Ruby said, and came back with a screwdriver in her hand. "Got it!" she said triumphantly.

"Good," I said, and stepped back. "See if you can get

that panel off." I held the light while Ruby got down on her knees and unscrewed the panel, setting it aside.

"Give me the flashlight." She shone it into the cavity. Her voice was muffled. "I don't see anything unusual."

"It's probably hidden," I said. "Put your arm in and feel around."

Ruby unfolded herself and got to her feet. "Maybe . . . maybe you should try, China. You're closer to Hank's size. You can probably get your arm in there better than I can."

"You're afraid of spiders, that's all," I said. "I bet Nancy Drew wouldn't let a dinky little spider keep her from searching for a hidden envelope."

Ruby frowned. "Probably not. But she might be intimidated by a great big scorpion. I got stung when I went looking for the cleanser under the bathroom sink last week."

"So you want the scorpions to sting *me*?"

"Well . . ." Ruby said. "Please, China?"

I snatched the flashlight from her and got down on my knees. The opening was about thirty inches square, and I could see pipes inside the cavity. I could see dust, too, and chunks of Sheetrock and construction debris. And spiderwebs. But no scorpions. Gritting my teeth, I stuck my arm inside as far as I could reach and groped around the opening on both sides.

"Nothing," I reported. And then, reaching above the opening, I felt a smooth, papery surface. "Here it is!" I exclaimed, pulling it out. "It was pushed behind a stud."

I clambered to my feet, holding a dirty white envelope by one corner. It was recycled, for there was a canceled stamp on it and Hank's name and address had been scribbled through with a pencil. The flap was taped shut.

"I vote for opening it," Ruby said eagerly.

"I agree," I said. "But we need to avoid disturbing the prints—and there are bound to be some." I motioned with my head in the direction of the kitchen. "Let's find a better place to work."

In the small kitchen—and yes, indeed, there was garbage here somewhere—Ruby held the flashlight while I put the envelope on the counter. I found a sharp-pointed knife in the dish drainer and used it to pull up a corner of the tape, carefully peeling it off, then used the point of the knife to open the unsealed flap and tease out the contents.

There was just one item: a Polaroid photograph, taken with a flash. It was very badly faded and the background was indistinct. I could just make out the subject: a man, lying full-length on his back on the floor of what looked like a stone-sided corridor. There was a jagged hole in his head above his right eye, with a slight welling of blood. The eyes were open, the lips parted in a grotesque grin, and I saw the gleam of what looked like a gold tooth in the ghastly mouth. I pulled in my breath sharply.

"Oh, my stars!" Ruby exclaimed. "It's . . . it's Andy Obermann!"

"You're sure?" I asked, although that gold tooth was confirmation enough for me. "No mistake?"

"Positive," Ruby said, staring at the photo. "And he's . . ." Her voice died away. She gulped audibly. "China," she whispered, "you were right. Andy *is* the skeleton in the cave!"

"Well, that's one question answered," I said soberly. I turned the photo over, using the tips of my fingers. On the back, in faint penciled script were the initials "GD" and a date: "10/21/76."

"GD," Ruby breathed. The flashlight trembled. She looked at me, her eyes large, the pupils dilated. "So Gabe Dixon killed him! And the photo proves it!"

"Well . . ." I said.

"Gabe must have been selling drugs," she went on, the words spilling out. "He took Andy out to the cave to do a deal, and they got into some sort of argument over the stuff, or maybe over money, and Andy got shot."

I shook my head. "I don't think so. If Gabe was selling Andy drugs, they didn't need to trek all the way out to the cave. They could have done the deal anywhere." I pointed to the photograph. "That bullet wound above Andy's eye—Alana has identified it as an exit wound. He was shot from the back, so it wasn't an argument. It was more like an execution."

"But why did they go out to the cave, then?" Ruby demanded. "And why did Gabe take a photograph, for Pete's sake, and put his initials and the date on it? Didn't he realize that it might incriminate him?" She flapped her arms. "And come to think of it, why the heck did he have a camera with him? This doesn't make any sense, China. No sense at all!"

"It makes sense if you remember what Hank told Juan," I replied steadily. "He said his father had done something really big for the Obermann sisters. They paid him for it—remember?"

"But they didn't pay him enough," Ruby said, snapping her fingers. "Yes, I remember! So you're saying that . . ." She stopped, looking horrified. "No, that can't be right, China! He must have done something else for them—something like painting the house or saving them from a terrible accident. Those women wouldn't . . . Florence couldn't—"

"Wouldn't? Couldn't? How can you be so sure? We know what a manipulative, controlling woman Jane is—has been, most of her life. And there was certainly plenty of financial incentive. Doctor Obermann gave the bulk of his fortune to his two sons and left his daughters only an annual allowance. They didn't even get the family house."

"But I thought that it was their house!" Ruby exclaimed, startled.

I shook my head. "It was left to their brother, Harley, with instructions to allow his sisters to live there as long as the house remained in the family. And Andy was Harley's son, so he inherited the house—as well as the family fortune—when Harley died."

"How do you know all that?" Ruby asked, startled.

"McQuaid dug up the information as background. The sisters wanted to hire him—to protect them from Hank."

Ruby's eyes narrowed. "Protect them from . . . Hank?"

"That's what they told McQuaid on Thursday—or what they implied, rather. They didn't actually get around to naming names. Florence became ill, and the rest of the interview was postponed until Saturday. But by then, Hank was already dead. They didn't need McQuaid."

"I see," Ruby said thoughtfully.

"Bob told me that Andy was pretty well broke when he came back here, and that the bulk of the estate was tied up so that he couldn't get to it for the next few years. Lila said Andy was trying to borrow money from his aunts. He got a bit from Florence, but Jane wouldn't give him any, so he began talking about selling the house. In that case, the sisters would have been out on their ear—with only their annual allowance to cushion the blow."

Ruby was staring at me, a slow acceptance dawning on her face. "And from all reports," she said in a low voice, "Andy was a serious addict by the time he got out of those army hospitals. Maybe Jane thought there was no hope for him."

"It's possible. I can imagine her telling Florence that Andy would be dead soon anyway, at the rate he was going."

"So they ordered Gabe to kill him," Ruby whispered.

I nodded. "And I think we can guess why Gabe took Andy out to the cave."

"To dispose of the body there?"

"It was as safe a grave as any, and safer than most. Anywhere else, and he'd run the risk that the body would be found." I paused. "There's something more, too. After Gabe took this photo, he turned Andy face-down and bashed in the back of his head with a rock. If somebody found the body, it would look like a caving accident."

"And he took the photo," Ruby said softly, "to prove that Andy was dead. How awful, China."

"Maybe he took two photos," I said. "One to give the

Obermanns, to prove that Andy was dead, so he could get his money. And this one to keep—just in case."

"Maybe he took more." There was an edge in Ruby's vice. "We can't know how many times he might have given them the 'last' photo—and how many times they paid up."

"Right. But I suspect that at some point, Gabe became afraid of the Obermanns. Perhaps that's why he refused their offer of a room in their house."

"And Hank knew all this," Ruby said wonderingly. "Or guessed it. From the photo, maybe."

"I think he knew it," I said. "I think his father told him before he died. And Hank foolishly decided it was his turn to get something out of the Obermann sisters. Ten thousand somethings, actually." I shook my head. "Sounds like there's enough guilt here to go around, with some left over." The only real victim was Andy, whose crime, if that's what it was, was a desperate longing for the relief that the drugs brought him. And perhaps Florence, who had been under her sister's control for most of her life.

Ruby put her hand on my arm. "China," she said in a frightened voice, "Juan said that maybe Hank was tricked. I think he was right!"

The gun cabinet, locked on Thursday afternoon, when McQuaid was there, unlocked on Friday night, when Jane needed to use it. "I agree," I said grimly. "They invited Hank to come to the house, at a time when they knew there would be somebody at the theater, celebrating at the cast party. Somebody who could hear the shots and come running. Hank thought they were going to pay him off. But what they really had in mind—"

"What Jane had in mind," Ruby said firmly. "I can't believe that Florence would have agreed to murder Hank. Or Andy, either, for that matter."

"Why not?" I asked. "We know that Jane bullied Florence. Why couldn't she have bullied her into a conspiracy to murder Andy, especially if Andy was half-dead already?

And to murder Hank, who might reveal their part in Andy's murder?" Then I thought of the look—half-frightened, half-defiant—on Florence's face the afternoon before, at the hospital. "But maybe Florence was tired of being bullied," I said thoughtfully. "Maybe she was ready to tell what she knew about the past, about Andy. About Hank."

Ruby stared at me. "That's right, China! Remember what she said when Jane was throwing us out of the room? We'd been talking about Andy, and she asked us to come back and see her. She said she wanted to talk."

"And Jane heard her," I said. I thought of Helen Berger's suspicions. "And may have killed her for it."

"Killed her?" Ruby asked faintly. "What makes you say that?" Her hand went to her mouth. "Oh, China, I knew there was something wrong! A little voice kept telling me—"

"In this case, your little voice may have something. That call from Helen Berger tonight—Juan interrupted us before I could tell you why she phoned. Helen says that Doctor Mackey didn't put anything into Florence's chart about a heart condition—and Mackey was Florence's personal physician. The doctor has ordered an autopsy, and Helen suspects that Florence might have died from some sort of plant poisoning. She's an expert on herbal poisons, you know."

And as I said the words, I was thinking of Friday night. After the shot had been reported, Sheila and I had hurried to the Obermann house up a dark path lined with oleander bushes. Oleander, a deadly plant poison, responsible for a rash of recent suicides and murders in Sri Lanka, where the shrub is native, plentiful, and readily available. Oleander, which had been featured as a murder weapon in a movie that had been reviewed not long ago in the *Enterprise*. Which can cause gastric inflammation and cardiac irregularities. Which can kill, especially the very young and the very old.

I reined myself in. There is a substantial evidentiary gap between noticing oleander bushes in a backyard and proving the owner guilty of murder. Without a confession or eyewitness testimony, it's notoriously difficult to make a poisoning charge stick.

"I think we'd better get moving," I said, returning the photo to its envelope. I opened the pantry, found a box of plastic zipper-top bags, chose one, and slid the envelope into it. The picture was evidence. I didn't want to be accused of contaminating it. Finding it, yes—and maybe even a tad bit illegally. But not contaminating it.

Ruby was rummaging under the sink. I turned just as she dragged something out.

"What are you doing?" I asked.

"I'm taking out the garbage," she said. "There's no point in leaving it to stink up the house, is there?"

"Leave it," I said. "If the cops come back here—and they might—they'll want to search the garbage."

Ruby looked down at the bag, a curious expression on her face. "You don't think there's anything interesting in there, do you?"

"Not interesting enough for me to go through it," I said, wrinkling my nose. "We need to leave Sheila and her boys something to do. Come on, Ruby. We still have to get Juan some clothes."

Juan's room was even messier than Brian's, and it took a few minutes to find reasonably clean shirts, jeans, underwear, and a pair of running shoes. While Ruby was doing that, I took a quick look through the small desk in Hank's room.

In the drawer, I found what I was looking for: Hank's checkbook. He had been meticulous about keeping the check register, with checks, cash withdrawals, and deposits duly noted. If the Obermann sisters had given him money to persuade him to keep his story to himself, he hadn't noted it in the register.

Ruby came to the door with a large paper bag in her arms. "Ready?" she asked.

"Ready," I said, and closed the drawer. The cops would want to look at that checkbook, too.

When we walked out of the house, we took two things that didn't belong to us, the Polaroid photograph of Andy Obermann's corpse and the bag of Juan's clothes. We left Hank Dixon's garbage behind.

Chapter Nineteen

PERSONAL FRAGRANCES

To make your own personal fragrance, add 20 drops of essential oil to 2 tablespoons jojoba oil. Some combinations to try: bergamot and lemon (perky, citrusy); patchouli and sandalwood (luxurious, musky); ylang-ylang and rose (sweetly exotic).

"Okay, Sherlock," Ruby said, getting behind the wheel. "Now what?"

I'd been thinking about that. "The corpse in the photo belongs to Blackie," I said. "It's his case and his jurisdiction, and normally I'd turn the photo over to him. But if we're right about who killed Andy Obermann and why, that puts the matter into a whole different light. One of Andy's murderers is still alive and at large." It didn't matter who pulled the trigger—if the Obermann sisters had paid for the job, they were as guilty as the man who fired the gun. "And she may have murdered again," I added.

"Murdered again *twice,*" Ruby muttered, starting the car. "Hank . . . and Florence."

"And that's Sheila's case," I said, taking my cell phone out of my purse and punching in her number. "What's more, a hot case takes precedence over a cold one. Let's go talk to Sheila."

Sheila didn't answer the phone until the third ring, and

when she did, her voice sounded groggy. "The lights have been off for a couple of hours," she said. "I've had a helluva day. I decided to go to bed early."

"Well, you'll have to get up again, Smart Cookie. Ruby and I have uncovered some important evidence in the Hank Dixon shooting. We're bringing it over."

"Evidence? What evidence? What are you talking about?"

"Seeing is believing," I said. "We'll be there in ten minutes. Don't go back to bed."

"I wouldn't dream of it," Sheila muttered, and banged down the phone.

After I finished talking to Sheila, I phoned to check on Brian and make sure that everything was all right at home. McQuaid picked up the call.

"Where the dickens are you?" he asked, sounding aggrieved. "I thought you were going to be home this evening."

"Ruby came over, and we decided to go out," I said evasively. The explanation was long and convoluted. I needed to be looking into his face when I told him what had happened—otherwise, he'd never believe me. "We're going over to Sheila's," I said. "Don't expect me home right away."

"Girl talk, I suppose," he said, and chuckled in an irritatingly patronizing way. "What are you and Ruby up to now? Trying to get Sheila and Blackie together again?"

"Not . . . exactly," I said. The two of them would have to collaborate to assemble all the pieces of this complex puzzle, past and present. If they were going to reconcile, they'd have every opportunity. But that was beside the point. And there was that troubling business of Sheila's relationship to Colin. Even under ordinary circumstances, I wouldn't have attempted to play peacemaker between Sheila and Blackie. With Colin involved (and he was involved, I was sure of it), it was definitely hands-off.

"Well, enjoy yourselves," McQuaid said, and added, "Brian said you helped him bury his lizard."

"With full military honors. It was an impressive ceremony. How come you never manage to be present at these occasions?"

There was a smile in McQuaid's voice. "Just unlucky, I guess. See you later, babe."

I made kissy noises into the phone and clicked it off as we pulled into Sheila's driveway.

When Sheila was appointed chief of police, she bought a modest frame house on the west side of town—a move that I see now, in hindsight, as indicative of her reservations about her engagement to Blackie. The house was built in the thirties, in one of Pecan Springs' first subdivisions, before developers discovered that people would actually buy houses built from lot line to lot line, with lawns the size of a paper napkin. Sheila has a large fenced yard, with an enormous old pecan tree out front. A couple of the tree's smaller limbs had come unhitched and were lying in the drive, and the grass was littered with pecans, but the storm didn't seem to have caused much damage.

The power had been restored, too, and Sheila had turned the porch light on for us. Barefoot and wearing a pair of lace-trimmed red silk pajamas, she opened the front door to Ruby's ring.

I raised my eyebrows. "Woo-woo," I said, glancing at her attire. "The chief's sexy sleepwear."

"They're almost too pretty to sleep in," Ruby said.

Sheila looked down at herself and colored. "Oh, these," she said, as if she'd forgotten she had them on. "They were a birthday present. I thought I'd try to get some use out of them." She knuckled her eyes, smearing her mascara, and yawned sleepily. "This had better be good, you guys, and I do mean *good.* I was dead to the world, and I meant to stay that way until the alarm clock went off."

I sniffed. She was wearing perfume—ylang-ylang and rose, I'd bet. I suppressed a quick quip about women who slept in their makeup and perfume and handed her the plastic bag with the envelope in it. "This'll wake you up, Smart Cookie."

She held the bag at arm's length. "And what the hell is *this*?" From the tone of her voice, you'd have thought she was already smelling Hank's garbage.

Ruby flapped her blue sleeves. "It's a photo of a corpse," she announced triumphantly. "Listen, Sheila, China and I have just solved three murders. The story is so incredible that you'll never guess it, not in a gazillion years."

Sheila looked her up and down, eyeing the blue batik top and mermaid earrings. "Is that your official crime-solving getup?" she asked grumpily. She turned to me, her hands on her hips, her head tilted to one side. Not only was she wearing mascara, but lipstick and blusher. "And you've only solved three murders? Well, heck. I figured you'd cleared my entire cold case file."

"I'm really sorry we got you up," I soothed. "We'll explain the whole thing, but we'd better have some coffee."

It took a couple of cups of hot coffee (and more important, a plate of double-chocolate brownies) to get all three of us through the explanation and the subsequent questions and answers. But by the end of the story, Sheila was definitely awake and listening.

When we concluded our narrative, she gave her head an I'm-not-believing-this shake. "I know for a fact that Howie Masterson is planning to ask the grand jury to no-bill Jane Obermann in the shooting of Hank Dixon, on the grounds that she killed him during an attempted armed robbery."

"Oh, lordy," Ruby said, rolling her eyes. "Howie the Ding-Bat Masterson. I forgot about him." Ruby and I are among those who have no respect for our new D.A.

"Yeah," I said bleakly. "Howie's probably looking forward to it. A made-for-TV production, starring himself as guardian of the Second Amendment and defender of every citizen's right to self-defense." Howie would go through the ceiling when Sheila put a revised list of criminal charges in front of him.

"Yeah, right," Sheila said ironically. "So now you're saying that I have to tell Howie to forget his plan to canonize Jane. Instead, I have to tell him that I want her indicted on three counts of murder." She ticked them off on her fingers. "She hired a hit man to kill her nephew. She lured the hit man's son to her house and shot him. And then she poisoned her sister to keep her from spilling the beans." She paused for effect. "Anything else you two amateur sleuths want me to add to the list? A little embezzlement, maybe? Drug smuggling? Gun running?"

Ruby cleared her throat. "This isn't going to be easy, is it?"

"As my father used to say, it is going to be tougher than a horny toad's toenails," Sheila replied grimly. "To make matters worse, Miss Obermann was a big political contributor this year. And Howie's campaign spent one helluva of a lot of somebody's money on those billboard ads—could've been hers."

I had to smile at that, even though there was nothing funny about it. Howie's billboards had shown up all over the county, featuring a twelve-by-twenty-foot photo of himself in chaps, leather vest, and a white Stetson, sitting behind the steering wheel of his Dodge Ram truck, equipped with a grill guard heavy enough to shove an elk off the road, mud flaps that looked like they belonged on an eighteen-wheeler, and a .375 H & H elephant gun slung in the rear window. The ad had a two-word caption: Texas Tough.

"I didn't think about that," Ruby said. "Politics is everywhere these days."

"It's not just politics, or Howie's plan to set himself up as the Defender of the Faith," Sheila said, sounding resigned. "It's community reaction. Jane isn't much liked, but the Obermann name carries a lot of weight. There's the hospital, the library, the new theater—" She stopped, pursing her mouth. "None of which means that she's safe from prosecution, of course. It just means that this won't be an ordinary case. And the evidence against her is going to have to be pretty extraordinary—if only because the D.A. is not going to be anxious to try this case."

To say the least. "I'm sure you won't go to Howie until you have all the evidence lined up," I said cautiously. "There's this photo, of course, which documents Andy Obermann's death—and probably has both Hank's and his father's fingerprints on it."

I stopped, momentarily distracted. Where the heck was Sheila going to get Gabe Dixon's fingerprints for comparison? Had he been in the armed forces, maybe? I took a breath and plunged on.

"You'll probably want to request that Florence Obermann's autopsy include several toxicological tests. Helen Berger's list will narrow down the possibilities. And McQuaid will be glad to give you a statement about his interview with the women, and about that gun cabinet." I frowned. There was something else. Now, what was it?

"You said that Gabe Dixon shot Andy Obermann from behind." Sheila was looking down at the photograph. "Was the slug found? Does the sheriff have it?"

Oh, for Pete's sake. "No," I said, reaching for my purse, "the slug hasn't been found—at least, not yet." I took out the little plastic bag containing the casing that Brian had given me earlier that evening. "However, this is the casing." I'd put it into my purse, intending to take it to Blackie in the morning. Now, it might be more relevant to Sheila's investigation.

Ruby was staring at the casing. "Where in the world did you get that, China?"

"Brian picked it up in the cave," I said, "before he knew that his caveman had been shot to death. He gave it to me tonight, when I told him what I'd learned from Alana Montoya. I was going to drop it off at the sheriff's office in the morning."

Sheila shook the casing out onto the table and peered at

it. Without saying anything, she left the table and came back with a magnifying glass.

"It's got *USCC* and the number *18* stamped in the base," I said, "but I have no idea what they mean."

"I do." Sheila studied the casing through the magnifying glass. After a minute, she put it down. "The letters are military identifications. The number refers to the year of manufacture. This cartridge is a .45 caliber ACP, made in 1918."

"1918," I said slowly. "World War One."

Ruby wrinkled her forehead. "What does ACP mean?"

"Automatic Colt pistol," Sheila replied. "It was used longer in the military than any other firearm—adopted in 1911, and not retired until 1985."

Ruby frowned. "So Gabe Dixon shot Andy with a bullet that was almost sixty years old? Isn't that kind of old for ammunition?"

"Not if it's stored correctly," Sheila said. "There's a lot of old wartime ammunition out there, both First and Second World Wars." She slid the casing back into the bag and looked at me. "The gun I took away from Jane Obermann on Friday night, China—it was a seven-shot .45 caliber Colt automatic. Her father's gun, if you'll remember. And the ammo she used had been in the gun for some time, and it bore the same markings as this. Somebody in ballistics can compare the two casings, but they look identical to me."

I thought about that. "You took the gun out of Jane's hand. How many bullets were in the magazine?"

"Four," Sheila said. "And there were two in Hank Dixon."

"And one in Andy Obermann," I said. "Four plus two plus one is seven."

"Oh, good Lord," Ruby said in a whisper.

"So it looks like Jane shot Hank," I went on, "with the same gun—and the same ammunition—that Hank's father used to kill Andy."

"We have the slugs we dug out of Hank," Sheila said. "If we can locate the slug that killed Andy, we'll compare them. With luck, we'll get a match."

"But the same gun!" Ruby protested incredulously. "That's just plain stupid—and Jane Obermann isn't a stupid woman."

"Maybe she never knew which gun Gabe used to kill Andy," I replied. "Or maybe she just forgot. After all, it was a long time ago. Or maybe it was the only one of the three guns in the cabinet that happened to be loaded."

"It was," Sheila said quietly. "I checked. The other two guns, a Mauser and a Luger, were both empty. And there was no ammo in the cabinet."

"And of course," I added, "Jane had no idea that Andy's remains had been found. She must have been feeling pretty secure after all these years. So even if she did know that Gabe had used that Colt, it might not have mattered to her."

"Or maybe she thought it was poetic justice of some sort," Ruby said darkly. "Somebody who is devious enough to invite Hank to her house and set up his murder so it looked like she was shooting a burglar—that kind of person is capable of anything."

"What about the knife?" I asked Sheila. "If Hank thought he was going to get his payoff, it doesn't seem likely that he would come armed—at least, not with a butcher knife. Is it possible that the knife is a throwdown? That it actually came from the Obermanns' kitchen?" "Throwdown" is cop talk for a weapon that is planted at a crime scene.

"I don't know," Sheila said. "I'll get a warrant and search the kitchen for similar items. Of course, the knife will already have been checked for Hank's prints. But I'll see that we get Jane's prints, too, and have them matched against anything else that might show up on the knife."

"So what's left?" I asked. "Florence's autopsy?"

Sheila nodded. "You say that you're getting a list of those plants from the nurse?"

"First thing tomorrow," I replied. "I'm thinking that oleander is a good bet. The bushes that line the path in the backyard—they're oleander. It's definitely toxic enough to do the job, and it matches Florence's symptoms."

"How would she . . . how would she have done it?" Ruby asked hesitantly. "Brew it up as a tea?"

"I don't think so," I said. "From what I know of oleander, the toxins aren't soluble in water. She might have chopped up the leaves and put them into something she baked."

"Be sure I get the list as soon as it's available," Sheila said. "The M.E. down in Bexar County won't have started the autopsy yet, so I'll have time to talk to Doctor Mackey and amend the request." She rubbed her fingers across her forehead as if she had a headache. "Got any other little problems I can solve for you?"

"Yeah," I said regretfully. "His name is Juan, and he's illegal."

"Oh, hell." Sheila looked at me. "I'm going to have to talk to him, you know. And if he really wants to clear Dixon's name, he'll want to talk to us. Where does he hang out?"

"I have no idea," I said, giving Ruby a sign that I didn't want her mentioning Taco's Grill. If Juan was going to talk to the cops, it ought to be his call.

Ruby fielded my concern and raised one eyebrow. "Why don't you discuss Juan's situation with Justine, China? She's handled immigration cases." Justine is Justine Wyzinski, a.k.a. The Whiz, a friend who does a fair amount of pro bono legal work.

"Now, there's a plan," I said approvingly. "I should have thought of that. Maybe Justine can arrange for Sheila to get his testimony without endangering—"

Sheila stood up. "Listen, I know you two are all fired up about this, but I've had a rotten day, and it is just the beginning of what promises to be a really rotten week—especially if I've got to tell Howie that his favorite donor may turn out to be a three-time killer. I'm not making any promises on this Juan business. We'll start looking for him tomorrow. If you know where he is, you'd better tell him to turn his ass in. Mucho pronto."

Sheila might look like a sexy deb queen in her red silk pajamas, but she has the mouth of a cop. I got up and gave her a hug. "Thanks for the coffee, Smart Cookie. We'll leave, and you can go back to bed. You'll keep us posted on developments, I hope."

"And if you need us, we'll be at the shops in the morning," Ruby said.

Sheila rubbed her arms. "Oh, don't mention morning. I don't want to think about it."

We were on our way out of the kitchen when I happened to glance at the counter next to the sink. An empty wine bottle sat there, with two wineglasses beside it. One of the glasses had a lipstick smear on the rim. The other didn't. I looked up and caught Sheila's searching glance. I held her eyes until she colored and looked away.

Conscious of Ruby beside me, I said nothing. But the speculations lingered at the back of my mind, like snidely suspicious neighbors trading nasty gossip over the back fence. Maybe Sheila—in her sexy red silk pajamas, designer fragrance, and makeup—hadn't actually been in bed when we called, after all. Or maybe she hadn't been in bed alone.

Chapter Twenty

In 1807, when the French invaded Spain, twelve soldiers in the French army cut some oleander branches and used them as skewers for shish-ka-bob. All twelve became desperately ill, and seven of them died.

Ralph W. Moss
Herbs Against Cancer: History and Controversy

I was right. It took quite a lot of talking and direct eye contact to convince McQuaid that my story of the night's events—every enthralling detail of it—was a hundred percent true. But by the time he had absorbed the tale, he agreed with my assessment of the situation, and added his own little twist.

"I'm thinking back to the day I met with the Obermann sisters," he said musingly. "Florence seemed distraught to me. When she left to go upstairs, Jane attributed her distress to illness. But maybe Florence was having second thoughts about the plan to kill Hank Dixon."

"But nothing was said about her heart condition until she was out of the room? I think that's what you told me."

"Right. It's entirely possible that Jane was laying the groundwork for a future 'heart attack'." Of course, neither of the women ever actually came out and named names. That is, they didn't actually say it was Hank they were afraid of. But they said enough so that—after Hank was dead—I'd be certain to come forward and tell the police that they were hiring me to protect them from him."

"And your testimony would substantiate the claim that he had broken into the house, intending to kill them."

McQuaid's mouth twisted into a bitter smile. "God, I hate to be used." He shook his head. "I'll bet Jane never intended to pay me a retainer, either. It was a setup."

"I agree," I said. I leaned over and kissed him. "But now that we know the full story—or we think we do—your testimony could be key to premeditation. Obviously, they were setting Hank up." I paused. "I hope Sheila finds Jane's prints on that knife. That would pretty well wrap up Hank's case. Florence's autopsy should reveal how she died. For Andy, there's the photo of the corpse and the cartridge casing that Brian found—and with luck Blackie will locate the slug itself when he does a thorough search of the cave."

"There's the financial motivation, as well," McQuaid added. "That should be easy to establish. Through their father's will, the sisters got only an annual allowance, while their nephew eventually inherited the estate and the house. When they arranged to have him declared legally dead, they got everything."

"And Bob and Lila can both testify to the fact that Andy was hard up for cash to support his drug habit and wanted to sell the house his aunts were living in."

"Sounds pretty tight," McQuaid said. He added dryly, "I don't see how even Howie Masterson can mess this one up."

"Don't be so sure," I said. "Jane has the bucks to hire herself the best defense. And she's an old woman—a big sympathy factor there. Her attorney will play that for all it's worth, and he'll have a lot of help from her. I wouldn't be a bit surprised if she manages to intimidate the jury into an acquittal." I paused. "The one I'm really worried about is Juan. He'll have to testify in court to what Hank told him."

"Yeah," McQuaid said. "That's a problem."

I glanced at the old Seth Thomas clock over the refrigerator. It felt to me like three in the morning, but it was only midnight. "I wonder if Justine is still up. I could call and see if she's willing to help Juan."

McQuaid pushed back his chair. "Well, if I were The Whiz, I'd be a heck of a lot more receptive if I were asked during working hours. Ask me at midnight, and I'd say no on principle."

I raised my eyebrow. "Wouldn't it depend on what you were asked, and who asked you?"

"It might," he said, and grinned. "Did you have something special in mind?"

On second thought, Justine could wait. I'd call her in the morning, first thing.

I connected with Justine, whose practice is in San Antonio, and got a promise from her to take Juan's case, if I could persuade him to talk to her. Leaving Ruby to mind both shops, I took the bag of Juan's clothing over to Taco's Grill, where I gave it to Rosie, who turned out to be a cute young girl, Juan's girlfriend, most likely. I also left him a note, saying that I had located a lawyer who was willing to work with him on his immigration situation and asking him to get in touch with me or McQuaid as soon as possible.

Since we'd been interrupted in our conversation about Cassandra's partnership proposal, Ruby and I used our free moments during the day to discuss Cass's scheme. Obviously, we needed to give Janet time off to rest her knees, and Cassandra was undoubtedly a skilled and experienced cook. Her offer to help with the catering was welcome, as well, since Ruby had booked two more events just this morning. And both of us were enthusiastic about the personal chef idea. We know quite a few professional people who would love to open their freezers and find a stack of tempting and healthy meals, as an alternative to the high-fat, high-sodium, high-calorie foods they're likely to get when they eat out.

"The big question," Ruby said thoughtfully, cocking her

head to one side, "is the partnership. There's no doubt that we could use the cash she's offering." Cassandra had made a straightforward business proposal: She'd put in a certain amount of cash for a certain percentage of the business—the amount and the percentage to be negotiated. "But when you and I went into business together," Ruby added, "we had already worked together for five or six years. I probably know Cass better than you do, and I honestly don't feel I know her very well. Mostly she's pleasant and helpful, but sometimes she's sort of in-your-face."

"Well," I said, "we certainly can't decide whether she'll work out as a partner until we know her better. The only honest thing to do is to tell her that. If she wants to take a chance on us, I guess that's up to her. But it's going to mean giving up a steady paycheck—maybe she won't want to risk a sure thing for something that isn't."

"She seems like a risk-taker to me." Ruby reached for the phone. "Okay if I have a chat with her?"

"Be my guest," I said, and went off to help a customer who was trying to decide whether she should give lavender another try, having failed for the last two years in a row. Growing lavender is a little dicey in the heat and humidity of central Texas, but I introduced her to some Spanish lavender that might do better in her garden than the English lavender she'd been trying to grow. I also told her that I amend the planting soil with plenty of sand to improve the drainage, and mulch the plants with three or four inches of pea gravel or granite chips. And then I wished her luck. Sometimes I think that the world is made up of two kinds of people. Those who can grow lavender and those who wish they could.

Tuesday was a busy day, and Wednesday was its twin. When we closed the cash registers at five-thirty on Wednesday evening, Ruby and I were both pleased. And not only that, but Ruby and Cassandra had had a couple of productive phone conversations. Cass was not only willing but eager to take the risk. She'd be taking over for Janet in the kitchen a couple of days a week, and would be helping Ruby with the catering, starting on Saturday afternoon. We agreed to revisit the partnership question in a couple of months, when we knew each other better. Ruby and I were excited—in a restrained, cautious way—at the prospect of being joined by another pair of helping hands, and Ruby said Cass was excited, too.

I was closing up when Ruby came through the door between our shops.

"Would you mind giving me a ride home?" she asked. "Amy's car conked out this morning, and she's borrowed mine."

I went to lock the front door. "No problem. Do you want to stop somewhere along the way?"

"At the theater, if you don't mind. I need to pick up one of my costumes for repair." Ruby bent down to give Khat a good-night pat. "Max stepped on my skirt in the Sunday matinee. I was darn lucky not to be standing there in front of everybody in my bare minimums."

"Fine with me," I said. "I've got three more large salvias to put into the landscaping. I'll do that, while you get your costume."

It took only a few minutes to pop the plants into the ground, which was still moist under its thick blanket of mulch. Just as I finished, Ruby came out of the theater, her costume over her arm, and we started to walk back to Big Mama, who was parked in the lot. There was a shout behind us, however, and we turned to see Jane Obermann, dressed in black, standing at the back of her garden, gesturing at us.

"Ms. Wilcox," she called in a peremptory tone, "I want a word with you about your performance!"

"Oh, no." Ruby gave me an apprehensive look. "Do you mind coming along, China? I need some moral support. And knowing what I know about that woman—" She shuddered. "Why hasn't Sheila arrested her yet?"

"Because she doesn't have enough evidence to persuade

Howie to sign off on the case," I said. "Things don't happen in real life the way they do in mystery novels, Ruby. Even when the cops have a pretty good idea who the killer is, they have to be able to make the charge stick, especially in a high-profile case like this one. Otherwise, they risk lawsuits."

When we reached Jane, she gave me a haughty glance, then turned to Ruby. "What I have to say to you, Ms. Wilcox, is better said in private."

"China is my friend," Ruby said with dignity. "I want her to hear."

Jane peered at me. "Ah, Ms. Nails," she said.

"Bayles," I said. "China Bayles."

Unflustered, she turned toward the house. "At least we can go indoors. I don't intend for the neighbors to eavesdrop."

"Looks like I'm in for it," Ruby muttered.

"I'll be with you," I said comfortingly, although I wasn't sure I'd be much comfort. The truth was that Ruby and I were in the presence of a woman who, we were convinced, was a three-time killer, and both of us had every right to be frightened.

In the library, we were not invited to sit. Instead, Jane seated herself and began to tell Ruby, firmly and in no uncertain terms, what she thought of her interpretation of Cynthia Obermann. I stood off to one side, noticing that the bloodstained rug had been removed and another moved into its place. If Jane Obermann recognized me as one of the people who had responded to the gunshots on Friday night, she didn't give any sign—but then, she had me confused with someone else altogether. Someone named Nails.

"As a playwright," she began, "I must tell you that I am absolutely disgusted by what you and your so-called director have done to my script. In fact, I intend to consult with my lawyer to determine whether I should—"

She was interrupted by an abrupt rapping at the front door. With an imperial "Wait here," she rose from the chair and went through the hall. We heard a surprised exclamation, a muted exchange, and then Sheila came into the room, in uniform, followed by two uniformed officers, one male and one female. Jane Obermann followed the trio.

"I fail to understand what you mean by a 'warrant,' " she was saying, with an air of offended dignity. "This is a house of mourning. My poor sister has only recently died. You have no right to—"

"I'm sorry, Miss Obermann," Sheila said firmly, "but the warrant gives us the right to conduct a search. I would very much appreciate it if you would let Officer Beard and Officer Murray go about their business. And as I said, I have several questions to ask you, so you might want to sit down while we talk." She glanced at Ruby and me, pretending not to know us. "If you don't mind, I'll ask your guests to leave. This is a police matter."

I almost grinned at that, but I understood. If I were Sheila, I definitely wouldn't want an experienced defense attorney, friend or no friend, eavesdropping on my interrogation. But Jane Obermann had other ideas.

"No," she said, in a contrary tone. She sat down in her chair, folded her arms across her bosom, and glared at Sheila. "I demand that Ms. Wilcox and Ms. Nails be allowed to stay. I want them to be able to testify that I am being treated like a common criminal."

Hardly a *common* criminal, I thought wryly. A common criminal—somebody from East Pecan Springs, or somebody whose family name was Jones or Smith—might be in jail already. But I only nodded. Ruby gave a silent shrug, and Sheila pointed to chairs.

"Then I'll need to ask you to sit down and say nothing," she said to us. She reached into her bag and took out a notebook and a pen. "I'll note for the record that Ms. Wilcox and Ms. Nails . . ." She looked at me.

"Bayles," I said firmly. "China Bayles."

"Yes. Ms. Wilcox and Ms. Bayles are here at Miss Obermann's request."

We sat down as the two uniformed officers made their way to the kitchen and were heard to be opening and closing drawers—with some unnecessary loudness, I thought. Sheila must have wanted Jane Obermann to know that the kitchen was being searched.

"I have a request, several questions, and some information that I think might interest you, Miss Obermann," Sheila said, reaching into her bag again. "First, the request. I have here a fingerprint kit. I would like to obtain your fingerprints for—"

"My fingerprints!" Jane Obermann exclaimed angrily, curling her hands into fists. "Absolutely not!"

"—for the purposes of exclusion," Sheila continued smoothly. She put the kit back into her purse. "However, if you prefer, I shall be glad to arrange for a police car to call for you and take you to the station, where—"

"You're saying that I *have* to do this?" Jane narrowed her eyes to slits.

"I'm afraid so," Sheila said, with an apologetic smile. She took the kit out again. "It will take only a minute."

Ruby and I watched while Sheila deftly inked Jane's fingers and thumbs and pressed them onto the fingerprint card. She handed her a wipe with a "Thank you, Miss Obermann. I appreciate your cooperation."

From the kitchen, there was the sound of rattling silverware. "What are they looking for?" Jane Obermann demanded—more nervously now, it seemed to me.

"They have a list," Sheila said. She opened her notebook to a clean page. "Now, to the questions. I understand that you mentioned to several people that your sister had a delicate heart. When was her heart condition diagnosed? And what was the name of the diagnosing physician?"

There was a silence. "I . . . I'm not sure," Jane said finally. Her forehead was wrinkled, as if she were making an effort to remember. "It's something that poor Florence knew for quite some years. Where she learned it, I couldn't say."

Sheila was writing busily. When she finished, she looked up. "Thank you. Doctor Mackey, Florence's physician, was not aware of a heart condition. Can you tell me why?"

"I have no idea," Jane said fiercely. "And I don't know why you're asking these questions. My sister's health was between herself and her doctor."

"Thank you," Sheila said. She continued to write, her pen scratching against the paper. The silence stretched out. At last, she stopped. "Now, one additional matter, with regard to your sister. Before her death, she suffered nausea, abdominal pain, low blood pressure, and cardiac dysrhythmia." She paused, and I could see the question coming. "Are you aware that oleander is a deadly plant poison that can cause these symptoms and lead to fatality?"

Jane's face went white. "Oleander?" she managed. "What . . . what is that?"

"The large shrubs that line the path in your backyard are oleander bushes," Sheila said. "I take it, then, that your answer is—"

Jane gathered herself. With great dignity, she said, "I shall have no further conversation with you. You cannot force me to talk to you unless my attorney is present."

Sheila closed her notebook and put it away. "You are neither under arrest at this moment, Miss Obermann, nor in custody. You are not a suspect, only a person of interest. As such, you are free to refuse to answer any questions, at your discretion." She sat back in her chair, while we listened to the sounds of continued movement in the kitchen, the opening and shutting of drawers and cabinet doors, and the murmur of low voices.

I gave Sheila an admiring glance. She was handling this interrogation with real dexterity. The conversation was mannered and calm, but beneath its polite surface, tensions bubbled like hot lava.

I had learned a long time ago that silence can be as powerful a tool as words, especially if one party to the conversation has a guilty conscience. The silence in the sitting room continued. Ruby and I were quiet. Sheila said nothing. Jane thought about the kitchen noises, and Sheila's questions, and shifted uneasily in her chair.

"You . . . you said you had some information," she said finally.

"Yes," Sheila said. She raised an eyebrow. "I supposed that, given your unwillingness to talk further, you would not want to hear it. Was I wrong?"

Jane's need to know got the better of her. "Well, yes," she said reluctantly.

"In 1983, your nephew, Andrew Obermann, was declared legally dead, at the request of you and your sister." Sheila smiled. "Perhaps you will be glad to hear that he has been found and positively identified."

So Max Baumeister, Jane's pick to play the part of her father, had managed to find those X rays. Good for him, I thought. There was probably some irony here, if I dug far enough for it.

But Jane had heard Sheila's statement in a different way. "Andrew has been *found*?" she cried shrilly. "But that's not possible! He's been dead all these years. I know, because I—" She stopped, biting her lip, realizing that she had been about to let the truth slip out. "Where . . . where was he found?" she asked at last, attempting to recover herself.

Sheila was watching her coolly. "His skeleton was discovered in Mistletoe Springs Cave, south of town, by a team of anthropologists from CTSU. His remains have been identified by dental records supplied by Doctor Baumeister." She paused. "I don't suppose you have any information about your nephew's disappearance that you would like to share with me?"

Jane, finally flustered, seemed to have forgotten that she was not going to have any more conversation with Sheila.

"Information? Of course not. We . . . we got a letter from California. That's where we thought he'd gone."

Sheila said nothing.

Jane shook her head, her lips pressed together. "In a . . . cave, you say? Perhaps that's not so surprising. The boy was always one for exploring." Her voice seemed to be trembling slightly. "I suppose he lost his way, or fell down a cliff. Or perhaps he was killed by falling rock."

"That's what was thought at first," Sheila agreed. "However, after a careful forensic examination, it was determined that he died of a gunshot wound."

"He was . . . shot?" Jane's question was hardly audible.

"In the head," Sheila replied matter-of-factly. "From behind, execution-style. Both the cartridge casing and the bullet have been recovered."

That was fast work, I thought approvingly. Blackie must have sent somebody out to that cave right away, and they found the spent slug without difficulty.

Jane opened her mouth to say something, then closed it again. Sheila took the opportunity to add, "It turns out that the bullet that killed your nephew was World War One ammunition, fired from a .45 caliber Colt pistol."

"A Colt?" The word seemed to have jerked out of her.

"Yes. The same type of gun and ammunition that you used on Friday night, when you shot the . . . *intruder*." There was a peculiar emphasis on the word. Sheila smiled dryly. "In fact, this coincidence seemed so striking that I have arranged to have the slugs tested to see if they might have been fired from the same gun. I expect to have the report first thing in the morning."

Jane's face had paled and her hands were trembling. "It . . . sounds as if you are making an accusation."

"I'm not in a position to make accusations in this case," Sheila said pleasantly. "Not yet, that is." She looked up as the female officer came into the room. "Ah, here we are," she said, sounding pleased. "It looks as if we've wrapped up the search. What do you have there, Officer Murray?"

The officer silently handed her three plastic bags and a sheet of paper.

"Let's see," Sheila said, taking the bags. "It appears that we are taking a large wooden-handled fork and a small wooden-handled knife. The two appear to be from the same matched set." She looked at the third bag. "And what is this?"

"Four muffins," the officer said. "They seem to be home-baked. We found them in the refrigerator freezer."

"Ah, yes," Sheila said, with satisfaction. "Muffins." She scrawled her initials on the paper and handed it and the bag back to the officer. She stood. "Thank you for your time, Miss Obermann. It's entirely likely that I will have additional questions for you when the results of various analyses are in. It would be helpful if you did not leave town without letting me know your plans." She paused. "That won't be a problem, will it?"

"Of . . . course not," Jane managed.

Ruby and I didn't say a word until we got into Big Mama and closed the doors.

"But why didn't Sheila arrest her?" Ruby burst out. "I mean, it's as plain as the nose on your face, China! That woman is a killer!"

"Because Howie is probably insisting on taking the ballistics and fingerprint evidence to the grand jury before he goes for an arrest warrant. And of course, now that they have those muffins, they'll want to test them, too. Jane doesn't drive, so she's probably not a flight risk." I grinned bleakly. "And there's no one left for her to kill."

I was wrong about that.

Chapter Twenty-one

Ezekial connected dem dry bones
I hear de word o' de Lord

Disconnect dem bones, dem dry bones
I hear de word o' de Lord.

Dem bones, dem bones gonna walk around
Dem bones, dem bones gonna rise again
Dem bones, dem bones, dem dry bones
Now hear de word o' de Lord.

Thursday was another busy day, and by the time I got home that evening, bone-tired, I was glad to discover a note saying that McQuaid and Brian had gone to help with the school science fair. Howard Cosell, however, was there and covered with mud, from the tip of his nose to the tip of his tail.

"Howard!" I exclaimed, irritated. "You dirty dog! Have you been digging up rabbits again?"

Howard regarded me with an guileless grin and a cheerful wag of his muddy tail.

"Well, it doesn't matter where you've been," I said firmly. "It's where you're going that counts. Come on. You have to have a bath—and before supper, too. You can't go in the house looking like that."

A bath! Howard yelped in alarm. *Oh, bummer!* He ran in the direction of his hideout under the porch, as fast as his short legs could carry him. But I'm faster, and I was determined. Bummer or not, Howard was in for it.

Unless it's cold, Howard has his baths outdoors, with the hose. I fetched his herbal doggie shampoo and a couple of towels. Howard is not naturally fond of bathing, but when he was confronted with the fact that he had no other choice, he reluctantly joined me, and we had our bath. Yes, both of us. It's impossible to bathe a bassett without getting thoroughly wet yourself.

"There now, don't you smell good?" I asked cheerily, when I had finished toweling him off. Howard gave himself a mighty shake and ran to roll in the grass.

I was moving the towels from the washing machine into the dryer when the phone rang. It was Sheila, calling on her cell phone from her car. She was on her way over.

"Just for a few minutes," she said. "I won't stay."

"Yes, you will," I replied firmly. "McQuaid and Brian have gone out, and I haven't had supper yet. I'll bet you haven't eaten, either. This is an offer you can't refuse."

By the time Sheila arrived, I'd thawed Ruby's Better Bones Soup in the microwave, made a couple of sandwiches with leftover chicken, set out a bowl of chips, and poured iced tea. Everything was on the table when she knocked at the door.

"You look tired," I said, as she came in, wearing her uniform.

"You look damp," she retorted, taking off her cap.

"Yeah." I grinned. "Howard and I just had a bath. What's your excuse?"

She sat down abruptly. "Jane Obermann shot herself. Her housekeeper found her this afternoon."

"Oh, lord." I sat down across from her. I started to say, "I'm sorry," but didn't quite get the words out.

Was I really sorry? Jane was a malicious, manipulative woman who had earned the right to be called "evil." I am not a death-penalty advocate, but she'd been a candidate for Huntsville's Death Row, if I'd ever met one—although, given her age, a jury would have been more likely to lock her up for the rest of her life, rather than execute her. Facing a publically humiliating trial, the permanent loss of her way of life, and the bleak prospect of ending her days in prison, she had chosen a different route. Her choice. And maybe it was better this way, for her and for everybody else.

"She used the Luger this time," Sheila was saying, in a flat, hard voice. "In her bedroom. One shot, and it was over."

"Did she leave a confession?" I didn't think it was likely. Jane was not the kind of woman who would find comfort in spilling facts and feelings onto paper. She would leave us guessing at the things we didn't know such as whether she had actually pushed her mother off the roof, all those years ago.

"No such luck," Sheila said. "But we'd already assembled most of the evidence against her, and Howie was primed to take it to the grand jury early next week. The ballistics test we ran on the Colt is back. The three shots—the one that killed Andy and the two she pumped into Hank—were fired from the same gun."

"How about the autopsy report on Florence?"

"She ingested oleander—the autopsy turned up traces of the cardiac glycoside oleandrin. And the muffins were full of bits of green oleander leaf. I guess Jane was saving them in case the first one or two didn't do the job." She paused. "If it hadn't been for you, China, the poisoning would have gone undetected."

I got up and went to the stove. "Not me. It was Helen Berger who noticed the symptoms." I ladled soup into two bowls and carried them to the table.

"I've interviewed Helen." Sheila picked up her spoon. "She said she probably wouldn't have pursued the matter if you hadn't insisted." She tasted the soup. "Mmm, good, China. Did you make this just for me?"

"I thawed it out just for you," I said with a grin. "Ruby

invented it for her mother, who's been diagnosed with osteoporosis. It's called Better Bones Soup. It's got bok choy and kale and tofu—stuff to make your bones tougher."

Sheila gave a sarcastic laugh. "Yeah, well, along with a thicker skin, I could use tougher bones. I have to stand up to the city council again later this week." For the next couple of minutes, all you could hear was the clinking of spoons against soup bowls. Then Sheila added, "I haven't forgotten that you were the one who dug up the clues to Andrew Obermann's identity, China—and tied that killing to Gabe Dixon. If we'd had to go to trial, that photo you found would have been convincing evidence."

"But not conclusive." I pushed my soup bowl away and began on my sandwich. "A good defense attorney would attack the connection to Gabe, and—"

"The photograph had Gabe Dixon's fingerprints on it. We matched the prints against his military record. He was a Korean vet."

"Okay. But the prosecution would still have to connect the sisters to their nephew's murder. There's no proof that they actually paid Gabe for killing Andy. They—"

"Yes, there is." Sheila finished her soup and picked up her chicken sandwich. "You won't believe this, but they paid him by check."

I stared at her. "You're kidding."

"Nope. Ten thousand dollars. Dated October 23, 1976, payable to Gabriel Dixon, signed by Jane Obermann and countersigned by Florence Obermann. The bank still has a record of the check. Apparently, the signatures of both sisters were required because the check was so large." Her grin was mirthless. "What's more, he used the check to open a savings account. I guess he was figuring to hang on to his ill-gotten gains against a rainy day."

I rolled my eyes. "Of all the careless—" I stopped. Paying a hit man wasn't something the sisters did every day, and accepting blood money was probably new to Gabe, too. None of them were thinking about the possibility that the money could be traced. And it wasn't, either—for over a quarter of a century.

"It turns out that Gabe grew up on the Swenson Ranch, where his father worked," Sheila added. "He probably played in that cave when he was a boy." She finished her sandwich and licked her fingers. "And speaking of carelessness, the utensils we took from the Obermann kitchen—they matched the knife that Hank is supposed to have carried into the house. You were right. It was a throwdown."

"Figures," I said. "It probably didn't occur to Jane that her story would be questioned." I paused. "Fingerprints?"

"Jane's left thumb and forefinger, on the knife blade." Sheila drained her iced tea. "Which, together with the unlocked gun cabinet and Juan Gomez's testimony, pretty much cinches the matter. Howie said he'd go for premeditation." She chuckled. "He would have hated it, though. Pillar of the community, contributor to his political campaign. Oh, how he would have hated it."

I eyed her. "You've talked to Juan?"

"Justine Wyzinski brought him in this morning, and he gave us a statement. I didn't inquire into the details, but I gather that Justine thinks she can help him get out from under his immigration problem. He'll have to go back to Mexico for a while, but Justine says she thinks he can reapply for a student visa."

There was a long pause. Sheila leaned forward, and her mouth tightened. "I need to ask you something, China. It's about Blackie and Alana Montoya, the forensic anthropologist at CTSU. Do you know her?"

"Yes," I said cautiously.

"Are they . . . are they involved?"

"Do you care?" I countered.

She sighed. "I've been hearing things about her. That she drinks, for one thing. That she's in some sort of trouble at the university, for another. And I even heard a rumor that she tried to kill herself." Her expression was rueful. "I guess I'm feeling . . . well, protective. I don't want Blackie to get hurt again, that's all."

"If it'll make you feel better, I understand that they aren't involved."

"Well, that's good," Sheila said, sounding relieved.

"And that she's returning to Mexico."

"Returning—" Sheila stared at me. "You mean, she's taking a leave from the university?"

"I think she's resigned."

Sheila was puzzled. "Resigned? But why? What's going to happen to the new program?"

I shrugged. "You'll have to ask McQuaid about that. Maybe they'll look for somebody to replace her. The program is a good idea. It would be a shame to let it die."

She nodded. "Yeah. Well, I'm sorry she's leaving, but I'm glad that Blackie isn't . . . well, involved with her. He's pretty raw right now." She put out her hand and touched mine. "And thanks for the information."

"Maybe you can return the favor." I regarded her seriously. "Tell me about you and Colin Fowler—at least, that's the name he's using right now."

Sheila put both hands flat on the table and tensed her muscles, as if to rise. Her mouth was hard, her eyes remote. Her cop face. "I don't know what you're talking about, China."

"Sure you do, Smart Cookie. I have no way of knowing what this is about, but I do know that there's something between you and Colin. If it's over and done with, that's one thing. If it's current, that's another. Ruby is crazy about him."

"If I tell you it's over and done with, will you believe me?"

"Is it?"

The silence stretched tight as a soundless guitar string. "Yes."

Her "yes" was unqualified, but the silence had been

telling. "Then why all the secrecy?" I asked testily. "Why not just come right out and—"

She stood up. "I'm sorry, China. I can tell you that any relationship I might have had with Colin Fowler is concluded. However, I'm not at liberty to tell you anything else." Her voice was flat and hard. Her cop voice.

"But what—"

"I'm *sorry,* China. Lay off with the questions." Her mouth softened. "You're making me feel terrible."

"Yeah, sure," I said, unsatisfied, troubled. There were too many unanswered questions here, too many hidden things, too many secrets. It sounded to me as if Ruby was headed for trouble, and there was nothing I could do to head it off.

Sheila looked at her watch. "Now I really have to go. Thanks for the supper. Tell Ruby that my bones feel better already." Her mouth fitted itself into a smile. "And thanks for connecting the dots on the Obermann case."

"You're welcome," I said glumly. "Anytime."

She went to the door, put on her cap, and gave me a flinty-eyed glance. In her uniform, she looked a whole lot tougher than Howie Dingbat Masterson—real Texas Tough. "Okay, China. Here's the deal. I promise not to get between Colin and Ruby, if you promise to keep an eye on Blackie for me."

I folded my arms. "Keep an eye on Blackie?" I asked with interest. "Does that mean you still—"

"It just means that I don't want him making a fool of himself over women who don't deserve him," Sheila snapped. She pulled her hat brim down. "Deal?"

"Deal," I said. I regarded her. "Sheila, you are one tough cookie."

Herbs for Your Skeleton

Whether acute or chronic, diseases of the musculoskeletal system are almost always painful and are often debilitating. Learning to treat your particular condition with herbs—in a broader holistic context, of course—can help you reduce the intensity and frequency of your symptoms. In some cases, it may even alleviate the problem altogether.

David Hoffman
Healthy Bones & Joints

Before modern science came up with pharmaceuticals to help us maintain our bones and joints, herbal medicine offered an array of possible treatments. Here are some that have been used over the centuries.

Herbs with estrogenic effects

Declining estrogen is one of the causes of bone loss. Herbs that have estrogenic effects include black cohosh (a well-documented herbal alternative to hormone replacement therapy), dong quai, burdock root, Chinese ox knee root, alfalfa, and motherwort. Red clover, the subject of recent scientific study, has been shown to help increase cortical bone. Numerous studies have confirmed that soy slows bone loss, as well as lowering cholesterol and reducing the risk of breast cancer.

Herbs that boost the minerals in our bodies

Herbalists have traditionally recommended nettle, alfalfa, oatstraw, and slippery elm to enhance the minerals in the body and maintain strong bones. In a 1999 Italian study, horsetail was shown to improve bone density.

Herbs that help to relieve joint pain

Although it has not been scientifically studied, turmeric has been traditionally prescribed to reduce inflammation and relieve the pain of rheumatoid arthritis and osteoarthritis. Devil's claw (an African herb) and boswellia (a tree native to India, Africa, and the Middle East, which yields a resin known as *sallai guggal*) have been the subjects of several studies, but the results have been mixed. Other recent scientific studies have confirmed the traditional use of nettles, willow bark, ginger, St. John's wort, evening primrose, borage, and black currant as effective analgesics and inflammation suppressors. The remedy most thoroughly studied and most confidently recommended is capsaicin, the pain-relieving compound derived from hot red peppers.

Reading Resources

Bucco, Gloria, "Joint Relief: Herbs for Osteoarthritic Pain. *Herbs for Health*, November/December, 1998, pp. 50–54.

Hoffman, David, *Healthy Bones & Joints: A Natural Approach to Treating Arthritis, Osteoporosis, Tendinitis, Myalgia & Bursitis*, Storey Books, 2000.

Khalsa, Karta Purkh Singh, "Herbs for Bone Health," *Herb Quarterly*, Part One, Summer, 2003, pp. 43–49; Part Two, Fall, 2003, pp. 50–54.

Stengler, Mark, *Build Strong Bones: Prevent Osteoporosis and Enhance Bone Health Naturally*, IMPAKT Communications, 1998.

White, M.D., Linda B., "Pain-Free Joints, Naturally," *Herbs for Health*, July/August, 2001, pp. 38–42.

A Collection of Recipes from Dead Man's Bones

China's Curried Chicken

(CHAPTER TWO)

1 frying chicken, cut up
1 tablespoon vegetable oil
1 tablespoon butter
$^1/_2$ cup chopped onion
$^1/_2$ cup celery, sliced diagonally
$^1/_2$ cup carrot, sliced diagonally
1 cooking apple, chopped
1 green pepper, chopped
2 cloves garlic, crushed
1 16-ounce can diced tomatoes, undrained
3 tablespoons raisins
$^1/_8$ to $^1/_4$ teaspoon crushed red pepper
1 tablespoon curry powder
salt to taste
1 tablespoon cornstarch

In a large skillet, brown chicken pieces in hot oil and butter over medium-high heat. Remove chicken. In the oil, sauté onion, celery, carrot, apple, green pepper, and garlic until tender, but not brown. Stir in undrained diced tomatoes, raisins, crushed red pepper, curry powder, and salt. When the mixture boils, add chicken pieces. Cover and simmer until chicken is tender and cooked through. Remove chicken to a heated platter. Make a paste by adding a little water to the cornstarch, and use it to thicken the vegetable mixture. Serve chicken and vegetables over brown rice. Makes 6–8 servings.

McQuaid's Six-Alarm Chutney

(CHAPTER TWO)

1 pound Granny Smith apples (or other tart apple), peeled, cored, coarsely chopped
½ pound onions, chopped
½ pound raisins
4 cloves garlic, crushed
1 quart cider vinegar
1 pound brown sugar
2 tablespoons mustard powder
1 tablespoon ground ginger
2 tablespoons cayenne (more, if you dare)

Place all ingredients in a nonreactive (stainless, glass, or enamel) pan. Bring to a boil, then reduce heat and simmer gently for about 3 hours, uncovered, until the chutney is thick. Stir occasionally, to keep from sticking. Spoon into hot, clean jars and cover immediately with airtight lids. When cool, store in refrigerator for up to a month. Makes 4 or 5 half-pint jars.

Chilled Green Pea Soup, with Mint

(CHAPTER FOUR)

3 cups green peas (fresh or frozen)
2 tablespoons fresh mint, chopped very fine
1¼ cups whole milk
1¼ cups chicken stock
salt, pepper to taste
for garnish: sour cream, chopped green onion tops

Cook peas until soft in barely enough water to cover. Drain, place in a blender with mint, and puree. Add milk and chicken stock and blend until smooth and creamy. Season to taste with salt, pepper. Chill for at least an hour. Garnish with sour cream and chopped green onion tops. Serves 4.

Theresa Loe's Chive Dip in Harvest Pumpkin

(CHAPTER NINE)

8 ounces sour cream
4 ounces cream cheese, softened
2 tablespoons fresh chives, finely chopped
2 tablespoons scallions, finely chopped
¼ teaspoon salt
⅛ teaspoon garlic powder
1 small pumpkin, hollowed out
assorted cut vegetables
fresh chive blossoms
fresh lemon balm or parsley for garnish

In a small bowl, combine sour cream, cream cheese, chopped chives, scallions, salt, and garlic powder. Stir with a fork or whisk until well blended. Cover and refrigerate for at least 1 hour before serving. To serve, spoon dip into pumpkin and set on a tray surrounded by fresh cut vegetables for dipping. Sprinkle some chopped chive blossoms on top of the dip. Garnish tray with remaining chive blossoms and fresh sprigs of lemon balm or parsley. Makes 1½ cups. May be doubled or tripled for a large crowd or a larger pumpkin. (Reprinted with permission from *The New Herbal Calendar,* 2003, by Theresa Loe. To order Theresa's current calendar, book, and videos, go to www.countrythyme.com, or write to Country Thyme, P.O. Box 3090, El Segundo, CA 90245.)

Bob Godwin's Best Grilled Goat

(CHAPTER FIFTEEN)

4 goat chops, 1" thick (round bone or shoulder blade)
½ teaspoon salt
½ teaspoon pepper
½ teaspoon ground rosemary
1 8-ounce can crushed pineapple
½ cup Maria Zapata's Jalapeño-Apricot jelly (or ordinary jalapeño jelly or apricot jam)
¼ cup lemon juice
1 tablespoon Dijon-style mustard
3 green onions, chopped

Rub chops with salt, pepper, and rosemary. Combine remaining ingredients in a saucepan and bring to a boil, stirring until the jelly melts. Broil or grill chops 8–10 minutes on each side. Spoon sauce over meat during the last 5 minutes. Sprinkle chops with green onions, and serve with bowl of sauce.

Docia's Devil-Made-Me-Do-It Apple Pie

(CHAPTER FIFTEEN)

unbaked crust for a two-crust 9″ pie
8 medium apples, peeled, cored, sliced (about 8 cups)
1/2 cup granulated sugar
1/4 cup flour
1/4 teaspoon cinnamon
1/4 teaspoon ground nutmeg
1/2 cup Maria Zapata's Jalapeño-Apricot Jelly or 1/2 cup ordinary jalapeño jelly

Preheat oven to 425°F. Mix sliced apples, sugar, flour, cinnamon, nutmeg, and jelly. Spoon into pastry-lined pie pan. Cover with top crust, crimp and seal edges, cut slits in top. Bake 40–50 minutes, or until crust is brown and juice bubbles through slits. To prevent overbrowning, cover crimped edges with aluminum foil; remove during last 15 minutes.

Ruby's Better Bones Soup

(CHAPTER SIXTEEN)

2 tablespoons olive oil
1/2 cup onions, chopped
1/2 cup carrots, diced
4 cloves garlic, minced
1 14- or 16-ounce can crushed or diced tomatoes
2 quarts chicken or vegetable stock
1 4-ounce can water chestnuts, drained
2 baby bok choy, white and green parts sliced separately
1 bay leaf
2 teaspoons mixed dried herbs (try parsley, sage, summer savory, chervil, rosemary)
1/2 pound fresh kale, stems removed, chopped
6–8 ounces hard tofu, cubed

In a large saucepan or Dutch oven, sauté onions and carrots for 7–8 minutes. Add garlic and sauté for another minute. Add tomatoes, stock, water chestnuts, bok choy (white parts), bay leaf, and herbs and simmer for 10–15 minutes. Add green parts of bok choy and kale and cook until just tender (1–2 minutes). Add tofu and cook another 1–2 minutes. Remove bay leaf and serve hot. Makes 6–8 servings.

Howard's Herbal Doggie Shampoo

(CHAPTER NINETEEN)

1 quart liquid shampoo
2 drops pennyroyal or peppermint oil
2 drops lemon oil
2 drops rosemary oil
2 drops lavender oil
2 drops citronella

Mix all together, using amounts listed. Too much of a good thing can irritate a dog's skin. (And do be careful when you use essential oils. Ingested, they are highly toxic.)

MYSTERY PARTNERS WEBSITE

Susan and Bill Albert maintain an interactive website with information about their books, herb lore, recipes, a bulletin board, and Susan's online journal. To visit, go to www.mysterypartners.com. While you're there, be sure and subscribe to the Alberts' e-mail newsletter, which is sent at least once a month. *China's Garden* and the *Partners in Crime* print newsletter are no longer being published.

Susan Wittig Albert

A Dilly of a Death

China's otherwise sensible husband is bored with teaching and ready for a career change...say hello to Mike McQuaid, P.I. His first client is Phoebe the Pickle Queen, owner of the biggest little pickle business in Texas. She says her plant manager is embezzling, and she wants McQuaid to follow the money. But just days before the annual Picklefest, Phoebe disappears. And now it's up to McQuaid and China to search for her—and for clues in a case that promises to leave a very sour taste.

"Readers will relish this more-sweet-than-sour adventure." —*Booklist*

0-425-19399-3

Available wherever books are sold or at penguin.com